REVOLT

D1637265

Praise for Qaisra Shahraz

'A lean, lyrical meditation on tradition and independence, sensuality and sacrifice, set against the mortal background of modern day Pakistan, Shahraz's debut beguiles throughout' *The Times*

'Gripping, hugely involving and very satisfying' Kate Mosse

'Full of vivid details about the lives and loves, the duties and desires in Muslim family life' Yasmin Alibhai-Brown

'An international bestseller ... an extraordinary story of love and betrayal in rural Pakistan' *Manchester Evening News*

'An absorbing adventure, from a vivid imagination' *She*

'A riveting family saga' *Bradford Telegraph and Argus*

'Stunning debut novel. An intricate study of love, family, politics and sacrifice' *Eastern Eye*

'Compulsive reading ... An intriguing tale of love, envy and jealousy' *Asian Times*

'A real story-telling gift' Sue Gee

'A very moving tale of love, passion and Islamic traditions ... difficult to put down' BBC National Asian Network

About the author

Fellow of the Royal Society of Arts, Qaisra Shahraz is a prize-winning and critically acclaimed novelist and scriptwriter. Born in Pakistan, she has lived in Manchester (UK) since childhood and gained two Masters Degrees in English and European literature and scriptwriting. As a highly successful woman, Qaisra was recognised as one of 100 influential Pakistani women in the Pakistan Power 100 List (2012). Previously, she was nominated for the Asian Women of Achievement Awards and for the *Muslim News* Awards for Excellence.

Her novels, *The Holy Woman* and *Typhoon*, have been translated into several languages. *The Holy Woman* (2001) won the Golden Jubilee Award, and has become a bestseller in Indonesia and Turkey. She has appeared in many international writers' festivals and book fairs, including Abu Dhabi, Jaipur, Ottawa and Beijing. Her award-winning drama serial *Dil Hee To Hai* was broadcast on Pakistani Television in 2003. Qaisra's most recent novel, *Revolt*, is published by Arcadia in 2013. She has also completed two volumes of short stories: *A Pair of Jeans* and *Train to Krakow* and is working on her fourth novel *The Henna Painter*. Several of her prize-winning short stories are published in the UK and abroad, and her work is customarily studied in schools and universities. A critical analysis of her works has been undertaken in *The Holy and the Unholy: Critical Essays on Qaisra Shahraz's Fiction* (2011). Qaisra Shahraz has another successful career in education, as a consultant, teacher trainer and inspector.

REVOLT

Qaisra Shahraz

Arcadia Books Ltd
139 Highlever Road
London W10 6PH

www.arcadiabooks.co.uk

First published in the United Kingdom by Arcadia Books 2013

Copyright © Qaisra Shahraz, 2013

Qaisra Shahraz has asserted her moral right to be identified as the author of this
work in accordance with the Copyright, Designs and Patents Act, 1988.

A catalogue record for this book is available from the British Library.

ISBN 978-0-9573304-9-8

Typeset in Minion by MacGuru Ltd
Printed and bound by CPI Group (UK) Ltd, Croydon CR0 4YY

Arcadia Books supports English PEN *www.englishpen.org* and
The Book Trade Charity *http://booktradecharity.wordpress.com*

Arcadia Books distributors are as follows:

in the UK and elsewhere in Europe:
Macmillan Distribution Ltd
Brunel Road
Houndmills
Basingstoke
Hants RG21 6XS

in the USA and Canada:
Dufour Editions
PO Box 7
Chester Springs
PA, 19425

in Australia/New Zealand:
NewSouth Books
University of New South Wales
Sydney NSW 2052

in South Africa:
Jacana Media (Pty) Ltd
PO Box 291784
Melville 2109
Johannesburg

For my beloved sister Farah

Prologue

Barefooted, Massi Fiza panted up the marble stairs and dashed straight through the mosquito-netted door and the brocade drapes, into the village goldsmith's lounge. Clutching her jute laundry bag against her flat chest, she hovered over the seated figure of her friend Rukhsar, exclaiming: 'Another suicide bombing!'

Perched on a pile of cushions, an aluminium casket of gems in front of her, the village *siniaran* was engrossed in the nimble task of inserting tiny pearls into a gold bridal collar set.

'What?' Rukhsar cried, abandoning her work, not relishing this sudden intrusion late in the evening, just when the next episode of her favourite Indian drama was about to start.

Shabnum, Rukhsar's 24-year-old eldest daughter, sitting reading a play on the sofa, gawped; the house linen had already been collected. Nevertheless she cheerily offered:

'A cup of our Italian coffee, Massi Fiza?'

The jute bag slipped out of Massi Fiza's hand. Grimacing, Shabnum quickly reached to retrieve it from their *kashmiri* silk rug, rolling her *kajal*-lined eyes in disgust. The laundrywoman rarely had time to wash this item.

'Massi Fiza!' The goldmistress, now quite rattled, reached up to shake her friend's arm. 'You OK?'

'Another bombing!' Massi Fiza repeated as if in a trance.

Rukhsar was now on her feet. 'What? Where?'

'In two mosques in Malakand.'

'Oh, Allah Pak, not another one! What's happening to our poor country? So many innocent people killed by explosions and those American drones!'

'My sons! What if …?' Massi Fiza stopped short, lowering her gaze.

'What would they be doing in Malakand?' Rukhsar's eyes narrowed. 'Have you got their phone numbers?'

Massi Fiza shook her head; numbers just did not tally with her brain cells and technology of any sort frightened her. Therefore she had never learned to use those 'silly' mobile phones, as she called them.

'Sit and relax, Massi Fiza. Shabnum will make your favourite coffee from the *expensive* pot, whilst I finish the pearlwork on this necklace.'

Massi Fiza pulled herself out of her trance but remained standing.

'What are you reading, Shabnum?'

'Ruhi's book, *Othello* – a sad *Engrezi* love story. A drama by William Shakespeare.' Shabnum cheekily held it up, her cheeks heavy with laughter. What would the semi-illiterate laundry-woman know about literature?

'*Engrezi kitab*? Weelly Speer?' squeaked Massi Fiza, staring in awe at the English book.

The English alphabet had always intimidated her; her punishment for mixing up the upper and the lower cases in her fifth class was a good telling-off from her sour-faced teacher, who, as known to the entire village, had only been educated to a tenth *jamaat* class herself. Massi Fiza did triumph in some areas, however, managing to master words like 'cat' and 'dog'.

'Never mind "Willy Speer" – let's talk.' Rukhsar chuckled at Massi Fiza's struggle with the name of the great English Bard. The laundrywoman's five primary classes in an under-resourced village school never quite qualified her to sample Shakespeare's masterpieces. Rukhsar's twelfth class, however, in the posh college in town, did. *Romeo and Juliet* still remained the gold-mistress's favourite Shakespearean drama.

'Whose set are you working on now, Rukhsar-ji?' Massi Fiza's envious eyes were hawked on the necklace.

'Saher's … the lawyer woman's wedding.'

'Of course! What an exciting week, Rukhsar-ji,' Massi Fiza smirked, colour rushing back into her gaunt mahogany-brown cheeks.

'Is it?' Rukhsar challenged, settling back on the soft pile of cushions in the middle of the room, sure that her neighbour had plenty of salacious news to share; her keen eyes behind the large designer glasses assessing both the emotional landscape of her friend's face and the necklace still to be completed. Rukhsar happily forfeited her favourite Indian drama serial in order to acquaint herself with the goings-on in Gulistan.

'So! Tell me!' Rukhsar eagerly prompted, her high-cheek-boned face coquettishly sloped to one side, adding a healthy jowl to her neckline.

Forgetting about her wicked sons and the suicide bombers, Massi Fiza, her grey eyes alive and mischievous, took a deep breath and proudly announced:

'The landowners' "princes" are back this week!'

'Princes?'

'Yes, the *zemindar* "princes". Haughty Mistress Mehreen's son Ismail is coming from London for his wedding. Gentle Mistress Gulbahar's son Arslan is flying in from New York tomorrow morning. And sour Mistress Rani is busy preparing for her daughter Saher's wedding. And ...' Fiza stopped, tiptoeing to stand in front of Rukhsar's tall fan to cool a hot flush stinging across her shoulders and up her scrawny throat. Enjoying the welcoming breeze, she lifted the three amulets garlanding her neck.

'Go on then ...' her friend slyly goaded. The village *dhoban* was now in her element, ready to part with the juiciest piece of news.

'She's back!'

'Who?'

'Laila! The potter's ... after years!' Massi Fiza abruptly stopped again.

'Oh!'

'Well! Did you not expect it – with him returning? You must have seen her? The door is opposite yours.'

'No, I'm too busy with my work to peer over roof terraces and eavesdrop on the goings-on in my neighbours' houses, Massi Fiza!' Rukhsar scoffed good-humouredly before asking, 'What will happen?'

'We'll find out soon enough, won't we, as it's all happening at the white *hevali*? And that's where I'll be, first thing in the morning. Good old Begum tells me everything. Of course with quite a bit of bossing in between! Shabnum, my *ladli*, where's my coffee? You've heard everything now!'

The topic of bombing was duly thrust aside. What happened elsewhere could not be helped, as long as it had nothing to do with their Gulistan or intrude into their lives.

'In any event what can I, a humble laundrywoman, do to stop such atrocities?' she silently bewailed.

Then she paled, a sombre thought crossing her mind, remembering the long, thick, black beard framing her son's narrow face the last time he had visited her. 'What if my sons have got in with the wrong company? And been brainwashed by those horrible men!' Then laughed aloud at her runaway imagination, making her friend raise her head from the bridal collar set in her hand.

Massi Fiza immediately straightened her face; there were some things you did not share even with good trusted friends.

'Oh, Allah Pak! I forgot the box!'

'The box?' Rukhsar duly dropped the pearl between her fingers.

'The Gujjar's poor son … waiting thirteen years for the American green card is returning home in a box! Guess what, he got the card, but two days later snuffed it … heart attack or sugar problem. His poor family is at the airport to collect the body. Can you imagine it? All those years of waiting and cheating on his wife?' Massi Fiza hastened to explain as Rukhsar's neatly plucked, arched eyebrows had shot up. 'You know he kept a Hispanic mistress in Chicago! The *besharm* man made no bones about it, openly boasting, and in front of us women, too, about cohabiting with her … to get that yellow card! Fancy abandoning your wife and kids for years, and when it's time for the poor lot to join him he shoots up to the heavens! Bad timing or what! No one dares to mention his American *haram* brood he has left behind. Two lots of children on two continents! Terrible!'

Making a face in distaste, Rukhsar nimbly picked up another tiny pearl from the casket. 'I hate this modern curse – this migration thing, Massi Fiza! It destroys families! My heart bleeds for his poor Zubeda, patiently biding her time for years and now left with a house full of luxury items, tears, four children to wed, not to mention looking after his elderly parents for the rest of her life! She'll not see America, I tell you! Do you think anyone will let her go now – unless her son takes her!'

'Well, it's not that bad!' Bristling, Massi Fiza went on the defensive, thin mouth tightly pursed. 'Migration – going to *velat* must be good or why else would all these young people go raring off to foreign lands, with their families eagerly packing them off? Even their wives remain contented – delighted with their bank balances. Look at their homes, their standard of living, Rukhsar-ji!'

Massi Fiza would not eliminate the raw envy from her tone. That was how she felt. So why bother hiding it from her friend? How she craved that somebody would arrange for her two good-for-nothing sons to migrate to somewhere in the Middle East. Then she, too, could add a second storey to her house as her neighbours had done.

It still rattled her that the bricklayer had turned their humble dwelling into a grand two-storey villa entirely swathed in marble. Not an inch spared! All from their son's hard work, digging roads under the scorching Abu Dhabi sun.

Massi Fiza was particularly annoyed because the bricklayer's house not only dwarfed her three-roomed humble house, but its high walls aggressively blocked half the sunlight that her laundry business desperately needed. The bricklayer was now a bricklayer in name only, since his son's foreign remittances padded his bank account. And the airs of his womenfolk, especially the illiterate, big-mouthed mother Jeena, grated on Massi Fiza. Within months they had graduated into a class of their own on the village social ladder, particularly on the scale of snobbery.

'Rich but no manners!' Massi Fiza fumed in front of her many clients. The bricklayer's household delighted in repaying her animosity by packing off their laundry to the other village laundry house, the *dhobi ghat*.

'Well, it has not made a two *paisa* difference to the quiltmaker's home! Poor Zeinab is still digging holes in her fingers from all the darning she does with those long needles. The floors of her house are *still* brick-lined and the roof, I believe, *still* has a mud veneer that she annually slaps on herself with her calloused hands,' Rukhsar stridently reminded her friend, now quite worked up on the subject of migration; hating people who abandoned their families to migrate elsewhere.

Irritated, she was about to scold, 'Massi Fiza, I wish you would wear a bra sometimes!' but stopped short. Instead, she averted her gaze from her friend's brown nipples poking through the thin lawn fabric of her *kameez*. Rukhsar knew the cheeky answer her friend would throw her way. 'Allah Pak has not blessed me with your large bosom! There's practically nothing for the cups to hold! So why bother, and in the summer heat?'

Rukhsar proudly glanced down at her own perfect bosom to make sure that it was not 'swelling' out of the neckline of her *kameez* from her crouched position.

'That's because her son-in-law's wealth has gone into his parents' city house,' Massi Fiza scoffed, unaware of her friend's train of thought on nipples and breasts. 'Oh dear, I must be off.'

'Don't forget to keep me informed.'

'Of course I will! Especially about what's happening in the homes of the three *zemindar* sisters. Master Arslan is coming tomorrow morning. Begum tells me that there'll be a big homecoming party that Master Haider will host. But will they let *her* through the door? That's the *big* question. We'll have to see, won't we! It's going to be quite an exciting time in our Gulistan.'

'For you, Massi Fiza, yes! But I'm stuck here in *chardevari*, behind these four walls, working on these gold *machlis*!' Rukhsar gently teased.

'Must hurry. Need to soak the whites!' She scurried out of the room; for once without drinking Shabnum's Italian coffee. Meeting the grey-haired master goldsmith on the stairs, she blushed, hurriedly draping her red-dyed muslin shawl over her chest. With a shy smile Massi Fiza sidled past him, muttering her '*salaams*' at the bottom of the steps, whilst shuffling her feet back into her green, bleached, plastic sandals.

PART ONE

CHAPTER 1

The Girl

In Gulistan village, the morning sun was high up over the sugarcane fields. Nine-year-old Shirin, in a white frilly frock with matching *chooridaar pyjama,* her auburn curls swinging around her shoulders, hopped along the dusty path to her favourite spot – the large termite mound.

Thrusting back her thick fringe with her small hand, she excitedly peered at the mound; colander-like dotted with holes. Yesterday she had delightedly watched hundreds of lively ants swarming out and zigzagging down the dry cakey outer crust.

Disappointed, Shirin aggressively poked holes with her sharp twig. A small crust, alive with dozens of little 'beasts,' came away in her hand. Shrieking she dropped it. Scrambling out of the holes, the stringy rows of ants were marching down the sun-baked mound.

Startled on hearing the sound of horses' hooves and the imperious voice shouting, 'Get out of our way, girl!' she stepped back, stumbling over a stone.

Shirin fell straight onto a dry tuft of grass and tangles of brushwood, their sharp blades digging into her soft thighs. Howling in pain, she blinked up at the towering horse's white legs. The rider with his thick crop of reddish-brown hair glinting fire in the morning sun glared down at the girl. Her lower lip quivering, Shirin's vision blurred. Then Ali, another rider, appeared, coming to an abrupt stop near her, gripping tightly onto the reins of his horse. It was the girl!

The man with the reddish-brown hair pulled tightly at his reins and sped his horse towards the village, leaving a heavy screen of warm, dewy morning dust behind him.

'Are you all right, *piari shahzadi*?' Ali whispered.

His gentle tone and endearing words, 'lovely princess', triggered the flood of tears Shirin had been holding back.

Distressed on her behalf, he asked, 'Shall I take you home?' reaching down to pull her up onto his horse.

'Ali!'

Ali's hand tightened on the girl's arm as he faced his master. Trembling, Shirin turned a bewildered look at the other rider glaring at them from a distance and then pulled herself away, staring down in horror at the grassy stains soiling her favourite frock.

His mouth an angry slit, Ali asked. 'All right, princess?'

Shirin nodded; mouth a beguiling small pout and eyes two shimmering blue gems. She liked this man; he had brought them food the other night and always called her *piari shahzadi*.

Satisfied that the girl was OK, Ali sped up the path to the village square, stealing a look over his shoulder and flashing another kind smile at her.

Shirin remained staring after them, until she felt the tiny bites on her bare toes. Ants were scurrying around her feet.

Angrily wiping her tears with her small fist, she started to walk back, eyes on the white horse disappearing into the big white mansion, the *hevali*. Suddenly, a fully cloaked young woman in a pale blue linen *chador* stepped out from the tall sugarcane plants, startling her.

Shirin stared, innocently asking, 'Did you poo in the sugarcane field?' Her mother had told her once that in the old days, people used the fields to defecate at night or early in the morning.

Blushing, Salma, the quiltmaker's daughter, taken aback by the question, shook her head, trying her best to smile, and began to walk by her side. Shirin nervously glanced up at the woman, wondering if she would talk. It was only as they passed the *hevali* in the village square, that the woman murmured, 'You and I can't enter certain doors ...' Her fingertips brushed across the whitewashed railings 'These gates ... are closed to you! Two doors in the next street are closed to me.'

The small space between Shirin's dainty triangular-shaped

eyebrows furrowed. The word *pagaal* darted into her head. As if reading her mind, Salma drily murmured, 'I'm not mad … Ask your mum,' her eyes sweeping over the imposing building.

In the main village lane, the bricklayer's pregnant daughter-in-law with her reddish *sak*-stained lips and a basket of fresh vegetables held in the curve of one arm was sauntering towards them. Her other hand clutched the shawl discreetly draped around her shoulders to hide her heavily swollen, seven-month mound. Eyes averted, Salma raised the edge of her blue *chador* tightly to her chin and hurried away, protecting the other woman from her *perchanvah,* her evil shadow.

✳

Begum, Ali's wife, had his square-shaped *paratha* ready with a slice of mango pickle on a steel *chappati* tray. The dollop of fresh *makhan* churned before dawn in her clay milking pot had turned to a white fatty pool in the middle of it.

'Ali?'

Begum knew instantly that something was wrong when her husband reached for his mug of milky cinnamon tea, kicking aside the footstool. After three noisy, scalding-hot sips, Ali thrust it back on the tray, turning to leave.

'What's wrong, Ali?' Begum asked, quite vexed by his strange behaviour. What had got into him this morning? 'Your *paratha,* Ali!' she sternly reminded him. Four minutes to shape and cook, and the sizzling-hot ghee fat had burned her second finger on the blackened *tava* pan this morning.

'I don't want it!' he hissed. Why would the darned woman not leave him alone?

'What!' Scandalised, Begum leaned back on her footstool. Ali never missed his daily *paratha*. So today was a strange omission and he had a very busy day ahead of him.

'I said, I don't want it!' he aggressively rounded on her. Begum, equally annoyed, tugged at his trousers.

'OK! I'll eat the damn thing, woman!' Angrily he slapped her hand away.

'Forget the *paratha*!' she fumed. 'Tell me what's wrong!'

'The girl,' he muttered, his large Adam's apple, poking through the thin brown skin, bobbing up and down.

'I've bought a new dress for her. Massi Fiza will smuggle it out to ...'

'Master Haider shouted at her!'

'What?' Begum struggled to her feet, hand held against her mouth.

'The poor mite was in his way, Begum, nearly getting herself trodden! Master managed to pull his horse back!' Ali faithfully explained in a bid to excuse his master's actions. 'Then she fell, with big fat tears streaming down her lovely face. I wanted to jump off my horse and give her a tight hug, but Master called me – looking very fierce!'

'Well you had no choice, Ali. Comfort her or disobey our master.' Begum reassured her husband, her rebellious spirit tightening her mouth. 'And we've done quite a bit of disobeying,' she added, but he was already out of the courtyard, rattling the tall wooden door shut behind him.

Breakfast was not on Ali's mind. Master Haider wanted Ali to oversee the preparation for Arslan's homecoming village feast and get all the horses ready for the party parade.

In her soot-stained kitchen corner of the veranda, Begum made a face at the three-layered *paratha* dripping with fat and the half pot of creamy cinnamon tea left on the stove. Draping her *chador* carefully around her shoulders, she headed for Master Haider's *hevali* a street away.

*

Mistress Gulbahar was dreading her two sisters' simultaneous arrival at the *hevali*. With her beloved son's homecoming, she had plenty to do rather than having to put up with Mehreen's childish tantrums and Rani's supercilious looks. Gulbahar secretly hoped that Rani, her middle sister, would not be staying for long, for she was a law unto herself and stiffly rebuffed any attempt at 'sisterly' persuasion or friendship. On the other hand, Gulbahar was looking forward to having a good discussion with her brother-in-law, Liaquat, about the wedding arrangements for his son, Ismail.

'Thank goodness I have Begum. She'll see to the feast,' Gulbahar congratulated herself. She had not quite bargained on her housekeeper's sullen mood this morning, however, and was deeply offended by Begum's neglect in offering her customary morning *salaam*.

The girl, not a greeting, was on Begum's mind. Bristling with resentment at her employers and their 'cruel hearts', Begum headed straight for the kitchen but found herself annoyingly waylaid in the lobby of the back entrance by Massi Fiza, clutching a bulky sack of linen in her arms.

'Third round this morning, Begum!' A grinning Massi Fiza eagerly boasted, 'Here even before you! Mistress Gulbahar instructed me yesterday to wash lots of items.'

Begum angrily rounded on the laundrywoman, putting the *dhoban* in her place. 'I'm well aware of what goes on here, Fiza! Mistress Gulbahar shares all household matters with me.'

'How do you think I'm going to manage all this washing in one day?' Massi Fiza breezily asked, eager to start a conversation, blissfully unaware of the housekeeper's hostile mood this morning.

'As you've greedily grabbed all the washing from this household, I'm sure you'll find a way. Where you'll dry it all, I just don't know or care!' Then Begum cattily added, chuckling, 'Why don't you get your Rukhsar's glamorous college-educated daughters to lend you their manicured hands!'

Dismissing the laundrywoman, Begum entered 'her' domain, the large well-equipped kitchen with all modern conveniences and two marble sinks, both overlooking the central courtyard with its large marble shell-shaped fountain basin.

'Chance of a bowl of pink tea, Begum-ji?' Massi Fiza requested with a sheepish grin, head popped around the door, body poised to take flight in case Begum threw anything at her.

Begum glared back her answer, loathing the woman and her pestering this morning. If she had not been holding a basinful of flour, she could easily have wrung Massi Fiza's scrawny neck with its three dangling, black amulets, reverently purchased from the sweetmaker's wife's *pir*.

'Massi Fiza, take the laundry and get lost! I'm in no mood for your gossiping or to make you bowls of *sabz* tea!' Begum hissed, trying to still her panting heartbeat. 'Get your best friend Rukhsar to make you their Italian coffee! I've plenty to do with the guests arriving …' She stopped short, glimpsing the speculative look in Massi Fiza's eyes.

Always eager to know about the goings-on in the *hevali*, Massi Fiza inevitably ended up gossiping with her *siniaran* friend. Begum banged the door shut with her foot on Massi Fiza's shocked face.

*

Mistress Gulbahar entered the kitchen, highly mystified by her housekeeper's non-appearance in her bedroom this morning.

'Begum, I want the red rose china set brought out for the dinner. Make sure Jeena does not chip any more gold rims off the plates,' Gulbahar instructed.

'I'll wash the entire set myself,' Begum muttered, keeping her gaze averted from her mistress's. Deeply aggrieved by her housekeeper's tone and behaviour Gulbahar waited patiently for her to explain herself. Begum, however, appeared to be glued to the freezer lid.

'Begum?' Gulbahar prompted, smiling. They had been close friends for over two decades.

'Mother and daughter are back in the village!' Begum bitterly announced, waiting for some sound or word. She held her breath, nearly choking, hand frozen on the large bundle of lamb chops.

'Begum, don't forget to add yoghurt to the rice,' Gulbahar quietly ordered before walking out.

Her eyes squeezed tight in disbelief, Begum banged the freezer lid shut. 'What did you expect, woman?'

Leaning against the crockery sink, Begum stared out of the grilled window overlooking the courtyard. Mistress Gulbahar was feeding Mithu, their parakeet, its breakfast of seeds, her two fingers thrust in a cage dangling from one of the marble veranda colonnades. The parakeet mattered. Not the *girl*.

CHAPTER 2

The Closed Doors

Shirin's leather-sandaled steps threaded across the small veranda of the potter's home three lanes away. Through the grilled window bars of the main bedroom she saw her mother sorting out the bedding. A folded quilt propped on her head, Laila headed for the rooftop terrace to air it in the sun, carefully avoiding the two broken steps with their missing bricks. Smiling at her daughter, she returned to collect the other quilt.

Laila pulled her daughter into her arms. A loud wail was Shirin's answer. When her mother squatted in front of her everything swam before her eyes. 'Shirin?'

Alarmed, Laila peered into Shirin's eyes, now magnified into large sky-blue orbs swaying in a clear bed of water.

'Have you hurt yourself?'

Shirin nodded, pulling herself out of her mother's arms to show her dress. 'Look, my birthday dress, it's all ruined!'

'I'll buy you another one! Massi Fiza will give this one a special wash. How did you fall?'

Face screwed up in pain. 'I tripped, and ... and that horrible old man's eyes kept glaring at me ...' Shirin explained.

'The old man!' Laila's body stilled. 'What old man?'

'On a white horse – with face tassels. He ... he said, "Get out of our way, girl!" I hate him.'

Pressing her daughter's sobbing body against her chest, Laila planted kisses on her auburn curls, aflame in the morning sunlight peeping through the meshwork of the veranda tiles.

'This man, did he just appear?' Laila gently prompted.

'Yes!'

'And he had blue eyes and brown hair?' she whispered, a dull-ness spreading through her.

'Yes ... how do you know?' Shirin kept her eyes squeezed shut, blocking out the raw hatred in the man's face.

Laila stood up. 'You must have done something!'

'I didn't!' Shirin turned on her mother with a shrill, indignant cry, eyes flashing. 'I was looking at ants ... and I fell down. The horse's legs nearly hit me.' The loud sobs were back and this time with a vengeance.

'Guess what kind of *paratha* I've made you this morning?' Laila coaxed, keen to change the subject and wiping away her tears. 'And, by the way, he's not an old man!' she reprimanded.

Shirin shrugged at her mother's comment on the man's age – not caring.

'A spinach *paratha* – with an omelette – no onions, I promise,' her mother added. The mention of her favourite breakfast did the job; Shirin's rosebud mouth wedged into a reluctant smile.

Later on the rooftop, after hanging her daughter's dress to dry, Laila's head automatically turned to the other section of the village; to the *hevali*. With its light peachy paintwork and glossy white marble tiles gleaming in the hot sun, the large villa was a beacon to all. With its tall roof gallery, green and white flags flying high from two of the corners, Master Haider's *hevali* could easily be spotted at a distance.

Sighing, Laila sank down on the portable wooden bed to get on with an important task. A bucketful of roses had to be threaded fast. Begum's note tucked amidst the flowers had categorically stated two o'clock.

Laila dug the thick darning needle in and out of the rose stems, ignoring her sore thumbs and fingertips. Her daughter, now fed, bathed, dressed in a new frock and with her damp hair brushed flat against her scalp was sitting beside her.

'What're you doing, Mummy?' she enquired, feeling the soft petals between her fingertips.

'I'm making a *welcoming* flower garland, my darling.'

'Who for?'

'For a very special person, my darling,' she whispered, voice husky, kissing her daughter on her wet head.

'It's Daddy!' she shrieked with delight.

Laila's smile slipped. 'No! You can meet this person when he arrives. You've got a very special job to do, my princess. Look through those holes in the wall tiles. When you see three or four cars coming together into the village, with the big black Jeep in front, you must immediately call me, Shirin.'

*

Gulbahar stood lost beside the marble fountain, trying to recall the chore she had forgotten.

Face clearing, 'Begum!' she called. 'Have you switched on the air conditioning in *all* the rooms? Remember my beautiful son is coming from a cold country.'

Begum materialised from the main guest dining room, having given the last touches to the table with a vase of fresh orchids. The glass panels and mirrors in all the rooms had been thoroughly inspected for dust and smear marks.

'Yes, Sahiba-ji, it's on full blast – in all of the rooms! Ali will wheel in a water cooler near Mistress Mehreen's bed, for her hot flushes.'

'How thoughtful! What about the dinner? I wish you had let me ask Rasoola to help you!'

Begum vigorously shook her head, face creasing in distaste at the thought of *that* woman working in her kitchen. Rasoola, Mehreen's housekeeper, was cursed with a *complaining* disposition; about virtually everyone and everything, including her bad back. And the gravest sin of all – she had not one ounce of loyalty to her employers.

Begum did, however, gracefully welcome the town cook, Nalu, into her kitchen. To her surprise, not only was he wonderful at cooking but fantastic company, too; he had kept her giggling all morning with tales about his simple '*bholi*' wife, who continuously fell victim to the children's pranks. Before long, Begum had forgotten about the master's treatment of the girl and was delighted with Nalu's gift of a bag of his special freshly ground herbs.

'Sahiba-ji, please don't worry,' Begum reassured her mistress. 'Nalu has already cooked two large pots of meat. The rice is done and the watermelons are drowning nicely in icy water. I'm about to slice them ... Shall I use the crystal bowls, Mistress?'

'Of course!' Gulbahar gently chided. Everything had to be crystalware for her beloved son's homecoming!

'Oh, Begum!' Gulbahar exclaimed, as another thought struck her. 'What about the *halvie*? Did he say if the *jalebis* will be ready in the evening?'

'All sorted, Mistress. Ali is collecting three baskets at six; the sweetmaker, thanks to his wife's good nagging is punctual with the orders, unlike the horrid baker ... Remember how he kept us waiting for the *chappatis* with all the hungry guests to feed on Bakra Eid.'

'Great! Thanks, Begum. I must get ready. Can't wait to see my son!'

'Please, Mistress, don't worry. Will you stand and wait outside in the street with everyone else?'

'I think ...' Gulbahar frowned. 'I'll compromise this time, Begum, by standing inside, but peeping out of the door. You know I'm not in purdah but your master really hates men's eyes ogling me.'

Begum chuckled, eyes twinkling. 'Of course, he has every right to do so – he's very possessive about you and his family! Not surprising when he has a beautiful wife like you and a daughter ...' Begum faltered, as her mistress's eyes automatically squeezed shut, a shadow crossing her face.

'Excuse me ...' Begum stammered, cursing her stupid runaway tongue. 'Need to thread the garland!' she nervously added.

Gulbahar stiffly assented with her head, mood lightening. Her sisters were on their way. Saher, her lawyer niece, had taken a day off from her office work to personally welcome her cousin home, and she, his mother, hadn't even got changed!

*

'Mummy! Mummy! I can see the cars!' Shirin excitedly shouted from the rooftop to her mother down below in the courtyard. 'Are you there, Mummy?'

Laila stepped out from under the veranda, the *kajal* stick in her hand. Her daughter was peering over the low balcony wall from the rooftop. 'Be careful, darling. You'll fall!' Laila anxiously called.

A few moments later, her body swathed in a lawn *chador*, Laila stepped into the lane and collided with Massi Fiza and her bundle of clean laundry. Laila prayed that the laundrywoman wasn't heading for the same place and suddenly decided that she didn't want her daughter to accompany her.

'Shirin, please play at home or in the fields!'

'I want to go to the fields.'

Smiling, she left her daughter and hastened down the lane, the garland held tightly against her chest under the fold of her *chador*.

✴

The sweetmaker's wife, Jennat Bibi, had just been to see her *pir* in the next village. Face glowing, she hopped off the bus on the GT road and hurried home to tell her family the good news she had learned. Ahead of her, a large group of excited well-wishers had gathered outside Master Haider's *hevali* to welcome back young Master Arslan. With garlands of flowers proudly draped over their arms, some talked animatedly amongst themselves.

Jennat Bibi spotted her friend Neelam amongst the crowd of women well-wishers and hastened her pace.

'*Assalam alaikum*, Jennat Bibi. How are you?' Neelum turned, smiling.

'*Wa laikum salam*, with God's blessing I'm well and very happy.'

'Been visiting your relatives in the city?'

'No, my *pir*.'

'Why?'

'Good news! Tell you later – but why are you here?'

'Don't you know? Master Arslan is coming home from America. Did your husband not get the big order for the *mithai* for his homecoming party?'

'Oh … Yes, of course. I forgot. I'll join you, as I'm here anyway!'

'Yes, do! Look! See who else is here! Hiding behind that tree … it's her … '

Both women glanced surreptitiously at the cloaked woman half hidden behind the tree.

'Well, Sister Jennat Bibi. What did your *pir* say?' Neelum eagerly pressed, wanting to know the truth behind her friend's flushed face and laughing brown eyes.

'Go on then … You'll be the first to know. My *pir* tells me that Faiza is going to have a son!'

'How wonderful! Congratulations!'

'Thank you!' Jennat Bibi winked. 'This is going to be fun! Look at Massi Fiza – just because she collects the dirty linen from the *hevali*, she's hogging the gates as if she owns them,' she sneered, having never seen eye to eye with the laundrywoman since the *dhoban* had ruined her white silk shawl with red dye from another garment. She grimaced at the garland in her friend's hands, wishing that she had one, too.

And why was her foolish husband not here? Could he not spare a few measly minutes to leave his greasy *jalebi*-frying wok and syrup pot to attend this gathering? Did he not know the importance of remaining in the good books of the rich and the influential ones? Luckily for the sweetmaker's household, she was the blessed one – with plenty of worldly wisdom, augmented by her *pir*'s guidance. Her husband was only fit to make *ladoos*!

*

'They are here!' Begum excitedly shrieked to her Sahiba-ji, standing discreetly behind the door with a large china plate piled high with an assortment of sweetmeats in her hand, relishing the warmth of the freshly baked *ladoos*.

The three cars with the Jeep in front rode up the dusty road to the *hevali* gates. The well-wishers excitedly rushed to greet. Haider stepped out first, followed by his beloved son, Arslan.

Excited cries of '*Mubarak, Mubarak, Haider Sahib!*' jetted

loudly out of everyone's mouths. Arslan, a twenty-six-year-old young man, was immediately hemmed in by a circle of well-wishers and warm hugs. Grinning, he took it all in good grace, letting men eagerly drop their flower and money garlands over his neck.

Haider stood aside, proudly watching.

Unable to wait, Gulbahar boldly thrust the door wide open, desperate for the other people to leave her son alone, aching to smother his face with kisses. Her eyes scanned the heads of the villagers and then drifted to the old *neem* tree facing the *hevali's* gates.

Gulbahar froze, watching a woman's cloaked figure move forward. Wide-eyed, her fingers tightly gripped a plate of sweetmeats.

Ali, too, happened to look behind, eyes fixed on the woman's beseeching gaze, requesting his permission to either step forward into the crowd or to disappear into anonymity once more.

Laila drew her garland of thickly knotted rosebuds from under her *chador*. Ali closed his eyes tight. Hers continued to plead.

'Please let me!' they begged.

Ali surrendered, humanity kicking in. A smile of approval flickered across his face, head dipping. It was up to almighty Allah now.

Heart thudding, Laila took tentative steps into the crowd, pressing the flower garland to her chest, her other hand holding the fold of the *chador* up to her mouth. Some well-wishers, recognising her, let her pass and waited with bated breath.

Laila hovered three paces behind the tall broad-shouldered young man. Soft lips parting and voice husky, 'Arslan,' she whispered.

Arslan turned, his handsome mouth parting in pleasure, the cobalt-blue eyes scanning the partially hidden face of the woman standing in front of him. Laila heard the indrawn breath of Master Haider, standing two yards away.

Laila held her garland in her hands. Standing on her toes, she reached up for his neck, but another masculine arm neatly sliced between them, pulling him away.

Laila stumbled backwards and the garland fell to the ground. Arslan glared at his father, electrifying the villagers looking on.

Keeping his face straight in front of the well-wishers, Haider coldly announced, 'Your mother is waiting, my son!' digging his fingers hard into his son's elbow. 'Let's go inside!' Arslan felt the full ruthless strength of his father's fingers and surrendered, letting himself be pulled, his bewildered gaze fixed on Laila's lowered face.

Then, before his horrified eyes, his father's silver-embroidered *khussa*-clad foot fell flat on Laila's garland, crushing the neatly threaded rosebuds into the dust.

Laila raised a pain-filled face, but the head had already turned.

Attempting to salvage the situation, Ali dutifully stepped behind Arslan's figure, cutting him off from Laila. Ali's tearful eyes begged forgiveness of the woman who offered an anguished screen of shimmering blue water.

The shocked well-wishers nervously stepped aside to let Arslan and Haider pass. Some mischievous pairs of eyes remained on the crushed garland and the woman who mutely stared across at Mistress Gulbahar's stricken face peeping from behind the *hevali* door. Then Mistress Gulbahar hurriedly drew back as her two beloved men entered, thrusting the tall door wide open. A small group of relatives followed behind.

Ali, last to enter, shut the door behind him.

The village people, talking in hushed voices and casting their last glances at the woman still staring at the closed gates, made their way back to their homes.

Behind the *hevali* gates, a pair of keen eyes rested on the remaining pink and red roses scattered on the dusty ground.

*

In the *hevali* courtyard, Arslan stood stiffly in his mother's arms, letting her rain kisses over his face and shoulders in a bid to reassure herself that he was actually back – all in one piece. Gulbahar just couldn't get enough of her son.

'He's home, Haider Sahib!' her quivering voice addressed her unsmiling husband from across the courtyard. Then she looked expectantly at her son. Smile faltering, Gulbahar stepped back.

'Arslan?'

Arslan pointedly held his father's gaze, mouth parted to storm at them, but the words died on his lips as he watched the light of love slip from his beloved mother's face. The dull wary look was back, the beautiful mouth drooped. Where had that sparkle from his childhood days gone? But he knew – did he not?

'I'm tired from the journey, Mother,' he gently offered, masking his thoughts and feelings; after all, it was not his mother's fault. 'I need to rest.'

'Guests are waiting to meet you, my son,' his father mocked.

'They can wait!' Arslan swiftly rounded on his father. 'As someone else had to wait for ten years – just to have a door slammed in her face!'

Ignoring his father's stony face, Arslan entered his bedroom, slamming the door shut behind him.

Gulbahar nervously exchanged a look with her husband, feeling her chest tighten. Two shocks in one day – first the girl, then her mother. Begum, ever watchful and protective of her mistress's welfare, dragged a chair from under the veranda. Gulbahar collapsed into it, only to be threatened by the stiff looming shadow of her husband.

'What sort of children did you raise, Gulbahar?' he accused.

'Beautiful children, Haider,' she valiantly shot back, hysterical laughter rumbling through her body.

Ruefully shaking his head at his wife's words, Haider strode into the dining room and bid his male guests to eat and make themselves fully at home while Arslan rested.

*

In the dimly lit bedroom, Laila stared down at the crushed rosebuds in the fold of her *chador*, strangling a scream ripping through her throat. Shirin dropped her skipping rope and came running to see what was wrong with her mother.

'Are you crying again, Mummy?' she demanded, her young mind trying to judge whether her mother was upset.

'No! Stop badgering me, Shirin. Go and play outside!' Laila shouted, looking away.

Shirin did not obey; instead she watched her mother empty the crushed rosebuds into a small china dish on the dressing table and cover it with a crocheted-edged muslin cloth.

*

After serving the guests, Begum had sneaked home and was fast at work in her living room. The thick darning needle threaded with wool swung in and out of the remains of seven rosebud stems she had scooped from outside the *hevali* gates, her anxious eyes often straying to the wall clock. Mistress Gulbahar's two sisters, Mehreen and Rani, had probably arrived by now. Job done, Begum hid the garland beneath her *chador* and hastened back to work.

Sneaking in through the servants' entrance, Begum was crossing the central courtyard when Mistress Gulbahar caught her.

'Begum, I've been looking everywhere for you, even in the paddock!'

Sheepishly Begum pulled up her *chador* to show the garland. Her eyes widening, Gulbahar was about to reprimand her and then stopped short when she heard her husband's footsteps behind her. Meanwhile, Begum slipped into the young master's room.

The air conditioner noisily purring away sent jets of cool air swishing across the high ceiling of the whitewashed room. Master Arslan was wide awake, struggling with the reality of straddling two worlds. A lost traveller wedged between two lands – that of his homeland and America, yet belonging to neither; unable to come to terms with his parents' world and running away from the other that had become increasingly hostile to him since the awful events of 9/11.

'Master Arslan!' Begum stood beside the bed, lovingly gazing down at the young man she had looked after for many years. Arslan sat up, attempting to smile. 'Master Arslan,' Begum's secretive voice wooed, lifting her *chador* to show the remains of Laila's garland.

'Begum …' Eyes softening, Arslan was humbled by Begum's loving endeavour.

'See! Threaded it for you, my prince.'

Arslan stared at the clumsily threaded rosebuds, closing his eyes to smell the crushed petals.

'How could I let her garland, threaded by her beautiful loving fingers go to waste? I scooped every single petal into my *chador*! You know I love you both – I'd do anything for you two!'

'I know Begum!' Arslan slipped off the bed to place the garland around his neck. 'Thank you!'

Begum preened, advising, 'Wear it with pride, my little prince!'

'I will. No matter what the rest of this household thinks … or says!'

Begum followed him out of the room, keeping her triumphant eyes lowered. She was a traitor once again, but a happy and unrepentant one this time!

Haider, who was having his overcoat brushed down by Ali, stiffened when his son stepped out of his room with the garland around his neck.

Arslan nonchalantly walked to the marble fountain, cooling his hand under the spray of water in the large basin where as a toddler, dressed only in shorts, Begum used to sit him down and let him splash around. His gaze shot up to the roof terrace where as a young boy he used to play kites. As if reading his thoughts, Begum strolled over to caress him on his cheek, gaze softening with love.

'Master Arslan, you'll get sunstroke standing out in the heat. This is not America.'

'You'd be surprised, Begum. It gets really hot in the summer in the USA. Sometimes your skin begins to peel off!'

'Really!'

'Really!' he mimicked, bursting into laughter and splashing her with a scoopful of water as he used to do as a child. Shrieking, she stepped back wiping her wet face. Begum was still his favourite person, the woman who successfully weaned him out of many of his childhood sulks.

'Master Arslan, your two aunties have been waiting for hours. And have not eaten yet. Poor things didn't want to disturb your sleep. Guess who else is here?'

She paused, her eyes fixed on his face, anticipating the telltale tide of colour that would sweep his cheeks at the mention of a name.

'Saher,' she whispered and delightedly watched the colour jump into his face. 'Has America whitened your blood, my handsome prince?'

'No, Begum, it's still very red and warm! The American experience has given me an insight into another world and another way of thinking about my life, that's all. On the whole I loved my stay and study there. Made many friends and learned a lot about equality and celebration of diversity.'

'So you find our ways are not to your liking any more, Master Arslan?' Begum drily quipped, disappointed at his response.

'No, Begum, let's say we beg to differ! Shall we go and meet my dear ladies?' he gruffly offered, not in any mood to debate further about his life in America, its virtues and its vices.

As soon as he opened the dining-room door, his eyes sought Saher, joy rushing through him. Her face lighting up, she strolled over and planted a kiss near his mouth, shocking him into stillness, cheek smarting and eyes hooded.

'Well, our prince returns!' she teased, smiling, fingers resting on his bare arm and voice warm with laughter.

'My handsome graduate nephew returns!' His Auntie Mehreen gathered him in her arms.

'Yes, Auntie, a fully-fledged American postgraduate with a PhD – for whatever that's worth here,' he corrected, sauntering over to Saher's mother, Rani, who had remained sitting at the table, frowning at her daughter's action in kissing Arslan. She lightly patted him on his shoulder; the cool awkward smile did not quite reach her eyes. Inside, Rani was recoiling from the look she had glimpsed in his eyes as they fell on her daughter.

'The rascal!' she fumed under her breath. Why didn't anyone else notice it? Just as well, for her daughter's sake!

'Come and sit down, my beautiful son,' Gulbahar stiffly requested from across the room, her eyes shying away from Laila's garland around his neck. 'Your aunts waited to eat with you.'

Arslan pulled out a chair for Saher before sitting next to her at the table.

'Gorgeous as ever!' Leaning over he whispered into her ears, as his aunts busied themselves with the food. Blushing, Saher looked away from the wicked glint in his eyes.

'And America has made you a very impudent *badmash* man!' she retaliated, punishing him for his unwanted compliment.

A shadow crossing his face, Arslan spoke in English so that his mother and aunts could not follow their conversation.

'Things have become really difficult for some of us again as a result of recent events. Many innocent Muslims are detained and questioned, including at the airports.'

'OK, let's not talk about that now but it's so good to have you back,' she warmly smiled.

'But there was still some humanity in America even after 9/11!' he mocked, looking away, afraid to lose himself in the depths of her grey eyes.

'And there isn't any here, Arslan?' she enquired, sobering.

'Well, I see no sign of humanity in this household!' He had deliberately switched to Urdu, his eyes on his mother.

The three sisters listened, spoons poised nervously over their food.

'And you sisters are no better! Can you not make my mother see sense? Are your hearts made of stone, too?' His accusing gaze transfixed them into silence.

'Arslan!' His mother's aggrieved voice sliced across the table, watching Begum nervously hovering over Saher's shoulders with a large dish of pilau rice weighing down her arms.

'I'm not very hungry, Mother!' Noisily scraping back his chair on the marble floor, Arslan strode out of the room, leaving the five women staring after him.

'Rude boy!' Rani sneered.

'Saher, please go after him. You are good with him.' Ignoring Rani's hostile stare Gulbahar coaxed her niece, upset at her son's reaction.

'Arslan!' Saher called. Hearing her footsteps, he ran up the marble stairs, taking two strides at a time.

Smiling, Saher followed him up to the rooftop terrace with its elegant alcoves, wall niches, marble floor, and rows of earthenware-potted petunias and geraniums in full bloom, propped against the iron railings. Some bushes trailed over the railings, creating an attractive profusion of yellow and purple flowers.

Saher pressed her hand on his shoulder.

'Don't touch me!' Flinching, he rounded on her, 'I'm not a child!'

'I never said you were! I'm sorry.' Alarmed, she stepped back.

'Then why did you kiss me earlier?' he asked, confusing her further.

'Because I wanted to ... and missed you!' she stammered, trying to explain; she had followed the social custom of being able to kiss one's own younger brothers and cousins.

'I recommend that from now on you keep all your kisses for your fiancé!' he jeered, bent on hurting her.

'What's wrong, Arslan?' Saher was both shocked and offended. 'Why are you behaving so strangely and saying such nasty things to me?'

'I'm just reminding you about social propriety; that women in our culture do not go around kissing men or touching them physically unless they are very young or married to them or blood sisters! You are none of these!'

'You're being silly! You are like a brother to me!' she retaliated, flummoxed by his reaction.

'Does that make it legitimate for you to touch me?' he snarled. 'Why have you never touched Ismail?' Cynically watching the tide of crimson colour flooding her cheeks, 'Because he's your fiancé, is that why?'

'This is all mad talk! I'll not touch you ever again, you silly man! I don't know what has happened to you? Is this what America has turned you into? This horrible cruel beast bent on offending everyone?'

'No, you'll never understand! Leave me alone, Saher! Don't ever touch me again!' He turned his back to her.

Then the fight went out of him.

'Have you seen Laila?' he asked, changing the subject. 'I saw her earlier. Father publicly humiliated both of us and almost dragged me into the house. She just stood there … That look on her face, Saher – I'll never forget it!'

An awkward silence ensued.

'But surely you know the score, Arslan?' Saher lamely offered.

He beamed his full wrath on her. 'For how long is everyone going to go on scoring? Don't you think she has been punished enough?'

'I'm sorry!' Saher stepped back, distressed at his pain. 'Like you, I miss Laila.'

'I'm sorry, Saher,' Arslan shrugged, relenting. 'It's not your fault.'

'It's all right!' She smiled as she always did, reaching out to him, but he gripped her wrist hard before it reached his cheek.

'Arslan!' she whispered, lost for words, her wrist hurting in his tight grip.

'Please don't touch me, Saher, for I am a child no longer!' he whispered softly into her eyes before letting go of her arm and turning. 'Ismail will definitely not appreciate it. Believe me!' he shot over his shoulder.

Saher reeled; all this fuss about her touching him. He knew that she was a touching sort of person and had always touched him? He had come from the West, the land where men and women openly kissed in the streets and demonstrated their feelings publicly. So why had he become so paranoid about her touching him?

'I'm a man now, Saher!'

She stared at his back, mouth agape, before leaving him. Twice he had made a point of reminding her about that.

'Oh, Ismail! Please come soon,' she silently beseeched running down the stairs, her painted toes gripping her elegant mules. Three more days to go before her fiancé would join her. And in three weeks' time, she would be a married woman. In six months' time, upon successfully gaining a spouse's entry visa, she would most probably be with him in England. There was a lot to do in the run-up to her forthcoming wedding. Her mother had forgotten that they had an appointment with the goldsmith.

Later she drove her mother and Auntie Mehreen, her future mother-in-law, to Ismail's house. It was there that her future father-in-law, Liaquat Sahib, had invited two of the most prestigious jewellers, one from the city and the other from the village, Rukhsar's husband, for Saher's dowry jewellery.

*

Laila fingered the soft petals in her palm. 'His feet touched them,' she cried, doubling over on her bed beside her sleeping daughter.

The phone shrilled in the silent room startling Laila. Reluctantly she reached for the receiver, knowing it was going to be her husband. Begum's sweet voice welcomed her.

'Don't fret, young Mistress, he's wearing your garland!' Laila held her breath.

'Thank you!' she whispered, but the phone was silent in her hand.

At the other end of the line, in the *hevali*, Begum blushed, placing the phone back on its cradle when her mistress entered the room. Gulbahar's accusing eyes spelt that she had heard the entire conversation. Begum opted to brazen it out.

'I'll serve the tea, Sahiba-ji!' Sticking a full smile to her face, she hastened out of the room.

Gulbahar crossed the room to the onyx coffee table. Lifting the phone receiver, she pressed the redial button. And waited – her breath held.

'Hello?' the hesitant voice uttered. Seconds ticked away into silence.

Then a soft moan, 'Forgive me!'

Gulbahar clicked the receiver down onto its cradle. Cheeks flushed, she joined her sisters in the drawing room.

*

In her room, Laila quietly wept, holding the phone to her cheek. 'When will you forgive me? How long will you go on punishing me?'

A few minutes later the phone shrilled again, but she let it ring for some time before pulling the wire out. She knew it was her husband this time, and she only had bitter words to greet him: 'I have lost my world for you. Are you worth it, Jubail?'

The words taunted, as they did on most nights, in the humble potter's home. Closing her eyes, she ritually relived that journey; the previous life of young Mistress Laila, the beautiful daughter of Haider, who loved horse riding, dressed in men's clothing, with her father's stable boy.

CHAPTER 3

Laila

Jubail was busy grooming Master Haider's favourite mare in the stable, late in the evening, when his eyes fell upon the beautiful 22-year-old Mistress Laila. Strolling to the other horse, she patted its flanks and then laid her head on the horse's neck. Standing still, Jubail watched from under the shadow of the tree – intrigued. He had never set eyes on a woman who behaved in this intimate way towards a horse; Laila had definitely inherited her father's genes.

The horse under Jubail's hand shifted, immediately drawing Laila's attention to his corner of the stable courtyard. Startled, she stepped back, eyes wary. She knew who he was; the potter's son – the 'clever' young man studying at the prestigious university and whose passion for riding horses had won her father's respect and interest.

Master Haider took pride in breeding horses for the annual city race and for his personal use, little deterred by the fact that on a practical level horses were becoming obsolete in their part of the district. Only the *tangas,* the horse carriages, required a horse and those, too, were becoming scarce. The humble local rickshaws and cars had taken over both peoples' lives and the rural landscape.

When Jubail had tentatively asked if he could ride and look after the horses, Haider Ali could barely contain his delight. Arslan was too young to handle horses.

'Jubail, saddle this horse,' Laila commanded in a clear, authoritative voice, addressing him by his first name.

Jubail bristled at the tone – the one she used with the servants.

And he, despite being a clever student at university, here in the village, as a mere stable boy from the humble potter's household, was clearly in that league as far as Mistress Laila was concerned. He nodded, turning to hide his tight face, but she had already gone.

The horse prepared, he waited, perched on a small stool in the shadowed area of the veranda, wondering who was going to ride it. The sky was dark and he wanted to get home; his mother was waiting with his favourite dish of fried fish. A slim turbaned man entered the stable courtyard, briskly strolled up to the saddled horse and in one clean sweep had swung himself over it.

Before Jubail could utter 'Hey you', the man and the horse had already ridden out of the stable courtyard gates. Fearing that the horse was being stolen, Jubail swung himself up on the other horse and galloped out of the paddock courtyard.

'Hey! Stop!' Jubail shouted, enraged. The rider merely scowled and galloped even faster. His heart racing, Jubail kept his eye on the horse and the rider now crossing the fields. Incensed, Jubail dug his heels into the animal's sides and increased his speed until he was parallel to the other horse, reaching for the reins. Taken aback by Jubail's action, the rider lost his grip and fell straight into the spinach field.

Hearing a gasp of pain, Jubail peered down, eyes widening in shock. It was a woman. More to the point, Mistress Laila, sprawled on top of the leafy spinach plants, glaring up at him. The dark mass of hair tumbled around her shoulders, the yards of fabric of her hand-made turban lay in her lap.

'How dare you!' she raged, eyes shot with contempt.

'I dare because riding out in the darkness, all alone, is neither sensible nor sane for a young woman!' he chillingly reminded her, nostrils flaring, angrily reining his horse. Then added, softening his tone, remembering his subservient role. 'It's not the done thing, Mistress – I'm sorry that I startled you!'

He left her seething on the dusty path, letting her sort herself out, and waited at a distance. Laila shoved her hair under the turban cloth knowing full well how incongruous she looked in male clothing. For no one else wore a turban in the village.

From afar and with grudging admiration, Jubail watched her ride away into the fields. Only when she headed back towards the village did he think it was right for him to turn back.

In the stable courtyard, ignoring him, Laila merely tied the horse in its usual place. Before she went through the door leading to the *hevali* courtyard she couldn't help calling over her shoulder, 'Saddle the horse for me tomorrow evening for nine o'clock,' the tone soft, but a command nevertheless.

Bemused, Jubail stared after her, his coal-black eyes blazing in the dark. Did she think he had nothing better to do than wait around to saddle horses for her at night? The arrogance of the woman!

*

Jubail did, however, 'wait around' and saddle Mistress Laila's horse, melting under her smile of gratitude and gems for eyes. Before riding out of the stable courtyard, she leaned down and whispered, 'Thank you.'

The two softly spoken words lent wings to his body. He found himself clambering onto another horse and riding out after her. Laila heard him racing after her but preferred to ignore his presence, instead widening the distance between them. Then she let him join her on the way back. Their companionable silence was only broken when she returned to the courtyard.

'Would you like to ride him again tomorrow night, Mistress Laila?' he asked, reading her thoughts, loving the sound of her name on his lips.

She smiled, looking down, adding with a plea, 'Please don't tell my father! He doesn't know I ride.'

He laughed aloud. 'You really love horse riding!' he marvelled, his dark eyes caressing her face and his voice husky with secret laughter.

'I love it! But Father would never let me ride a horse; he says that it is unfeminine!' she revealed, eyes shyly taking in his masculine appearance.

'Well, I don't know about the "unfeminine" bit, Mistress Laila, but you can clearly handle these beasts pretty well.'

She beamed in pleasure. 'Thank you.'

'Your father is away for a week, isn't he?' Jubail probed. 'So do you wish to ride out each night?'

She nodded, head lowered and heat rushing into her face; she was entering a conspiracy with him, just as she had done with Begum.

'OK, I'll saddle the horse for you for nine o'clock. But on one condition!' She looked up sharply, face alert. 'That I accompany you! I'm not happy about you riding alone in the dark. What if you were to fall and hurt yourself? And suppose somebody discovered your true identity?'

Reluctantly Laila nodded, accepting his wisdom. Thus a pattern was established. Jubail would leave his home early, immediately after his evening meal, and go to the paddock to saddle the two horses. Chaperoned by Begum, Laila would sneak out of the *hevali* to Begum's house to change into her male gear and don a turban or scoop her hair under a cap. They would ride out into the darkness, under the shining stars, relishing the clamour of crickets around them. Begum held a vigil, grateful to Jubail for keeping an eye on her young mistress.

The initial companionable silence soon turned to a strange tingling awareness between them. And they began to not only enjoy each other's company, but found the experience of racing across the fields exhilarating. Twice Jubail let her win. They discussed, debated and argued over many things – from cynicism about Pakistani politics to books they had read and their future aspirations for successful careers. Laila was eager to learn about his university life and he in turn coaxed her for information about her life as the wealthy daughter of the village landowner. Both were intrigued by the other's very different background. Wealth on one side; poverty on the other.

Her father's return put an abrupt stop to the riding. Chafing under the restraint, she sneaked two visits to the stable to spend time with Jubail, drowning him with her wistful looks, forcing him to offer: 'Look Laila, I'm going back to university tomorrow. Tonight is my last night of riding. Want to come?'

'Please!' Laila entreated, giggling, only too pleased, her

cobalt-blue eyes sparkling. 'Let me go and change, and tell Begum.'

A few minutes later, like two guilty children, they hurried out into the darkness, Laila checking over her shoulders, heart racing.

'I'll miss you,' she stammered in the dark, 'I mean riding with you,' she hastily amended, looking away. 'It's much more fun ...'

'I've enjoyed riding with you, too! I'll be back during the holidays,' he promised, chest swelling with pride.

'Good,' she whispered, uncomfortable with the heat rushing through her cheeks.

Only Begum knew about her young mistress's clandestine horse riding and meetings with Jubail, the potter's son. Startled at catching a glimpse of shy warmth in her mistress's eyes, Begum felt duty-bound to warn her about the sheer impropriety of it all, not bothering to mince her words, 'So unacceptable for the landlord's daughter to be spending so much time alone in the darkness – with a man who is no blood relative, but happens to be the son of a lowly potter! What would your father think if he found out?' she had scorned.

Gulbahar, totally unaware of her daughter's movements and emotional involvement with the potter's son, was fully steeped in preparations for Laila's trousseau. A landlord with two homesteads and dozens of acres to his name from a nearby town was asking for her hand in marriage. Gulbahar had kept her daughter abreast of all the goings-on as she went her merry way in planning for the engagement over a period of months.

Laila ignored it all. Her thoughts were with Jubail; she was eagerly waiting for their next horse riding session when he returned after his final university exams. Arslan, her younger brother had been sworn to secrecy, as were Ali and Begum, albeit reluctantly, about her movements and relationship with the potter's son.

Laila's prospective fiancé and his family were coming to fix a date for the engagement party. Cheeks flushed with excitement, Gulbahar informed her 12-year-old son that his sister was getting married soon. Very close to his sister, and upset at the prospect of losing her, Arslan dashed out to tell Laila, but she wasn't in her room. He went searching for Begum.

'Has my sister gone out horse riding again?' Arslan innocently asked of Begum, hovering near the stable doors. A knot of worry tightening her throat, Begum's eyes peered out at the dark fields, on the lookout for her flighty young mistress. Young master's nails dug into Begum's arm as he recalled that his father, too, was out on his horse.

*

From under the shadows of the *minar* tree, Haider's proud gaze swooped over acres of land etched against the far horizon. 'All of this will be my Arslan's one day!' he uttered aloud, addressing the evening stars. 'For my Laila has no need of this land when she marries.'

Sitting back on his steed, Haider Ali congratulated himself on his fortune, revelling in Allah Pak's blessing; he had everything. Two beautiful healthy children, a dutiful wonderful wife, and wealth that would keep his future generations in splendid style and see his only son through an expensive foreign university education.

From the corners of his eyes he noted the approaching figures of two horse riders in the distance.

A few seconds later, he stiffened on hearing a peal of laughter, his head shooting up. One rider was bending down and, in the process, the cap had fallen off and long hair spilled out onto the shoulders. Haider's hand became a tight fist, clutching the horse's reins. Spellbound, he watched the other rider jump down from the horse, pick up the cap and then start to tuck *his* daughter's hair back under it.

Gritting his teeth, betrayal skewered Haider. 'That beast is touching my daughter!' Nausea spiralled through him at the thought of his daughter's defilement; eyes shut tight and beads of sweat erupting on his face.

'Surely it can't be my Laila riding out alone at night with him!' He crushed the urge to rush up to the 'beast' and lash him both with his belt and his words. 'Get your hands off my daughter, you rascal!'

Pressing his hand hard against his mouth to stifle his rage, and schooled with innate human wisdom, Haider did and said nothing, merely withdrawing from the scene – for it was impossible for him to look either of them in the eye.

*

Begum was standing tall on her heels at the stable door, peering into the dark – apparently waiting. Haider guessed correctly for whom. On catching a glimpse of her master, the housekeeper shrivelled on the spot, singeing beneath the full blaze of his wounded eyes, her wobbly legs almost giving way beneath her.

He knew!

Her waiting days for Mistress Laila were over; it was time to scuttle off home. God only knew what was about to happen in the *hevali*. 'Oh, Allah Pak, what calamity have my actions unleashed on this household!'

Once home and gasping for breath, Begum collapsed on the *charpoy* on the veranda. Her husband, leaning against the colonnade, dragged at the cigarette butt gripped between his three fingers, shooting her a speculative look.

'Our master knows about Laila!' Begum tried to sit up. The shock had done something to her back. The knot of pain had her flattened on the portable bed. She had heard about this form of paralysis but never believed it. In fact, she had scoffed at the idea.

Ali winced, 'Oh, Begum, what have we done? He knows nothing about her relationship with that scoundrel!'

From the bed, Begum, still in pain, dumbly nodded, licking her dried lips, bursting to explain. 'He knows, Ali! He looks like a man who has lost five inches off his height. I'll never forget that look in his eyes, Ali!'

'What do you expect, woman?' her husband bitterly sniped.

'Oh, Allah Pak!'

'What now?'

'Mistress Gulbahar! She knows absolutely nothing!'

The cigarette butt in Ali's hand was shaking, his Adam's apple energetically bobbing up and down.

'Just pray, woman!' he lashed out. 'A right dimwit you are. I told you not to indulge the young mistress!'

Begum miserably accepted the truth behind her husband's cruel and derogatory term 'dimwit'.

✳

Gulbahar was happily humming to 'Queen' Noor Jahan's famous Punjabi melody whilst leaning down into a steel trunk. Supporting its heavy steel lid with one hand, with the other she lifted the burgundy roll of chenille that was propped against other rolls of fabric; a beautiful collection of silks, chiffons and velvets for Laila's trousseau, purchased from many cities. The tantalising picture of her fair-skinned, attractive daughter draped in a dark rich velvet fabric had Gulbahar grinning. This had to be the one for her Laila's engagement party. 'First impressions matter,' she gushed.

Gulbahar was enjoying the sensual fingering of the chenille's softness when the door was aggressively thrown open.

'What do you think of this, Laila?' She held up the roll, her head still leaning over the trunk.

Stony silence greeted her question. Raising her head, Gulbahar's smile fled at the tight mask of her husband's face.

'Haider-ji?' she stammered, immediately sensing that something was terribly wrong.

'You have failed me, Gulbahar!' The granite-laden words pelted her from across the room.

Her heart plummeting, Gulbahar dully croaked, 'I don't understand, Haider-ji?'

'Where's Laila?'

'Laila?' She winced at the cutting tone, frowning. 'I ... I think she's in her room. Why?'

With a bitter male grunt he strode out of the room.

Gulbahar dropped the roll in the steel case and slamming the lid down ran after her husband. He had already crossed the courtyard; she followed him to the first floor and then went straight to her daughter's room, staring in puzzlement at the empty bedroom. When she returned downstairs, she found Laila standing by the fountain spring hurriedly winding her hair up into a knot. A long linen scarf was draped over her shoulders.

'Where were you, Laila?'

'I … I …' Laila's lowered head added to Gulbahar's confusion.

'Laila?' she demanded, voice rising. 'Your father just asked if I knew where you were?'

To Gulbahar's dismay, Laila paled and a frightened, childlike look scuttled across her face.

'Laila, what's going on?' Gulbahar asked, fear clutching hold of her. 'What did your father mean when he said that I have *failed* him?'

Under the moonlight Laila stared at the two little brown sparrows lightly hopping on the necks of the earthenware plant pots. Gulbahar shook her by the arm. Mother and daughter warily eyed each other, their heartbeats quickening as they heard Haider's steps thudding down the stairs.

Both froze.

Haider's eyes lightly skimmed over their heads and then he looked beyond into space, icily addressing his daughter.

'Laila, kindly inform your mother where you were and with *whom* this evening?'

In reply Laila's head hung in shame. Haider hastened away in the direction of his office, unable to look at his daughter.

'Laila!' Gulbahar asked, bewildered, her eyes on her husband's departing figure. Laila escaped, snatching her hand from her mother's grasp. In her room upstairs, she locked herself in, cheeks throbbing with shame. Her father had seen her with Jubail! If only the ground would open up and gulp her down whole.

Panting, Gulbahar stood outside her daughter's room, her small fist thudding on the wooden door. Then she drew back, the mist clearing in her head and eyes widening in horror. Her heart squeezed. What had her daughter done that merited her locking herself away in shame? And what was it that made it impossible for her Haider-ji to look at his daughter or to utter the words, as if they would soil his mouth?

Resigned to her fate, Gulbahar waited in her room for her husband. She didn't know what time he returned, but he was up before her and studiously avoided her eyes.

'Gulbahar, prepare for your daughter's wedding!' was his

morning greeting. 'Forget six months, now it's in six weeks' time,' he coldly instructed, leaving his wife breathless and panicking.

*

Ali was summoned to Haider's office. His master didn't honour his trusted male companion with eye contact, questions or a smile this morning. Instead his gaze remained fixed on the leather top of his desk. In two minutes he had scrawled a note in perfect *Nastaliq* Urdu. Nervously, Ali waited.

'This is for the potter.' Haider held out the note, his face averted.

Clutching the folded, crispy bond paper, Ali hurried to exit.

Away from the *hevali*, and with a pounding heart, Ali couldn't resist sneaking a look at the content of the note. The three cursive lines merely informed the potter that his eldest son's services were no longer required at the *hevali* and that he should present himself in the office to meet the landlord.

With only two living rooms cum bedrooms, a tiny kitchen annexed to a small corner of the veranda, and the top half of the outside wall knocked down by a camel and its load of Afghan rugs and Balochi dhurries, the potter's small courtyard was cluttered with stacks of clay cooking pots and dough basins. The glazed ones were left to dry on the sunny rooftop terrace.

The potter's clay-encrusted wheel, the central feature of the house, took up a large portion of the courtyard. His wiry body stooped over the wheel, the potter had spent decades in that spot, moulding the clay dough into various kitchen items; from water pitchers and round-bellied milk churning pots to dainty glazed tea bowls. His wife, after hurriedly dispensing with the early-morning household chores, started on the painting, glazing and the selling of the pots. Most fellow villagers applauded the pair for their hard, honest work and rewarded them by buying all their everyday crockery from them rather than from the shops in the nearest town.

The potter painstakingly worked at the wheel to pay for his two sons' city education. Jubail, with his university fees had required the most financial support. Master Haider had lately taken over paying for Jubail's fees. Proud of his young protégé, he was happy to support someone from a humble background, who would one day enjoy a better life than his parents. What had pot-making done for the poor potter, his wife silently mourned? Simply destroyed his posture, prematurely aging him – at 47 he looked 75.

Jubail was taking his morning shower under the water pump when Ali entered with his head stiffly held at an angle. As Haider Sahib's *munshi*, he enjoyed a significantly higher social standing than the potter in the village hierarchy.

Grim-faced, he handed the note to the potter's youngest son and quickly withdrew, ignoring the potter's wife's eager call of *salaam* from the kitchen area. He was in no mood for a pleasant chit-chat with the family that had caused his master a terrible *baesti*, a loss of face.

The potter, baffled by the content of the letter from Master-ji, meekly handed it to Jubail. His wet hair dripping over his bare brown muscular shoulders, Jubail quickly scanned the three lines.

'The master knows about us.' The words tapped in his head, but outwardly he remained calm, loathing his father's obsequious expression.

'I don't know why the master wants to see me, but I'll go. And why does he say that they don't need your services at the *hevali*, Jubail? Have they got a new stable boy?'

'I guess you'll find out soon enough when you see him,' Jubail replied cryptically, nonchalantly running a comb through his wet hair. Nothing would stop fate, he shrugged, a smile tugging at his mouth.

*

Fifteen minutes later, the baffled potter stood timidly outside Master Haider's office and was stiffly ushered inside by Ali. Master Haider's gaze remained averted. The three lines of the note matched the brevity of his spoken words.

'Your son has wounded us where it hurts the most – our *izzat*! He's no longer welcome in our *hevali* or this village.'

'Master-ji, why?' the shocked potter squeaked.

But 'Master-ji' didn't deign to reply; instead, he rose from his chair and signalled with his hand for the potter to leave. The potter sidled out of the room, his bent body sloped further under the weight of humiliation, and his gaunt brown face now a shade darker. Across the courtyard he caught Gulbahar's hostile glance, her graceful body held tall.

Only that morning she had learned about Laila's rendez-vous with the potter's son, having pulled it out of a guilt-ridden Begum. Seeing Hafiz, the potter, on their premises, was just too much for poor Gulbahar. Angrily, she climbed up the marble stairs to her daughter's room. Laila sat on her bed listlessly staring at the floor, a woman's magazine with Madonna's face on the cover lying on her lap.

Gulbahar emulated her husband's style. Like him, she was a woman of few words and had clamped down the wild urge to strike her daughter. Instead, she flung three, short, clipped sentences at Laila.

'I failed you as a mother! You failed me as a daughter! Let us both not fail your father!' Laila sighed with relief; her mother wasn't going to make a scene. It was not in her mother's nature to throw tantrums like her Aunt Mehreen.

'You were getting engaged to Master Zohaib,' Gulbahar continued in her cool, enigmatic manner. 'Your father and I have decided that we'll opt for one ceremony – a wedding in six weeks' time. That's best all round under the circumstances. So a lot of work has to be done, and I need your help, Laila!'

Throat dry, Laila merely gaped at her mother.

'Mother, no!'

Gulbahar was already at the door; her icy grey eyes lancing her daughter, colour flagged red in her cheekbones. 'There's no room for "no" after what you've done! The disgrace you've heaped upon our heads. A potter's son! Meeting him in the dark? Have you no shame – no *sharm*? Has he *touched* you or defiled you?' Laila vigorously shook her head. 'Count yourself lucky that your father hasn't blistered you with his tongue! You have escaped lightly, my shameless girl!' Then she was gone, the door firmly shut.

Speechless, and recoiling from her mother's harsh words, Laila curled her body into a ball of misery. Was she to obey her heart or her parents?

CHAPTER 4

Jubail

'He has no right to tell us what to do! Who the hell does he think he is? Does he own everyone in this village?' Jubail fumed, snarling at his father. The stricken potter blinked in disbelief at his son. Had their Jubail totally lost it, challenging the master – the laird of the village?

'Yes, in truth … he does own the village – more than half of its land belongs to him! Half the villagers are his tenants,' his mother bitterly reminded him, taken aback by her son's revolt and arrogance. Mouth dry and round eyes eagerly scanning her son's face for any telltale signs, she asked, 'What did Master mean when he said that you have hurt us where it wounds the most?'

Her son's answer was his lowered gaze.

'Jubail!' she screeched, wiping her sweat-beaded cheeks with her *chador*.

'I've been out horse riding with Mistress Laila at night. That's all!' he defiantly threw back at her.

'What!' they both shouted.

'So what!' he taunted, body aggressively poised, angered by their gaping mouths.

Brazen-faced, he announced, grinning, 'I want to marry Laila!' shrivelling his parents on the spot.

'My God!' His mother cried shrilly, the first to clear her head and find her tongue. 'Marry Mistress Laila? What heaven are you floating in? Are you insane, my lad!' she shook her clay-coated fist at him, matching her husband's incredulous stare.

Jubail's artificial smile slipped away. Spirit dipping, he leaned heavily against the flaking plaster wall. If his parents reacted like this, then how would the master ever condone this marriage?

Moments later, hot rage ripping through him, he aggressively rounded on his parents.

'Who says? And why can't I marry Laila, Mother?' A rebellious and rhetorical question, which his mother answered with her eloquent, piteous eyes.

'Because, my arrogant son, look around you!' his father stated simply, pointing to his potter's wheel. 'This is our humble world and Mistress Laila ... Well, she belongs to another *dunya* – another planet!'

Hating them, their words and preconceptions, Jubail stormed out. Why did his humble roots threaten to stand between him and his personal happiness? Laila loved him. He was capable of offering her a better world than a potter's wheel now that he had completed his university education. Did he as a human being not have a right to marry the person he wanted?

He ran to Begum's quarters – probably their only ally. He recalled that in Shakespeare's play *Romeo and Juliet* there was the nurse, Juliet's confidante, who helped the lovers. He had mentally assigned Begum a similar role. Surely, loving Laila as she did, she would help them.

∗

Begum was hosing down a thick layer of stubborn dust and dried leaves from her brick-lined courtyard when she caught sight of the potter's 'brat'. Resentment flaring through her body, Begum shot to her feet.

'Don't you think you've done enough damage already... Now you have the gall to show your face to us, you scoundrel?'

Face tightening, Jubail held his ground. 'I want to see Laila, please!' he pleaded with a determined look in his eyes.

'Are you mad?' Begum shrieked, throwing aside the gushing water hose and nearly wetting him with it. Striding up to him, she gave him a good telling-off. 'Listen to me, you lovesick brat! Mistress Laila is getting married to Master Zohaib, not to you – a potter's son! Master Zohaib is a landlord and from the same class. Can you not see that you've caused enough damage already! Leave my master's family alone – you scoundrel!'

'Don't abuse me, Begum – please pass on this message.' Hating her, Jubail persisted. 'Just this once, please? The master has forbidden me from seeing her.'

'Good, and so he should! You both made fools of me, and it's all my fault!'

'No, Begum, we did not! But do this – just once, Begum!' Jubail beseeched, wooing her with his liquid, coal-dark eyes. Begum snatched her gaze away, knowing she was a glutton for people's eyes, especially for her young mistress's magical sapphires.

'You are mad!'

Jubail turned to leave. 'I know you'll tell her. Six o'clock … behind the *jamuni* tree, please,' he boldly instructed, leaving an outraged Begum standing with her mouth open, but convinced nevertheless.

✳

Later in the afternoon, Begum tried to comfort her young mistress, as Laila wailed her heart out on her shoulder.

'Begum, I can't marry Master Zohaib; it's Jubail I love!'

'Oh, Mistress Laila! Shush!' Begum paled. 'What a terrible thing to say!'

'But, Begum!'

'Do you know how much you've hurt your parents already? If they hear you talking like this, what will they think?' she hastened to advise her young mistress.

Begum would bitterly remember the next few moments for eternity, as her beautiful young mistress inched her way around and straight into her big, soft, melting heart. For Laila was Begum's Achilles heel. And she invariably won and Begum invariably lost. This was no different from any other occasion.

That evening, Laila went to meet Jubail, smuggled out of the *hevali* by a loyal and loving Begum.

✳

Begum was petrified; the courtyard clock had already struck

ten and the night sky was forbiddingly dark, but no young mistress.

'Are you still here, Begum?' enquired a surprised Gulbahar coming down to the kitchen to check if the yoghurt mixture had set in the clay basin. Arslan loved his mother's home-made yoghurt with its thick, pinkish, creamy skin on top. 'Go home, my dear, your Ali will be waiting! You can finish clean-ing the *dal* tomorrow,' she kindly advised her housekeeper, blissfully unaware of the typhoon sweeping through Begum's head.

Begum peered out of the courtyard. Any minute now her young mistress's head should have popped in behind the kitchen door, winked at her and then disappeared.

And Mistress Gulbahar imagined her daughter fast asleep in her room.

Rage suffocated Begum. How could her young mistress betray her like this? Did she have no shame or sense? Staying out all night with a strange man and especially after what had happened. For the first time in her life anger and resentment clawed. Above all, she hated herself, the gullible old Begum who was exploited by her spoilt young mistress!

By midnight the *hevali* was in total silence. Mistress Gulbahar and Haider Sahib were in bed. Arslan had gone to stay at his Aunt Rani's home to spend time with his cousin Saher. A stiff figure of misery, Begum stood in the middle of the courtyard, leaning on the cool marble basin of the fountain.

Gently, she let herself out of the side door, but made sure that it was left slightly ajar so that her young mistress could sneak in without waking her parents.

Away from the *hevali* and under the moonlit sky, Begum's desperate eyes sought two figures. But the landscape remained dismally flat. Listlessly waiting under the shadow of the large *jamuni* tree, Begum tucked her night shawl around her head, protecting herself against the cool breeze.

'Please, Allah Pak, return our Laila safely to us and with her *izzat* intact!' Begum begged of her almighty Allah Pak.

Finally, afraid of the dark shadows and the scuttling movement of a rattlesnake in the undergrowth around the tangles of brush-wood, Begum gave up her vigil and hurried home.

As soon as she bolted the door, her husband leapt off his port-able bed on the veranda, rushing across the courtyard, hand raised to strike her. Begum fearfully crouched against the wall as he gripped her arm.

'I've been worried sick, Begum! I was about to go to the *hevali* to look for you! What time do you call this?' He shook her hard, her shawl falling off.

'Ali, please! Don't shout,' Begum cried, in tears. 'Please, just go to the potter's house and find out if his devil is at home? These children will kill us!'

'What are you saying?' Ali stiffened, eyes fearful.

'Mistress Laila is not at home!' she whimpered, looking up at the starry sky. Surely those stars were privy to the couple's whereabouts, Begum wondered.

'Where is she, then?' he thundered, voice threaded with steel. Begum's heart plummeted.

'With Jubail … somewhere! I don't know where!'

'What?' The look on his face would stay with her for life.

'And do you know who's to blame for this?'

Hysteria gripped Begum. 'Yes, blame me. Ali, I am a stupid, gullible woman, who falls into Laila's trap every time. I gave her the message from Jubail! I sneaked her out! Ali, if I am not stupid, I don't know who is …?' Begum wailed, recoiling from the horror smeared across her husband's face.

'What have you done, Begum?' he whispered, feeling faint and reaching his hand to his sweat-beaded forehead.

'I'm stupid!' she repeated, groaning aloud, wallowing in her misery. But her husband had gone!

Ali sprinted through the dark village lanes, stumbling over small rocks, pebbles and avoiding dry cow-dung cakes. Panting, his low hurried knocks on the wooden door prompted the potter to come running with his wife in tow. On seeing Ali, their gaunt faces became pictures of fear; it meant only one thing – Jubail.

'Where's your son?' Ali hissed into their faces. The potter

visibly shrank, as if willing himself to melt away into nothingness, his bent back even more stooped.

'Come inside!' he croaked.

Ali gingerly stepped down into the narrow, dark hallway, afraid of stumbling against a stack of pots lined against the wall, or the open gutter outside the potter's door.

'We don't know where he is!' Jubail's mother rushed to explain, not easily cowed by Haider-ji's overbearing *munshi*. 'He's a commoner like us and so I'll not be intimidated by him!' she defiantly reminded herself. 'And our son has just become a graduate.'

'Well, you had better find out!' Ali thundered in her direction, irked by women like her who spoke up first these days and who, unlike his Begum, had their wits about them. His Begum had truly lost hers!

'Our young mistress is not at home, fools!' he jeered, unable to disguise his contempt for them.

The potter and his wife shrank against the wall, eyes standing large in their gaunt faces, mouths fallen open. Hearing their shallow breathing, Ali took pity on them, fearing that either of them might have a heart seizure. He even felt sorry for the potter's rude 'outspoken' wife. Nevertheless, he brutally had to spell out their predicament to them.

'If the master finds out that your son has dared to speak to his daughter again, specifically after his instructions yesterday, he'll have your hide. The audacity of you foolish "little" people amazes me! The landlord of the village and a mere potter!' Ali sneered. Which cuckoo land were these people living in?

'You don't have to insult us!' The potter's wife bitterly snapped back at the *munshi*, recoiling from his harsh words. 'We know … We told him … Stupid boy! But what about her – that madam of yours? Who's keeping an eye on her? She left her home. Our son did not drag her out of the *hevali*!' Resentment had flared. Ali had no right to insult them. Who was he anyway? Just a peg or two above them!

Ali blushed. The arrow had struck home and he immediately went on the defensive. His master and his *izzat* couldn't be sullied by anyone.

'My mistress is a naive young woman, I admit. But your son is a conniving snake, bent on raising himself up on the social ladder by pursuing our mistress – you know just as well as I do, you foolish folk, that both our class and caste system has firm boundaries. Even if you could jump from one to the other, it would still be unthinkable for your clan to even glance at the daughter of the most powerful man in this village, let alone contemplate anything else between them.'

'*Munshi-ji*, we know what our son has done.' The potter meekly intervened, scowling heavily at his wife. Trust her to make it more difficult for them.

Ali mellowed. 'Please find your son and send him packing back to the city. Otherwise there'll be hell to pay! Goodnight!' Then he melted into the night.

The potter, shuffling behind his wife, returned to his portable bed, sick at heart. Sleep forgotten, they huddled inside their cotton flattened quilts, keeping a vigil for their son, ears alert to the smallest of sounds.

*

Ali returned home, screaming in his head, 'Where are they?'

His wife eagerly ran to open the door. He shook his head. Begum stood still, a crushing weakness sweeping through her body.

'Go to bed!' He sank heavily down on his portable *charpoy*. 'You can be sure that a long day awaits us!'

Instead of sleeping, she raised her two hands in *du'a* to Allah Pak, fervently beseeching: 'Please protect my Mistress Gulbahar's household! Let nothing destroy or tarnish the honour of our master and mistress – they are good people, and don't deserve to suffer. Please keep evil away from my master's door!'

'But evil is already at our door!' an inner demon sneered. 'In the shape of a foolish infatuation between the young mistress and the potter's son.' Were they both blind to the social situation, the incompatibility of it all?

'I'm just a humble servant!' Begum beseeched. 'I do what my superiors ask of me. In obeying Mistress Laila, I have betrayed her parents. Allah Pak, let the *divas* of their home be forever lit!'

Still praying, with hands raised, Begum stared up at the stars above her, chewing her lower lip and tasting blood. She had pulled her portable bed out into the courtyard, feeling suffocated in the small shaded space of the veranda. Her mistress and master slept peacefully in their comfortable king-sized beds, little guessing at the evil fast knocking on their door! Begum nearly fainted into her pillow.

*

Gulbahar happily entered her daughter's room to show her a silver-plated tea set for her trousseau. Imagining Laila to be on the rooftop gallery she went down to see if breakfast was ready, and saw her housekeeper just coming in through the back door.

'Begum?' Frowning, Gulbahar softly called, but the housekeeper had crossed the courtyard, ignoring Mithu's morning 'salaam' calls from the cage, and was already on the stairs. Confused, Gulbahar followed her housekeeper into her daughter's room.

She found Begum sitting on Laila's bed.

'Is Mistress Laila upstairs having breakfast?' Begum enquired, her guilty face lowered.

'Not seen her yet …'

To her alarm, Gulbahar saw Begum's body double over; with her face buried in her lap, she sobbed loudly into her *chador*.

'Begum! What's wrong?' Gulbahar's heart had taken flight.

'You won't want to know!' Begum wailed aloud.

'Is it to do with our Laila?' Gulbahar commanded, her face level with Begum's.

Begum raised her tear-stricken face and nodded miserably. Her mistress's look of horror would remain etched in her mind for years to come.

'Where is she?' Gulbahar stuttered, barely able to breathe, fear gripping her.

'I don't know!' Begum replied dully, her vacant eyes on the picture of her young mistress on the wall. 'She's gone!' she whispered, watching her mistress's eyes squeeze shut. Gulbahar slid down on the bed next to Begum.

'Gone, Begum! It can't be true!' The broken words were threaded with fear and disbelief.

Gulbahar tried to claw her way back to reality. Her daughter's reputation couldn't be compromised, even in the eyes of a faithful housekeeper.

'She'll be around the *hevali* somewhere,' Gulbahar brusquely replied. 'Please, no word of this to your master or anyone else,' she added softly, head lowered, before leaving the room.

Begum wanted to shout out: 'Laila has gone! She's been out all night with her lover!' But love and respect for her mistress prevented her from uttering the terrible words aloud. Instead, she picked up a large framed photograph of Laila taken under the moonlight. 'Little Mistress, we never knew that you would become so self-destructive and do this to your parents!'

Begum wearily stood up. Breakfast still had to be prepared; there was the shopping for fresh vegetables to organise for the afternoon dinner. Laila's new in-laws were coming this evening to discuss dates and practicalities relating to the forthcoming wedding. The new maid assigned with responsibility for the upper-floor rooms had to be supervised, especially to ensure that she had dusted behind the bed posts and other items of furniture.

Downstairs in the large courtyard, a nightly breeze always meant a thicker layer of dust to sweep away the following morning. Everything had to be ritually polished, scrubbed or hosed down before the guests arrived. Women guests often had a tendency to wander and look around the beautiful *hevali* out of curiosity.

'I haven't slept a wink all night. How will I be able to do anything today?' Begum groaned to herself, going downstairs to inspect the work of the new maid, and scowled. The silly chit was still watering the plants around the colonnades; the hanging baskets of geraniums were leaking water everywhere onto the marble surface. Begum could not be bothered to remind her of the safety hazard.

Her thoughts were elsewhere. 'I must keep out of Mistress Gulbahar's path today!'

CHAPTER 5

The Elopement

Begum was sitting at the kitchen table dicing aubergines into quarters for the afternoon dinner when Ali apeared in front of her under the ceiling fan, wiping his tanned forehead with his fingertips. The look in his eyes made Begum stagger to her feet; eyes automatically darting to the door, fearful of someone entering.

'Ali?' She felt faint. 'Please say it's not bad news?'

'No, Begum, it's *very* bad news,' he contradicted. 'Our spoilt Mistress Laila has eloped with the potter's brat!'

Mouth fallen open, Begum swayed. Ali reached to catch her. The knife and the piece of aubergine were on the tiled kitchen floor.

'Run off with the potter's son!' Begum cried, voice faint.

'Manzoor, our taxi man … said that he had dropped Jubail and a veiled woman at the bus station. He thought that it was a female relative of his, but it was our Laila. He saw her face – saw them get on the Islamabad bus. I've told him not to utter a word about this to anyone.'

Begum sank into a heap on the footstool. 'All my fault … I gave her the message … Allah Pak help us!'

'Yes, Begum, beg Allah Pak to help us *all*!' he corrected. 'That selfish pair has thrown us into the middle of the flour-grinding machine, a *chaki*,' he taunted.

'What are we going to do, Ali?'

'The potters are already frightened out of their wits – poor souls. I must get to them before the master finds out.'

Then he was gone. Putting her head in her lap, Begum wept bitterly, unaware of time and space until she heard footsteps.

'Begum, are you all right?'

Begum raised fearful eyes at her mistress, unable to contain the bad news inside her any longer. 'Laila has gone, Mistress!' she wailed aloud. 'Left the village last night with Jubail!'

Gulbahar froze, eyes now orbs of horror. Begum stumbled up from the footstool to reach her mistress, but Gulbahar blindly turned and left the room – the dinner forgotten.

*

Ali sprinted through the village lanes to reach the potter's home. Once there, he pressed his face to the door, knocking hard and not caring who heard. It was immediately opened by the potter, his wife hovering behind him. The sight of both their faces clearly told him that neither had slept.

Ali shot them a bitter look. 'You'd better pack your bags and leave immediately! Your devil of a son, *shaitan,* has eloped with our Master Haider's daughter. His pure impudence is unimaginable!' He ignored their shocked, indrawn breaths. 'As to where he gets it from – I really can't fathom? Not from you simple folks. You can imagine what will happen once Master Haider finds out. You'd better reach him!'

His eyes swept over their stricken faces; he could almost hear the flutter of their timid heartbeats, and he relented, feeling sorry for them, but then reminded himself that it was their responsibility to guide their wayward son. They had let everyone down.

The potter's hands were shaking as he bolted the front door. His wife was rubbing her two calloused palms together in a traditional gesture to demonstrate outrage.

'What has our son done?' she croaked in disbelief.

'*Education,* Rahmat Bibi – giving people foolish illusions! Making them fly high in fairy lands. *Spend more money on him,* you said,' the potter jeered. 'Well, this is the result! Now deal with it.'

*

Ali was fixing the broken leg of the veranda *charpoy* when the shrill ringing tone of his mobile phone made him drop his hammer. It was Mistress Laila.

'Where are you, Mistress? We're worried sick ...' Ali stammered, maintaining his code of respect in addressing her, although he wanted to deliver spades full of anger over the phone. She abruptly vanquished him with her brazen anouncement.

'I've married Jubail! Please inform my parents – ask them to forgive me.'

'Mistress Laila ...' he croaked but the line was already dead. Laila was in no mood for angry lectures from a *mere* servant.

Ali slid onto the nearby chair, brushing his moist palm over his flushed face. His Adam's apple was energetically bobbing up and down.

'Mad Laila! What have you done?' he mourned aloud, frightening the two black crows hopping on Begum's linen *kurtha* on her washing line.

He remained slumped for a long time on his old chair, under the shade of the veranda, not knowing what to do. How could he keep this bombshell buried inside him?

'Allah Pak, please help them!' He fervently prayed that the potter's lot had fled. For there would be no corner for them to hide in the village from the master's wrath!

Shame scorched his face. No child did this sort of thing! To disobey was one thing; to marry in secret was another, and to such an unsuitable man simply unthinkable!

His heart bled for his Master Sahib. A proud man and admired by all; used to holding his head high up in his village community. How would he ever recover from this catastrophe?

'Oh, God! No!' Ali cried. Laila's prospective in-laws were due to arrive that very night. 'Shameless girl! Laila, if you were my daughter, I'd have strangled you by now!'

'But she's not the only one to blame!' the inner voice mocked. His idiotic Begum had played a pivotal role in this family's destruction. It looked as if they, too, would be fleeing with the potter's family; two faithful servants had turned into traitors.

*

Ali peeped from behind the *minar* tree in the open ground.

When the Jeep had disappeared over the horizon, he dashed into the *hevali*. Face flushed, he wandered around the building looking for Begum. To his dismay, he eventually found her in Mistress Gulbahar's room where two keen pairs of eyes assessed his face. Their intuition immediately alerted them that he had some terrible news to impart about Laila.

Hovering awkwardly near the door, Ali shuffled his feet, studiously avoiding eye contact with them. Begum leaned back against the bed post, afraid of falling in a heap on the floor from her panting heart if her husband didn't speak up soon.

'Begum, can I see you for a moment?' he ventured to ask.

'Ali, whatever you have come to say to Begum, please say it in front of me – that is if it's to do with my daughter?' Gulbahar coolly chided.

Ali desperately sought escape. 'It's our portable bed … I want to show it to Begum for one minute, if you could excuse her, Mistress?'

'Ali, you've never lied before!' Gulbahar stiffly mocked.

Ali turned and bowed his head against the wooden doorframe. The two women nervously waited.

'Mistress Laila has married the potter's son!'

Reaching her mistress's side, Begum gently held her in her arms and guided her to the armchair. She crouched on the floor, clutching her mistress's legs, fearing they would give way beneath her. Ali's forehead was still pressed against the doorframe. Begum stared at the clock as if her whole life depended on it. The master was due back in half an hour.

Hearing his mistress's steps, Ali sidled away from the door, head lowered.

'Ali, I'll tell your master myself … Please phone Laila's in-laws to cancel their visit … say that we have left for the city because of a family bereavement or something,' Gulbahar instructed, before leaving.

Begum sobbed loudly into her muslin shawl, unable to meet her husband's accusing eyes.

*

Gulbahar leaned against the cold marble surface of the veranda colonnade, her eyes shut tight.

'Sahiba-ji!' Begum timidly asked. 'Are you all right?'

Gulbahar ignored her question and the chattering call of the parakeet swinging in his cage and returned to her bedroom. Husband and wife exchanged nervous glances.

'What are we going to do, Ali?' Begum beseeched.

'Run!'

Begum nodded, fear etched across her face.

Ali's bitter laugh frightened the two crows pecking the pomegranate fruit sewn inside little cotton bags in one corner of the courtyard. 'Sometimes I wonder what your head is stuffed with – sawdust?'

'You are cruel, Ali. I never expected our Laila would do this!'

'She always had you wound round her pretty little finger, didn't she? And you always became her puppet, her *phutley* that she manipulated to her heart's content.'

'You indulged and loved her too, Ali!'

'Yes … but not in the reckless way you doted on her. She *used you*, Begum. For God's sake, wake up woman!' His words were her undoing.

Begum wept in self-pity. It was true; she had been thoroughly manipulated by her selfish young mistress.

'Where's my sister?' young Arslan demanded from the rooftop, peering down over the railing. The question was innocent enough, but Ali and his wife, down below in the courtyard, stared up wide-eyed at the young master-ji flying a green kite.

'She's about somewhere!' Ali lightly quipped, recovering first.

'I want to fly my other kite with her. Tell her to come up when you see her!'

'OK, Master Arslan.' Begum whispered to her husband, 'There will be more things flying tonight!' Her heart bled for young Arslan, wondering how he would cope with Laila's elopement.

Begum shuffled back to the kitchen. The dinner preparation and the household chores had to be got on with. Above all, the *hevali* had to be emptied of all eavesdropping servants, and soon.

'Farida, wash everything quickly! I don't need you this evening! I'll manage – the visitors are not coming,' Begum explained to the young maid, ignoring her confused look.

'Yes, Mistress Begum!' came a meek reply.

With exasperation, Begum eyed her leisurely scrubbing strokes. Why couldn't the chit swing her arms out properly and give the pots a really good shine. What was wrong with the hands of the youth these days – weaklings!

'Oh, God!' Begum dropped the ladle in the curry sauce. She had to stop the guests from coming. And who would be the one to tell Master Haider? Begum agonised.

She needn't have worried.

*

Haider had personally decided to call on Jennat Bibi, the local sweetmaker's wife, to order the sweetmeats for his daughter's wedding. Jennat Bibi loved taking orders from Haider's household, as the delivery of baskets of sweets gave her an opportunity to visit 'that wonderful magical palace' as she boasted to her family and friends.

The sweetmaker's front door was open and Haider overheard two female voices from within, locked in a hushed conversation; one speaker was Jennat Bibi.

'Have you heard that Master Haider's daughter, Laila, has eloped with the potter's son? And the poor potters have all fled! See for yourself! A huge padlock is dangling from their door!'

Transfixed, Haider leaned heavily against the wall for support. He heard the peal of bells from the milk buffaloes trundling past him and the mumbled greeting, '*Salaam*, Master-ji' of the cowherd, shepherding them down the lane.

A dog barking brought Haider back to reality and he hastened away down the lane – to the potter's door. A rusty old aluminium padlock hung heavily in the middle of the bolted wooden door. Haider stood lost in thought, wondering how to verify the truth of what he had overheard.

'Just gossip by bitching women!'

Not wanting to meet anyone, Haider slid quietly through the

hevali side door and went straight up to his daughter's room – it was empty.

With a thudding heart, he padded through all the rooms. In the kitchen, Begum was stirring the ladle in the cooking pot; he quietly closed the door.

His last destination was the rooftop, where he found Arslan flying his kite alone.

'Arslan, have you seen your sister today?'

His son was squinting in the hot afternoon sunshine, tugging at the kite string. His kite was swaying in the sky, and about to crash straight into his friend Saleem's large, blue, striped one.

'No.'

'When was the last time you saw her?'

'Don't know,' he mumbled, annoyed at being pestered about his sister.

'Did you see her at breakfast time?'

'No!' was the quick surly answer. Arslan did not like his father's harsh tone of voice.

'Did you see her last night?' Frowning, Arslan tried to remember. 'Leave the damn thing alone and answer me, boy!' Haider demanded.

Arslan lost his grip on the string and watched in horror as his kite floated away. For the first time he felt the stirring of hatred for his father.

'Yes!'

'What time?'

'Don't know!' Arslan's eyes fell before his father's. He remembered seeing his sister leave through the back door at nine o'clock, with Begum standing behind her. 'Begum knows,' he volunteered, wanting to get rid of his father. Haider was already sprinting down the marble stairs.

Arslan gazed up at his beautiful kite drifting away, wondering which lucky boy would pull it down.

*

When the door slammed shut, Begum knew that this was the moment she had been dreading. Heart pounding, she failed to greet her master.

'Begum, just answer one question!' the dignified voice commanded. 'Were you the last person to see our Laila?'

Begum trembled. 'Yes.' The wooden spoon fell with a loud plop into the large pot of milk and carrots for the *gajar halva* pudding.

The door was slammed shut.

Begum turned the stove off. It didn't matter if the carrot *halva* got burned, for the master would not be eating anything from her hand today. Her days at the *hevali* had come to a piteous end. After ensuring all the servants had left, she let herself out by the side door – the family needed privacy.

Arms tightly folded against her chest under her cotton *chador*, Begum shuffled back to her home, stepping twice on the sun-baked cow pats on the footpath. Where would they find employment like this one, Begum mourned? For years they had enjoyed privileges that not even other family members could anticipate. Their house furnishings were specially ordered for them. They had three well-balanced meals each day at the *hevali* with plenty of meat. Moreover Mistress Gulbahar had generously given the order to the Gujjar boy to deliver a large jug of milk to Begum's home first thing every morning. She had even got them a fridge to store their milk and meat.

Begum did not wear Mistress Gulbahar's cast-offs, but velvets in the winter, and in summer her body was caressed by the softest of lawns and silks that felt like *malai* cream, even between her chapped fingertips.

'Mistress Laila, you have robbed us of our livelihood,' Begum groaned aloud, gaze fixed longingly on the beautiful homestead. 'I'm saying goodbye to the *hevali*!'

At home, her faint whisper barely reached Ali's ears, 'He knows!'

'It's all your fault, you stupid woman!' Leaping off his seat, Ali vented his wretchedness on her.

Colour drained from Begum's cheeks, shocked at her husband's hostility and a fearful thought crossing her mind. Would he actually beat her? Her elder sister's bruise-ridden body had scarred her youth. And she had vowed that she would never let any man touch her!

'Ali! You don't have to tell me what I already know!' she coldly reminded him, her body rigid with hurt and indignation.

'Can you imagine what will happen to Chaudharani Gulbahar when she faces her husband?' Ali taunted, continuing his sexist tirade. 'You women are all the same – weak, with your hearts ruling your heads!'

'Ali, you are cruel! You loved Mistress Laila, too!' Begum retaliated.

'Just go and shove yourself in a big hole, Begum!' Ali jeered, hating her sullen tone.

That was the turning point – the moment in Begum's humble life – that provided her with the answer to their predicament.

'I don't need to shove myself in any hole!' she mocked, standing up tall. 'I'm a faithful servant and I'll not run away! I'm going back to the *hevali*. Even if they throw me out, Ali! I'll station myself outside their front door until they forgive me. And I'll go on begging for their forgiveness until they do!'

'Good for you! But don't come wailing to me later if they send you packing!' he jeered.

'Ali, stop being so childish!' Loftily dismissing her husband, Begum retraced her steps back to the *hevali*.

She had learned something new today; that when it came to a crisis, her husband completely lost his head. And that women were not weak, but men were cowards.

Smiling, Begum cried, 'On the contrary, we are strong, my silly Ali,' sidling back into the *hevali* through the servants' door. It was like a silent mausoleum.

Where were her master and mistress?

*

Gulbahar's dull eyes lifted from her husband's feet and slowly journeyed to his face. His expression signalled everything. He knew. As she opened her mouth, it crossed her mind that she was going to dash years off him.

'Haider Sahib, your beloved daughter has married the potter's son.' They were quiet words, but had a vicious sting. Her husband's hand clutched the air, fingers reaching for support.

Gulbahar steeled herself for the punishment: the thunder that would pelt her body; the abusive rainfall of sharp words. But there was only a cloying, crushing silence.

Her mighty stony-faced husband did nothing; he simply walked away.

'Laila!' An anguished scream rent though Gulbahar's body. As if in a surreal dream, she dashed after her husband, panting up the stairs to their bedroom door but the handle wouldn't move.

'Haider-ji,' she whimpered, panicking, 'Please open the door!'

No sound. Gulbahar slid down on the marble floor and resting her head against the walnut-lacquered door she wept. She felt his pain, but hers was sharper. 'We've all betrayed him.' Gulbahar sobbed into her silk *dupatta* with the hand-embroidered lacework, given to her by the wife of the governor of Punjab as a present when they hosted them in Lahore.

'Mother!' Arslan exclaimed. Gulbahar blinked, a large tear trembling on her lower eyelash. 'What's the matter, Mama?'

'Your sister has swept the world from beneath our feet, my son!' Gulbahar opted for honesty with her young son, but failed to use the word 'eloped'.

'What has she done?' he asked eagerly, unable to make sense of his mother's words.

Gulbahar debated with herself. He was only young. 'Your sister has married the potter's son.' Gulbahar assessed his face for his reaction. No surprise. No condemnation. 'He doesn't understand – he never will,' she thought, envying her son's innocence. 'Arslan, please go and study in your room, my son!' she advised, before entering her daughter's room.

There, her eyes fell on her daughter's picture frame. 'Laila, how could you do this to your father?' Gulbahar sat on her daughter's bed and wept again.

Haider had locked himself in and her out of their bedroom. Gulbahar made dozens of journeys to their door that day and the next day. He had not eaten. Only drunk the tap water from the en-suite bathroom.

'Please, Haider-ji!' Begum, too, pleaded outside the bedroom.

'It's all my fault, if only I had told you!' Begum wept on her mistress's shoulder.

'You didn't tell her to elope or get married, did you, Begum? So please don't blame yourself, my dear. If anyone is to blame, it's me, her mother. How ignorant I am.'

'Please, Mistress, don't blame yourself – we are all at fault.' The housekeeper offered generously, touched by her beloved mistress's kindness.

Even Ali's appeals were ignored.

*

It was the new kitchen maid in Haider's household who became the village loudspeaker, clearly letting everyone know about Laila's elopement with the potter's son. All waited with bated breath for the volcanic explosion at the *hevali*, wondering what the landlord would do to the potter's family? Would he track them down? Speculations, speculations, but nobody knew for sure. They all agreed on one thing – that they expected something to happen; some momentous event to erupt in the village that would scorch everything and everyone in its path.

They were in for a mighty big disappointment; the volcano didn't erupt and there was no village scorching. No chasing after the potter's family. Begum and Ali were not dismissed or thrown out of their living quarters.

Master Haider had simply withdrawn – from everyone and everything. Even from his family. For it was rumoured that no one had seen him for three days. And of course the rumour of Laila's elopement soon reached the ears of Laila's prospective in-laws. The jilted landlord, humiliated though he was, counted himself lucky to escape from such an unsuitable match. No matter how gorgeous Laila was, she had become a *besharm* woman. And all for a potter's son! Was she deranged?

*

'Can you believe it – locking yourself in?' Massi Fiza teased her best friend, Rukhsar, peering longingly at the new gold necklace set that she was working on.

'Apparently there'll be no jewellery for Mistress Laila now! Would any parent give a dowry to a daughter who has disgraced them in this manner?' The rhetorical question had the goldsmith's wife's head shooting up from the rows of rubies she was nimbly stringing.

'Disgraceful, Massi Fiza!' she loftily agreed.

'Be careful, Mistress Rukhsar, you have three daughters yourself. You'll need to watch them all!' Massi Fiza slyly reminded her.

'Oh, I do! I don't know what our almighty Chaudharani Gulbahar was up to with her daughter. Fancy not even having an inkling of what was going on? These "big" people are so smart in so many things but apparently blind to a daughter's *izzat*! It's not as if she has half a dozen children – only two!'

'Well, whether two or a dozen, children are very conniving these days. Thank goodness I don't have any daughters to disgrace me,' Massi Fiza preened.

'Well, see that your boys don't "disgrace" you by chasing after girls above their caste and station in life!' Rukhsar returned equally cattily, bristling at her friend's aspersion that she had only produced females.

'My boys are quite sensible – you know what they are like.' The feeble words did not quite ring true even to Massi Fiza's own ears. Rukhsar dropped her gaze to her beads. It had dawned on her lately that her friend had a tendency to talk in glowing terms about her sons. As if everyone did not know what good-for-nothing sons they were. The realisation jolted through Rukhsar that Massi Fiza was after her daughter's *rishta!*

The goldmistress's body trembled with indignation, nausea spiralling inside her, pricking her finger with the sharp tool as she poked the hole in the tiny pearl bead. A goldsmith's daughter was no match for a laundrywoman's son! The situation was almost the same as the incongruous match of Master Haider's daughter with the potter's son. No! Her *ladli* daughters were destined for more 'elevated' households, where gold flowed in abundance in the form of gold bracelets, not a home that overflowed with every *Nethu Pethu's* dirty laundry.

CHAPTER 6

The Return

Four months later, heavily veiled up to her eyes, Laila returned with her husband to the village in the middle of the night. Like bandits, they stole into Jubail's family home, stealthily breaking open the ugly aluminium padlock.

Inside the potter's home, Laila saw her new home for the first time – a hovel. Everything was caked with dust and cobwebs – the two pillars, the rusty grilled windows, the veranda floor with patches of cement missing, even the washing line. In disgust, Laila withdrew from the kitchen washing area with its moss-encrusted water pump and went to inspect the rest of the house. That was it – just two rooms! No proper kitchen or bathroom. She hadn't quite expected a replica of her parents' palatial *hevali*, but this humble dwelling, devoid of any modern facilities, a few pieces of shabby furniture and stacks of ugly pots of all sizes littering the place was too much for poor Laila. At one stage, panicking, she was about to run out; and out of Jubail's life. But to where and to what? Luckily, their Islamabad apartment was far better, rented with the money from the eight gold bangles she happened to be wearing the night of her elopement.

Where would she cook? On that small portable oil burner stove, squatting on a rickety footstool? When she looked around for a rolling pin, her husband cheekily reminded her: 'What wretched village woman uses a rolling pin to make *chappatis*? Only for *puris*! The first village task young women master on reaching their teens is often the art of making perfect round *chappatis* by hand! There are no Begums in the neighbouring households to help with the cooking.'

How Laila wished she had learned the skill of making soft, round *chappatis* from Begum. This wasn't Islamabad where they could fetch ready-made meals from cafes. Everything had to be prepared by her hands. And she was in no position to hire servants to scurry around doing her bidding. Shrugging her shoulders, Laila reminded herself that they were here on a special errand – to ask for her parent's forgiveness and to return home to the *hevali*, where there were plenty of servants to take care of her needs. Jubail had strongly advised her against coming, saying it was too soon. Laila, however, wouldn't rest until she had seen her parents and asked for their forgiveness. Each passing day had been agony.

'They can't do anything to me now. I'm legally married,' she emphatically told herself. 'And parents always forgive.'

What Laila hadn't bargained on was that in her absence her beloved parents had swapped hearts for stones. Tossing and turning on the hard, jute-woven portable bed, she longed for the soft, wide breadth of her queen-sized bed in her family home and wondered how poor people slept on these narrow uncomfortable things. Even with two thick towels tucked under the bedsheet, she knew her back would be sore and lined with the jute-woven pattern marks.

'I miss you so much, my darling Arslan. I can't wait to see you,' she wept, wetting another corner of the pillow. Unable to wait until the morning, Laila crept past Jubail, fast asleep on the other portable bed.

Out in the open courtyard, she stared around in bemusement. 'This is my new home …'

Her own bedroom in the *hevali* was the size of the potter's courtyard. Laila crushed the thought; the potter's wheel was no match for her father's acres of land and dozens of pedigree racehorses.

Guided by the light of the moon, she located the staircase to the rooftop, semi-hidden behind a tall stack of round-bellied milk churning pots. Her father's *hevali*, including the rooftop terrace, was elegantly dressed in marble from top to bottom. Half of the potter's rooftop terrace, used for stacking pots and

portable beds, was brick-lined. The other half had a small heap
of coal and a pile of chopped wood to use for the rooftop *chappati tandoor*. No plants, or flowering bushes, or marble floor.
Just three old rickety portable beds, one with a missing leg.

Laila had very rarely viewed her home from any of the villager's rooftops. In fact, she could not recall ever crossing to the
other side of the village. The *hevali* was the first building in sight
when one entered the village, and she had always travelled by car.
Her everyday life had little to do with the local village people. As
the daughter of the wealthy landlord it never occurred to her or
her parents to befriend the village children. Similarly the villagers shied away; Laila was beyond their reach as a playmate or
sphere of influence, even for the 'fashionable and very modern'
goldsmith's daughters.

Her reputed friends were daughters of politicians, media
celebrities and other landowning families from the boarding
school and city college. Her knowledge of the village extended
to Massi Fiza, their laundrywoman, who was now practically a
neighbour – her front door literally opposite theirs.

'I have returned home, Mother!' Laila whispered up to the
shining stars.

*

Gulbahar was standing on her prayer mat, about to start her
afternoon prayers, when Begum whispered in Gulbahar's ear.

'She's here, Sahiba-ji!' Her mistress heard but betrayed no
visible sign that she had.

'She's here!' Begum croaked louder.

'Who's here, Begum?' Gulbahar's harsh voice challenged,
turning to confront her housekeeper.

Begum shrivelled, the light of hope snuffed in her eyes, her
heart retreating to a low, dull beat. Her mistress had indeed
killed not only her daughter in her thoughts, but had also slain
her own heart.

'No one!' Begum mumbled in confusion, turning away, wondering what was going to happen. For Massi Fiza had excitedly whispered that Mistress Laila had arrived during the night

and was now living in the potter's home, whilst her rascal of a husband had gone to work in the neighbouring town.

'She's here!' Gulbahar softly repeated Begum's words to her husband's back, feeling duty-bound to alert him. Haider was standing ready to say his *maghrib* prayers; he neither replied nor showed any indication that he had heard but merely started his prayer sequence, raising his hands over his shoulders. Gulbahar let the moment pass – at least he was prepared. She had not expected a discussion, as Laila's name had become a taboo.

✳

The small footstool, with its one uneven leg, on which Laila crouched to make breakfast, kept toppling to one side, giving her a painful stitch at the side of her leg. Her eyes remained on the outside door, expecting her father to storm in at any moment followed by a tearful mother with open arms. Breakfast and dinner was cooked. She had specially made her father's favourite dish, semolina *halwa*, syrupy the way he liked it.

In the end, nobody came.

No storming father, no weeping mother crossed the potter's threshold. The second day also passed. Laila's life swung on the face of the clock and the outside door – waiting. She knew that the *dhoban* had passed the message. 'Why has no one come?' she mourned in bewilderment.

On the third day, after her husband had left for shopping in town, Laila determinedly stepped out of her home, an ugly fortress of her own making, daring to walk out into the village lane and show her face.

'I'm Haider Ali's daughter and will not hide myself!' The pelting storm had to be borne. And she was ready both to face the wrath of her family and the sniggers of the villagers.

Her body discreetly cloaked in a large grey muslin *chador* and her face partially hidden behind its folds, Laila stepped warily out onto the cobbled lane. Once upon a time, the elegant Miss Laila would never let a *chador* come anywhere near her body. Now, she sought refuge in its ample width and length.

Her destination was her father's *hevali*.

As she entered the lane, her heart thudding, she felt faint; her beloved father was walking towards her.

'He has come!'

Her heart singing, she let the fold of the *chador* fall from her face as he came nearer. His eyes dutifully looked down in a modest fashion adopted by the village men whilst passing women. He therefore didn't notice or recognise her and was about to pass her; Laila panicked.

'Father!' Her urgent voice sliced across the small space between them. A mere flicker of an eye was his only response; the gaze had barely lifted from the ground. Then the head dropped down before his eyes reached her face.

And he walked on, passing her still figure in the lane, staring after him.

'Father!' Stunned, Laila shouted after him, past caring who heard her, born out of a need to be recognised and heard. Her father's feet didn't stall. The head didn't turn. She watched his tall stiff figure disappear down the side street.

Mouth dry, Laila leaned against the gate of the bricklayer's villa, wiping her wet cheeks clean. The bricklayer's two chattering teenage granddaughters coming out of the house made her briskly walk off.

She had lost the father but still had a mother.

Pushing open the *hevali* gates of her parents' home, Laila experienced an awkwardness, as if she was entering it as a stranger. Her hungry eyes devoured the spacious beauty of the courtyard, its central marble fountain overflowing with a steady spray of clear water, rows of marble colonnades garlanded with the lush growth of plants and flowers and the two trees now swollen with fruit; oranges and guava. The small pomegranate tree bushes with pomegranates hanging from them were protected from the pecking crows behind the small cotton bags sewn by Begum's skilful fingers.

Begum herself was hard at work in the courtyard. On her toes, she was reaching up to brush down a tiny row of spiralling cobwebs hanging from one of the veranda colonnades when Laila called.

Electrified, Begum swung round.

The bundle of *boker* sticks with sticky cobwebs slipped from Begum's hand as she clamped her hand to her mouth, gasping.

'Laila-ji,' she whispered, automatically adding the respectful term of 'ji' to address her young mistress. Joy flared, fear raged. What would happen now?

'Begum, where is my mother?' Laila demanded, hovering nervously on the threshold. Begum's eyes swept angrily over her irresponsible mistress; the imperious voice didn't match the pathetic appearance. This wasn't the fashion-loving, elegant Laila with her fine stitching, tight-zipped dresses, tiny three-inch sleeves showing off her slender, youthful arms, the one bred in the lap of luxury in her parental home, but a weighed-down specimen of womanhood and symbol of humility.

'Any other village woman, for that matter,' Begum mentally scoffed, eyes widening. Did she see lines on Mistress Laila's forehead? Obviously, the expensive Western pots of face creams and body lotions that Ali purchased for her from the city's top shopping plazas no longer featured in her life. Her Mistress Gulbahar still had porcelain skin and she was twenty years older!

Seething, Begum climbed up to her Mistress Gulbahar's room, followed by Laila.

*

Gulbahar was in the middle of her *zuhr nafl* prayer sequence, her forehead touching the soft surface of the velvet prayer rug, ready to rise to start a new *rakah*. The shallow, hesitant breathing, the light tread of her daughter's feet on the floor tightened Gulbahar's chest. When two feet stood beside her, the Arabic words of prayers deserted her, her mouth only forming the words *Ibrahima, Ibrahima*. Bemused, she turned her head first to the right and then to the left to signal her exit from her prayers.

Her eyes fleetingly swept over her daughter's cloaked figure but avoided the face.

'Mother!' Laila beseeched, now squatting, touching her mother's feet.

'Please forgive me, Mother,' she begged.

Alarmed, Gulbahar pulled her foot away. Only two thoughts banged with clarity in her head: betrayal and shame.

'Begum, have I not warned you about letting beggars into the house.' The voice sounded chillingly aggrieved. 'You've disobeyed me yet again, Begum!'

'Mother!' Laila cried, lying in a heap on the cold marble floor. Gulbahar turned her back to the two women.

'Begum, please show *this* beggar the door! And guard it well!' Gulbahar cruelly instructed, mouth quivering.

Begum's distressed gaze swung from the daughter's face to the mother's back. Gulbahar, unable to pray, walked out of the room, heading for the open air and privacy of the rooftop terrace.

Tears streaked down Laila's face. Begum helplessly watched, before turning to follow her mistress, the words 'you have disobeyed me yet again' throbbing in her ears. Yes, she had brought Laila up to her mistress's room. What had she expected – a reconciliation, a pat on the back? Did she not know that Laila was dead to her parents? How could she allow Laila's shadow to cross their paths?

As if in a dream, Laila followed the faithful housekeeper down the stairs. Begum's body language neither signalled her love nor her anger. Her loyalty was to Mistress Gulbahar and Master Haider; her mission now was to quickly usher Mistress Laila out before her father returned home. Striding across the courtyard and opening the door wide, Begum kept her face averted from the accusing glare of Laila's eyes.

'Don't look at me like that!' Begum taunted. 'You burned all your boats, Mistress Laila, on that night when you eloped with your lover,' she angrily continued, with throbbing red cheeks. 'You killed your parents with your cruelty! Stamped on their joy of life! Snuffed the light out of this house. Did you know that this is the house of the dead, Laila? I never knew that the young mistress I so lovingly cared for could be so selfish and cruel to the very people she loved. Your parents do not mourn for you! Don't flatter yourself! But I mourn for my master and mistress and for the empty vessels that they have become! What does the potter's son have that the landlord didn't – that led you to lose your female modesty? What did you see in his father's clay pots that made you turn your back on the casket of gold jewellery and acres of land offerd by the other man?

'Your father hasn't spoken to anyone for months – neither friends nor relatives! Do you know he has lost two inches in height because his head is forever stooped in shame? He barely lifts his gaze or looks anyone in the eye! Do not mislead yourself, selfish Laila, that anybody will come running to bring you home! The night you married him, you slammed shut the door of the *hevali* behind you and said goodbye to all of this! Your mother has just made that perfectly clear.'

'No! No!' Laila wept. 'Don't say that, Begum, please listen – I'm pregnant!' she whimpered.

Begum struggled with her thoughts and breath. At last, dry-mouthed, she coldly uttered, 'I wish you joy of your future newborn. I pray that as a parent you will never taste the pain you've caused your parents.'

'Please, Begum, don't lecture me! I, too, have died a "thousand" times.'

'You are the guilty one!' Begum snapped bitterly. 'What wrong did your parents do to deserve the punishment you meted out to them? You used me, Mistress Laila, as you've always done. No more! Do you hear me?'

'I *hear*, Begum, but what can I say! My crime was to fall in love and to want to be with him!' Laila's tone was equally cutting. This was not the Begum she adored and who always played to her tune.

'I wish you joy with your "love" and your lover then. Please go now! You are lucky – some fathers have killed their daughters for less than what you've done!' Begum almost wanted to push her out. 'Master will be back soon! I don't know what he'll do when he sees you!'

'I have met him already!' Laila's voice tapered away.

'You've met him?' Begum panicked.

'Don't worry. It appears I've indeed killed everyone in this household with my action – even you! Forgive me, Begum.' Laila pulled the *chador* lower over her forehead.

Begum's heart leapt in pain as she fought the urge to hug Laila tightly, her expression now softer. 'I pray that perhaps your child may bring back to life the dead in this home,' she whispered. 'And I'll pray for your health, my little princess,' she finished, her eyes now swollen and leaking with tears.

Flushed with gratitude and sobbing quietly in the fold of her *chador*, Laila nodded. 'Thank you and goodbye, Begum. I will return to Islamabad, for there is nothing for me here: no home, no parents – not even Begum! Where is Arslan, Begum? I would like to see him so much. In all my little life you've arranged things for me, from climbing up the tall *jamuni* trees, to arranging late night horse riding, to letting me escape from an unhappy engagement … Please do this for me – for a sister longing to see her brother,' she ended, noting the look of incredulity on the housekeeper's face.

'Begum, this "beggar" has not come to beg for food but only for a glimpse of her baby brother! Is that too much to ask from your well of humanity?' Laila begged, opening out the fold of her shawl in front of her body – in a manner reminiscent of a street beggar. 'I was cruel, you say, but have mercy, Begum; Allah Pak says forgive and offer forgiveness!'

'OK! I'll see what I can do. Now, please go,' Begum urged, unable to cope any more with Laila's emotional blackmail, her knack of weaving her magic around her heart with her sapphires for eyes.

Laila stepped out of the *hevali* she loved, closing the gates behind her. Through the small window, Begum watched the shadowy veiled figure walk away. 'Oh, Laila, what have you done?' Begum kept muttering all evening as she went about her chores, imagining her young mistress trying to cook in the potter's hovel of a home.

Nobody mentioned Laila's name. Her husband had quietly informed her the following morning that the *dhoban* saw Laila leaving the village with her husband. The potter's house was once again padlocked. Begum sighed in relief. Laila had entered and departed like a shadow. The storm had brewed but not burst. The sky was clear again, but the shadowy greyness lingered, casting its mantle of doom over the *hevali* and the lives of those within its walls.

*

'My sister was here and you didn't tell me?' Arslan accused his mother, soaking up the early morning sunshine on the rooftop gallery. Gulbahar blinked, taken aback by her son's outburst.

'You have no sister!' Gulbahar harshly reminded her son, knowing full well that he was very fond of his sister. For more than two weeks, he had sulked and refused to eat when Laila had left.

'Yes, I have!' came Arslan's belligerent answer, tugging at his mother's arm. 'She was here! Our Laila is alive. I want to see her!'

'*Khabardor!*' Haider Ali thundered, coming from behind. 'Don't talk to your mother like this again! You have no sister! Grow up, my son!'

Arslan beamed an angry gaze at his father, his rebellious mouth opening, but the look in his father's eyes dammed the angry words. He marched down the marble stairs in pursuit of Begum, running to her house, not bothered that he had ruined his newly polished shoes with a thick layer of dust. Without knocking, he burst through the door, startling husband and wife, eating bananas. Two peels on the plate and two in their hands. The sight – their preoccupation with fruit – galled him. He lashed straight out at Begum.

'You knew she was here, Begum!' The words pelted like pointed darts into Begum's body. The small half-peeled banana went back on the plate as Begum turned to her husband, desperately seeking some direction.

'You knew, Begum!' Arslan accused, very much the landlord's son, his body aggressively poised over the housekeeper's figure in the bamboo and raffia chair.

'Yes, I knew!' Begum steadily held her young master's gaze.

'And you never told me?' Aggrieved, Arslan squeezed his eyes to prevent the tears from shaming him.

'Beloved little master …' Begum's heart melted in pain. 'I

couldn't, Arslan. You know how it is,' she appealed, hoping for his understanding.

'No, I don't know,' he lashed out. 'Everybody has gone mad! My *baji* is not dead!' he sobbed aloud. 'I want to see her!'

Ali decided that it was time to take a firm hand with Arslan. His wife, as usual, in her soft-hearted way, was getting nowhere.

'You've no sister, Master Arslan! For us she's dead, because she abandoned all of us. Did she give a thought to you, Arslan? No, she just ran away!' Ali's taunting remark struck home, making Arslan want to retaliate. Begum quickly stepped in, pulling Arslan's stiff body into her arms as she had always done since he was a toddler.

'I know it hurts, Master Arslan. I know you love her very much, as I do,' she said, ignoring her husband's look of strong disapproval. 'But your sister did something terrible.'

'She only got married, Begum!' Arslan scoffed. 'What's wrong with that? Don't people usually get married when they are grown up?'

'Yes, people do get married, Master Arslan,' Begum stuttered to explain. 'It was the way in which it was done! She only thought of herself and killed us all!'

'Don't be silly, Begum? She hasn't "killed" anyone. Now you are talking rubbish.' He angrily pulled himself out of Begum's arms.

'You are right, Arslan, she didn't kill anyone, but there are different sorts of deaths and killings. She "killed" your parents in spirit. Can you understand what I'm trying to say? They live, Arslan, but as shadows. They are not the same people; their lives are empty. How long is it since you heard any laughter in the *hevali*, Arslan? Have you ever noticed your father looking you directly in the eye? Your mother has just become a tomb of silence. Remember one thing, when you grow up, never hurt your parents, my darling!'

'But Allah Pak is merciful and forgives,' beseeched the boy. 'Will my parents never forgive her?' he asked, his eyes now openly overflowing.

'I don't know, my pet. But I promise you one thing – when she comes next time, I will take you to see her.'

'Can you find out where she lives, so that I can phone her?' He eagerly asked.

Begum sobered, eyes evasive. 'I'll just arrange for you to meet her.'

'What if she never returns?' Arslan petulantly offered, his spirits sinking, angrily brushing away the tears from his cheeks. 'I miss her so much, Begum.'

'I know, Master Arslan, but believe me, she'll return, my son. I know she will.' She pulled him into her arms and let him sob on her shoulders.

*

Begum was proved right; Laila did return to the village a few months later. This time, she brought Shirin with her – her baby daughter. Again she arrived at dusk, a shadowy, cloaked figure, hurrying through the dark lanes; keen to avoid meeting anyone she knew. Again it was the *dhoban* who was first alerted of her arrival when her eyes fell straight on the door; the padlock was gone. With excitement rushing through her, Massi Fiza charged straight into the potter's home, cheerfully offering '*salaam*' and startling Laila breastfeeding her baby girl on the veranda. Massi Fiza's eyes widened in disbelief; she was not prepared for the sight of a baby.

Disconcerted by the intrusion, Laila hurriedly pulled down her shawl to hide both her breast and her daughter, scowling at her husband for not bolting the door. Jubail sat on the chair scribbling business notes for the engineering firm he was working for in Islamabad.

Laila's confounded glance immediately spelt to the *dhoban* that she was not her favourite person, nor was she welcome in her home. Massi Fiza's narrow shoulders stiffened with mock outrage, unperturbed by the landlord's daughter's open show of hostility. The potter's hovel was hardly a place for Master Haider's imperious daughter to display her 'queenly' tantrums, Massi Fiza silently scoffed. On the contrary, Laila was now one of them, downgraded to the same class, living in the same lane, in a house worse than hers! There were no Alis or Begums to serve her night and day. It was time the haughty young mistress dispensed with her airs and came to accept her new station in life with grace.

Even she, a humble laundrywoman, had one room with chipped marble floors. In the potter's house, not one tiny piece of marble graced any floor surface, let alone the stairs and the two sorry-looking, cement-coated pillars. Moreover, Massi Fiza was sure her home was bigger by at least two *merlas* than the potter's humble dwelling.

On glimpsing the burning resentment in the tall, wiry, middle-aged woman, Laila schooled her face to form a welcoming smile. Whether she liked it or not, the *dhoban* would be a useful errand woman – the ideal messenger and go-between for herself and Begum. Laila discreetly kept her *chador* down over her naked breast, shielding it from the interested gaze of Massi Fiza who had been on the point of jabbering aloud, 'You have beautiful breasts, Laila-ji,' but stopped short in embarrassment. Female breasts were of special interest to her. For Allah Pak had been particularly mean to her, in furnishing her with only tiny pads of flesh. She always kept herself covered not for modesty's sake, but in shame at having a flat chest.

'Massi Fiza-ji, please inform Begum that I have arrived with my baby,' Laila curtly instructed. 'Here, please take these for your errand.' The smile and the cold, blue eyes mocked Massi Fiza and her greed.

Reluctant to proffer her hand, Massi Fiza's fingers nevertheless folded the two crisp red 100-rupee notes in her tight fist. Money always came in handy – no matter from what source. Pride never helped, and similarly it was idiotic to offer an empty gesture and reject the offering.

Massi Fiza excitedly flew to the *hevali*. 'She might be living in the humble potter's home, but Laila still has her father's blood drumming through her veins,' Massi Fiza reminded herself.

In the *hevali*, Begum was in the midst of the sensuous throes of Queen Noor Jahan's delightful Punjabi melodies. Her eyes firmly shut and reddish-orange *sak*-stained mouth softly parted, Begum was humming the lyrics when Massi Fiza burst in with her message. Begum stopped the kitchen cassette recorder, annoyed at the rude interruption. But on learning the news, she ran out of her kitchen.

Her first port of call was Arslan, and she found him playing cricket with other boys in a school playground. Begum watched him whack the ball high into the air, bringing a smile of pride to their housekeeper's face. Laila loved horses and Arslan played cricket. Begum wistfully wondered if their young master would be the next Imran Khan of Pakistan.

Ignoring his angry scowl at being interrupted, Begum whispered in his ear. Face lighting up, Arslan dropped his bat and ran after Begum. Later, like two guilty thieves in the night, they sneaked into the potter's home, with Begum glancing fearfully over her shoulder before entering. She could not risk being seen entering this home with the young master!

As her wretched luck would have it, Massi Fiza materialised from behind her door and treated Begum to a smug conspiratorial smile before entering the goldsmith's house for a good natter with her friend Rukhsar.

'Damn the woman!' Begum cursed, gritting her teeth. Was the *dhoban* spying on them from behind the crack in her door?

*

The goldsmith's living quarters were on the second floor. And the workshop with its shutters always down was on the first floor, where business and the real 'gold' work took place. Everyone knew where they had to go. The actual gold jewellery was locked away in cabinets upstairs, or tucked into little parcels and kept in a large pillowcase carefully guarded by the goldsmith's wife and his three daughters. At night, the pillowcase was always placed next to the goldsmith's bed on a chair, for one never knew with thieves. Burglars wouldn't pick up a pillow and run away. The funny thing was, courtesy of Massi Fiza-ji's slip of the tongue, everyone in the village knew where he stored his gold items. And it wasn't in the safe, where he kept old jewellery other people handed in to be repaired.

Upon entering, Massi Fiza excitedly announced to Rukhsar,

'Master Arslan is here with the potter's grandchild!' Then continued, 'A beautiful little girl – not at all like the potter's son, thank goodness!'

'Hey, what's wrong with him?' Rukhsar challenged her friend, affronted by her supercilious manner. 'Does Master Haider know?' she mischievously asked. All this drama was going on two doors away and she did not know, thanks to her work keeping her busy all day long!

'No, I doubt it,' Massi Fiza proclaimed. 'Begum looked as if she was going to have a heart attack when she saw me, which is mean of her; after all, I was the one who told her. But I forgive her.' Smiling, she glanced down at Rukhsar's hands.

'What are you doing, my friend?'

'Only what I'm destined to do in this home – stringing these wretched pearls onto this thread! You know how tiny these things are? I'm fed up with my lazy daughters. They never lend me a hand. The only thing they love doing is trying on other people's jewellery and preening themselves in front of mirrors – silly girls.'

'Rukhsar-ji, don't be harsh on them. They are girls after all, and bound to love jewellery. Well, having said that, my niece doesn't. She always has her head in one of those fashion magazines.'

'Don't let her read all those women's magazines with stories about love and all that rubbish! They'll turn the girl's head, you know. I supervise my daughters' reading habits quite closely,' Rukhsar commented before adding, with a twinkle in her eyes: 'Have you ever been in love, Massi Fiza-ji?'

'Ooh! What a question to ask?' Massi Fiza blurted, blushing beetroot. 'No, Sister Rukhsar. Love played no part in my humble life.'

'Don't be silly, Massi Fiza-ji, everybody falls in love. It's nothing to do with your station in life,' Rukhsar innocently commented.

'Then, Rukhsar-ji, you must have been in love yourself!' Massi Fiza slyly prompted, neatly turning the table on her friend. It was now Rukhsar's turn to blush, with tides of colour flushing through her olive-skinned cheeks.

'No, my friend,' she glibly lied, her eyes determinedly fixed on the bead and the needle. Not for anything would she utter a word to Massi Fiza about the college boy who lived next door to her parents' home and her secret pining for him. All those afternoons of peering over the rooftop gallery. Oh, how she loved him. That was until he got married to another college student. Love then turned to hatred for him and self-loathing! Thank goodness her reputation and *izzat* hadn't been sullied, and her parents didn't have to get involved at the end

'Thankfully love didn't darken my parents' door,' her lying tongue loftily preached. 'I'll tell you, my friend, love means trouble – big, mighty trouble.'

'It sounds as if you are an expert in this matter and know what you are talking about, Rukhsar-ji,' Massi Fiza chuckled, not easily fooled, her small round eyes interestingly noting the flush which had, by now, sunk to Rukhsar's rounded throat.

'Yes, definitely so,' Rukhsar assented, carefully avoiding her friend's eyes, painfully aware of her heated face. 'Trust my cheeks to betray me,' she chided herself.

Aloud she continued, 'See where it has landed the potter's entire family … exiled because of their son's foolish infatuation. And where has the mighty daughter of Haider Ali ended up? Cooking her own meals on an old stove next to the muddy potter's wheel! Save us all from this pathetic mad disease, my friend. Love is not worth it, I tell you!' Having said that with passion, Rukhsar was now boldly able to raise her eyes to her friend.

'We're not the ones who need to worry about this, Rukhsar-ji. We're too old, and not likely to elope with anyone to anywhere, are we? Nor will anyone offer to elope with us older ladies for that matter! You just need to keep your eye on your daughters and make sure that they don't go out horse riding. After all, that was what did it for that pair.'

'Horse riding – my daughters! Massi Fiza-ji, they would never go near such a beast, let alone ride one. I think Haider Ali's daughter is totally mad. They spoilt her rotten because of those big blue eyes of hers that she always flashed at everyone. How could poor Jubail resist such a woman, and if she was throwing herself at him!' Rukhsar sneered. She could never stand the elegant, beautiful daughter of the landlord. And, in particular, she resented Laila's eyes. That young woman had always eclipsed her daughters' looks and their education.

'Yes, Rukhsar, I can't help melting into those eyes myself!' Massi Fiza admitted. 'All she has to do is to look at you and you become her slave! Imagine what it must be like for the poor potter's son – what chance did he stand when a beauty just throws herself at him? I had better get home – three sacks full of laundry from the butcher's family waiting to be washed. You know what their greasy, blood-stained clothes are like? My hands get worn down with all that scrubbing! Even my two washing machines are no good for their clothes.'

The thought of the mountain of laundry waiting for her at home, and most of it white linen, was now sending waves of panic through her.

'Well, you had better hurry up, but don't forget to tell me what's happening in the potter's house, won't you? I just can't seem to get out of my house these days. Customers keep coming and I have to entertain the wives with tea and *mithaei*, whilst the husbands bargain away. By the way, do you know if Gulbahar's younger sister's son has gone to England?'

'You mean Mehreen's son, Ismail – yes, why do you ask?' Massi Fiza was puzzled.

'Well, you know ...' Rukhsar stuttered, dropping her gaze and unable to continue, pride making it impossible.

Massi Fiza immediately understood her friend; it was her turn to be deliciously catty. 'I don't think any of your daughters will be going to England. If it's anybody he takes with him it will be Saher, Rani's daughter. I am sure the sisters have an unofficial agreement that their children will marry one day. He's only young – 21, I think. He's not likely to come back to marry for some time, you know. Your daughters are too young yet.'

'One has to plan for daughters,' Rukhsar stiffly reminded her. 'By the way, what if he marries a *goorie*, a white woman, out there?'

'Oh, gosh!' Massi Fiza's mouth gaped open in wonder. 'Allah Pak, he wouldn't do something like that, would he?'

'You never know, these things happen all the time, my friend.

Young men have been known to bring home foreign brides.' Rukhsar stopped, grimacing as she saw her youngest daughter come in with two china cups of coffee. Why did her Ruhi always treat everyone the same? Did the village *dhoban* really deserve to be served in their best china, the same as their local council-lor's wife? Her face straight and smiling, she skilfully signalled her displeasure to her daughter. Understanding her mother perfectly, Ruhi, in a rebellious mood for having to sort out her mother's wardrobe, just as skilfully ignored her mother's look. She offered, instead, a packet of their best biscuits, richly dipped in chocolate, to their humble visitor.

Massi Fiza happily dunked the whole round biscuit into her hot drink and saw the chocolate melt into the coffee. Shocked, she dipped her fingers into the cup to grab the soggy wet biscuit, popping one half into her mouth whilst the other plopped back into the creamy dark liquid. Massi Fiza shrugged. It was all going to end up in her stomach anyway. Noisily she slurped down the rich chocolatey coffee to the last drop and, smiling her thanks, handed back the china cup.

'You're a very kind girl, Ruhi ... always treating me to life's little luxuries.'

If only Ruhi ... Massi Fiza halted her errant thoughts there and then as she remembered the washing. Her two sons and their future brides could wait!

'Yes, she is!' Rukhsar drily agreed.

'Imagine a *goorie* in our midst, Rukhsar, in our village!' Massie Fiza was lost in thought of a white, European woman visiting their village. Her friend merely smiled; she would let the *dhoban* dream on. One had to have some luxurious daydreams in life.

*

Laila proudly offered her daughter to her brother, before hugging him herself. 'Oh, how you have grown, my beautiful prince!' Arslan was glaring at his sister's husband over her shoulder, the man who had robbed him of his beloved sister.

Jubail coolly returned his young brother-in-law's gaze, under-standing his resentment perfectly.

'She's beautiful, *baji jan!*' Arslan whispered, looking down in wonder at his little niece and touching her tiny fingers.

'Yes! Just like her uncle.' Beaming with pleasure, Laila proudly claimed, 'She has our eyes and colouring.'

Lovingly tucking the shawl tightly around her little body, Begum smiled down at the baby girl. Inside, her heart wept, feeling the coarse texture of the nondescript baby blanket between her chapped fingers and scanning the humble surroundings in distress. Was this her young mistress's destiny?

'Oh, Mistress Laila,' she mourned later on her way home. 'If you had this first child inside the walls of your parents' home, you would have been spoilt rotten – Mistress Gulbahar would have purchased the finest of woollen cashmere! But this … this …' She couldn't continue as utter despair hit her hard. It was so unreal to imagine her young mistress living amidst such squalor and poverty.

She had so many questions to ask: about the birth; the after care; who helped her mistress in her hour of need; did she breast-feed? Had she given birth at home or did she go to a proper hospital? Did she need anything and, above all, was she happy? Yet, she had asked none, only behaved as a criminal who had stolen into a forbidden world and wanted to scurry away – eager to be gone from that street.

'I did not want to betray our masters, but I have done so yet again, Ali!' She could never keep anything from her Ali, even though he always gave her a hard time. 'But how could I not take Master Arslan to see his beloved sister?' she defensively cried, baulking at the horror-struck look in his eyes.

'*Beloved sister,* you said?' her husband snarled into her face. 'If she had an ounce of love for her family, Begum, she wouldn't have abandoned them. How I despise you! See how *she* manages to use you every time. You fall for that enchanting face of hers. Tell me, what magic potion does she give you? What light, *noor*, flashes out of those blue eyes that beguile you so much? I don't know what to do with you any more!' He capped his verbal abuse with a look of utter contempt, making his wife recoil in outrage.

'I take no magic potion from her, you silly man!' Begum

bitterly retorted. 'Go on, give me another one of your lousy lectures. But I believe that we are destroying this child. He cannot make any sense of the situation – too young to feel or understand his parents' suffering. We'll end up destroying him, emotionally, if we carry on like this – just you wait and see, Ali.' Her eyes scanned her husband's face, hoping that he understood. 'He sees no wrong in his sister's actions. In his eyes she has only got married. He misses her terribly and wants her back home. In fact, he blames his parents for the whole thing. I'll tell you this, Ali, Arslan's resentment is destructive. One of these days he is going to blow up – he will turn on his parents, hurting them even more than Laila. Can you bear that to happen? The next time, our Master Haider may never come out of his room. So please allow Arslan to meet his sister secretly. It means so much to him.' Her impassioned words melted Ali's anger.

'I really don't know where you get your twisted reasoning or strange wisdom from. Certainly not from your basic primary education,' Ali good-humouredly mocked, giving in to his wife's logic, his eyebrows arching up to their thin, grey peaks. 'All I know is that one day you'll have us both turned out onto the streets in disgrace!'

'Don't be silly!' Begum added, her eyes sparkling. 'Do you think we should show the baby to Mistress Gulbahar? She's the grandmother, for goodness sake.' She quickly defended herself, noticing the angry glint leap into her husband's eyes.

'I don't think it will be Arslan who will break this family, but you, my foolish wife. Do you think that the master and mistress will want to look at the potter's son's brat? It'll be like sprinkling salt onto their gaping wounds, you foolish woman! Don't you have any common sense?'

Begum turned on him, resenting his derogatory term 'foolish woman'. 'It's their daughter's baby, too – their grandchild!'

'Yes!' Her husband sneered back, rising to his feet. 'In their eyes their daughter is dead, and her personal belongings were thrown out. Now, you want to foist a baby in front of their eyes. For God's sake, woman, wake up! Just forget your foolish dreams for once. Laila, with or without a daughter, is a doomed shadow passing through the village. Nobody will acknowledge her or go near her! They'll do what the landlord is doing – ignore them! The girl will be ignored all her life.'

'Oh! That's cruel, Ali,' Begum stammered, tears brimming. 'The baby's lovely. I tell you that little girl will one day bring her grandfather and grandmother to their knees!'

Ali was now striding across the courtyard. He had had enough of his wife's passion for the foolish young mistress for one evening. 'God forbid that *manhous* day, their granddaughter bringing our masters to their knees! Their daughter has killed them, never mind a granddaughter!'

'I … I didn't mean it like that!' Begum stuttered. 'Please listen! The baby is called Shirin, Ali, and she's gorgeous – with Haider Sahib's eyes! Why don't you visit Laila? Allah Pak is merciful and forgiving, my husband, as Arslan, a child, had to remind us. The baby has done no wrong and is innocent. Laila has come to feast her eyes on her parents' home. Give her some sustenance for her journey. We cannot be judges, Ali.' Her voice had risen. 'Her parents can, but we can't!'

Her husband shook his head in derision once more before slamming the wooden door shut behind him and muttering to himself. 'You are insane, woman!'

Satisfied with her lecture and a smug smile lining her face, Begum sat down to chop the *akros* for their evening meal; she knew that she had won and that Ali would visit the baby. He had never let her down when she requested anything of him. He blustered quite a bit, but ultimately always gave in, as he loved her in his own strange fashion – even her so-called stupidity. Begum chuckled. 'My Ali is quite daft at times, but ever so nice most of the time.'

That night after dinner, Ali sheepishly let slip that he'd given the baby girl a 500-rupee note, in his role as godfather. With eyes lowered, he sipped the almond milk drink that Begum brought back home on most days from the *hevali*. Almond milk drinks were one of the luxuries that they enjoyed in the house of their generous employers. Begum pretended not to have heard, but smugly smiling inside, she gloriously thanked him as she lay on her side of the bed.

Ali omitted to tell his wife how he, Ali, hadn't acknowledged Jubail even with a glance. Their mistress could be forgiven, but not him – the *shaitan* – the devil who had pulled her out of her parents' home. That beast would never be forgiven for destroying both Laila's and his own family. It was rumoured that the poor potter and his family had fled far away over the mountains to Abbottabad, abandoning his potter's wheel as well as dozens of pots ready to be sold.

When any of the villagers happened to see Jubail, they all averted their gazes, but they never told him off, aping their superior, Master Haider. For Mistress Laila, there were no particular words of greeting or a show of animosity, but a sly, semi-averted acknowledgement in the eyes of many.

*

After a week of waiting in despair for her parents to come and take her home Laila bitterly chided herself: 'You are living a foolish dream, Laila. Wake up!'

Over the next few years, she kept to her punishing ritual of returning to the village every six months. She never gave up hope – where one loved, one never did. For the three-year-old toddler, without a care in the world, the village lane became the most natural place for her to run around and play. As she giggled and hopped on the cobblestones around her mother, she was totally oblivious of people's reactions, their indrawn breaths and, in particular, of one older man with reddish-brown hair whose shadow and eyes had momentarily grazed her face and then immediately shifted. For her mother, watching from behind, it was a crushing blow.

'This is how they must feel,' Laila bitterly acknowledged.

Her daughter was lovely and people in the city often commented on her appearance wherever she went. Here in the village she simply did not exist.

'At least Father's eyes have fallen on her face,' Laila wept. 'Mother, how could you be so callous? Don't you want to see your granddaughter?' Night after night the same words bitterly echoed.

Desperate to show her daughter to her mother, she had smuggled photographs into the *hevali* via Begum's unwilling hands, with an appeal, 'If Mother will not see my Shirin in person then at least in a photograph. Begum, take them! Do this for me, please!' she had beseeched.

As always, unable to watch her young mistress cry, Begum's soft heart melted. Her reluctant hands clutching the small envelope hidden under her *chador*, she went up to her mistress's bedroom. Taking out two pictures, she propped them strategically on the dressing table, one behind her mistress's favourite *athar* bottle, the other against the silver-plated hand mirror.

Later in the evening, as Gulbahar bent to comb her hair, the photos sent a shock wave searing through her. Hand trembling, Gulbahar's eyes took her fill of the beautiful smiling face of the young child with her crop of curly, brown hair. Breathing ragged, she took stock of herself. Gripping one edge of the photograph, and with a steely will, she turned it upside down. With shaking fingers she turned the key in the lock of the bottom drawer of her dressing-table. Pulling it open, she carefully placed the two photos inside – face down.

'My ultimate test – my duty to my husband!' she vowed, firmly turning the key to lock the drawer and then hiding it behind the leg of her dresser, part of her dowry. Haider would never be looking for things down there.

That particular drawer, its wood studded with pieces of onyx, was only opened again for depositing the next photograph a few months later. It, too, was cruelly placed face down on top of the previous pictures. Gulbahar never looked at them again. Nor did it occur to her to tear them up or show them to her two sisters. The child remained a tabooed topic. If any members of her family glimpsed Shirin in the street, nobody mentioned it. Not even her sisters had the audacity to discuss the girl – Shirin simply didn't exist.

By now, an inch-high pile of photographs of all sizes had accumulated over the past four years in her locked, bottom drawer. Two had been cut in half and Gulbahar could only guess who had been in the other half.

Gulbahar stiffly passed her test of endurance with flying colours, remaining true to her words and her husband. She had betrayed her Haider-ji once but she would never do it again. A wife she was, but one who had happily opted to kill the mother inside her. The grandmother, on the other hand, just didn't exist and definitely not for the daughter of a man who had robbed them of their daughter and swept away their world from under their very feet.

As Shirin grew older, she got used to the regular visits to the village. Passing her grandparents' *hevali* every day, she never entered it or learned about the people who lived in it. Eyes squinting in the shadow of their small lobby, Shirin had gazed up in wonder at the tall young man her mother quietly talked to behind their closed door. She was equally curious as to why her mother had wept against the shoulders of this man. Who was he? Why had this man also kissed her mother's cheek? Her innocent mind did not learn that a brother was bidding his sister goodbye. Arslan was going to the United States to study, for a long time.

A few years later, when he was expected back in Pakistan, Laila returned to the village, eager to welcome her brother. Although he had refused to write or phone her following his parents' advice, he never stopped her from doing either. Her husband often taunted her for the way her family was treating her. Feeling vulnerable and defensive, she would then bitterly turn on him: 'If you hadn't crossed my path, I wouldn't be in this mess.' By now, their earlier passion had long been extinguished in the melting pot of grief and bitterness. Laila ached for her family.

'I don't know what I saw in you, anyway,' she cruelly lashed out one day, wanting to punish him in frustration.

They both ended up hurting and blaming one another and then resignedly making up, for there was no one else to support them individually. Recriminations and a cloud of bitterness always hung over them. Both had lost their families. Jubail's parents never forgave him. The potter, missing his village, taunted his son's loins for turning their world into a nightmarish existence. 'What was wrong with the other girls? Did you have to reach to the sky to pluck a star and in the process make us homeless, my greedy, arrogant son?' Jubail would aggressively argue back. In their hearts, however, both he and Laila knew that their decision to elope and marry without informing either of the two families was a despicable and cruel thing to do.

Laila had decided to come alone for her brother's homecoming, fearing her husband's presence would blight her stay.

PART TWO

CHAPTER 7

Daniela

In Liverpool, England, Dave watched from his kitchen window Mrs Patel's peacock-green silk sari flying all over the washing line, one end clutched in her tight fist. Grinning, he suppressed his urge to jump over the garden fence dividing the two semi-detached houses and lend a hand to the poor woman in pinning down the seven yards of dripping-wet fabric. Unable to resist, he pushed open the double-glazed kitchen window and shouted, 'Mrs Patel, look at those clouds. Is it worth the bother, dear?'

The sixty-one-year-old Ugandan Indian woman merely grinned, sweeping back tendrils of hair slipped from her small immaculate bun, the red marital *tikka* proudly sitting on her forehead above her nose. 'I know, Mr Harrison, but the wind will soon dry my saris! By the way, I'm making aubergine and potato *bhaji*. Would you like some?' she offered.

'You bet!'

'I'll get our Nita to bring it round.'

'Thanks a bundle, Mrs Patel!' He pulled the window shut, his mouth already salivating at the thought of Mrs Patel's wonderful *bhaji*. His wife, not keen on curries, hated him for this.

'How shameful to take food off a neighbour, never mind asking!' she had stiffly jeered last time and had nearly thrown the plate of cauliflower curry into the bin, declaring, 'Now the whole kitchen will reek of this ghastly, garlicky stuff!'

'Ghastly!' Dave had fumed. 'Mrs Patel makes delicious curries! It's a pity that you don't like them.'

'It's a *pity* about a lot of things in this household, David!'

Dave's good humour fled, catching the hard glint in her eyes. The time for reasoning with her was gone. And they both knew the matter went beyond curries. It was just another opportunity for her to mock him on the differences between them.

His mobile phone bleeped a text message: 'Outside,' he read. His fingers quickly tapped a reply: 'OK, honey.'

Slinging his jacket over his shoulder, he was at the front door before he shouted up to his wife. 'I'm off to the Central Library, Liz.'

'OK!' Elizabeth grimaced, drying her wet hair in the bath-room. Why couldn't he get 'Elizabeth' out of his mouth rather than that common 'Liz'?

Outside in his front garden, Dave immediately spotted the silver car parked halfway down the street. He sprinted down the road and bumped into a young Yemeni woman, living four doors away, pushing her three-year-old toddler in a buggy, a bag of groceries hanging at the side.

'Sorry, love!' he mumbled.

'It's OK,' she politely nodded, straightening her *hijab* and feeling for any stray strands of hair that may have escaped from under her scarf.

Upstairs in the front bedroom, Elizabeth swept aside the venetian blinds and looked down at the street, massaging expen-sive Dior lotion onto her slim throat, roughened from recent sunbathing on the island of Crete, her eyes on the silver car and its driver.

*

Dave took a long tender look at the young woman sitting in the driver's seat. Leaning over, he brushed his mouth across her cheek.

'How are you, honey?'

'Fine. I needed you with me today – I'm having my first scan.'

'Gosh, really! How exciting, love! Come on then, what're we waiting for?'

As the car zoomed past his home, Dave's smile slipped.

They drove in silence for a while before she softly asked, 'You've not told her, have you?'

'No! You told me not to. Remember!' He looked away, face tight.

'Good. It's better this way.'

'I'm not so sure, but if you say so.'

In her bedroom, Elizabeth stood back from the window, hand clutching one of the long strips from the window blinds, feet sinking into the plush pile of Axminster carpet.

*

It was just like any other morning at the antenatal clinic, with women lounging in different stages of pregnancy, displaying baby mounds of all shapes and sizes, some rounded whilst others protruded at strange angles through their maternity garments. Some were alone; others came with their partners or parents. Lively toddlers were playing in the play area. Bemused, Daniela let her senses absorb the scene.

An hour later, they were back in the car, parked in the same place on Dave's street.

'You sure, Daniela, that you don't want me to tell Liz?'

'No!'

'Don't fret, my gem. Are you going back to school?'

'Yes, we couldn't get supply cover for this afternoon.'

Dave sighed, looking through the windscreen. The refuse men were emptying the bins into their truck. Dave hopped out, remembering his rubbish bag in the kitchen.

'Take care. Need to dash before those rascals drive off.'

'Thanks. I love you so much!'

'I know, and remember I'm here for you! Bye, honey.'

The car sped off down the road.

'Hi guys, just hang on a sec, will you?'

'Sure, mate!' the eldest man answered, tipping the contents of one wheelie bin into the truck.

Elizabeth went out into the garden to check her bedding plants. The geraniums were doing really well, she noted absently. The ivy creeping up the garden fence provided them with more privacy from the neighbours. Elizabeth peered over the fence, staring at Mrs Patel's five tiny, silk, sari blouses in turquoise, pink, black, green and brown, wondering how the Indian woman managed to dress so discreetly with not an inch of her midriff flesh showing.

Two hours later, they were eating their lunch out on the patio near the apple tree. 'I saw you get into her silver car, David.' Elizabeth toyed with her microwaved chilli con carne, eyes steady on his face, challenging him to look up from his shepherd's pie.

'So you told me earlier!' he replied, taking another swig from his bottle of shandy.

She placed her fork neatly back on her Laura Ashley china plate and continued staring at him. Dave simply refused to make eye contact. Meal finished, he stood up to leave, but couldn't help the outburst, though he knew the outcome all too well. 'You can't stop me, Liz. You can do what you want, but you won't stop me!'

There would be a full-blown argument later, followed by the inevitable cold-shoulder treatment. Even at the dining table, her academic books would neatly divide them.

'Do what you've always done, David, run!' The contempt was apparent in the arch of her neck and the eyes resting on their well-manicured, landscaped garden. Inside the house, a tuneless whistle on his lips, Dave grabbed his jacket and headed for the local pub.

Pushing aside her plate, Elizabeth picked up her book from the table and soon forgot her husband; absorbed in her PhD research on Plato's *Republic* and the Roman historian Tacitus.

CHAPTER 8

The Jewels

Liaquat, Mehreen's husband, had eagerly obtained the services of two goldsmiths, one from the city and the other from Gulistan – Rukhsar's husband – to display their finest jewellery items on the large table in the drawing room for Saher to inspect.

The afternoon sunlight jumping through the window lit the rubies, emeralds and sapphires on the chunky necklace sets that would be worn on the main wedding day. There were also many delicate, gem-encrusted sets for evening wear and parties, as well as pendants and *matr malas* for casual wear. Over sixty rings of all shapes and designs sat cushioned in dainty, velvet boxes laid out on a silver-plated tray.

Liaquat, a proud 55-year-old landowner, wished to honour and bestow many gifts on his son's bride. Extremely fond of Saher, he could not wait to have her live with them. The wedding had been planned many years ago, but their son had kept putting it off.

The doorbell rang. Rasoola, the housekeeper, abandoned her tedious task of chasing away the flies swarming over the tray of pastries in the kitchen and rushed to open the door.

Saher found herself blushing, extremely annoyed at the sly knowing smile in the housekeeper's eyes.

'Only two weeks to go before you are the new mistress in this *hevali*!' were Rasoola's teasing welcoming words.

'Rasoola, stop yapping and let us inside!' Mehreen irritably scolded, hating her housekeeper for her gossiping tongue. Well chastened, seething and with a fallen face, Rasoola stiffly stepped back. Her mistress had a very special knack of humiliating her and doing her *baesti* in front of other people.

'*Bismillah*, Mistress Rani,' she welcomed in her syrupy tone. 'Please go into the drawing room. Sahib-ji and the two goldsmiths are waiting with lots of boxes of jewellery for you ladies to see. I'll be in the kitchen cleaning out the rice for Ismail's wedding.'

'I must get Begum to lend you a hand for the wedding feasts,' Mehreen loftily announced.

'No need, Mistress,' Rasoola sharply replied, bristling at the suggestion. The last thing she wanted was to have bossy Begum in her kitchen. That woman was already blighting her life, her ears aching from hearing glowing praises about her. Mehreen neither praised Rasoola nor stopped lecturing her about Begum's 'excellent' work and was always commenting, 'Begum does this, why don't you?' Many a time Rasoola had cattily wanted to blurt out, 'Why don't you get Begum here?' But her cowardly lips remained tightly sealed. Master Liaquat was a generous man and had helped with her two younger sisters' wedding costs – thankfully all now happily wedded off.

She just prayed that Saher, the new bride-to-be, a successful lawyer working in the nearby city and driving a smart car, wouldn't bring too many changes into their lives. And she, Rasoola, hated change above all!

*

Saher, gazing down at all the open velvet boxes, blushingly requsted of her future father-in-law, 'Please buy one small set only!'

'Such modesty, our Saher!' he cajoled, eyes shining with affection. 'Choose at least fifteen. Otherwise I'll be very offended – I mean it, Saher!'

'I can't!' Saher shook her head, horrified at the thought of all that gold touching her body.

'Half of these sets I'm giving you in my role as a surrogate father, my dearest Saher. You know that your aunt and I absolutely adore you, and what better way to demonstrate our affection than with these sets.' Saher gently sidled away from the table.

'Please remember our pride, Saher. Everyone expects you to have a lot of gold jewellery as the daughter-in-law of a wealthy *zemindar*,' he good-humouredly reminded her. 'One set is unthinkable!'

Saher cast an appealing glance at her mother, bringing Rani to her aid.

'You are very generous, Brother Liaquat. Fifteen is too much! Please remember, there will be future occasions,' she added.

'OK! I'll leave you women to it! I need to phone Ismail to confirm what time his plane is arriving on Wednesday.'

CHAPTER 9

The Surprise

In her primary school, Daniela glanced at the wall clock, waiting for the morning break.

'Sharon, can you manage here for the next fifteen minutes, please? I need to pop into Mrs Dixon's room.'

'Sure!' The 22-year-old assistant teacher was listening to young Mandy reading from the picture book about the naughty dinosaur.

'Thanks.' Daniela swept her gaze over her class of 30 five-year-olds. Jonathan and Eric were still enjoying a good bout of giggles, dumping more jugs of water into the playing sand and making little wet craters. Rebecca's dear little face, fringed by heavy, overgrown, brown curls was screwed up in deep concentration as she charcoaled a picture of her nana with a large red party hat. Jaswinder was thumbs and fingers, totally engrossed in working out her sums on the abacus. Ahmad and Chen were still excitedly tapping away at the computer keyboard, watching the different icons popping up on the monitor.

Emily Dixon, the headmistress of the Church of England primary school, was on the phone when Daniela entered and smiling signalled her to sit in front of the desk.

'Could I discuss something with you?'

'What, now?' Emily's eyebrows arched. The morning teaching session had not ended.

'Please. It's urgent, Emily,' Daniela earnestly appealed, as she perched on the edge of the leather armchair. The headmistress watched the young woman nervously pushing her hand through her short-cropped fair hair. 'I need to take about three weeks off work – beginning literally from tomorrow!'

'What!' The headmistress's mouth dropped open at this strange request – and right in the middle of a very hectic school term; they had just received notice of their Ofsted monitoring inspection.

'Daniela, you can't be serious, my dear. We've just had our half-term holidays.' A thought struck her. 'It's not the inspection that you want to escape from?'

'Of course not!' A very conscientious teacher, Daniela was deeply offended. 'I know it's at a bad time, but I really do need to take time off.'

'Why?' Emily Dixon asked, now completely mystified.

'For personal reasons – I'm sorry, I can't discuss the details.'

'But this is most irregular! Our school play, Daniela? You play the piano! And as the teacher governor you were going to report on the key stage literacy! On Friday you are booked for the IT training in Birmingham. There's so much going on, Daniela.'

'Please, it's urgent … I need to save my marriage!'

The headmistress was nonplussed. 'I see! In that case, I'd better ring immediately for supply cover. Shall we try Sally?'

'Oh, thank you! I would not have asked for leave if it was not urgent. Yes, Sally is excellent … The kids loved her story-telling.'

A few hours later she was home, sorting out her clothes and hiding her suitcase carefully under the stairs.

*

Saher stood with the wardrobe door wide open, hand poised on the sleeveless cherry chiffon outfit. Sporting naked arms in front of her future father-in-law was out of the question. The warmth in her face made her slam the wardrobe door shut. That outfit was for her own private moments with Ismail. Arslan had called her gorgeous, but what would Ismail say?

She smiled, pulling out her fiancé's photograph from her diary to have a quick glance before leaving. She was late for work and her client, a feudal landlord she was representing today in court, expected the whole world to play to his tune. What was worse, he had begun crudely wooing her, unashamedly harping on about his single status in life, in front of his two male companions.

Saher had abruptly dismissed his overtures with a cold smile. He was her client and she wasn't cut out to be the wife of a feudal landlord. No, she was destined for a life abroad, fervently hoping that her Ismail would quickly find her a partnership with a law firm in Liverpool.

In the bright beautifully landscaped central courtyard, eyes shaded by her sunglasses, Saher breathed in the scent of the rose bushes and the foliage on the tall potted plants soaking up the sun.

'Come home early, Saher, there's a lot to be done before Ismail's arrival!' her mother urged, calling from the dining room.

'I will! *Khuda Hafiz*!' Saher crossed the courtyard, letting the manservant respectfully escort her to her car through the *hevali* gates. Within a few yards the village road, winding through the fields of wheat and orange groves, had brutalised the car's shiny body with a thick layer of dust. In a buoyant mood, Saher turned on the radio, listening to her favourite love song 'Aja Soynaya', a woman calling out to her lover to come home. The song also sadly reminded her that her days in Pakistan were numbered, leading her to speculate on what life in England had to offer her. Would she fit in or learn to adjust both to the icy cold climate and the British culture? Ismail had never properly talked about his city. She knew that she would really miss her village, especially her mother and car. How she longed to take all three with her.

*

Daniela stood patiently in the standby queue at Manchester Airport, her straw hat propped at an angle that hid almost two thirds of her face. From beneath the wide brim, her eyes urgently skimmed the faces of the people around her.

Once checked in and clutching her boarding pass, Daniela excitedly headed for the departure lounge. Her heart stopped thumping only when she was in her seat and the plane was high up in the sky, her face buried in a glossy magazine, biding her time.

The flight attendant was wheeling the food trolley down the

aisle when she saw *him* rise from his seat. Adrenalin gushed through Daniela.

'Hello, Ismail!' she whispered, raising her face as he was about to pass. The man swivelled round, as if shot in the stomach. Daniela stared back, her throat, all of a sudden, parched. Eyes tightly closed, his hand clawed at the headrest of the seat in front of her.

'You silly woman!' he ground out under his breath, finding his tongue.

Daniela's head shot up in indignation.

'Aren't you pleased to see me?' she croaked.

'Pleased?' he stammered, moving his head from side to side in disbelief. 'You don't know what you've done!' he glared down into her face.

Daniela blushed scarlet, embarrassed by the glance of the elderly Pakistani woman sitting beside her. The flight attendant, too, had heard everything.

'The lady needs to pass, Ismail, please move aside!' she coldly instructed in her best public school tone, ready to demolish him, colour flooding into her cheeks.

The toilet was forgotten as Ismail's world swayed before him. Returning to his seat, he told himself it had to be a nightmare. Daniela couldn't possibly be on the plane! He looked back down the aisle, just to check that he was not dreaming! Daniela's cold stare, ten rows back, sent the shivers through him.

'What's wrong, Ismail?' she accused, her green eyes bright with condemnation, now standing in the aisle beside him.

'What's wrong?' he mimicked, livid. 'You don't know what you've done, you fool!'

'Ismail!' Colour drained from Daniela's cheeks.

'Go and sit down! And don't make a scene!' he hissed under his breath, eyes averted from the man coming down the aisle.

Seething, Daniela returned to her seat. It was an overnight journey and she had anticipated the sharing of laughter and jokes, enthusiastic discussions about Pakistan, but this? What had she done? All she had wanted to do was to surprise him – to go to Pakistan.

Her heart sank, cheeks burning. What was the matter with him? She had managed to get leave, granted under such difficult circumstances, so that she could meet his parents. And he, the beast, wasn't even pleased that she was going with him.

Daniela was attacked by insecurity again. She knew for sure that Ismail loved her passionately, yet he always shied away from talking about his family in Pakistan, not even letting her say 'hello' to them on the telephone. When she had once suggested meeting them in Pakistan he had laughed away the idea, offering her platitudes that she would be totally out of place in that society, as a *goorie*, a white woman in a different culture. To prove him wrong had thus become her mission.

She felt she owed it to him and especially to their future children, wanting them to be proud of their two different heritages. She could tell intuitively that he came from a wealthy background. She was always asking her young Pakistani pupils and their parents about Pakistan, wistfully listening to their enthusiastic stories and letting her imagination wander away to the world of her husband's homeland. She loved wearing *shalwar kameez* suits and envied the women who had received them as presents from Pakistan – she had received none.

As she imagined her mother-in-law refurbishing her wardrobe in the local Pakistani style, as befitting the daughter-in-law of a wealthy landlord, it didn't occur to her that they might not even know of her existence.

CHAPTER 10

The Evil Shadow

On the same day in Gulistan, there was chaos in the sweetmaker's household; unexpected guests had turned up late in the afternoon. Two separate families, in fact, and neither had planned to arrive on the same day, nor informed their unsuspecting hosts. Now, both the hosts and the guests ardently wished that they had. Everyone's embarrassment was clumsily apparent for all to see. As hosts, Jennat Bibi and her daughter-in-law Faiza nervously battled to stitch on brave faces. With steely smiles they scurried around offering hospitality, starting off with carting in a crate of bottled soft drinks. Indeed it turned out to be a hectic time for the women and their housemaid, as they shopped, cooked and entertained the guests including preparing the smoking hookah pipes for the two elder male relatives with small twists of fresh tobacco.

Faiza's nightmare started in the kitchen whilst making a stack of *chappatis*. She froze, leaning against the worktop, tightening her pelvic floor muscles to stop the uterine fluid gushing out, her eye on the eighteenth *chappati* burning on the flat-topped pan.

'Oh, Allah Pak,' she groaned as a sudden spasm hit her abdomen. Panic gripped her. She was four months' pregnant, therefore she shouldn't be menstruating.

Nobody else was in the kitchen; her mother-in-law was animatedly entertaining the guests after preparing the pudding of semolina *halwa*, whilst the maid had been despatched to sort out all the bedding for the guests in the back storeroom. Switching off the stove burner and plucking the charred *chappati* from the *tava* pan, Faiza sidled out of the kitchen to get to the *ghusl khanah*. Unfortunately, the bathroom was on the other side of the house and so she had to pass the two lively elderly men under the veranda, happily taking turns at the hookah pipe and sharing jokes with her father-in-law, Javaid.

Her soaking *shalwar* was now sticking uncomfortably to the inside of her thighs with the amniotic fluid trickling down to her ankles. She nearly fainted at the thought: 'What if the two men see my blood-stained garments?' Head lowered, she nimbly crossed the courtyard, passing the two middle-aged women guests and their three grandchildren, with Jennat Bibi sitting on a cane chair happily entertaining them with village stories about Master Haider's son's homecoming and of poor Laila, the land-lord's daughter, who had eloped and was now back in the village.

'Has she no pride – to keep coming back to be treated like that? Imagine having a door slammed shut in your face by your family and in front of everyone. The poor girl, how she must have felt!' commiserated the younger of the two women guests. Her own daughter had married for love, so she felt an obligation to show some sympathy with that poor woman's fate.

'And guess what – there's a big wedding coming up. Mistress Mehreen's son, Ismail, is coming back from England to marry Saher – the lawyer – Mistress Rani's daughter.'

The two men were still heatedly discussing Pakistani politics and the recent elections. 'Will the Karachi situation get better? Will this new government be at the beck and call of America? Let's see who leads our country, Obama or our new politicians? Will the "load shedding" matter be urgently dealt with by the new party? My poor son's shoe factory has come to a standstill with all the electric cuts!' ranted the younger of the two men.

Faiza hurried passed them, draping her long shawl around her down to her ankles. In the bathroom, her hand feverishly prised open the trouser's *nallah* string, nervously peering down at her navel area. Feeling faint, she closed her eyes, leaning against the tiled wall. It was what she had feared – she was losing her baby!

'Oh, God help me!' she cried, squatting down on the toilet bowl, letting nature take over. After five years – Allah Pak couldn't be so unjust!

Remembering the guests, she hurriedly sluiced her legs and changed into a pair of old trousers hanging on the door hook. Head lowered, Faiza returned to the kitchen. After making the last two *chappatis*, she whispered into her mother-in-law's ear that she wanted to rest.

'Of course, my dear, go and lie down.' Jennat Bibi affectionately ushered her out of the kitchen, her tender caring look cutting Faiza to her soul. 'Oh, God, she doesn't know and she wants the baby so badly!'

Unobtrusively Faiza sneaked to her bedroom at the back of the house. Laying an extra layer of quilt padding in the middle of the bed and a sanitary towel wedged between her thighs, Faiza waited; she was still bleeding. An hour later her husband, Anwar, returned from their sweet shop – Faiza pretended to be asleep.

*

When Faiza next woke up, she saw the stars in the dark night winking down at them through the steel bars of the window overlooking the veranda. As it was summer three of the guests had wanted to sleep in the open courtyard on portable *charpoys* to enjoy the cool night breeze. The eldest male guest leaning over the side of the portable bed was still puffing away on his hookah pipe, the water in the steel base making a gurgling noise in the silence of the night. The other man, on his *charpoy,* was happily snoring away.

At about three o'clock in the night, her abdomen somersaulted into a strong contraction. Her high-pitched scream shattered the silence of the night, startling everyone in the house awake. The older of the male guests, who had only just dozed off, sat bolt upright, spluttering and coughing, knocking down the hookah pipe.

Faiza clamped her hand on her mouth, but too late. Lights were hurriedly switched on and the running of feet could be heard throughout the house. Her husband, lying beside her, leapt up in alarm.

The first person to appear at her bedside was Jennat Bibi,

concern etched across her features. Her father-in-law, Javaid, peered into the semi-dark room over his wife's shoulder. He switched on the light and everyone stared at Faiza's sweat-beaded face and stooped body.

'Are you all right, my dear?' Jennat Bibi's voice trembled with fear. Faiza shook her head, discreetly pointing to her lower abdomen.

Jennat Bibi's mouth dropped open, eyes widening in horror. Then collecting her wits about her, she signalled for her son and husband to leave the room. Jennat Bibi's pointed gaze fell on Faiza's pain-racked face as she gingerly lifted the quilt off Faiza's body and immediately dropped it, stumbling away from the bed, one hand clasping the back of her head and the other at her throat. Faiza, doubling over in pain, howled out another piercing scream.

Through clenched teeth, Jennat Bibi called her son, anxiously waiting in the adjoining dressing room, to hurry and get the village *dhai*. Jennat Bibi, perched on one corner of the bed, first rocked herself backwards and forwards as if in a trance, then reaching out to Faiza gently began to massage her shoulders and wept as the reality of the situation hit her. Hopes dashed; there would be no grandchild. As her pain subsided, Faiza, too, sobbed – for her mother-in-law's personal loss.

When Birkat Bibi, the midwife arrived, Faiza was lying in Jennat Bibi's arms, eyes closed and body weakened by the uterine contractions. Birkat Bibi began to work quickly, discreetly expressing her sorrow at this misfortune. Normally she found her role as the local midwife and nurse very rewarding, particularly when she delivered healthy, bouncing baby boys resulting in her payment being amply topped up by lots of other presents. On sad occasions like this, however, she kept a very low profile, and felt guilty at receiving any payment for her services to the woman miscarrying or delivering a stillborn child. Like everybody else in the village, Birkat Bibi knew how important the arrival of this baby had been for the sweetmaker's family.

With Faiza refreshed and resting in clean clothes in another bed, Birkat Bibi accepted some tea and *halwa*. It was then that she ventured to ask Jennat Bibi as to why Faiza had lost her baby? Hovering listlessly in the room, Jennat Bibi's head shot up at Birkat Bibi's words, struck by sudden pain.

'Salma! That *charail*, that witch! It's her evil shadow! She's been after my Faiza since the day she learned of her pregnancy.'

'What? Which Salma, Jennat Bibi dear?'

'Salma, the quiltmaker's daughter, who else! The one who lives with her mother whilst her husband is away working in Dubai,' Jennat Bibi spat out. 'Miscarried three times! You've dealt with her miscarriages yourself ... The wicked girl has not left my Faiza alone! Just yesterday she was here, hugging my Faiza! I saw her with my own eyes ... Can you believe it, Birkat Bibi? Everything in this house is now soaked in her *perchanvah*, her evil shadow.'

Birkat Bibi tactfully kept silent. She knew only too well about Salma's problem and it was she who had suggested that Salma see a city gynaecologist. Familiar with the superstitious beliefs of some of the village women that she had to work with, at times she despised herself for pandering to their whims by her silence and geniality. As a trained midwife and a local nurse, her credibility would be in question if she started to believe in some of their ideas. However, it wasn't in her business interests to argue with them as they were her prospective employers and likely to financially reward her for her services, and often very generously.

She felt sorry for Salma, knowing that she had been made the scapegoat for the tragedy in this household. Faiza had quietly told her about the fall, but had pleaded with her not to tell her mother-in-law. Nodding her head, Birkat Bibi left soon after, promising to return in the morning to offer a hot-oil body massage. For the rest of the night, Jennat Bibi sat in vigil by Faiza's bed, her eyes staring in the dark.

'You thought I was crazy and that these were only old wives' tales!' Jennat Bibi jeered at her husband when he returned from the mosque after saying his *fajr* morning prayers. 'Now see what has happened in our house – lost our grandchild within one day of *that* woman being in our house. You ridiculed me and my beliefs, saying that I spouted nonsense! Now I suppose you will say it's all a coincidence? But don't you agree that it's strange that our healthy daughter-in-law suddenly miscarries the very next day after hugging a woman doomed with an evil shadow? Do you still think I spout nonsense, Javaid-ji?' her shrill voice accused.

Bemused by the whole episode, Javaid-ji didn't reply. There was nothing to ridicule. He didn't believe his wife's ideas but, on the other hand, how strange that his daughter-in-law had miscarried at this time. Were these women right after all about amulets, *tweez* and so on? Wryly shaking his head, he strode out of the room.

The male guests, of course, couldn't discuss the matter openly, though guessing correctly as to what had transpired in the middle of the night. They had come, expecting to spend a few pleasant days in Javaid Salman's house, and therefore did not relish the cloud of doom now hanging over the household. With Faiza confined to her bed, they were wondering whether they would be served proper meals or if the breakfast of carrot *halva* they had been really looking forward to from Faiza would materialise that morning.

Staring politely at each other, the guests sat quietly around the courtyard in the morning. The only audible sound was that of the raucous cawing of the black crows perched on the veranda wall.

At nine o'clock, straight after supervising the breakfast served by the maid, Jennat Bibi pulled on her outdoor *chador* and hurried out on her important errand after collecting her best friend, Neelum, from the neighbouring street, dragging her away from her morning household chores. 'What, right now! Not swept my floor yet,' her friend had gasped.

*

The village quiltmaker, Zeinab, was brusquely clearing away breakfast dishes in the *bavarchikhana*, when they were disturbed by a thudding sound on the outside door. Mother and daughter exchanged alarmed glances.

'Who can be knocking like this? The postman has already been, Salma.'

Zeinab opened the door offering the customary Muslim '*Bismillah, Bismillah,*' greeting to the two female visitors. Straight away she was struck by Jennat Bibi's stiff demeanour and hostile expression, standing tall under the veranda.

'Is everything all right, Sister Jennat Bibi?' she gently asked.

'No!' Jennat Bibi exploded. 'Our Faiza miscarried last night.' She pinned her full hostile gaze on Salma, who appeared to shrink back against the broomstick she was holding.

'Oh, I'm sorry, Sister Jennat Bibi, I truly am!' Like everyone else, she knew how precious the baby was for Jennat Bibi's family.

'So you should be, Zeinab.' She deliberately omitted to say the complimentary word 'sister'. 'Your evil daughter has been after my Faiza since the day she conceived. Just because she keeps miscarrying herself, she made sure that our Faiza couldn't have a healthy baby, either.'

Zeinab's parched mouth opened and closed three times before she found her voice. 'Hang on, Jennat Bibi!' She, too, had dispensed with the word 'sister'. 'This is utter nonsense! What has my Salma got to do with your Faiza's miscarriage? It's her body, nothing to do with my daughter. How dare you say such things? I have tolerated your superstitious ways about *perchanvah* and *chillah* rubbish, but this is madness.' Zeinab was fuming, her chest under her shawl heaving and falling, pigmented cheeks now fiery red with anger.

'Huh! Sister Neelum, are you listening to this woman? Don't you think that it's a great coincidence that I saw Salma, in my own home, hugging the life out of my Faiza, and the very next day that poor girl loses her baby? I suppose you think that I imagined all that? Didn't you go to our house yesterday, Salma, you witch? Speak up, girl!' Jennat Bibi took an aggressive step forward and her vindictive pointed stare demolished Salma who was leaning for support against the veranda pillar.

'Did you, Salma?' her mother screeched, flabbergasted, turning her wrath on her daughter.

'Yes, Mother,' Salma whimpered, distressed and mortally terrified of Jennat Bibi.

'You see! If I were you, Zeinab, I would lock away your *manhous* daughter until the babies in this village are born. Instead of letting her gad about and spread her *perchanvah* on healthy pregnant women!'

Done with her speech, Jennat Bibi dramatically swished her *chador* shawl over her shoulders and stormed out, with Neelum hurrying after her, throwing an apologetic stare at Zeinab.

For a few seconds, the mother and daughter remained standing, as if turned to stone, buried under the cruelty of Jennat Bibi's accusations. At last, Zeinab sank on the *charpoy* in the courtyard and turned her wrath on her daughter, who seemed to have melted against the pillar.

'Salma, Salma, how many times have I told you not to have anything to do with your friend until she's had the baby? I know that we don't believe this *perchanvah* rubbish, but these village women do. Why did you go to her house yesterday and why, of all things, did you hug Faiza? You've just played straight into Jennat Bibi's hands.'

'It was Faiza! She hugged me and fell on the marble floor, right before my very eyes! Her miscarriage has nothing to do with me, Mother. Believe me!'

'You daft girl! Why didn't you tell Jennat Bibi that Faiza fell?' Zeinab was up on her feet in outrage.

'I was so afraid! I'm sure that Faiza hasn't told her.'

'But this is an outrage! Allah Pak, that vicious woman is spreading rumours that you have caused her daughter-in-law to miscarry. Come on, my girl, grab your *chador*. I'll not let her victimise you any more. She's made you a scapegoat for her daughter-in-law's own carelessness! I'll deal with this woman once and for all!'

'Where are we going, Mother?' Horrified, Salma drew back, lips quivering in distress, not relishing the thought of being drawn into the unsavoury limelight any further.

'We're going to Jennat Bibi's house to sort this matter!'

'Mother, no!' Salma whimpered, dreading meeting that woman again.

✳

Zeinab grabbed her reluctant daughter by the arm and, a few minutes later, was racing through the village lane to Jennat Bibi's house. In a daze, Salma allowed herself to be dragged, thinking about Jennat Bibi's vindictive word *manhous*, evil. Perhaps if she hadn't gone to see Faiza, her friend might not have slipped and thus lost the baby. Perhaps *perchanvah* did affect women. How could her mother persuade the village women to believe otherwise?

When a fuming Zeinab, with her daughter in tow, entered the sweetmaker's courtyard, Jennat Bibi's houseguests were lounging around and treated them to speculative stares. The two elderly men, puffing away at the hookah pipes, who were hitherto engrossed in the ability of the new government to tackle the problems that the previous group could not deal with, also stopped short. Cheeks shot red with embarrassment, Salma sidled to hide behind her mother, not having bargained on meeting all these people. The reverse was true for Zeinab; she congratulated herself on having a healthy audience of all ages and deeply relished a confrontation with Jennat Bibi.

Stepping out of her kitchen and catching sight of them, Jennat Bibi narrowed her eyes in disbelief, her body stiffening.

Zeinab calmly skimmed the faces of all the people in Jennat Bibi's home, and stared back. Apart from the cheery morning cawing sound of the crows, complete silence reigned. The women guests were particularly keen to witness the next scene. They had already learned of the reason for Faiza's miscarriage and immediately guessed the identity of the two women visitors; one with the *perchanvah*.

They had just finished a hearty breakfast of *parathas*, tomato omelette and fresh homemade yoghurt and were now about to savour a second cup of *sabz* tea. Luckily, the two grandchildren were playing with kites on the rooftop terrace. The guests were struck by Jennat Bibi's rudeness; she hadn't issued a single word of greeting or welcome for the two female visitors.

Zeinab, too, had dispensed with the customary greeting and

gestures of social etiquette. Nor did she care a *paisa* for the sly glances of Jennat Bibi's two female guests. Today she was in for the kill and would not spare their host. Now it was her turn. Zeinab straightened her back, standing supremely tall in the middle of the courtyard, reminiscent of Jennat Bibi's stance a short time earlier in her home.

The silence was only broken when the sweetmaker followed his wife out of the kitchen. Irked by his wife's abject rudeness, he warmly welcomed the visitors, drawing out a high-backed chair for Zeinab under the guava tree. 'Welcome, Sister Zeinab, please sit down here. If you've come to see Faiza, she's resting in her room.'

'Thank you, Brother Javaid, but are you sure that we are *permitted* to see Faiza? For you see, your darling Jennat Bibi has forbidden us from entering your home, never mind seeing Faiza!' Zeinab enjoyed watching the fleeting expression of irritation pass over his face.

'I've come to see Jennat Bibi, and her *pir*.'

'Oh!'

'Why do you want to see my *pir*?' his wife quickly interrupted. 'What has he done?'

'A lot! He's responsible for stuffing the heads of silly and gullible women like you with sheer nonsense and for making my daughter into a scapegoat for Faiza's miscarriage.'

For the first time in her life, Zeinab didn't mince her words; after all Jennat Bibi hadn't minced hers. She had nothing to be afraid of and Jennat Bibi had almost accused her daughter of murder and witchcraft. Therefore she felt no shame in openly talking about miscarriages, a tabooed subject like sex and pregnancy, whilst in the presence of the two elderly male guests.

Anyway, today wasn't a normal day, and she didn't feel normal, either. Javaid had been irritated and bemused for years by the influence that the *pir* had on his wife, and so in a perverse way he welcomed the speech, even though it was a *baesti* to have his wife called 'silly' in front of all these people. He was extremely angry now and suspected that his wife had done Zeinab and Salma a great wrong to have brought this normally pleasant and dignified woman to speak in such a manner.

'Jennat Bibi, what have you done? Been blaming the loss of our grandchild on that *masoum*, innocent child? This is ridiculous!'

'Trust you, Javaid, to delight in me being insulted and ridiculed.' Outraged at her husband for taking that woman's side, Jennat Bibi could barely speak – anger choking her.

'It's not a matter of ridicule,' Zeinab angrily explained, 'but a matter of religious and social debate. Where does it say in the *Holy Quran* or *hadiths* about *perchanvah*? These are the sources of our beliefs and anything else is *shirk*, against the teaching of our faith, as you well know. Where has the *pir* got his ideas from? Is he a woman? Or a doctor? Or an authority on all female health matters? What does he know about the functions of our *female* bodies?'

Jennat Bibi paled under the onslaught. 'We all know that you don't believe in *pirs*. That doesn't give you the license to ridicule *ours*.' She bitterly stressed the word 'ours', hoping that her husband would support her. However, from Javaid's hostile stare, it seemed that the contrary was true. In fact, the wicked man appeared to be gloating; apparently his god-sent opportunity to discredit and rubbish her *pir*. Jennat Bibi felt very much alone.

'No. It doesn't. You're right, Jennat Bibi. I respect religious people like *pirs;* they are normally very intelligent men. People like us do need them, to guide us in religious and spiritual matters. It's their ignorance in female matters, meddling with superstitions passed down through the centuries and brainwashing you women that I abhor. Some of you women have been brainwashed to such an extent, that you not only shun, but deeply offend women like my daughter, who have tragically miscarried on more than one occasion. Silly woman, it's not a disease that you can catch! Some of you have even shunned the food that my poor Salma cooked and put in front of you. All this I've silently and bitterly observed and tolerated. You've harmed the minds of young women like my daughter … and insulted the whole essence of your womanhood,' Zeinab ended, pursing her mouth tightly.

'Shut up! I'll not listen to any more of your nonsense!' Jennat

Bibi aggressively stood in front of Zeinab, her body quivering with rage.

'Not so easy, I haven't finished yet, Jennat Bibi,' Zeinab scoffed. 'I suppose it's all right for you to come storming into my house early in the morning and accuse my daughter of witchcraft – that my Salma caused Faiza's miscarriage. Well, has your precious Faiza told you that she fell yesterday and hurt herself on the marble floor?'

Her mouth dry, Jennat Bibi stared at the woman she utterly loathed.

'What fall?' she blustered.

'Why don't you go and ask that madam?' Zeinab goaded.

As if in a terrible dream, Jennat Bibi walked to her son's bedroom, with Zeinab, Salma, Javaid and one of the women guests following behind her.

In her room, Faiza lay panicking. She had overheard everything in the courtyard. Hearing the footsteps, her heart thudded, dreading this moment.

Then the door was thrust open and they all entered, hovering around her bed. Faiza spied her friend Salma hiding behind her mother and studiously avoided looking her in the eye.

Jennat Bibi eyed her daughter-in-law with a particular message that she desperately wanted Faiza to interpret correctly.

'These silly women are making up tales. Salma said that you fell yesterday. Did you fall, my dear?'

Faiza looked her mother-in-law steadily in the eye. She was confronted with the moral choice of either betraying her friend or allowing her mother-in-law to lose face.

'No,' she said emphatically, out of the corner of her eye catching sight of the crushed look on Salma's face. Faiza ruthlessly looked away; she could only save one. Knowing how much the baby had meant to her she couldn't bear to cap her mother-in-law's loss with a *baesti*, a public loss of face. The baby was lost through her own carelessness; she had been warned about wet floors.

Highly distressed, her eyes brimming with angry tears, Salma had rushed out of the room, unable to believe what had happened. Her friend, by her lies, had sealed her fate with the evil shadow.

'Well, apparently your daughter-in-law is not only a liar but a mighty big coward, too!' Zeinab, red-cheeked and with a pointed stare at Faiza's lowered face, strode out of the room and out into the courtyard. She turned to look over her shoulder at Jennat Bibi.

'Don't think that the matter is now closed, Jennat Bibi. I'm going to invite ... No! In fact, force your *pir* to come to our village and give his version of the ideas you have cruelly perpetuated in the village.' Then with a dramatic gesture of her hand, pointing around the courtyard and the house, she continued:

'Moreover, *perchanvah* is now in your house; now your daughter-in-law has miscarried, and therefore according to your rules and *ressmeh*, no household with a pregnant woman should welcome her nor will they visit your house. Now, it's your Faiza who will and should be shunned – that is what you preach and think, isn't it? If, in the next two or three months' time, any woman miscarries it will be due to your Faiza's evil shadow not my daughter's. I will keep my Salma at home; anyway, the poor girl hides herself in the sugarcane fields half of the time – you people have mentally scarred my daughter. She can't think straight any more! As you have made the rules by your preaching, you must now live by them! You cannot have it both ways! No other pregnant woman will visit your house and you must not let your lying, two-faced, serpent of a daughter-in-law, Faiza, visit other houses!

'Correct, Javaid-ji? You and all your guests are our witnesses today. And you'll ensure that Jennat Bibi lives by the rules of her own making.'

So saying, Zeinab ended her visit. Fuming and with her head held high, she made a dignified departure. Her daughter had already ran ahead, mortified to her very soul at her friend's betrayal.

Jennat Bibi stood in the middle of the courtyard, amidst the amazed glances of her unwanted guests, her mouth opening and closing. For once in her lifetime, she was lost for words, bringing a reluctant smile to her husband's face.

CHAPTER 11

The Goorie

Mehreen had no inkling that she had an English daughter-in-law, flying high up in the sky, heading to her home. Smiling in her sleep, she opened her arms wide to greet her beloved son.

'Liaquat-ji! Wake up! Our son is coming!' Her husband stirred.

'Mehreen! The Imam hasn't even opened the mosque gates for the morning *azan*,' Liaquat gruffly reminded her, peeping at the clock on the wall with one eye open, and turning on his side.

'But you've to be at the airport in two hours' time. Can I come with you?' she appealed, excitement running through her voice.

'Mehreen, you know very well that there will be no space in the car!'

'No space for a mother?' Mehreen exploded.

'He's coming home, Mehreen! Be reasonable!' His voice hardened, fearful of a full-blown tantrum at this time of the morning. 'Just think, you'll see him in a few hours' time. Your sister, Gulbahar, never goes to the airport.'

'Stop comparing me to Gulbahar! I hate it when you do that. She doesn't like aeroplanes! Well, I love them. And I want to watch the one with my son in it land!'

'Now you are being childish, Mehreen. Remember that Arslan and his father are going, too.'

'OK!' Mehreen's high-pitched voice didn't bother her husband. Frustrated, a few minutes later, she poked him in the arm, but he simply ignored her, a smile on his face. Gulbahar was in his dream again.

*

Daniela savoured the adrenalin surging through her on hearing the pilot's authoritative voice informing the passengers that the plane was due to land in half an hour's time.

'At last!'

For so long, she had fantasised about visiting this land. A whole new world lay before her; meeting new people, hearing another language and learning about different customs. Over the bent head of the sleeping elderly fellow-passenger, she caught her first glimpse of the landscape below rapidly changing to a rich green carpet. Just then, her husband's head turned – his look lanced her. She mutely stared back. What had she done to transform her husband into a beastly stranger?

The plane shuddered and the wing flaps lowered in preparation for landing. As soon as it came to an abrupt stop, some over-zealous passengers scrambled to their feet to retrieve their luggage from the overhead compartments. Daniela panicked. Grabbing her handbag and box of duty-free chocolates, she reached her husband's side.

'Ismail. All I wanted was to give you a surprise!'

'Yes, you've done that all right, you mad woman!' Daniela paled. Ismail had never uttered an unkind word to her before.

He had pushed ahead. Daniela did the same, smiling apologetically at two of the passengers letting her pass. Clutching tightly onto her hand luggage, she ran down the metal steps of the plane, ignoring the sudden blast of May heat attacking her bare legs as she attempted to keep up with her husband. Breathlessly, she hopped on the waiting bus, gripping the arm of an older gentleman. Seeing that it was an Englishwoman his expression was all sweet and saintly. Ismail's eyes spat fire, as he stood behind her, urgently whispering in her ear.

'Daniela, please,' he pleaded, desperation now written all over his face. 'I can't take you home. Please forgive me – I will explain everything later. Just get on the very next plane back to England. You can't meet my family yet.'

'I don't understand, Ismail!' Daniela choked back her tears

before being jostled against a bearded man as the bus came to a sudden halt outside the arrival hall. Her husband had already leapt off the bus. Horror-stricken, Daniela saw him disappear amidst a crowd of people.

She merely nodded when the smiling immigration officer checked her passport, finding everything so surreal. Listlessly, she joined the large crowd of passengers in the baggage reclaim hall. Their prying, speculative gazes didn't matter to her, knowing that she looked out of place with her white skin and bare legs, amidst the group of brown, newly-arrived Pakistanis, and wishing that she had either worn a long skirt or a pair of trousers.

'Daniela!' Ismail was by her side again. 'It's the wrong time, I tell you!' He raised her chin.

'Leave me alone!' Daniela hissed. Tears were threatening to stream down her cheeks.

'I'll bring you myself next time – I promise. Just check into a hotel, my darling. Speak to the people at the information desk, they'll guide you further … Have you got enough cash? I must go. They are waiting for me.'

'Who?'

'My family!'

'But I want to meet your family!' Daniela wailed aloud, uncaring that people were looking at her with sharp interest. A *goorie* crying aloud at the airport! Why?

'You can't – not now!' he stepped back, panicking.

'But why?'

'Because they don't know you exist! Oh, God! There's my cousin, Arslan, I must go!'

And he was gone.

'I don't exist!' Swaying, Daniela watched her luggage go round on the carousel. She pushed aside the eager porter expecting a fat tip. His jaw dropped. The woman had hauled her suitcase onto a trolley and was now wheeling it out of the hall.

'Wow! What a woman!' he announced to his fellow porter, his forehead shining with beaded sweat.

'Well, she's a *goorie*!' was the other's dismissive reply. 'They are supposed to be sturdy women – not like some of "our" frail ones.'

In the arrival lounge, Daniela spotted her husband with a young man. Rage stormed through her.

'Ismail,' she called. Other passengers stared at her. The man Ismail was hugging also turned.

Hearing his wife, Ismail started to steer away his luggage trolley. 'Come, Arslan, let's go!'

'But, Ismail, that woman is calling you!' Arslan's eyes were on the attractive Englishwoman, with her straw hat and a skirt that just reached above her knees, standing looking lost and out of place amidst the native Pakistanis.

'What woman?' Desperation paralysed Ismail.

Arslan sprinted to Daniela's side. She was whimpering her husband's name. 'Ismail!'

Ismail felt faint, mouth drying as his father entered the arrival lounge. Pushing his trolley and summoning a smile to his face, Ismail reached his father.

Liaquat was looking at Arslan and Daniela, a frown creasing his forehead as he hugged his son.

'Who is Arslan speaking to?'

'She's *only* a woman tourist,' Ismail jabbered. 'Arslan is helping her in English. Let's go and meet the others.' He steered his trolley in the other direction, diverting his father's attention.

*

Arslan stood in front of Daniela. 'Can I help you, madam?' Her streaming eyes were fixed on her beloved husband – deserting her in a foreign place amongst strangers.

'I don't know!' Animal-like noises tore at her throat.

'You called my cousin "Ismail". Do you know him?'

'He's my husband,' she cried. 'And he's abandoning me here!'

Arslan's mouth dropped open, face paling.

'Am I so ugly or something?'

'No, no!' Arslan hastened to add, trying to regain his bearings. Ismail's strange behaviour and his haste to be off now all made sense. 'You don't understand, madam,' he coldly informed the Englishwoman.

'Try me!' she stammered, choking on her tears.

Even though Arslan's own head was spinning, he felt sorry for her. The full implication of his cousin's actions hit him then. It was important that this woman was acquainted with the truth at once.

'The problem is far worse,' he began, realising that he was going to hurt her, but she had to understand the gravity of the situation. 'Your husband has a fiancée waiting for him here in Pakistan. Our cousin, Saher! They are supposed to be getting married in three weeks' time!'

'What!' Daniela's body swayed against the trolley, her breathing shallow and the colour draining from her face.

'What shall I do?' Arslan debated fast, now also panic-stricken. They were all waiting for him, but he couldn't abandon this poor woman, especially as she happened to be Ismail's wife.

A volcano burst through Daniela.

'I'm his wife and expecting our first child! He told me to go to a hotel and catch the earliest flight back to Manchester. I only wanted to meet his family.'

Arslan saw his father coming over, a speculative look gleaming in his eyes. He snatched the trolley from Daniela and began to steer it towards the exit. Decisions had to be made and fast.

'Let's move. My father is coming,' he whispered. 'I'm going to pretend that you are my guest,' he quickly explained. 'You must not tell anyone that you are Ismail's wife. Understand?'

Expecting the worst, Daniela nodded. Disconcerted, she stared back at the older man whose eyes coolly slid over her body, down to her bare calves.

Haider had watched Arslan's intimate exchange with the white woman; his head dipped close to the woman's face had sent alarm bells ringing in Haider's head.

Striding to his son's side, he demanded, 'Who's this woman, Arslan?' the words coming out more harshly than he had intended, his eyes fixed on the woman's tear-smeared face.

'She's a tourist, Father, from England. I know what you are thinking but she's not from America – she has lost the address of the people she's supposed to be visiting. I'm taking her to our home,' Arslan explained, face taut.

'What! Why?'

Daniela looked on helplessly, unable to understand what was being decided about her.

'Because I speak her language and she's afraid of being on her own.'

'And why should you be responsible for her?' Haider ground out, angry with the stance his son was taking. Fear was fast clutching at his heart. Had Arslan brought home an American mistress?

Ignoring the last comment, Arslan turned to the English guest, 'Come!'

Daniela gratefully followed, nervously glancing at the older man and intimidated by the hostility darting from his eyes. It dawned on her that perhaps the older man thought that she was with his son. With mounting hysteria, Daniela wanted to giggle aloud.

'Father, you go with Ismail. We'll follow in another taxi.'

Angrily Haider walked off. Looking back over his shoulder, he saw them get into a taxi together and, still in a daze, he joined his brother-in-law.

'Where's Arslan going and who's that white woman with him?' Liaquat enquired.

'My son has gone mad. He's taking a *goorie* to our home!' Haider replied.

'Did that woman come from England, Ismail?' Liaquat asked.

'I've no idea!' Ismail promptly lied, flushing and looking out of the window. 'Can we just get home please, Father?'

The car sped away from Islamabad's airport. The scenery held no nostalgic appeal for Ismail; instead, he kept looking back, cursing his cousin for being such a gentleman. 'She would have gone back and nobody would have been any the wiser if Arslan had not seen her!' he thought.

Now he had lost all control over his life; a puppet in a puppet theatre in which the master puppeteer was unknown.

'You silly woman! What have you done?' Ismail inwardly cursed his wife whilst beaming at his father.

*

The passing scenery, the shops, the people and the sunshine held no interest for Daniela. Everything was a blur. The words 'his family doesn't know about you' and 'there's a fiancée waiting to marry him in three weeks' time' zoomed through her head.

'I can't believe it!' she said.

'I'm sorry, but you had better believe it! Your appearance is going to turn Ismail's family's world upside down – especially that of his fiancée, patiently waiting for him to take her back to England as his bride!' Arslan bitterly reminded her, the polite smile slipping from his face.

'God help me!'

The intrigued, Pushto-speaking driver kept peeping at the 'special' passenger in his rear-view mirror, the first white woman ever to sit in his taxi – who was she? And more interestingly did these two people have a sexual relationship?

'Yes, God help us all!' Arslan echoed in his own head, recalling the face of the woman he adored. 'I'll kill you, Ismail, for doing this to our Saher.'

He turned to the woman beside him. 'What's your name?' he coldly asked.

'Daniela.' Wetting her dry lips, Daniela raised her face to him. The two green orbs of misery melted Arslan's heart.

'Don't worry, Daniela,' he reassured her, touching her hand. 'I'll take care of everything. You shall stay in my father's house as my guest until your husband comes clean and claims you as his wife. He'll not be marrying Saher. You have my word on it, Daniela!'

Glad to see her visibly relaxed he had to remind her nevertheless: 'You must understand, Daniela, that you have unleashed a storm upon my clan. Many people's dreams, including those of my two aunties and Saher, are going to be shattered. It would be cruel to foist you on them straight away … a bombshell. For they have no inkling about you, Daniela. We'll have to try the softly-softly approach. I think that's how you say it in English, isn't it? This will buy your husband time to reflect on the situation and to prepare his family. From what I could see at the airport he was going out of his mind already. Sorry to have to warn you, but be prepared to become an object of hate!'

'Oh!' Daniela was thoroughly shaken.

'I'm sorry, but that's the reality! And you must remember you are my guest. I really don't know what else to do under these circumstances.'

'Thank you,' Daniela accepted in a broken voice. 'That lousy husband of mine would have abandoned me at the airport. How could any man do this to his wife?'

'A cowardly one, Daniela, and one who doesn't know what to do, other than to scamper!' Arslan angrily shot back, his fist was itching to thrust into his cousin's face. 'I'm going to kill him!'

'Yes, do,' Daniela smiled at her companion for the first time. 'Let him meet his mother first in one piece – then we'll both finish him off together!' Daniela giggled, making the driver look up sharply into the mirror.

Arslan settled in his seat for the two-hour journey back to the village; eyes closed, thoughts on Saher, vowing to spare her the pain.

Sympathy welling up for their unwanted guest, he generously offered, 'Daniela, I'll show you my country – some very beautiful sights, I promise you. I'll look after you. Don't worry about anything.'

✳

'There's a *goorie* with our prince!' Begum's awed voice reached Gulbahar who was stirring the *kheer* rice pudding in the big silver pot.

'A white woman!' Gulbahar's heartbeat plummeted. A vision of a *goorie* arriving from America with her son had haunted her many a night. Today, when her fearful eyes fell upon the European woman with the golden, boyish haircut and bare white legs stepping into their courtyard, Gulbahar bitterly resigned herself to her fate; she was not destined to witness her children's wedding ceremonies.

In despair, she inwardly wailed, 'He has brought home a

goorie!' Many a mother's dreaded fear of their migrant sons marrying a foreign woman had come true for her, too. Gulbahar recalled the heartache of a city friend, whose son had brought back a lovely Korean woman.

Arslan accurately read his mother's face. 'So quick to jump to conclusions – how right and yet how wrong you are, Mother!' he silently taunted.

His 'unwanted' guest stood awkwardly beside him in the middle of the courtyard, the hot sun scorching her head, her freckled cheeks reddening, eyes marvelling at the seashell-shaped sculpture of the central fountain, wanting to dip her face in the flowing water.

The gazes of the two middle-aged women draped in shawls signalled to Daniela that they had never come face to face with a European woman before. Nor did it appear that they relished the idea of coming across one, from their startled, hostile looks. Their body language boldly cried out for them. This foreign woman was a threat to their world.

Arslan burst out laughing, startling the three women. 'Daniela, pardon me, but they are probably thinking something else. It's so embarrassing … Let me introduce you properly before they faint or eat both of us alive with their eyes,' he chuckled, ignoring his mother's disconcerted look as she heard him speak in English and was unable to understand.

'This is my mother, Daniela. I have yet to find a convincing explanation as to why you are here, without betraying Ismail. As you can see from their expressions, they've both got this crazy idea in their heads that you are my lover and have now followed me here.'

'Oh, no!' Cheeks crimsoning, Daniela shyly gazed back at the two women.

'Yes! I must quickly reassure my mother – she suffers from angina!' He smiled explaining in Urdu, 'Mother, this is a tourist from England … she has lost her ticket and needs to stay for a few days.'

'Stay? Here?' Gulbahar's heart thudded. Losing ticket? Couldn't he come up with a better excuse?

'Begum! Prepare the large guest room for our special guest!'
Arslan loftily instructed their housekeeper. 'We need to offer her
excellent hospitality as befits our family, *handan*! So that when
she returns to England she'll tell everyone how well we look after
our guests here!'

Gripping his arm, his mother's icy voice accosted Arslan, 'Is
she married?'

'Yes, Mother.' Arslan's answer was equally icy, his face rigid
as he looked at her fingers pressing into his flesh. 'She's somebody else's legal wife, not mine – if that's what you want to hear?
Allah Pak is my witness. I can say it with my hand on our *Holy
Quran* if you like … I only met this woman three hours ago, at
the airport, and that's the truth, Mother!' he ended, relieved to
see his mother's face relax. He reached forward to gently caress
her right cheek, looking deep into her eyes.

'I'll never hurt or cause you any personal pain or embarrassment, Mother. And I'll marry with your blessing, and someone
from our clan – my countrywoman. That I can tell you now!'

'What? Who?' Gulbahar excitedly prompted, intrigued, her
body suddenly light, wanting to fly into his arms.

'Can't say much at the moment, only that I care for her very
deeply and will make her my wife, one day!' The smile was that
of a triumphant man, echoing once again the words he had
vowed as a 13-year-old.

'You sound so certain. Is it Nafisa?'

'No!'

'Bano?'

'No!'

'Will you not tell me?'

'No, Mother. I don't know if she'll consider me yet. Today I
know what I want. Everything I do will be with your blessing!
You'll witness your son's *nikkah*!'

'Please tell me who she is! Stop talking in riddles, Arslan!'

'OK – somebody you know and love!' he teased.

'Tell me!' Gulbahar cried in frustration.

'No! I can't until I have her permission. Now that you know
where my marital inclinations lie, please treat this English guest

with the courtesy for which we are renowned. She deserves the best hospitality – as she's a very special guest.'

Daniela stood listening; her ears were familiar with the rhythm of the Urdu language, although she did not understand what was being said.

'I've just explained at length to my mother that there is nothing going on between us. Now, you can see how relaxed she is.' Arslan switched to English.

'Well, she's wrong about us, but spot on in another way. I feel so strange being here, Arslan.'

*

Rani went to her daughter's room and patiently waited. Saher was on the prayer mat, offering her midday *zuhr* prayers, with an extra set of thanksgiving *nafl* sequence for Ismail's safe arrival. Prayers completed, Saher plucked off the white muslin scarf from her head, freeing the loose waves of hair to tumble down to her shoulders. Her mother's eloquent eyes forced her shy gaze to fall to the car keys on the table, her heartbeat accelerating.

'Ready?'

'Yes.' Saher would have liked to meet Ismail alone, shying away from the prospect of speaking to him in public.

*

'We have a *goorie* in the house!' Begum excitedly shouted to Ali as soon as she saw him.

'A *goorie*?' Aghast, his eyes widened. What was a *goorie* doing in this part of the world and in their master's home? Their village wasn't exactly a favourite international tourist spot despite its scenic surroundings.

'Arslan brought her from the airport. A real *goorie*, Ali! With golden hair and milky white skin and ...' her voice lowered to a whisper, 'naked legs.'

'I see.' Mind ablaze with images of bare flesh, Ali was deeply offended. Female modesty was something he dearly valued in the village women around him. In the city, he was always uncomfortable in the company of women with naked arms.

He wanted to condemn his wife's excitement.

'She has nothing to do with Arslan, in case you are jumping to any conclusions!' Begum hastened to explain, accurately reading his mind. 'If you think that she has followed him from America, then you are wrong. Arslan told us that she has lost her ticket and needed somewhere to stay … In fact, she was on the same plane as Master Ismail.' She stopped, glimpsing a wary look enter her husband's face. 'What's wrong, Ali?' she croaked.

'Nothing,' he muttered, turning his face away, hiding his raw feelings.

'Tell me, Ali?'

'I said nothing, woman – leave it!' He brutally cut her short, hearing footsteps outside the kitchen. 'Don't you dare open your mouth to anyone, or say anything about the *goorie* being here!' Ali ordered, seeing the door open as Gulbahar entered the kitchen, catching his last words.

'Is anything the matter, Ali?' Gulbahar quietly enquired, confronted by the nervous look on both their faces.

'No, Mistress,' he muttered, hurrying to leave. From behind Gulbahar's shoulders he signalled to his wife to zip her mouth. Begum stared blankly, her heart nearly exiting from her body, wondering at the new disaster about to assault this doom-ridden family. The *goorie* could only mean one thing – trouble!

'Is everything all right, Begum?' Gulbahar coaxed, determined to find out the truth.

'Everything is fine, Mistress.' Begum turned to chop the salad, wondering whether to slice rings or chop into small dice. She had not prepared a meal for an English guest before.

'Use less chilli powder in the curry – we don't know if this Englishwoman has tasted our food or has the strength for red chillies,' Gulbahar instructed.

'Mistress …' Her runaway mouth had opened.

'Yes, Begum?'

'Who is this woman?' The question hung heavily between the two: employer and employee – trusted lifelong friends.

'She's a visitor!' Gulbahar's gaze fixed sharply on Begum's face.

'What do you think? You heard what Arslan told us, he wouldn't dare lie to me.'

'Yes, but she came on the same plane as Ismail?' Begum pressed, unable to stop herself, spurred by a niggling fear.

Silence.

Mithu's repetitive chanting of '*salaam*' from the courtyard was the only audible sound.

'What are you insinuating, Begum?' Gulbahar's faint voice pelted.

'I don't know, but is there a connection?' Begum's eyes opened wider.

'*A connection*? Please don't!' Gulbahar beseeched, panic-stricken for the second time in one day, desperately warding off the unwelcome thoughts and images prompted by Begum's words.

'I ... I ...' Begum stuttered, but her mistress had already gone. Begum abandoned the half-cut tomato. In the courtyard she heard her mistress calling her son, her tone urgent. Begum hastened after her mistress into the guest room.

Daniela was lying on the bed with her legs dangling over the edge, cheeks wet, staring up at the swirling ceiling fan when Gulbahar and Begum entered. She sat up, blushingly pulling her skirt down over her bare knees. Gulbahar had one magical word poised on her lips.

'Ismail!' It performed its magic on the white woman. Daniela's eyes grew large in her face and then she lowered her gaze. Heart thumping, Gulbahar swung her gaze to her woman helper, and repeated the word 'Ismail!' her eyes calmly fixed on the Englishwoman.

Daniela licked her lips, colour slowly reddening her cheeks, and stared back at Arslan's mother.

Nausea heaving through her, Gulbahar fled outside. They had Ismail's whore under their very own roof. Gulbahar leaned against the marble wall for support, gulping fresh air into her lungs.

'Begum!' she uttered. Her housekeeper's face mirrored her own misgivings. 'Our children will kill us.'

'Mistress, you don't know the truth ...'

'Begum, did you not see how she reacted to Ismail's name? Allah Pak, what's going to happen to my two sisters?'

'I don't know …' Begum pitifully raised her hands in defeat, eyes brimming with tears.

'What will we tell Saher?'

'You'll tell her nothing!' Arslan harshly commanded from the veranda.

'Whose *whore* have you brought to our home, Arslan? Tell me the truth! If she's not yours, is she Ismail's?'

'She's not a *whore*, Mother,' Arslan shouted, outraged. 'She's someone very special in your nephew's life. Are you ready to hear it?' He waited, his eyes on their faces.

Gulbahar nodded, her head was dizzying to new heights.

'She's Ismail's wife … not his whore!' her son jeered. 'Are you happy now?'

They weren't 'happy' at all – he had crushed them. A whore was one thing, but a wife! Unthinkable. Saher!

Gulbahar gave up, seeking solace on her woman helper's shoulders. Begum's arms went protectively around her mistress. Arslan watched the two women locked in their grief with piteous eyes. 'Please don't tell Saher yet! It'll kill her!' he pressed.

'Your sister destroyed our world ten years ago when she left this village. Today Ismail has done the same. Why does passion hit our families, Begum? What have we sisters done to deserve these misfortunes with our children?'

Arslan left the two women bewailing their lot. His thoughts were with his cousin, Saher.

*

Saher sat quietly beside her mother in the large drawing room, trying to recover her lost poise. Her fiancé had disappointed her. Although she hadn't expected him to greet her with hugs, a cool smile and a shy hello didn't quite merit years of patient waiting as his fiancée.

'My son is even more shy than your Saher!' Mehreen had paradoxically boasted, nudging her sister.

Rani nodded stiffly, not at all amused with Ismail's behaviour.

In fact, she was downright fuming. Ismail hadn't even bothered to greet her properly, and she was Saher's mother! Is that what *velat*, foreign lands, did to people – turned warm blood into icy water?

The contours of Rani's beautiful, unsmiling face grew harsher as the evening wore on – the grooves at the side of her mouth widened and her eyes hawked over Ismail. When Arslan entered the drawing room, mother and daughter noticed the exchange of pointed stares between the two cousins and watched him follow Ismail out of the room.

'You had better face the consequences!' Arslan burst out, pushing the bedroom door shut behind him, body aggressively poised. 'The news about Daniela is going to reach this *hevali* soon.'

'What have you told them?'

'Mother and Begum found out. I've left them buried in shock and grief.'

'That stupid bitch!' Ismail spat, aghast. His auntie knew!

Arslan dived at his cousin, throwing his tight fist straight across his jaw. Ismail fell on the marble floor, reeling from the pain.

'That was for using such an awful term for your wife and for wasting five years of our Saher's life, you louse! I'll not let you marry her! You don't deserve her!'

'I'm already married, you fool!' Ismail stiffly reminded him, lifting himself up.

'How could you do this to her and to your family?'

'The same way that *your* Laila did with the potter's son!' Ismail taunted. 'In your parents' eyes she married beneath her. I married a woman from another race and country! So what?'

'Yes, so what?' Arslan jeered, eyes sparkling with pure hatred. 'Laila damaged my family, just as you are now going to make two sisters into bitter enemies. Do you think Auntie Rani will ever forgive you for jilting her beloved only child, the *chirag*, the *noor*, the light of her life? Or that your parents will accept a *goorie* into their household, ever?'

'Well, why do you think I've not told them?' Ismail snarled

back, now really hating his younger cousin. 'I knew what their reaction would be. I came home, not to marry Saher, but to gently wean my parents into accepting my marriage to Daniela, now pregnant with our first child. I can't keep it a secret any longer. I hadn't bargained on her foolishly following me here, however. I'm still in a state of shock myself.'

'Well, you had better make an honest woman out of Daniela soon, by claiming her as your wife. Otherwise they'll think that she's *my* mistress who has followed me here … I can't go on lying for you … only until I can break the news gently to Saher myself. And don't you dare go near her!' he threatened, ignoring the speculative gleam in his cousin's eyes.

'What is it to you, anyway?' Ismail scoffed, taken aback by his cousin's impassioned behaviour and scanning his face with interest.

'Don't push your luck, Ismail. You had better find some excuse to visit Daniela! Or you'll have neither a wife nor a child after the disgraceful way that you treated her at the airport. It would send any woman off the rails,' Arslan brutally reminded his cousin before leaving.

Ismail stared at his luggage, wanting to flee back to England with Daniela. But it was too late; he was cornered, and all because of Arslan. A wife he had disowned – how despicable of him! 'But what could I do?'

CHAPTER 12

The Visit

Laila stood on the potter's rooftop, her eyes fixed on her parents' *hevali* in the other section of the village.

'Your *velati* cousin Ismail has arrived!' Massi Fiza, the laundrywoman had cheerily announced. 'And a *goorie* from *velat*, too! Guess where she's staying? In your parents' home. Who is she?' she asked eagerly, expecting Laila to have the answer.

Laila's response was an open mouth. Did the white woman have anything to do with Arslan?

'Massi Fiza was saying that there's a *goorie* in the white *hevali*. Is there one, Mummy? I want to see a real *goorie*!' Shirin had excitedly asked later.

'Yes, Shirin, but she can't be as white as you,' Laila indulgently told her daughter, priding herself on her daughter's colouring. 'Come on, let's go downstairs, it's getting dark soon. I still need to wash your dress.'

'For Daddy's arrival?'

'No. I've asked him not to come.'

'But why? I want him to come.'

Laila's eyes were on her foot, poised on the broken step. She had nearly twisted her ankle two days ago.

'We are going back soon.' Laila remembered to answer her daughter's question, once she was safely down on the veranda.

'When?'

'Soon.'

'But, Mummy, you said we were going to stay here for many days?'

'Well, I've changed my mind. We are going back tomorrow.'

'But …'

'No buts, Shirin, we'll be going back to Islamabad.' She glared down at her daughter's petulant face.

Away from her daughter, Laila mourned, 'I just want one more glimpse of my Arslan and to hug him.'

Then she would disappear, for there was nothing else to keep her here. Her parents had slammed the door on her. The image of her mother's peeping face still wounded her – over ten years of waiting to see that beloved face. 'When will you forgive me, Mother?' Laila bitterly wept, picking up the unwashed crockery. 'I want to see you!'

Her formerly elegant hands, 'worthy of being wrapped in cotton buds' in Begum's words, had fingertips crisscrossed with lines from the daily scouring of pots. As she tipped another greasy clay pot under the water pump, the image of her father's foot crushing her garland in the dust and the village women smirking behind their *chadors* bitterly flashed across her eyes. It was the ultimate humiliation; the mighty Haider's daughter on the ground, scooping up the remains of the crushed garland.

'Mummy, are you all right?' Shirin had run down the stairs, anxiously peeping up into her mother's face. She recognised the tear-choked tone – having lived with it all her life and sometimes wondering why her mother cried so much.

'Why have you been crying a lot here, Mummy?'

Laila turned her face away, heart melted. 'OK, we'll stay another week. Go and watch TV! I'll go across to the *dhoban*'s to collect your frocks.'

*

Laila's timid knocks on the door of Massi Fiza'a home went unheard, for Massi Fiza had a more interesting mission than getting through the laundry bags littering her small courtyard. 'Most of my clients have suitcases and wardrobes stuffed with clothes. So they won't go naked if I am a day late with the washing!' Massi Fiza made a point of reminding herself.

Ensconced in the goldsmith's drawing room, Massi Fiza was in full reel entertaining Rukhsar and her three 'fashionably dressed' daughters whilst slurping down her cup of milky coffee and plucking another delicious ghee-fat *ladoo* from the steel plate. Two streets away, the village butcher had been blessed with a baby son. As well as being entertained by the transvestites' – the *khusroos* – merry dancing and singing, most households in the vicinity had been rewarded with a basket of *ladoos*. Only the households that his wife had fallen out with were deliberately omitted, openly shaming them. For the butcher's wife was unable to hear any criticism of her husband's skill as a butcher, in respect of his mean cut of meat or that he weighed in too much of the fat.

'Honestly, she's as milky white as that tablecloth of yours!' Massi Fiza excitedly elaborated – fascination with skin colour, tones and facial marks was one of Massi Fiza's favourite topics – pointing her greasy, chapped finger towards the dining table next to the window.

'Really!' Rukhsar voiced in wonder.

'I was collecting the laundry from Begum then. Oh, Rukhsar-ji, you should have seen the look on poor Begum's face as the *goorie* entered their *hevali*!'

'I see!'

'It was her legs, Rukhsar-ji, long, muscled, white legs – not thin ones like mine and not a single hair in sight!'

'Everyone has hairs on their legs!' scoffed Rukhsar's youngest daughter, Farah, not fully appreciating the picture and irritated with their *dhoban's* knack for exaggeration. 'Her hair is golden. So either you can't see or it has been shaved off – women do shave, you know,' she explained drily.

'I don't!' Massi Fiza looked horrified. 'I would never let the razor come near my legs. Look!' She pulled up her *shalwar* to her kneecap. 'See, my leg is smooth – thanks to the vigorous scrubbing with the pumice stone.'

'Please do go on!' Rukhsar prompted, interested in the *goorie*, not Massi Fiza's smooth, thin, brown legs!

'And her hair, Rukhsar-ji! I'm sure it can't be more than two inches long. Can you believe it? Your husband's hair is at least three inches longer.'

'Are you insinuating that my Sharif-ji keeps his hair long?

Come on, my friend, girls here in Pakistan now also have these *boy cuts*, especially in the city. And this woman is a *goorie*, from a different land. The important question we should ask ourselves, however, is who is she? That's what I'd like to know,' Rukhsar finished. They exchanged meaningful glances.

'What is this white woman doing in our village?' Rukhsar continued, being the first to open her mouth. 'It's not every day that a *goorie* from *velat* ends up on our doorstep. And then to arrive on the same plane as Ismail! Also, why is she staying at Master Haider's *hevali*? Whose sweetheart is she? Arslan's or Ismail's?' She lowered her voice to a whisper, seeing her daughters delicately drop their gazes, but exchange sly glances beneath their Max Factor-streaked eyelashes.

'Your guess is as good as mine, Rukhsar-ji. I tell you, there is a drama in the making here. And what's more it's going to explode all around us soon. And I can't wait!'

'What, for the explosion?' Rukhsar chuckled, daintily sipping her coffee from her best china, holding it by her little finger. Massi Fiza was not interested in copying her actions. Instead, she cupped the china cup in her two hands, her favourite mode of drinking.

'You know what I mean, Rukhsar-ji!' Massi Fiza stammered, shamefaced.

'Well, if that *goorie* has anything to do with Ismail, there'll definitely be an explosion, destroying two families. My husband has just sold eight necklaces for Saher's lovely neck. The question is – will they now go on the even lovelier neck of the *goorie*? I would love to see her with my own eyes. I've never been inside Haider Sahib's *hevali*. We lost some good business with them! Before Laila's elopement, Haider Sahib garlanded that beloved daughter's dainty neck with at least two necklaces a year.'

'Well, I visit the *hevali* every two days for their laundry. Thinking about it, I might get the washing tonight. I am sure the ungrateful madam across the lane, Mistress Laila, will appreciate some news of her family. I'm her errand woman at the moment! Smuggling both food and messages from Begum. Mistress Laila is her pet.' She stopped abruptly and her thin greyish-black eyebrows shot up.

'What's the matter, Massi Fiza?' Rukhsar noted the strange look in her friend's eyes.

'I'm in a really wicked mood, Rukhsar-ji. I feel like doing something very daring!'

'What?' Rukhsar's round, khol-lined eyes were fixed on Massi Fiza's wide, thin-lipped grin displaying a set of uneven teeth jigsawed tightly together. 'Do tell me!' Rukhsar urged, excitement surging through her body.

'Only after I've done it, Rukhsar-ji,' she teased with a wink.

'Oh, you are simply wicked!' Rukhsar chuckled. Even her daughters with their condescending gazes were staring agog at their neighbour.

'No, don't say that, but it will be daring! I'd better get going!'

Her fingers eagerly reaching for the second portion of her third *ladoo* and neatly popping it into her mouth, she stood up. She had provided a lot of news and free entertainment – three *ladoos* were therefore a poor compensation! The girls were glad the laundrywoman had finished the *ladoos*, otherwise they would end up adding to their father's girth. As caring daughters they were determined to keep sugary and fatty things out of his way. Massi Fiza tiptoed around them on the Persian silk rug.

'Thank you, my daughters, for the milky coffee.'

'By the way, Auntie,' the middle sister corrected, 'it was cappuccino!' She grinned at the look of puzzlement on Massi Fiza's tanned, weather-beaten face. 'Feel honoured. Now, in which household in this village would they be offering you cappuccino – most of the villagers haven't even heard of such *velati* drinks.'

Smiling, Massi Fiza expressed her gratitude. 'You are such nice, hospitable girls. Why do you think your suits are the stiffest in the village? They have the most starch in them.'

'Thank you, Auntie,' Farah dutifully mumbled, looking away, remembering one of her stiff dresses that had stood out like a bag around her body.

*

As Massi Fiza stepped out of Rukhsar's two-storey house, Laila was entering the potter's house.

'Mistress Laila!' Massi Fiza loudly called.

'Yes, Massi Fiza?' Laila stiffened, tightly holding onto her daughter's arm. Massi Fiza was one of the women who had witnessed her humiliation outside her parents' *hevali* the other day and Laila hated her for that.

'I'll do your daughter's entire washing for you!' Massi Fiza generously offered, assessing the hostile look on Laila's face.

'I came earlier but you weren't at home!' Laila rebuked, eager to disappear inside her home.

'Sorry, I was next door. I'm going for a walk in the fields. Would you like me to take your lovely Shirin … so that you can rest for an hour or two? It'll be good for her to see something of the village,' she sweetly offered, gaze now lowered.

After a pause, Laila arrogantly deigned to accept, remembering her daughter's petulant mood. 'Yes, Massi Fiza!' She would today allow the laundrywoman the *honour* of taking her daughter with her. The villagers might ignore Shirin, but they all knew that Master Haider's blood ran through her veins – and he was their landlord. 'Shirin, please go for a walk with Massi Fiza.'

'Also, I'll be collecting some washing on the way, so will that be all right?' Massi Fiza quietly added, dropping her gaze again. Laila did not see that look of pure triumph and malice; she had already stepped into the dim brick-lined entrance of the potter's house, glad to have Shirin off her hands for a while and supervised.

Massi Fiza could not contain her excitement about where she was going. And it wasn't to the fields.

'Where are we going, Auntie-ji?' Shirin innocently asked, skipping alongside the tall, wiry woman, with a rolled laundry sack bundled under her arm.

'I'm going to collect some washing from the big, white house – the beautiful *hevali*. Do you know there's a *goorie* living there?' her voice dipped low, a smile on her face.

'A *goorie*!' Shirin exclaimed, standing still in the village lane, looking up at the laundrywoman. 'Oh, I've only seen a *gora* in Islamabad – not a *goree*!'

'Perhaps we'll see her. I wouldn't want you, our little darling, to miss out on such an exciting event as this! You would like to see her wouldn't you, my pet?'

'Oh, yes, thank you, Auntie-ji! You are so nice.' Shirin's excited face was raised up to Massi Fiza. The older woman smiled back, treating Shirin to her two rows of overcrowded teeth. Shirin was more fascinated with the bulbous black mole, with three grey hairs sprouting out of it, on Massi Fiza's chin.

With a thudding heart, Massi Fiza fervently prayed that the master's Jeep would not be there.

*

'Phew!' Massi Fiza sighed in relief. Only two cars were parked outside the *hevali* and the Jeep was definitely gone. Nevertheless the servants' side door it had to be – with Shirin by her side.

As they were about to enter the *hevali*, Shirin let go of Massi Fiza's hand, her mouth a petulant slit.

'What's the matter, my pet?' Massi Fiza's heartbeat quickened.

'Don't want to go in there!'

'Why not?'

'Because …' Shirin stopped. Her intuition forbade her from telling the washerwoman about the old man from the *hevali* who had made her cry.

'You'll love it … the *goorie's* in there!' Massi Fiza eagerly coaxed, seeing her careful plan going to pieces.

As expected the word '*goorie*' had a magical effect; Shirin forgot the 'horrible old man' and drifted happily into the big house, innocently setting her foot for the first time in her mother's family home.

Massi Fiza went straight into the kitchen to seek the housekeeper's permission. As soon as Begum saw Shirin hovering behind the laundrywoman, her mouth dropped open, goose pimples standing on her warm arms. The wooden spoon in her hand remained poised over the simmering *haleem* curry on the stove.

'Just doing my rounds, Begum,' Massi Fiza breezily explained, her gaze cheekily averted before Begum's outraged face.

'And you just decided to bring *her* here?' Begum hissed, not meeting the little girl's eyes.

'She wanted to see the *goorie*. I could not say no to her!' Massi Fiza hissed back, determined not to be bullied by the *hevali* gate-keeper this time.

'You're mad!' Begum screeched into her face.

'Shush, Begum-ji, she's listening!' Shirin was indeed listening, intrigued by the hushed, heated exchange between the two elderly women, wondering what was going on. The woman in the kitchen often brought food for them. So why were they angrily shushing each other? Her inquisitive eyes hopped over the large, immaculately clean kitchen with its marble floor and worktops, and wooden units with glossy white veneers. Her eyes opened in wonder at the marble pillar in the middle of the kitchen, from where a birdcage dangled with a chirping para-keet. Begum had brought Mithu into the kitchen this morning, relishing his *runak*, his merry noisy company. He actually mim-icked her name; the way Mistress Gulbahar called her.

'Take her out of here!'

'Oh, Begum. Don't be mean! Now that she's here, let her have a look around and meet your *velati* guest.'

'What? You're going to get us both beheaded today!'

But she had not bargained on Massi Fiza's rebellious wicked mood. That 'lowly' laundrywoman merely smiled, and pulling Shirin by the hand, cheekily sauntered out of the kitchen.

'Come on, Shirin, you can play with that bird another time … We're here to see a special lady … a *goorie*. Go and look around the *hevali* – it's a lovely place. Look at that fountain!' Massi Fiza pointed to the central architectural monument in the courtyard, with its healthy spray of water making a soothing, gurgling noise.

'Thank you, Auntie.'

'The *goorie* will be in one of those rooms upstairs, I'm sure. The stairs are over there.'

Shirin was off, excitedly sprinting across the marble court-yard to the stairways. Smiling and brazen-faced, Massi Fiza turned to face the panting figure of Begum. They watched Shirin disappear up the stairs to her grandparents' quarters.

'What have you done, Massi Fiza? They are sleeping upstairs!' Begum could hardly speak, nearly fainting with worry.

'Who?' Massi Fiza paled.

'Who do you think, you stupid woman?'

'But …' Massi Fiza stammered, her heart had now fled from her body. 'The Jeep's gone.'

'Master Arslan has taken it to Mistress Rani's house,' Begum angrily spat at the foolish laundrywoman.

'Oh, God, I must get out!' Massi Fiza was petrified. She had not bargained on Master Haider being in the villa. The bravado of her cunning mission deserted her.

'Yes, you should, you fool! Have you any idea what you've done? Mistress Gulbahar has not set eyes on her granddaughter in the flesh to this day. Don't you understand?'

'Oh!' It was now Massi Fiza's turn to sway, but Begum was already pushing her out of the courtyard.

Ashen-faced, Massi Fiza scurried out, leaving Begum to deal with whatever catastrophe befell that household. As she stepped out of the back door, Massi Fiza closed her eyes, feeling nauseous. Her wicked sense of humour was now replaced by primitive animal fear and a need for self-protection.

'Why, oh, why did I do it? What will Master Haider do to me if he finds out that I took Shirin to the *hevali*?'

*

Mouth parted in wonder, Shirin stared at the veranda gallery on the second floor. She had never seen so many beautiful marble columns. Colourful profusions of flowers were everywhere, some strategically draping the pillars from hanging baskets, others generously trailing over the wrought-iron railings.

A row of four, wide, lacquered wooden doors lined the top corridor. Shirin's small fingers pressed tightly on the large shining brass knob of the first door. It creaked as she gently pushed it open. Heart beating fast, Shirin peeped inside and glimpsed a large, beautifully furnished bedroom with a king-sized bed, a matching dressing table and a tall wardrobe. On the table was a pile of novels and magazines. It was a woman's room, Shirin could tell, little guessing that it was her mother's.

She tried the next two rooms. Both locked. She excitedly

reached for the final door, sure that the *goorie* would be in that room, putting her head round before entering, eyes narrowing; she could hear breathing. The curtains were fully drawn across the large window. Shirin squinted in the darkness.

Two people were sleeping in two separate king-sized beds. One of them had to be the *goorie*. Shirin tiptoed across the room, hoping that the soft clicking sound of her new sandals on the marble floor would not wake the man, but they did awake the other person.

Gulbahar lifted her head from the pillow and froze, staring straight into a beautiful young face framed with a curly crop of hair.

'I'm dreaming!' Gulbahar whimpered, feasting on the vision before her. 'This is my Laila!'

With no sign of recognition the girl calmly stared back, disappointed that the woman was not the *goorie*. She had expected a woman with white skin and golden hair. Not one with grey hair. Shirin turned to leave, dismissing the woman. The man on the other bed shifted, turning on his side. Adrenalin rushing through her, Shirin's eyes were on the man who had shouted and made her fall on the road. Gulbahar was fascinated by the fierce look chasing across the girl's face and, bemused, watched the girl slide out of the room, softly closing the door behind her. Her sandal heels echoed down the gallery outside.

Chest tightening, Gulbahar gasped for breath. Her muffled groan of pain startled her husband to sit up in the other bed.

'Gulbahar?' Haider anxiously asked. His wife was striding out of the room. Out on the gallery veranda, Gulbahar leaned over the wrought-iron railings, eyes on the girl below, her sandals clip-clopping across the courtyard before disappearing out of sight. Gulbahar drew back from the railings, her arms resting heavily by her side; her husband stood behind her.

'Gulbahar, what's wrong? Why did you run out?' His voice was anxious.

'It's nothing!' Gulbahar cried, hiding her flushed face from him.

Begum also appeared on the gallery terrace, having passed Shirin on the stairs, her face tight. As soon as she caught a glimpse of her dear sahiba's face, Begum knew that Gulbahar had met her granddaughter. She timidly stood beside her master, bent over his wife's stooped figure.

'Don't just stand there, Begum, call the doctor!' he shouted, voice threaded with fear.

Gulbahar shook her head.

'I'm fine – don't worry,' she stammered, breathing heavily, but trying her best to reassure her husband.

'Begum, find Arslan!'

'I don't need a doctor,' Gulbahar snapped, turning an ashen face to her husband and seeing her employee's gaze fall – they understood each other.

'Please don't make any fuss!' Gulbahar reprimanded, rising to her full height. 'I'll go back and rest in bed.'

'Good, come on!' Haider urged, taking her by the arm, really worried that his wife was having another angina attack. He followed her into the cool, dimly lit room, totally unaware that only a few minutes earlier, his granddaughter had come, glimpsed his face and fled.

Gulbahar gently eased her body onto her bed, whilst Haider gave her the angina tablets and poured a glass of water. Taking one of them, she smiled her thanks, promising herself that Haider would never find out who had caused her attack. Laying her head on her pillow, she recalled the beautiful young face. 'Why did the child flee when she saw Haider-ji?' Gulbahar asked herself, perplexed. 'Begum has a lot of explaining to do!' Her mouth tightened.

Gulbahar suddenly remembered the other 'unwanted' visitor in her home – the *goorie*, also taking an afternoon nap in the guest room downstairs. Arslan had phoned Begum to enquire if Daniela was being well looked after.

The housekeeper had huffily informed him: 'The *goorie* has had a shower and is now draped in a long *pathani* dress, thank goodness, discreetly covering her legs, and she's eaten a plateful of peas pilau, and after all that she is fast asleep under the AC.'

'Thank you, Begum!' Arslan had laughed aloud

*

'Did you see the *goorie*?' Massi Fiza eagerly asked, materialising from behind a tree. Ignoring Massi Fiza's proffered hand and question, Shirin sprinted away from the house. 'No, I didn't!' was the surly answer.

'Oh, was she not there?' Massi Fiza slyly prompted.

'I don't know.' The monotonous tone and Shirin's reluctance to speak intrigued her adult companion.

A few minutes later, at home, Shirin omitted to tell her mother about her visit to the *hevali*. It was only when she was rubbing her eyes with sleep in bed that Shirin had her outburst.

'I saw that beastly man! He lives in that big *hevali*, Mummy!' Her mother's indrawn breath was lost on her.

'What man?' Laila whispered, pretending to wave a mosquito away with her raffia hand fan.

'The man who shouted at me from his horse!' Shirin's shrill voice stung her mother into silence, mystifying her daughter. 'Mother, did you hear me?'

'Yes, I hear you, Shirin! And he's not beastly. Go to sleep now.' Laila coaxed her daughter to lie down, knowing that she herself would lie awake for a long while.

*

Wanting to escape to the fresh, cool breeze, Gulbahar left her room for the rooftop gallery. There, she gazed up in awe at the merry dance of the evening stars. 'How far away the stars are! And how mighty big is the space for them to roam about?' Gulbahar marvelled, craving to pluck one from the sky and hold it against her heart, letting its magical light into the empty place deep within her.

Her stiff neck tilted in the direction of the potter's house for the first time in over a decade.

The soft sound of Begum's footsteps had Gulbahar guiltily turning.

'You've not eaten anything, Mistress. The *goorie* has eaten a much bigger meal than you!' Begum commented, gently smiling at her mistress.

'I'm glad that our foreign guest is well fed, but I'm not hungry, Begum,' Gulbahar replied coolly. Begum paused before asking, 'Was that an angina attack, during the afternoon, Mistress?'

'I don't know,' Gulbahar lied, her vacant eyes fixed on her housekeeper's face. An awkward silence loomed between them, destroying the easy rapport they always shared. 'Begum …'

'Yes, Mistress.'

'Nothing.' Misery swamped Gulbahar. Begum waited, hoping for the thawing – but nothing. She turned.

'In my dream, I saw …' Gulbahar ventured, halting her housekeeper in her tracks.

'Yes, Mistress?' Begum croaked, and waited.

'Nothing.' Gulbahar eventually uttered, tone flat. Begum had had enough and escaped.

Gulbahar turned her head in the other direction towards her Rani's village. 'Laila gave me angina. What will Ismail give my two sisters and my beloved niece?'

CHAPTER 13

The Jilted

'Saher!' Arslan called from under the veranda of Ismail's home. Saher turned, not in a mood for her cousin's teasing, dull eyes clearly spelling that for him. This was her second visit to Ismail's home and he still treated her with studied politeness.

'Please meet me at our grandfather's old farmstead!' Arslan whispered, as she was about to pass him by. His serious face added a sense of urgency to the word 'please'. She assented with her eyebrows, a habit she had adopted with her career in the courts, where subtle head movements and eyebrows played a significant role.

✳

'Why the *deira*, Arslan?' Saher asked a few minutes later, laughing, enjoying the cool evening breeze from the car window playing with her hair. Was Arslan up to one of his old pranks? As a child he had often got them into trouble. She couldn't afford to be foolhardy – after all, she was getting married soon.

'I have my reasons.' His quiet, noncommittal answer had her intrigued.

'I see.'

The flippancy and the laughter was missing, she noted, fondly sketching his neat profile with her eyes. His strong, straight nose was like that of his father but he had the thick, wiry hair and colouring of his sister.

He pulled the Jeep to a standstill outside their grandfather's old farmhouse, scattering a neat line of glossy-coated, black crows that were perched on the wall greeting them with a chorus of cawing. The farmhouse was now a desolate place as the family had given up farming. Where the buffaloes had once sheltered at night, the huge barns and open verandas had now become storage places for old furniture.

'How have you found Ismail's behaviour?' Arslan's question stung Saher into stepping down from the Jeep, not ready to explore her own reaction to Ismail's aloofness, let alone share with Arslan how peeved she was.

Saher walked up to the tree, its branches heavily laden with small dark purple *jamounoo* fruit, the ground around its trunk littered with crow-pecked seeds. Clenched fists dug through the fabric of his white linen trouser pockets as Arslan walked up to her, his eyes tenderly tracing the contours of her face.

Feeling the heat under the intensity of his gaze, she poked him in the chest. 'Well, tell me! Why bring me here?'

His answer was a solemn look, as he debated what to say and how to soften the blow.

'Tell me about Ismail, please,' he requested, buying time.

'You've brought me all this way, just to ask me that?'

'I've my reasons, Saher!'

'Reasons?' she lashed out. 'Stop talking in riddles and get on with it!'

He paused, his gaze on her soft mouth. 'It's Ismail.' How he wished with all his heart that she could read his mind.

They stood there – gazes locked. In Saher's head thoughts somersaulted, a strange dullness gripping her and reaching down to her painted toes.

'Shall I say more?' Arslan softly prompted.

'Stop it!' Saher shouted. 'Stop the riddles!' Then she saw his eyes redden with pain.

'I wanted you to hear it from me, rather than anybody else.'

Saher dumbly nodded, now painfully aware that this was no teasing matter.

'There's a woman.' He let the quiet words sink into Saher's brain. 'She's a *goorie*,' he continued '… and she's staying at our house,' he ended, desperate for her to work out the rest for herself.

Saher froze, a soft moan fluttering through her lips. Then thrust her tight fists into Arslan's shoulder blade, making him stiffen at the aggressive contact.

'Are you telling me that this *goorie* is Ismail's woman friend?' She was pounding his back.

Slowly he turned, shocked by the wild look in her eyes. Her arms fell to her side.

Time stood still. The crows and the two parakeets in the branches above carried on pecking at the dark purple fruit, raining down some more seeds.

'No, she's not only Ismail's *lover* ... but much more,' he whispered, lowering his head, wanting to run away, but remaining there; duty-bound to break it to the woman he had loved his whole life. 'She's Ismail's lawful wife,' he quietly finished.

Colour deserted her face; she wound her arms tightly around her chest. It was a sight that Arslan had wanted to spare himself. Helplessly, he watched her tall frame slump against the tree; he was afraid to touch her.

It was a long time before she lifted her head. 'Arslan, please say you are joking!' Her poignant appeal shearing him, Arslan squatted down to her level and cupped her chin gently in his hand.

'This is no joke, Saher! I'm so sorry,' he whispered, his eyes shining with tears.

Saher wrenched her chin from his hand.

'Then leave me alone!' she cried, pulling her arm from his grasp as she struggled to stand upright. Arslan caught her.

'Don't touch me!' She ran off, pushing her way through the gates of the old *deira*. Arslan returned to the Jeep and was staring pensively through the dust-smeared windscreen when he was startled by a muffled scream renting the air.

He ran into the *deira* courtyard and saw her standing with her head pressed against the wall.

'Saher, don't!' he cried, and then stepped back, giving her the privacy she needed.

*

It was some thirty minutes later when Saher reappeared. Arslan stood waiting for her outside the gates, and in silence, they drove back to her home.

'Will you be all right?'

'I hate you!' she lashed out, jumping out of the vehicle. Stunned, Arslan switched the engine off and followed Saher inside. She had already crossed the courtyard and entered her room on the other side of the veranda. Rani came out of the drawing room to greet them, scowling at Arslan.

'Saher is very tired, Auntie!' Arslan hastened to explain, unperturbed by her hostile manner. 'Please don't disturb her!'

'Oh?' Rani's frown became more pronounced. 'She was fine earlier!'

Arslan faltered. 'I'll go and see if she's OK!'

Rani was about to stop him, but he had already sprinted across the courtyard. Tempted to follow, in a bid to chaperone her daughter, she then returned to the drawing room – seething.

Not bothering to knock, Arslan had entered Saher's room, firmly closing the door behind him. She was standing at the far side, looking out at the rear courtyard. She heard him enter the room, and imagining it to be her mother, braved a smile. On seeing Arslan, her poise deserted her. Lips quivering, anguish choked her. Unable to bear her distress, Arslan gently pulled her into his arms and held her in a tight embrace. Forgetting who held her, Saher wept like a child.

'Please don't tell my mother! Not yet!' she sobbed, her face buried against his neck.

'I won't,' was his husky promise, mouth touching her hair. It was only when she moved her head that her mouth brushed against his lower lip. Shuddering, she pulled herself away, prompting his arms to fall to his side. The wary look was back on her face; she tried to mask it with banter.

'You don't like being touched by me!' she teased, trying hard to smile.

'Oh, I think I can survive you touching me just this once!' he shrugged, sheepishly looking away. 'You're upset and needed a shoulder to cry on. What are you going to do?' he asked solemnly.

'What does a jilted woman normally do? Is there a guidebook written on this subject that I can consult?' she quipped drily.

'You're not a jilted woman.' His voice hardened. 'The beast didn't tell anyone what he was up to in England.'

'Will you, too, fall for a woman from another country?'

'No, I will not!' came his sharp retort.

'He's done it!' she bitterly reminded him. 'What's there to stop you? For all we know, you, too, might have an American woman tucked away somewhere.'

'No, I haven't! But there's a woman locked away here!' With a veiled look he pointed to his chest. 'And she's from here – I can assure you.'

Absorbed in her own misery, she neither noticed the words nor the special glint in his eyes.

'Saher, I'll try to protect you from any embarrassment, but I can't guarantee against people finding out.'

He turned to leave. 'I'm sorry,' he added dejectedly.

She nodded, her face folding in distress at the thought of people knowing that she had been jilted for an Englishwoman. The gossip would reach every corner of the village. She, the woman who had supposedly everything going for her, was to be ridiculed at the expense of a foreign bride. Her eyes swelling with tears, she abruptly looked out of the window.

'You've seen her. Is the *goorie* very attractive?' she asked, just as his hand turned the door handle.

'Yes, but not as beautiful as you!' came the quick curt answer.

'I want to see the woman who has robbed me of my fiancé,' she shouted after him, plagued by the image of the *goorie*, but he was gone.

*

Later, her mother tiptoed across the cool, marble floor and sat on the edge of the bed, resting her loving gaze on her daughter.

'What's the matter, Saher?' She knew something was amiss; her daughter was evading eye contact. And she, herself, was too afraid to voice her fears.

'Nothing,' was the dull reply.

'Look at me, Saher, and tell me the truth! Is it Ismail?'

Saher's head shook vigorously on the pillow.

'Then what is it?'

'Nothing – just tired.'

'Why did Arslan come to your room?' Frowning, her mother accused, 'Is there something going on between you two?' Her naive daughter might have missed the signs, but she hadn't – the possessive look in Arslan's eyes. As a mother she felt obliged to warn her daughter about social proprieties. Soon to be married, Saher could not afford to compromise herself with anyone, Arslan or otherwise.

'You couldn't be more wrong, Mother!' Saher sat up in outrage, hysterical laughter making her press her hand against her aching ribs.

'Don't be too friendly with Arslan! Remember, it's Ismail you are marrying.'

An animal wail ripped through Saher's mouth, making her mother leap off the bed in alarm. Rani pulled her only child into her arms, horrified at her daughter's mental state.

'What is it, my beautiful daughter?' she cried, hugging Saher tightly. 'You're frightening me – please, tell me what's wrong?'

Saher merely wept in her mother's lap. Eventually she pulled herself out of her mother's arms, bemused at her own behaviour, vowing never to show a weak side to the world, no matter how life treated her.

'I'm sorry.' She made an effort to smile and reassure her mother. 'I suppose I'm getting wedding nerves …'

Her mother couldn't believe it. 'Afraid of leaving me or of getting married?'

'Both … Mother,' Saher lied, eyes filling up again at the irony behind her mother's words. Unconvinced, Rani nodded and decided to leave her daughter in peace for the time being.

*

Daniela was taking a walk in the open fields of Gulistan with Arslan. She hadn't slept well. Vivid images of her husband's strange behaviour on the plane and at the airport had her waking up in a sweat many times. In the morning, she remained in her room, not knowing what to do with herself and too timid to step outside – for she couldn't speak Urdu and the women probably couldn't speak English. How she would have loved to have mastered some Urdu words and phrases from some of her young pupils before she had embarked on this mad journey.

A silent Begum had brought breakfast to her room. Sipping the syrupy-sweet milky coffee – Begum had got carried away with the sugar to reduce the bitterness – Daniela marvelled at how Arslan had come to her rescue, otherwise she didn't know what would have happened to her. When he suggested that he take her out for a walk around the village, Daniela had eagerly accepted.

'You understand, Daniela … that in order for you to blend into this society and way of life, you will need to cover your body discreetly. Your legs, for example …' he tried to explain, too embarrassed to elaborate further.

Daniela nodded. 'Of course, I know!'

'OK, I'll borrow one of my mother's *chadors* for you to wrap around your shoulders, as it gets cold in the valley.'

He met his father on the upstairs gallery.

'I think your mother has had one of her angina attacks,' his father informed him coldly. 'It's not to do with you, is it, Arslan?' Haider accused his son.

'No, it isn't! Probably to do with the woman you all slammed the doors on!'

'We've suffered for a long time because of your sister's wrong-doing. Don't upset your mother with your cruel jibes, Arslan.'

'I've no intention of hurting anyone, Father!' Arslan shot over his shoulder. 'I'm going to take our English guest for a walk in the fields.'

'Tell her to cover herself well,' his father reminded him. Arslan's mouth tightened.

'It's not necessary for you to cover your head,' he advised Daniela, helping her to straighten the garment around her shoulders before he led her out of the *hevali*. As they passed through the kitchen door, he thought it prudent to tell Begum, in case Ismail came.

'I'm taking our guest for a walk around the village.'

'Does Saher know?' Begum enquired. 'About *the goorie*, I mean.'

'Er … yes … Begum.' He looked down.

'Is she all right?'

'What do you expect, Begum?' Arslan bitterly rounded on their housekeeper.

Begum looked accusingly at Daniela as she closed the kitchen door.

'Arslan, that woman hates me!' Daniela couldn't help commenting at the *hevali* gates. 'What were you talking about?'

A ghost of a smile touched his face.

'Saher. Remember that she's supposed to be Ismail's fiancée, and then you turned up.'

'Oh, God, yes!' Daniela felt her mouth dry up again.

'Everyone loves Saher! A favourite amongst all our relatives. So you can just imagine what their reaction will be. They'll feel for her!'

'Does she know about me?'

The tentative question wrenched Arslan.

'She knows! I told her.' His voice had hardened, recalling his cousin's distress. He had never seen Saher break down and weep like that before.

Daniela stood still, imagining the predicament of the other woman. 'I'm so sorry,' she whispered.

'Those words will not help my cousin.' He turned to face his European companion. 'For you've robbed her of everything she had – her fiancé, her dignity, her self-esteem as a woman! I left a distraught bundle of humiliation last night, and do you know what she asked me before I left?'

'What?' Daniela's moist eyes stared at the hard lines of her young male companion's face.

'She asked me if you were beautiful? It's strange that the first thing a woman wants to know about her rival is her looks.'

'And what did you say?'

Arslan was in no mood to be gallant. 'You're a stunning-looking woman, Daniela … But in my biased eyes, I find Saher very beautiful and I told her so.'

'I'm glad you did that, Arslan … A jealous woman needs her pride.'

'I didn't say it for her pride's sake – I meant it … our Saher is very beautiful,' he taunted.

Daniela's gaze faltered, jealousy gnawing; now very keen to have a glimpse of this 'very beautiful' fiancée of Ismail's. A woman her husband had simply forgotten to mention.

'Let's not talk about them!' Arslan added, catching a vulnerable look in his guest's eyes. 'Let's go on pretending that you are a guest of mine. And I am taking you down to the valley. Have you got some sensible shoes on? Those *chappals* are perfect!' he applauded, glancing down at the sandals that Begum had lent to their English guest. Laughing, he offered his hand to support her, watching her step on the small boulders and rocks before dipping her feet into the clear blue running stream in the valley below.

'You are not planning to drown me here, are you?' Daniela teased. As he showed no sign of understanding, she elaborated, 'Well, it would solve everything if I did not exist.'

'Don't be silly!'

'I hope you don't mind me asking?' Daniela was intrigued. 'What does Saher mean to you?'

'She's my cousin.' Taken aback by her question, he stopped dead in his tracks, his foot half poised over another slippery boulder.

'Is she special?' Daniela probed, her woman's instinct guiding her along.

'I … I …' Arslan stopped, unwilling to discuss his feelings for Saher with his woman guest.

'I need to know! I'm Ismail's wife,' she appealed. Arslan understood and let down his barriers.

'Let's say she's very special to me. And now, I wouldn't allow Ismail to go anywhere near her. Does that satisfy you?'

'Yes, thank you,' she sighed, somewhat relieved. The hand in his grasp relaxed and he gave it a reassuring squeeze. She looked up and smiled back.

'I needed to know where I stood with you, and what support I could expect from you.'

'You are my sister-in-law. Saher will never be that, if I can help it!'

Daniela's rippling laughter rang through the valley. The young goat herd up on the grassy slopes watched, with a speculative gleam in his eyes, the foreign woman with short golden hair holding hands with the Pakistani man.

'Why do I get the feeling, Arslan, that you have some designs on her yourself?'

Arslan's laughter had her in giggles. 'I didn't say that!' He sobered, wanting to change the subject.

'Well, it would make me feel better and my position stronger, if you were to have designs on her.'

'She'd have a fit if she heard our conversation. And she definitely doesn't have any designs on me!' he bitterly added. 'For the last five years, Ismail has been the centre of her world! Even when I phoned from America, our conversation always gallingly centred on him. As she keeps reminding me, I'm only a younger brother to her – just because she's six months older than me.'

'I want to meet her!'

'You will, in due course. Listen, that's enough about me and Saher. Tell me about yourself?'

'Well, I work in a primary school, teaching lively six-year-olds, including some children of Pakistani parents.'

They had now waded through a good stretch of the stream. Daniela's face glowed with delight; appreciating the feel of the cool, sparkling water over her bare, white feet.

*

'Mummy, I can see the *goorie*!' Shirin shouted to her mother lying on the portable bed up on the rooftop. 'Look, her hair is shining like gold.' Laila joined her daughter at the low wall of their home, looking down at her brother and the Englishwoman as they turned into another lane. Heart swelling with happiness, she was about to shout down to them, when she remembered Shirin. Listlessly, she turned away from the roof wall, wondering who the *goorie* was and what she had to do with their Arslan? Her brother could not possibly be marrying a woman from another country!

CHAPTER 14

The Fairy

Gulbahar was awake, whilst her husband in the other bed slept on. Finding her *chappals* from under the bed, she walked to her dressing table. Unlocking her special drawer, she pulled out a wooden casket with an intricate onyx patchwork pattern. Holding it under her arm, she left her room and stood still outside the third bedroom she hadn't entered for more than ten years. She squeezed her eyes shut for a moment as she stepped inside her daughter's room and then steeled herself for the sight. The quilt had neither faded with time nor was it coated in dust. 'Begum has been secretly looking after this room,' was the first thought that whizzed through her mind. The magazines lay stacked on the bedside cabinet, next to the tall, marble lamp, just as they had the day Laila had eloped. Gulbahar did not need to look in the two wardrobes; their hollow depths had been stripped bare of all her daughter's belongings at her command. A grey, square shape made of dust could be seen on the white-washed wall where the large, hand-painted portrait of a beautiful 18-year-old Laila had once hung.

Sitting on the bed, Gulbahar emptied the casket's contents on the quilt; a stack of over 40 photos of Shirin, smuggled over the years by Begum. Fingers trembling, she turned one photograph over, showing Shirin as an eight-year-old, in a *gota kinari lengha* suit, standing against a background of two artificial pillars in a photographer's studio.

Gulbahar flicked over another, with Shirin in a pink smocked frock, her hair trimmed very short. In the third, the child's long hair was curling magically around her chubby face. Gulbahar looked closely at the small cut on the girl's chin in the fourth picture, showing a petulant five-year-old. Her mouth curved into a smile; the child had probably enjoyed a good tantrum with her mother. Another picture was a close-up one, the gem-like eyes sparkling with mischief, and the wide grin happily showing a gap where the tooth was missing. Gulbahar saw her granddaughter visibly grow up before her very eyes, from a small toddler to a defiant nine-year-old.

'Oh, Allah Pak!' she cried, a raw guttural sob choking her. 'My daughter lives in this child!'

Abandoning the pictures, she fled to the rooftop gallery where her son stood next to the railing wall, overlooking the sugarcane fields.

'Could you not sleep, either, Mother?' Arslan asked, his eyes fixed in the direction of his sister's home.

Gulbahar read his thoughts and painfully followed his gaze.

'A fairy floated into my home today, Arslan.'

'A fairy?'

'Yes!' Gulbahar smiled, fixing a tender gaze on her son. 'A beautiful little fairy!'

'Mother, there are no fairies!' Her son's cynical laugh dispersed the fog in Gulbahar's head.

'You are right. There are no fairies!' Gulbahar muttered to herself, pressing a hand hard against her chest. 'Only the dead and the living, and in this house we have both.'

'Mother!' Arslan prompted, taken aback by her train of thought and strange, nervous manner. Gulbahar wasn't in the mood to explore what was in her head or heart and left her son staring after her. Arslan's eyes remained on the far horizon – to the village where Saher slept.

'How can she get to sleep? The jilted one! May you rot in hell, Ismail, for doing this to her. You coward!' Arslan cried in his head.

Only two days ago, his aunt had proudly displayed Saher's trousseau for him to inspect. Saher had handed in her notice at work. He, himself, had purchased a diamond ring for her from a prestigious New York jeweller.

'Aunt Mehreen will never see her only son get married – a day she has been longing for for years! There will be no wedding bands playing outside her home. Ismail has robbed them of that day.'

His bitter thoughts turned to their foreign guest. The inevitable could not be delayed; Saher knew, and it just remained for Rani and Ismail's parents to find out.

CHAPTER 15

The Servant's Revolt

Mehreen and Liaquat Ali were in the throes of entertaining visitors for a third day, and preparing for their son's wedding, relishing every minute of it. For their servants, however, it was another matter. Rasoola was utterly fed up with all the extra wedding chores and the constant arrival of guests, many of whom had decided to arrive well before the wedding. Every day, there was the tedious task of scouring the big curry pots and stacking the best china crockery into the tall china cabinets. Barely fifteen minutes would pass before the dishes were carefully taken out again. The lavish wedding feasts meant that no sooner had one meal ended before it was time to start on the next one. The poor errand man was constantly shooting off on his motorcycle to fetch more meat, fresh vegetables or cakes and pastries. Even though it was a well-stocked home, with so many wedding guests, things like crates of soft drinks and fresh fruit, including boxes of mangoes, were constantly running short.

Rasoola's back was in a bad state from carrying the china-laden steel trays from the drawing room at one end of the *hevali* to the kitchen at the far end. Moreover, in the afternoons she had to cross the full length of the courtyard, the scathing rays of the sun beating down on her covered head. The sun was particularly punishing later in the afternoon.

The doorbell rang for the fourteenth time that day and Rasoola's hand shook, losing its grip on the heavy tray. Mistress Mehreen's precious Venetian china teapot and a couple of matching cups wobbled and fell. As soon as they touched the marble floor the dainty handles, crafted in some Italian factory, flew off the cups.

As if in a weird dream, Rasoola stared with a gaping mouth at the remains of the rosebud set and the mess of cakes and *samoses*. Hearing the crash, Mehreen came running out of the ground-floor bathroom, her beautiful china being one of her life's passions, her heart and soul. She delighted in collecting special china pieces from all over the world. Her recent holiday trip to Italy had cost a lot in excess-baggage charges, with four large boxes of delicate chinaware to pay for. Horror-stricken eyes on the broken china, Mehreen's plump cheeks reddened.

'You clumsy woman!' she raged, the words jamming in her throat. 'What have you done?'

Already upset, the harsh words were Rasoola's undoing, her eyes filling, to her shame.

'It was the bell!' she explained, feeling faint, 'I'm sorry!'

The bell rang again.

'Don't stand there gawping, you clumsy woman! Go and answer it!' The look of pure loathing on her mistress's face had Rasoola cringing. Her back throbbing, she hobbled to the door, cursing whoever was on the other side for startling her into dropping the tray.

Their visitor was none other than her hated rival Begum, from Mistress Gulbahar's household, standing there frowning, with a large sack of rice propped on the crown of her head. Very cross, Rasoola, instead of greeting, treated Begum to a deadly stare, opening the door wide.

Begum was extremely offended. Not to be welcomed with a '*salaam*' was intolerable.

The explanation for Rasoola's obnoxious behaviour, however, soon became apparent as Begum saw the ruins of Mistress Mehreen's most prized china set on the floor, and a livid sahiba of the house staring down at it.

'Begum, how many pieces of Mistress Gulbahar's best china have you broken?' Mehreen challenged. 'Look what this clumsy woman has done!'

Begum nervously glanced at Rasoola.

'In fact, at least two!' she tartly supplied the white lie. 'These marble floors, Mistress Mehreen, are terrible. Don't get me wrong, but one can easily slip on them, and these trays don't help, either.'

'The doorbell, Begum, made me jump!' Rasoola explained, grateful for the other housekeeper's support.

'Well, let me put this sack of rice down and I'll help you clear up.'

'Oh, Begum, please do!' Mehreen gushed. 'I wonder if Gulbahar can spare you for a few hours? There's so much to do here, especially with all the guests and wedding preparations.' She missed Begum's conspiratorial look at Rasoola.

'Certainly, Mistress.' Tugging her *shalwar's* hemline up to her ankles, Begum squatted on the floor to give Rasoola a hand.

'They keep increasing my workload! I can't take any more of this, Begum. They need more people to help run this place. Carrying trays around the *hevali*, sometimes more than fifteen times a day, is killing me.'

'That's not going to happen, so relax,' Begum offered without thinking.

'What? What do you mean?' Rasoola's eyes had become two glittering saucers.

'Forget it!' Begum hissed, reddening. It was too late.

'Tell me, Begum, please!'

'I wish that I had never opened my mouth,' Begum cursed herself under her breath. Master Arslan had especially tutored her to keep quiet. And here she was gossiping with Rasoola, who like Massi Fiza could not keep a thing to herself.

'Are you saying that the wedding is off?'

'No …' Begum said hesitantly.

'Then what?' Rasoola doggedly pressed, straightfaced.

'Oh, look, you silly woman, you're trying to wriggle this out of me, aren't you!' Begum surrendered. 'All right, I'll tell you – but please keep it quiet!'

'Yes, I will, Begum!' Rasoola nodded.

'Ismail already has a wife! The *goorie* staying with us at the *hevali*!' Begum heard the loud intake of breath as the broken half of the teapot slipped once again to the floor.

Rasoola stood up with a look of pure wonder on her face. The heat in the courtyard had become a cool breeze fanning over her body. Miraculously, the pain in her back had relaxed its grip, for she stood tall. Tall with the blessed knowledge in her possession!

'Are you telling the truth, Begum?'

'Shush, Mistress Sahiba is coming.' Begum quickly bent down to lift the broken pieces of crockery from the floor. Mistress Mehreen was crossing the veranda to join her guests. The men were animatedly talking about the recent elections, and were encouraging Liaquat to get more actively involved in the new governance by becoming a local councillor. Cynical about all parties, Liaquat shook his head firmly, pronouncing, 'All have their own personal agendas, whilst the country is going down the drain and terrorist activities on the rise – it's a nightmare! Can the new government rid us of the Taliban? Nowhere is safe at the moment. And the poor continue to suffer with rising prices, no electricity and low incomes!'

*

In a distinctly superior position this evening, nothing could wipe the smirk off Rasoola's face. 'If she dares to taunt me tonight about too much chilli powder or calls my *chappatis* "wonky shaped", I'll snuff that light out of her mean miserable eyes!' Rasoola vowed, utterly detesting her employer.

Grinding the almonds into the simmering hot milk for the family's night drink, and watching the skin thicken into *malai*, Rasoola enjoyed a wicked smile, ready to confront her catty mistress.

At times, Rasoola had reflected on why she hated her mistress so much, why she resented her own demeaning role as a servant, and the craving she was plagued with to own all of Mehreen's lovely possessions. The gorgeous feel of her mistress's luxurious fabrics against her fingers as she ironed them became a daily torment. Whilst her mistress's jewel boxes brimmed with gem-encrusted gold necklaces, Rasoola's small, garishly-painted, plastic trinket box only housed a paper-thin two *thola gulaband* necklace and a pair of earrings which had done the rounds at the goldsmith's workshop.

Envy was a terrible character flaw, but Rasoola offered no apologies for drowning in it, stoically telling herself, 'This wealth would turn even a saint's head, let alone poor old me!'

Later, from the top gallery, Mistress Mehreen shouted down to her housekeeper in the courtyard. Rasoola stiffened, hand still on the cotton *chador* she was rinsing in the washbasin. After ten o'clock at night, Rasoola had time for her own chores, which included washing her clothes as well as dyeing her greying hair. She hated peering in the mirror with no sunlight to guide her dye brush over the fine grey strands of hair at the front. The back of the head was overlooked, since it was always covered by her shawl. The next morning the darkened patches of skin around the temples always made her the butt of jokes from the old gardener. 'I can see you've been at the *kala kola* hair dye in the dark again, Rasoola!'

'Coming!' Rasoola shouted, grimacing at the twinges of pain in her back as she climbed the stairs. Outside the master bedroom, Rasoola braced herself for another bout of bickering from her highly strung mistress. Mehreen was alone, sitting on her bed, holding a mug of hot milk with an inch-thick layer of *malai* skin floating on top.

'Rasoola, you stupid woman, you know I don't take any sugar in my milk!'

'I … I didn't put any in your glass!' Rasoola took the china mug from her mistress.

'Are you saying I'm lying?'

'No!'

'Then taste it yourself!'

Rasoola took a big sip, tongue automatically reaching for the thick chunk of *malai*, savouring the wonderful buttery feel of the congealed milk against the roof of her mouth, sugar or no sugar.

'Well?' her mistress demanded.

Rasoola reddened. 'I'm sorry. It's Master Ismail's mug – he wanted sugar in his!'

'You're useless and senile, Rasoola! You have begun breaking things.' Mehreen paused, looking hard at her housekeeper. 'How will you cope with the wedding work? I think you're becoming lazy!'

That was the last straw for Rasoola; nobody ever called her 'lazy' and got away with it. Even her mother regretted calling her that once. Mistress Mehreen did not realise the storm she had unleashed with that mere word. Rasoola happily grabbed the cue to wipe the smile from her mistress's plump face.

'That's if there's to be a wedding!' she taunted over her shoulders, pausing at the doorway, loud enough for her mistress to hear.

'What did you say?'

Rasoola smirked, now in a delightfully wicked mood. She turned, her eyes glinting with pleasure, 'I don't think there's going to be any wedding in this household, Mistress Mehreen!' she repeated, enunciating each word clearly.

'You wicked woman – explain yourself!' Mehreen sputtered, barely able to speak.

'Your darling son is already married!' Rasoola announced with full malice, openly smirking at her highly distressed mistress.

'What are you saying?' Mehreen hissed, unable to breathe, a ball of oxygen jammed in the small pocket of her throat.

Rasoola stood tall in her hour of victory, relishing her revenge. She had suffered many years of verbal abuse from this woman. Triumphant, she breathed in, ready to strike the fatal blow.

'Your prince, Sahiba-ji, is married to a *goorie* – the one who's staying at your sister's home.'

Mehreen reeled, collapsing on the bed.

'What nonsense!' she cried, thrashing her way out of the nightmarish images in her head. 'You mad, vindictive woman!'

'I'm not mad. Ask your son!' Rasoola flung tartly over her shoulders before leaving the room with the mug of milk, head held high, delighted by her performance.

Outside in the corridor, she slurped down the sweet milk all in one go, savouring the delicious feel of the large chunks of *malai*.

Unperturbed by the havoc she had unleashed, Rasoola calmly

laid out her quilted bedding in the servants' quarters annexed to the courtyard. Her mistress had already verbally abused her. What more could she do in the middle of the night. Dismiss her? Well, come morning she would be gone anyway.

'But where shall I go?'

Rasoola shrugged her bony shoulders, feeling infinitely light-headed as a new thought sprung in her head.

'Mistress Gulbahar's *hevali* is a far better place to work and I like Begum. They will hire me there, I am sure.'

Brushing aside the mosquito buzzing over her face and unable to contain her curiosity, Rasoola tiptoed across the courtyard, hiding in the shadows of a colonnade near Master Ismail's room, and listened to the muffled, angry voices within. Someone was crying. Mistress Mehreen. The son merely repeated the words: 'Mother, please!'

Chuckling, Rasoola tiptoed back to bed.

*

Liaquat was late returning home. Three hours spent in Haider's office discussing land deals had not dampened his good mood for the preparations for his son's wedding. The three marquees had arrived. The six best cooks in the district had been hired for the wedding feast with thirteen dishes negotiated and agreed upon. Mumtaz, their local butcher, was honoured with the order for the wedding meat worth thousands of rupees. The quiet man with a large family to feed, educate and marry off was mightily pleased. The goldsmith had finished the work on the emerald set for Saher.

Liaquat had affectionately purchased two pairs of *karas* from Islamabad for Rani as a wedding gift; he was very protective of his widowed sister-in-law who had never remarried and stoically raised her daughter by herself. As a good brother-in-law, Liaquat had tenaciously supervised the financial side of Rani's land and its management, making sure that she obtained the best deals.

Saher was like a daughter to him and he had seen it as a fore-gone conclusion that she would become his daughter-in-law one day. That day was soon to become a reality and he could not help feeling sorry for Rani in losing an only child, and to a faraway land, too.

About to go upstairs, the sound of weeping from Ismail's room stalled Liaquat. Upon entering his son's room, Liaquat's heartbeat plummeted as he saw Mehreen sitting with her face buried in her night shawl and Ismail standing awkwardly beside her.

'Mehreen, what's wrong?' he asked, striding to his wife's side. She carried on sobbing. 'Ismail, why is your mother crying?'

Ismail stepped back, eyes lowered, contrite. He was supposed to break it gently to them. Now everything was out of his control.

'Mehreen!' Liaquat raised his voice.

Face hidden behind her shawl, Mehreen ran out of her son's room.

'What's going on, Ismail?' Liaquat demanded. Ismail remained silent. Mystified, Liaquat followed his wife to their room, mind ablaze with ideas and images, afraid to probe, and convinced that something terrible had happened. His wife often threw tantrums but very rarely wept.

'Mehreen?'

Mehreen wept louder, sniffing into her shawl. Liaquat waited, instinctively knowing that she was about to break his heart. At last, steeling herself, Mehreen was ready to shatter her husband's dreams.

'Gulbahar and Haider were unable to accept the potter's son as their son-in-law. Are you,' she asked with quiet dignity, voice roughened with tears, 'able to accept a *goorie* as your daughter-in-law? For that is what we've now got!'

Liaquat blankly stared, unable to make sense of his wife's words.

'What're you saying, Mehreen?' He asked, tone dull, mouth dry. Everything now fell into place – the *goorie* that came on the same plane as Ismail, staying at Gulbahar's house. This was no coincidence!

Utterly betrayed, he raged, 'How could our son do this to us?' They had been preparing for his wedding for years. Therefore how could he foist a woman from another country, culture and faith on them? Unbelievable!

Liaquat leaned his head against the armchair, eyes closed, weighed down by his son's betrayal. The energy Mehreen normally expended on a tantrum was now spent on loud wails and chants.

'Oh, God help us all!' she chanted, remembering her sister. 'What will Rani do to us? What will people say?'

'People!' Liaquat echoed bitterly. 'It's Saher I am thinking of. The poor girl – she doesn't deserve this. Say it's all a lie, Mehreen. Please tell me that there will be no white whore entering my home!'

Her husband's racist, explosive words alarmed Mehreen who was waiting for guidance from him. His gaze was steady. There was grief and there was anger, but rebellion, too. Their son couldn't get away with this.

CHAPTER 16

The Betrayal

Gulbahar was not only taken aback by her niece's appearance at the *hevali* so early in the morning, but also by her request.

'I want to see her, Auntie!' Saher announced, alarming Gulbahar and studiously avoiding eye contact, afraid to see pity reflected in those velvety brown eyes. The *goorie* hadn't even been served the special breakfast of *chana halwa puri*. Begum was still fishing out oily *puris* from the hot wok. Arslan was out horse riding, while Gulbahar herself had still been in bed dreaming of the beautiful young 'fairy'.

'Have you seen her?'

'Who, the *goorie*?'

'No! Laila's ...' She stopped short, reluctant to utter her granddaughter's name.

Saher nodded – understanding dawning. She had once visited her cousin in Islamabad two years ago, upon Arslan's request.

'Begum will bring you breakfast.' Gulbahar changed the subject, straightening her shawl around her shoulders. 'Do you want to have it with Arslan when he gets back?'

Saher shook her head. She hadn't come to take breakfast with anyone nor had she slept much. She had risen early – to seek out her *sokan*, her marital rival.

'Auntie, I have come to see her!' The dull voice tugged at her aunt's heart. Very uneasy about her niece meeting the 'other woman' Gulbahar asked:

'Do you have to?'

'Yes, I have to see her!'

'I'm so sorry, my dear.'

'Why do men do this to us women, Auntie?'

Gulbahar cynically choked on her tears. 'It's not just men who do this to us, but women, too! Remember my selfish daughter destroyed this home!'

Saher looked away, afraid to glimpse the lingering devastation in her aunt's eye.

'What madness is it, Auntie, that makes people so selfish – hurting their loved ones?'

'The madness of infatuation!' came the bitter cry. 'Lust has wrecked this home.' Gulbahar blushed. Saher's gaze fell.

'Is the *goorie* beautiful, Auntie? I prided myself on my looks, but how could I compete with a *goorie's* milky whiteness and her golden hair?'

'How dare you compare yourself with her!' Arslan accused the woman he adored.

Entering the room he strode across to his mother's bed; both looked up, startled. On his return from horse riding, Arslan had seen Saher's car and immediately went looking for her. His anger scorched them; he was unable to bear Saher talking in this vein – belittling herself.

'Auntie, I had better go!' Saher stammered, finding his company oppressive.

'You've come to see Daniela, haven't you?' Arslan prompted as he followed her down the marble stairs.

'Yes, I have!'

'I'll introduce you!'

'No!' Stung, Saher turned on him. 'I don't need any introductions from you!' Arslan grinned. This was the woman he enjoyed baiting.

'She's downstairs!'

Hearing the amusement in his voice, Saher's eyes filled up. 'Allah Pak, help me, he finds all this funny!' she cried, battling with humiliation.

*

Three deep breaths and then Saher was in her *sokan's* room, gently pushing the door open, forgetting to knock.

Standing on the threshold, she braced herself for the confrontation. Daniela was blow-drying her hair in front of the mirror and looked up with a smile, expecting Arslan or Begum with the breakfast tray. Gasping, Daniela instantly knew who the visitor was. The look in the woman's eyes said it all.

Spellbound, the women feasted on each other. Daniela felt the pangs of jealousy surging through her body. The fiancée was indeed beautiful, just as Arslan had said. Daniela noted the well-coiffed layers of hair falling gracefully over her shoulders and framing her face; the stylish cut of the elegant outfit accentuating the youthful body contours; a sculpted face with well-defined feminine features, kohl-lined, dark eyes and glossy plump lips. At the back of her mind she heard herself muttering, 'Ismail, were you both mad and blind to have forgotten a fiancée like this?'

Lost in wonder, Daniela forgot her own appeal as a woman. Saher had mentally fortified herself for a meeting with the *sokan*, but now standing in front of her, it hit her hard. This was the foreign woman that Ismail had taken to his bed and shared intimate moments with. Averting her gaze from the woman's full, thrusting, braless breasts pressed against the thin fabric of her cotton nightdress, Saher's inner demons echoed in disgust, 'He has touched that body!'

She battled the urge to flee. Strangely there was no envy, just resigned acceptance. The English woman's short, newly brushed hair glowed like gold. The gem-like eyes staring back at her were greenish-blue, fixed in an attractive naked face with high cheekbones.

'She's gorgeous. What must she be like when she's all made up?' Saher marvelled at the glowing translucent pink skin after the hot shower. The freely scattered freckles across the cheeks and nose added to Daniela's beauty, a woman in full bloom, glowing from her pregnancy.

She spoke first. Saher was the wronged one. Daniela had to make the first move.

'Hello!' she greeted, putting the hairdryer down on the dressing table, unsure of the other woman's reaction.

Saher snatched her gaze from Daniela's hair, trying to collect her wits about her. Ismail may have married this woman, but the *goorie* had known nothing about her and was as much a victim as she was.

'Hello!' A wry smile peeping through her features, Saher echoed back, taking a small step forward into the room and closing the door behind her. Smiling in return, Daniela gestured to the armchair.

'Please sit down!' she gently requested. 'Can you speak English?' Saher nodded. Their gazes momentarily locked and then shifted apart.

'I'm Saher!'

Daniela glanced down at her hand, afraid of it trembling, sure that Saher was able to hear her heartbeat. The silence was suffocating.

'I came to introduce myself … you're a visitor to this land. Welcome!' Inside, there was another poignant utterance, 'You're the woman who has robbed me of my fiancé!'

'I'm so sorry!' Daniela's anguished words fell between them. Saher paused, and then, head held high, gently withdrew from the room. Daniela sank onto the bed and wept.

'I've taken her fiancé and she comes to welcome me! Oh, God!' she agonised. 'I didn't know! The beast never told me!' Now, having met Saher, Daniela felt depressed and even more vulnerable.

*

Arslan was standing under the veranda when Saher, in tears, careered straight into his shoulders. She stepped back, but he pulled her gently by the arm.

'Saher! Please wait!'

'Leave me alone!' she cried, drawing away, voice roughened by a sob.

'Shush!' Wanting to give her privacy, he pulled her into one of the empty guest bedrooms, closing the door behind him.

'Satisfied now that you've met her?'

'Yes!' was her defiant answer. Arslan had seen her in tears

many times in her life – so when he held her close, she leaned her head on his shoulder and wept. Arslan let her. Unable to bear the warm mouth nestled against the base of his throat, he pulled himself away. She didn't realise what she was doing and he couldn't compromise her in any way; for the room had become an intimate cavern.

'Saher, this is silly! Why are you crying?'

'Silly? Yes, have a good laugh!'

'Yes, I'm laughing, Saher. If you'd like to know I never did want Ismail to marry you. He doesn't deserve you!'

'You are a beast for saying such a thing!' Bitterly, Saher stood back, staring at him. 'Then tell me who deserves me?' was her flippant question, little guessing at the response it would elicit.

'I do!'

'What?' She had heard his words but was deaf to the agony.

'Marry me, Saher!' he urged, though knowing that it was the wrong time.

'Are you mad, Arslan?' she cried, hysterical laughter nearly choking her. 'What childish games are you playing?' She stormed out of the room. Arslan stood staring and then ran after her; pride had to be restored.

'Sorry, Saher!' he called, 'for my childish joke! I never meant it!'

'I don't need jokes like that!' she fumed. 'Especially in pity, Arslan!'

He nodded. There was nothing to laugh at – she had made herself perfectly clear.

*

The telephone rang while Gulbahar was looking at photos of Arslan's American university friends. She stiffened, holding the receiver tightly to her ear.

'Gulbahar …' The mere wisp of a whisper.

'She knows!' Gulbahar's heart wept. 'Hello, Mehreen,' she dully greeted her.

'*Hum loothey ghey*,' Mehreen cried. 'We've been robbed!'

Gulbahar's tongue tried to lie but could not.

'I know.' She pressed her palm to her chest, alarming her son.

'Is it true?' Mehreen pleaded for a lie.

Gulbahar paused. What should or could one sister say to another? Deny the reality when the Englishwoman literally sat in the next room?

Voice rough with tears, Gulbahar confirmed, 'Yes, Mehreen, I'm so sorry.'

'Tell me!' Mehreen pleaded, still seeking a denial.

'She's staying with us, Mehreen …'

The receiver clicked down at the other end. Panic-stricken, Gulbahar stared at her son.

'Arslan, please take me to your poor aunt! God help us! How's she going to survive this? You must first drop me off at Mehreen's, then take me to Rani's – she doesn't even know yet. We need to gently break it to her.'

Arslan left his mother outside his Aunt Mehreen's villa, in no mood to face his cousin Ismail again or to witness his aunt's wretchedness. From a wedding to a catastrophe – what a nightmare!

At Saher's home, he was informed that his Aunt Rani was out shopping in the bazaar.

'And Saher?'

'She's in her room, Sahib-ji,' Neeli, the young woman helper, shyly explained, throwing aside the broom in her hand and running to open the door of the guest room for him. His arrival always elicited a deep blush from the 18-year-old daughter of the village cook. Their worlds and backgrounds were so different, but that did not halt the rapid flutter of her heartbeat.

Saher was in bed, gazing up at the ceiling and showed no visible sign of surprise when Arslan appeared. Smiling, he greeted her and asked, 'Where's Auntie?'

'Shopping for my trousseau, looking for a mink blanket!' The hysteria in her voice had Arslan squatting on the bed beside her, painfully watching the swollen teardrops spilling down her cheeks. Distressed by the look in his eyes, she buried her face in the pillow.

'I know,' he murmured, reaching to pull her up against his body. Saher surrendered and wept, burying her face against his chest, body shuddering. Arslan's grip tightened. Heaving his legs up, he was now half reclining on the bed. Head thrust against the pillow, he moved his hand gently over her hair to support her, and stared down at her body lying in his arms.

Her weeping had slowly stopped.

'How will I tell my mother? I'm going crazy, Arslan,' she whimpered, raising her face up to his, feeling the warmth of his breath.

'We have to.' His breath caught, his heart beating fast; he was sure she could hear it. Her lips were just inches away. But her eyes were not seeing him. When her hand reached to touch him on the face, he flinched.

'You don't like me touching you, do you?' she gently taunted, her palm soft and warm against his skin.

'I think I can survive,' he drily returned, his voice ragged, 'under the circumstances.'

Her eyes dulled. 'She's very beautiful, isn't she?'

He brushed his hand against her tear-stained cheek. 'Not as beautiful as you!' he whispered, gently pressing one fingertip into the plumped softness of her lower lip.

Taken aback by his words and the feel of his hand on her face, something speared through Saher. 'You always say such nice things.' A flirtatious smile lined her mouth, 'Such a gallant boy.'

'I'm not a boy!' Stung, Arslan pushed her aside, sliding off the bed, an angry tide of colour flooding his cheeks. Disconcerted by his reaction, Saher stared at his back, her breathing shallow.

'For God's sake, woman! Wake up! Has Ismail blinded you to everyone else?' he bitterly accused.

'What!'

'I'm not a boy!' He was bent on having his outburst. 'It's you … still *a little girl*. When will the sleeping beauty finally wake up? Do you think it's normal in our culture for a single man to enter a woman's room and then hold her in his arms? Would you let any man do it? Why let me? Because I am the *little boy* – the young cousin? I was just on the point of kissing you on the lips.'

'Stop it!' Saher shouted, horror-stricken. 'You stupid man!'

'Thank you, my darling, for this immediate graduation into manhood!'

'How dare you say such terrible things to me?' She was now sitting bolt upright. 'Kissing me! Have you gone mad? I'm not some American tart.'

'As if I don't know!' his voice now hollow, his back to her.

'Why are you being so cruel – just when Ismail has betrayed me! Do you feel sorry for me?'

'Sorry!' He swept round, eyes pointed daggers. 'Forget it! You are still blind!'

'Blind?' she hotly queried.

'I've wanted to say and do those things to you for over a decade!' he glared, cupping her face in his two hands, fingers digging into the soft flesh of her cheeks, before touching her lips. 'I've wanted to kiss you and marry you since I was 13!'

Saher drew back, pushing his hands away from her face.

'*Khabardar!*' she shuddered. 'Stop right there! Listen to me hard, Arslan, and for the last time – for I'll not repeat it. You are like a *little* brother to me!' She stressed the word 'little', wanting to hurt him in the way he had just hurt her.

'The *little* brother is only six months younger than you and is not so *little* any more,' he scoffed, wanting to strangle her.

'You're right – I've been blind …' she paused, her tone equally jeering. 'I may not be marrying Ismail, but you'll never take his place in my life, either. Thank you for your very considerate and well-timed offer to marry me, but Saher doesn't take pitiful crumbs nor is she interested in teenage crushes. And yes, you are right – I don't invite strange men into my room. I only let a 'younger brother' in, not a man who wants to kiss me! So get out!' Her finger pointed to the door, face scarlet, throat arched to its full slim length, chest heaving.

Head reeling, Arslan strode across the room and was about to turn the door handle when he remembered the reason for his coming.

'I only came to let you know that Aunt Mehreen and her household all know about Daniela!' he coldly informed her, shutting the door behind him. The blushing young maid with a lowered gaze was still hovering near the pillar under the veranda – waiting to catch another glimpse of him. Arslan ignored her and left the villa.

Inside her room, Saher sat stunned, head buzzing with Arslan's words.

'Oh my God!' she groaned aloud, shuddering. 'Arslan, how could you say those things to me – you are like a brother to me!' she cried, touching her mouth where his finger had lain. 'He wanted to kiss me. Arslan, have you gone crazy?'

＊

Rani excitedly headed to Mehreen's *hevali* with her shopping. What was the point of taking her daughter's trousseau presents home, when they were going to be carted back there. It was the expression on Mehreen's face that she wanted to witness when she felt the soft mink blanket between her fingers, which the seller had bragged was 'the finest in the land'. Her daughter's trousseau was a demonstration to both her sisters that being a widow didn't make her a charity case. On the contrary, as they all knew well enough, she was blessed with ample wealth, thanks to her father's foresight! And so could get her daughter married off in style, without touching a single *paisa* of Saher's earnings.

'Allah Pak, would I touch a penny from my daughter's salary? Never!' she loudly announced on a number of occasions to whoever was listening. What her daughter did with her money was her business – whether she invested it in another car or bought the so-called stocks, Rani didn't care a dime. She had sold one acre of land for the wedding expenses. Even if Saher took not a hankie to London, she would still furnish Mehreen's home from a mere humble sewing needle to a brand new car for her daughter to drive.

＊

Upon entering her sister's courtyard, Rani sensed immediately that something wasn't quite right. No one was in the courtyard to greet her. And where was Rasoola? she wondered, signalling to her chauffeur to place the luggage on the *takht paush,* the prayer table under the veranda.

'Mehreen!' she called.

Upstairs on the first floor, three hearts thudded to a halt.

'Rani is here!' Mehreen hissed, arms flailing, ready to faint in her eldest sister's arms. 'She knows, Gulbahar!' she stuttered, her lower lip quivering.

Gulbahar held tightly onto her sister's trembling body. 'She had to find out sooner or later, Mehreen.'

'Yes, Gulbahar-ji!' From his seat, Liaquat watched the two sisters locked in an embrace, his head throbbing with rage. Why had he not paid heed to the warning bells in his head when he saw Arslan talking to the *goorie* at the airport? After all, the woman had come off the same plane as their son!

'I cannot face Rani yet – please don't tell her where I am,' Mehreen pleaded with her eldest sister.

'Poor Mehreen is petrified!' Gulbahar's mouthed the words to her brother-in-law over Mehreen's shoulders, her heart aching for her two sisters who were about to become enemies.

'Mehreen, you must not be afraid – you've done nothing wrong, remember that!' she firmly reminded her. 'Our selfish children have put us in these predicaments. I'm so sorry that this has happened to you, too, my darling sister.'

'I have only one son, and now I'll never see his wedding!' Mehreen wailed, her heart breaking.

Liaquat had had enough and exchanged a knowing look with his sister-in-law. Gulbahar nodded her head in understanding, a ghost of a smile touching her face. They often managed Mehreen's tantrums together and as a result an intimacy of some sort had grown between them. He caught the smile and returned it with a wide one of his own. Head bent over her sister's shoulders, Mehreen missed both their smiles.

'No more tears, Mehreen. Mop up your face. You'll meet Rani – why should you have to hide? We've done nothing wrong, nor are we criminals. I will go and get her.' Her husband's grim and logical words sobered his wife.

He left her staring wide-eyed after him, lips still quivering. Gulbahar sat down, massaging Mehreen's trembling hand, her own heart beating fast. She loved both the sisters – but she was about to get caught in the middle of crossfire.

'What shall I do?' Gulbahar was assailed by the same sense of helplessness that had followed Laila's elopement. 'Which sister shall I support?' she dully echoed in her head.

＊

Downstairs in the courtyard, Rani was struck by Liaquat's averted gaze and stiff demeanour. Something wasn't quite right in this household today. Mouth dry, Rani quietly followed her brother-in-law up to Mehreen's room.

'Where's Rasoola?' she ventured to ask on the way, licking her lips.

'She's been dismissed – I mean she's gone on holiday,' he quickly amended.

'What? With the wedding coming up! Has my sister finally lost her marbles, losing yet another good worker? Mehreen is hopeless!' Rani contemptuously scoffed at her sister's handling of domestic workers.

Bristling, Liaquat's step briefly faltered. Then he took the cue she offered before entering their bedroom, 'The wedding, Sister Rani … There are new developments, shall we say …' he let his voice peter away.

'Oh!' Rani stood still, her heart plummeting to a faraway place.

In the bedroom, Mehreen's downcast face greeted Rani. Gulbahar was holding her tightly by the arm.

The tableau was set.

And it provided Rani with her answer, her misgivings spelt out. Like a stranger and an unwanted guest, she hovered awkwardly near the door. As usual, the other two sisters were in collusion and she was the 'outsider', just as it had always been since their childhood. Mehreen always managed to appeal to Gulbahar's good nature with her tears. Her gullible elder sister always fell for her sister's guile and tantrums. Gulbahar had actively adopted a surrogate-mother role and had been very protective of her two sisters, especially the youngest, plagued as she was by nightmares, whimpering in terror in the night and always ending up in her sister's bed, winding her arms tightly around her neck. The tight affection of the skinny arms bonded them. And so from an early age, Mehreen had delightedly discovered how easy it was to wind her way to her sister's heart.

Even though Rani was the young widow who raised a daughter single-handedly, it was Mehreen who demanded and commanded all the attention and invariably got it; it was her home that Gulbahar most visited. Also galling for Rani was the fact that her brother-in-law admired Gulbahar and enjoyed spending time with her. Unable to cope with the jealousy, Rani merely withdrew into herself and into her own world. They did not matter – only her daughter. Rashid, the man she had fallen in love with after her husband's death, had mattered once, but he, too, was lost. And it was all her own fault.

Eyes lingering bitterly on Gulbahar's protective arm around Mehreen's shoulders, Rani tasted bile.

The two sisters peered back, ridden with guilt and wearing exactly the same expressions as on the day Mehreen had accidentally ruined Rani's wedding dress with mustard oil and Gulbahar had valiantly risen to her sister's defence. Mortified and seething, Rani had gone to her new home smelling of oil. It was the talk for months amongst the women guests from her husband's side. Rani never quite forgave her sisters for that day, only just managing to crush her own childish desire to damage her sister's dress on Mehreen's wedding day.

Rani had her answer. She had seen Ismail's reaction to her daughter with her own eyes. Now these conspirators were going to break the news to her that he was jilting her Saher! Rani's eyes filled up, but she wouldn't give them the opportunity to humiliate her further – she would get in first.

Lowering herself onto the nearest chair, head down, Rani waited for someone to say something to her. The seconds ticked away. With her hands neatly folded on her lap and brimming eyes downcast, Rani echoed aloud her depressing thoughts. 'I went to the bazaar today and bought a lot of things for Saher's wedding. But it looks as if my Saher's trousseau isn't destined for this house, is it, my beloved sisters?' She now pinned them with her bitter stare.

Their heads shot up.

Rani waited for their denial, but none was forthcoming. Their tongues were tied in knots – electrified. She knew! What next?

'It's all right, my dear sisters. You don't need to gang up on me or insult me further with your silence – my daughter will not be the first nor the last to be jilted, especially by men who have lived abroad. I could not help but notice your son's behaviour towards Saher since he returned. It's not your fault, so please, all of you, don't be nervous on my behalf. I'll bid you all good day.'

She left them with their mouths open and strode out of the room, a lone dignified figure. Inside, however, she was a ball of misery, feeling just as wretched as she had felt following her phone conversation with Rashid many years ago.

'Rani!' Mehreen called, her heart leaping towards her sister.

'Let her go, Mehreen.' Gulbahar quietly advised, resigning herself to another situation where she had become the reluctant go-between; favourite with one sister and strongly disliked by the other; one forever clinging; the other loftily keeping her at arm's length. Caught between the two, loving one was a matter of betraying and hurting the other.

Whose side was she going to take in this crisis – Mehreen's or Rani's? As usual Mehreen had already emotionally monopolised her. Rani, true to her nature, had scornfully walked away – shunning them all.

*

Rani, blinded by tears, returned home, her daughter's wedding gifts, lovingly purchased that day, forgotten in Mehreen's *hevali*. As soon as her eyes fell on Saher, Rani burst into loud sobs, startling her. Saher pulled her mother into her arms.

'Mother, it's all right. Don't worry about me! I've seen her!'

'Who?'

'His wife – the *goorie!*'

Rani swayed in her daughter's arms, feeling faint.

'The *goorie?*'

Bewildered, Saher held onto her mother.

'Oh, God, I thought you knew, Mother?' Saher hid her own ravaged face.

'What *goorie*?' Rani cried, staring into her daughter's grey eyes. 'Has he brought home a *goorie*?'

'He hasn't just brought a *goorie* back with him – she's his *wife*, Mother!' she bitterly exclaimed, turning her back, unable to look her mother in the eye.

Rani's world fell apart. 'Wedded a *goorie*! Jilted you for a *goorie*!'

Blindly, she reached for the hammock swing-seat under the shade of the veranda and collapsed onto it.

CHAPTER 17

The Sisters' Agony

Daniela sat on the rooftop gallery of Arslan's home wondering what was going on in her husband's household. So many questions were rocketing through her head. 'What are they thinking and saying about me? Have his parents found out about me? What will Ismail's fiancée do? And what am I doing here in this strange land, amongst these people who hate me? Even their servants! That Begum woman in the kitchen has daggers for eyes. What storm have I unleashed upon this family?'

Distressed and loathing herself, Daniela wept openly, not caring if anyone saw her. 'My husband has abandoned me. Jesus, what am I going to do?' she groaned aloud. 'I'll ask Arslan to take me to the airport – I cannot stay another day in this god-forsaken place where I'm not wanted!'

An angry tide of colour chased through her freckled cheeks. 'But he's the father of my unborn child, so how can I abandon my marriage? How can I fight these people – for they will never accept me? I'm a thorn in their lives!'

After pacing the rooftop gallery several times, Daniela peered down at the untidy rows of streets crisscrossing each other and the green sugarcane fields circling the village. She marvelled at the ability of a veiled woman passing the *hevali* gates to maintain her balance whilst carrying a basket of vegetables on her head.

'Apart from Arslan, no one in this household understands a word I say.' A scowl of frustration marred her forehead.

*

Elizabeth was listening to the ten o'clock BBC news from her desk, whilst typing the last chapter of her doctoral thesis. Dave, in the leather armchair, with his legs up on the recliner, made a sudden incoherent sound. Elizabeth looked up sharply. Dave was staring at the screen, his face pale. Elizabeth switched her gaze to the news report; another bombing in some city in Pakistan.

Arching her eyebrows at his reaction Elizabeth turned to her laptop screen. Dave was now on his feet, nervously raking his fingers through his hair.

'She's there, Liz!'

Elizabeth glanced up, frowning, then baulked at the look in his eyes.

'Daniela's there,' he whispered. Elizabeth's hand went to her throat. They carried on staring at each other.

'Are you telling me that my daughter is … in that country?' She pointed to the screen, showing men in traditional Pakistani *shalwar kameez* suits running away from the wreckage of a bus blown apart.

'She's with her husband,' Dave added. 'She'll be fine. Probably she's far from that region.'

Elizabeth carried on staring, feeling sick, unable to say a word. Though she had washed her hands of her daughter since she married Ismail, unable to cope with the differences of her son-in-law's culture and faith, and bogged down by her own prejudices regarding colour and race, now fear for her daughter's safety seized her.

She switched the computer off and was about to leave the room. At the door, she accused, 'You did not stop her or have the decency to tell me, David!' her voice rough with animal fear for her daughter's safety.

'Liz, no need to worry. She's texted me recently, saying she's fine and having a wonderful time.' He omitted to tell her that Daniela had not even told him that she was going there. Only at the airport had she texted him.

'She's amongst strangers! In a foreign country, with a different culture …' Elizabeth shook her head at him before shutting the door. Dave stared back at the TV screen, then texted his daughter, expressing his fears for her safety. Her immediate reply, 'I'm fine, Dad!' brought a smile of relief to his face. He was about to text the words 'Your mother is worried sick', and paused.

*

With Rasoola gone, there was nobody to do the cooking in Mehreen's home and worried Gulbahar, albeit reluctantly, took on the supervisory role of her younger sister's household, first making tea for them all. The young errand boy and old male servant, employed for outside shopping chores, were both of no help in the making of meals. Their Mehreen had remained ill equipped for domestic chores. Putting a *chappati* on a hot *tava* pan was an ordeal for her. In her parents' home, Gulbahar, as the elder sister, had taken on the responsibility for running their household, only delegating certain tasks to the servants.

Gulbahar phoned to request Begum's help in her sister's home. Begum agreed with alacrity, knowing that the three sisters were having a terrible time and they needed her support.

As she sat sipping tea, the sudden image of the beautiful fairy before her eyes made Gulbahar smile. Mehreen caught the smile and her cheeks flagged red. Was Gulbahar gloating at her expense?

'Mehreen, I saw a beautiful fairy the other day ...' Gulbahar dreamily shared, failing to notice her sister's indignant look.

'A fairy?' Mehreen's eyebrows shot up.

'Yes, a nine-year-old fairy.' Gulbahar kept her eyes tightly shut, revelling in the picture of the fairy now dancing before her eyes. Mehreen smiled in understanding, warming to her sister once again. At last her sister had acknowledged Shirin, even if indirectly, and with a smile.

'Yes, a beautiful fairy indeed. I, too, saw her once.'

'What, here?' Gulbahar asked, wide-eyed.

'No, out in the fields – the day Arslan arrived.'

Gulbahar shut her eyes in pain. She was the grandmother and had set eyes on her granddaughter in person for the first time.

'Rani will never forgive us – how did she find out?' Mehreen changed the subject back to their present crisis.

'I don't know,' Gulbahar replied, her heart going out to

her middle sister. 'I ought to be with her. If you are suffering, Mehreen, imagine how it must be for our poor Rani! Her only daughter jilted for a foreign woman, just as she's feverishly making arrangements for her wedding. It's cruel, Mehreen.'

'Please don't say any more. When will this nightmare end?'

Gulbahar sank on the edge of her sister's bed, face pinched.

'It never ends, my sister.' Her soft voice was barely audible. 'It's a slow mean death, licking away into your soul and tearing you apart inside, leaving a hollow well into which one sinks – never to return!'

'Please don't!' Mehreen pleaded, staring aghast at her sister.

'I'm sorry, Mehreen, but that's the reality. Either you let it kill you or you kill the love for your children inside you, as I did with Laila. But I gained nothing … just ended up half killing myself. My sister, it's like a cancer that spreads, eating you away.'

'I know,' Mehreen replied, eyes filling up again. 'I'm so sorry, Sister Gulbahar. What you must have gone through – with Laila's elopement! Children make us suffer, don't they? But Sister Gulbahar, remember I only have one son while you still have your Arslan to wed!'

'Therefore … you have to start facing the facts and bring the *goorie* home.'

'Never!' Heat rushed into Mehreen's already fiery cheeks.

'You may well have to!' Gulbahar coldly returned, equally fiery and standing her ground. 'She's your daughter-in-law!'

'Did you bring your Laila back home, or the potter's son? You emptied your home of any traces of her!' Mehreen aggressively mocked her elder sister. 'I'll bring no foreign slut into this house – usurping our dear Saher's place!'

Gulbahar sighed, holding her hands up in defeat. 'Mehreen, do what you think is best. I need to get back. The *goorie* has to be fed. I don't know if Arslan is at home or not.'

*

Instead of returning home Gulbahar ended up on Rani's doorstep – shamefaced. Whereas Mehreen actively engaged her sister's attention with tears, Rani merely buttoned up into a sullen silence – a silence that with time had shrunk her two beautiful full lips. Her mouth rarely curved, but became a forbidding messenger of her miserable life of widowhood.

It was as if, with the disappearance of her mother to an early grave, someone had banged the door shut on Rani's vocal cords. She never made any sounds, never wailed or ranted like her impetuous younger sister. Nor would pride let her sink her head into her elder sister's lap and weep. Whereas the other two sisters as children had hugged themselves to sleep in each other's arms, seeking human solace as they wept for their beloved mother, Rani slept alone, choking on her silent, painful sobs.

Gulbahar timidly stepped into her sister's home, feeling like an interloper, unable to recall ever having spent a night at Rani's.

On seeing the forbidding straight line of her sister's mouth, Gulbahar's heart sank. In silence, they settled on the wooden hammock under the shade of the veranda. Intimidated by Rani's body language, and afraid of being rebuffed, the only physical contact Gulbahar permitted herself was to place her palm on her sister's back.

After ten minutes of awkward silence, Gulbahar lightly pecked the side of her sister's cheek with a kiss, for something still needed to be said.

'Rani, our *kismet* and children are cruel … I never wanted you to go through the pain I experienced with Laila's elopement. Our suffering, like our happiness, is the will of God. Human beings are destined to suffer in many ways. Imagine yourself in my or in Mehreen's shoes, for at least Saher has done nothing wrong. She's a beautiful and talented woman; so believe me when I tell you that hundreds of suitors will flock to your door for her *rishta*. At least you can now keep her in Pakistan as you've always wanted to.

'But imagine poor Mehreen's situation – no wedding to look forward to, no Pakistani daughter-in-law to welcome into her home. She has no dreams, no hopes, just a dead end. Both husband and wife are battling with these cruel facts of life. But they will survive, for nobody truly dies. I thought that I was dead for a long time, but there's still part of me that is alive – a beautiful fairy made that happen. There's always hope, my sister, but you'll need to be strong … Saher needs your support, Rani dear. Don't let this eat into your soul. Laila's actions ravaged our lives for ten years, and my husband and I lived as "shadows". Why did we punish ourselves? Who suffered? We did! And we are still suffering. Rani, you know I have a heart condition. One day, my heart will just stop beating, but I'll still have two wishes left.'

'What?' Rani asked quietly, breaking her ominous silence at last.

'To see the beautiful fairy again with my own eyes and see my Arslan wed the woman he loves.'

'Who does he want to marry?'

'I don't know, but he has promised me that she will be from our clan.'

'Well, every time I see him, he's with Saher,' Rani retorted.

A light flared and then immediately dimmed in Gulbahar's eyes and she turned her face to hide the look from her sister.

'I must go, Rani, I would like to take you to my home, but …'

'Yes – that English bitch is there!'

Gulbahar baulked at her sister's venom.

'Saher has met her,' she said softly.

Rani turned to her sister, her hand tugging at her *chador* on her head. 'Oh, God! My poor darling.'

She ran in the direction of her daughter's room, dismissing her sister. Gulbahar rose heavily to her feet. Outside, she informed the chauffeur to take her back home.

CHAPTER 18

The Goldsmith's Wife

Rukhsar's nimble fingers carefully embedded the ruby gems into the appropriate tiny grooves of the necklace and earring set. The goldsmith left it to his wife and daughters to check the minutiae – including whether all the little *machlis*, the dangling bits, were strung in the correct sequence on the earrings.

Rukhsar had just counted ten rubies in one ear stud and eleven in the other. Feverishly, her fingers began to count again: loudly reciting '*ek, do, teen*'. Each ruby cost extra rupees and they couldn't afford to make generous mistakes, particularly with three daughters to wed and with inflation on the rise. The *atta,* flour, was so expensive and there was sugar rationing, too; it was back to *gurh* tea for many villagers. Rukhsar wondered how the poor coped, especially those with large families.

'Massi Fiza is here!' her youngest daughter crisply announced, obeying the house rule to first warn their mother and then to help her quickly shield the gold jewellery from the visitors' prying eyes. Rukhsar either tucked them under a cushion or covered them discreetly with a newspaper if a tablecloth was not available. This time, however, Rukhsar didn't rush. It was only Massi Fiza, a good and trusted neighbour, whose eyes had been fully corrupted by hundreds of *tholas* of gold, but she had no knowledge as to where the goldsmith family stored their cash or gold at night.

The sturdy wooden door leading to the rooftop was forever bolted with three large, clumsy bolts. Only the master gold-smith's solid masculine fingers could prise them open. So Rukhsar and her daughters were deprived of the luxury of sleep-ing on the open terraces, under the gleaming, heavenly stars in the summer. They had to make do with the ceiling fans and air conditioning that their loving father had generously provided for his *nazak*, his delicate, 'boarding school educated' daughters as he proudly liked to describe them. Daughters aside, security was the number one priority for all. And no female in the household complained, especially since the trauma of an overnight robbery via the rooftop door, when thieves who had climbed over from the neighbouring terrace had made off with half a pillowcase of gold items. Poor Master-ji never forgot or quite recovered from that tragic incident. Rukhsar was adamant that it was then that her husband's hair had started to go grey, almost overnight. Insurance was unheard of in the village; loss was loss and had to be philosophically borne.

So from that day on, somebody from the family always had to guard their goods. 'Business was business after all,' Master Goldsmith had briskly drilled into his wife. No customer was ever left alone with the gold, irrespective of their status or their relationship with the goldsmith's family. Today, Massi Fiza-ji could not help gawping at the gleaming gold and emerald choker set lying on a bed of velvet. The counting finished, Rukhsar snapped the velvet box shut and peered up at their neighbour through her large blue bifocals.

'Welcome, Massi Fiza.'

'Oh, what a lovely necklace! Whose is it?' Massi Fiza squinted to take a closer look. Unlike her friend, she hated wearing her glasses, loathing the weight of them on her nose, and was therefore content to remain semi-blind when it came to examining minute details.

Not bothering to answer, Rukhsar passed the box to her hovering daughter. Massi Fiza-ji was just as persistent this morning.

'Was that necklace ten *tholas* in weight? Is it meant for that lawyer woman, Saher?'

'Actually, yes,' Rukhsar reluctantly divulged. Her head shot up as her friend's body had doubled in laughter. 'What's so funny, Massi Fiza-ji?'

'Well, I can tell you one thing – that necklace you have been working on, Rukhsar-ji, won't go on Saher's pretty neck.'

'What do you mean?' Rukhsar looked up, aghast.

'I mean that she'll not be wearing it. If anybody – it will be a lady with a very white neck indeed.'

'What are you insinuating, Massi Fiza-ji?' the goldmistress asked sharply, not caring for Massi Fiza's tendency to embroider events this morning. They had worked tirelessly on this set for the last few days and she had the arthritis in her finger joints to prove it. They were still glowing with the honour that the landlord had chosen them, the village jewellers, rather than the sophisticated urban ones, with their posh display cabinets and a team of workers to design and sell the goods.

'Well, I might as well tell it to you straight, as half of the village probably already knows by now.'

'What? Please don't exaggerate!' Rukhsar urged, already irked by what she had learned.

'That *goorie*, the white woman staying at Mistress Gulbahar's house, is Ismail's wife!' Massi Fiza triumphantly blurted out and eagerly waited for her friend's reaction.

Result.

Rukhsar was shocked into silence, mouth pursed into a tight line, a glazed look behind the designer frames.

'Well, what do you think of that?' Massi Fiza prompted, scanning Rukhsar's face with interest.

Her neighbour merely nodded, struck dumb at the thought of all that money possibly lost. Landlord Liaquat had kept her poor Sharif-ji busy for days, working tirelessly on scores of jewellery items of all shapes, styles and sizes. And now this! Would the landlord buy all these sets if the wedding was not even going to take place?

'Oh, no!' she cried out aloud. The cost of her eldest daughter's trousseau was partly invested in the landlord's commissioned jewellery items. The lavish engagement party had already put them in arrears by thousands of rupees and there were the college costs for their youngest daughter, Farah. Rukhsar turned a pained gaze on her friend.

'Have you heard what I've been saying, Rukhsar-ji? Are you OK?' Massi Fiza was now genuinely alarmed.

'Massi Fiza-ji, what cruel news you've given us! I knew something like this would happen. When you send your sons abroad and they bring back strange parcels – including foreign wives. Just as well my daughters aren't getting married abroad. My daughter is only going to the nearby town.'

It was Massi Fiza's turn to first stare and then button her mouth into a straight line.

'Who's getting married?'

Rukhsar blushed, her eyes falling. 'Oh, didn't I tell you that my Shabnum is engaged?'

Massi Fiza-ji was most aggrieved on two accounts. Firstly, that her friend hadn't told her anything, and she visited them every day, and secondly, that she had planned to ask for the girl's hand for her eldest son. Rukhsar glimpsed the disappointment in her friend's eyes and just as slyly and skilfully ignored it, knowing exactly what Massi Fiza was thinking. Inside she was churning with fury. Did the laundrywoman actually have the audacity to think that she, the goldsmith's wife, would stoop down to wed her town-educated, Murree boarding school daughter to a village lout, and to have her live in a village home stacked with other people's dirty laundry!

'Poor Saher, being jilted like that,' Rukhsar forcefully dragged her thoughts back to the matter in discussion, 'and by a woman from another race! Please, Allah Pak, save all our daughters from such a tragic fate as being jilted! I can't imagine what it must be like in those three mighty *zemindar* sisters' households. They are probably all going crazy. All are affected by this in some way or other – aren't they?'

'Yes, they are, Rukhsar-ji. Do you know that Mehreen sacked her housekeeper, Rasoola? Apparently Rasoola is going around everywhere, telling tales about her mistress and the white bride. Can you imagine having such a housekeeper? It's disgraceful – that woman hasn't one ounce of loyalty in her!'

'You're right!' Rukhsar agreed. 'What a thing to do – to betray the very hand that feeds you.'

'Talking about betrayal, the children of those landowners have done a fair share of that – letting their parents down, I mean.

First the daughter of one sister marries a potter's son, and then the only son of the third sister brings home a foreign woman; the daughter of the second sister to be jilted in the process. I feel so, so sorry for that poor woman. Haughty though she is! I've once or twice tried to speak to her when she is visiting her aunt's home, but she looks right through you. It's so humiliating. Why are we treated with such contempt? Do we … people of the lower classes not matter?'

'Poor you, but to those people you are just the servant – your detergent-stained clothes – that probably puts her off … And why should she, a famous lawyer, enter into discussion with you? You two have nothing in common.'

'I'm human, too! Allah Pak made me, too!' Massi Fiza heatedly reminded her friend, hating her for the remarks and feeling demeaned by them.

'Of course!' Rukhsar hastened to mollify her neighbour. 'By the way, I've heard about Jennat Bibi's daughter-in-law, Faiza, miscarrying and she blamed it on that poor girl – Salma!'

'Yes, I forgot to tell you, that poor girl is in a real state according to her mother, Zeinab. In fact, I've heard she has locked herself in her room and says that she'll not leave!'

'What?'

Massi Fiza energetically shrugged her shoulders. 'She's daft! When Jennat Bibi told her not to visit their house, why did the silly girl bother going there? Who knows, it might be her *perchanvah* that has caused it!'

'Oh, come on, Massi Fiza-ji. This is silly!'

'Well, Jennat Bibi's *pir* can't be wrong, can he?' Massi Fiza bristled, a true follower of Jennat Bibi's school of thought, wearing one of the amulets that the sweetmaker's wife had 'kindly' bought from the *pir* for her. Every time she visited Jennat Bibi's home for the laundry, Massi Fiza was supplied with a good dose of the *pir's* teaching. And Massi Fiza was an extremely avid listener and a faithful follower, intent on pleasing Jennat Bibi, a good customer for the laundry and supplier of sweets and snacks. Massi Fiza hated washing the sweetmaker's syrup-stained overcoat, but the added bonus was that she always ended up picking the leftover sweets from the shop. So in Massi Fiza's house, her steel plate of *ladoos*, *gulab jamuns* and *patesas*, her three favourite sweets, was never empty. And, unfortunately, she had three missing back molars to prove it!

'Oh, well, if the *pir* says so,' Rukhsar drily acquiesced, not bothering to debate the matter on superstitions further.

'By the way, I spotted Ismail entering the potter's house right now, as I was leaving my house. I wonder what those two are getting up to,' she winked, eyes sparkling in mischief.

'Well, your guess is as good as mine – both have made their parents suffer. They are probably commiserating with each other. And he's made my family suffer, too – for making those wretched necklace sets for his wedding!'

CHAPTER 19

The Kidnapping

Zeinab stood under the veranda outside her daughter Salma's bedroom, her knuckles hurting from banging on the old mahogany door, which dated to the period preceding the partition of India and Pakistan. Her father-in-law had gone back to their village house near Delhi and carted their special wooden door back to Pakistan.

'Open the door, you silly girl! Come out and eat. If you carry on like this people will believe that there is something *seriously* wrong with you … with your silly habit of hiding in the sugarcane fields and now locking yourself in. I've called your husband to take you away from the village.'

'Leave me alone. I don't want to eat anything.'

'Will you not help your poor mother? I've three quilts to darn for Gujjar's daughter's trousseau.'

'Leave me, Mother!'

'Stubborn girl!' Zeinab angrily muttered, despairing at the thought of the stitching yet to be done. The quilt needed to be fully stitched in the next hour and she could not afford to lose her next order. Gujjar, the village milk supplier, was a good customer, as his wife was devoted to annual spring cleaning and also tended to order new bedding every year. For Gujjar's wife, airing quilts on rooftop terraces was not enough; she insisted on new ones, just before the Bakra Eid festival.

Daughter or no daughter to lend a hand, the quilt had to be finished; this was her livelihood. The basket of thick darning needles tucked in the crook of her elbow, Zeinab climbed up the mud-baked steps to the rooftop terrace to continue her work under the sun. The raw, lumpy bits of cotton buds for the deep blue velvet quilts had to be flattened out first before being stiched by hand. With her long, thick darning needle, Zeinab's dexterous fingers dug in and out of the thick quilt border.

Down below, Salma peeped out of her door, listening for some sounds. Guessing that her mother was up on the terrace with her work, she sneaked into the small, dimly lit kitchen, annexed to one side of the veranda, with a small hole for a window. The clay *tandoor* shared with their poor widowed neighbour who had three young children to feed was still warm from her after-noon *chappati*-making. Salma poured herself a cool glass of *lassi* from the round-bellied clay pot and gulped it all down.

Then, veiling herself carefully in her long blue *chador*, she tied the item she had picked from the kitchen in one corner of it. With her face half hidden, she scurried out of her home and through the village lanes.

*

Shirin was playing alone, as usual, for the village children had been schooled by their parents to keep away from the girl. Though none of their mothers or fathers had ever explained the reason why to their children, it was out of respect for their landlord. If he ignored the potter's child then they should follow suit. Like him, they averted their eyes from Shirin's longing looks; she wished so much to play hopscotch with Chanda, the little girl who lived next door. From the age of six, Shirin got used to spending time on her own. Laila let her play out in the lane, expecting the village to be a safe place. In the city, Shirin would never be allowed to step out of the home without her parents.

What Laila had not realised was that the girl was wandering further and further away from the village on her exploratory jaunts. Today, Shirin had already climbed her favourite tree, snagging the hemline of her frock on one of the branches. Now, she was excitedly hopping to her second favourite place – the termite mound – to play with the little creatures again.

Hearing hurried steps behind her she looked over her

shoulders, her curls flying around her cheeks and mouth parted open. It was the *pagaal* woman in the blue *chador* who talked funny. The greeting of '*salaam*' died on Shirin's mouth as the woman dashed into the sugarcane field, thrusting her body through the tall, sturdy sugarcane plants.

Bemused and shrugging her small shoulders Shirin carried on walking to the termite mound, now armed with a large twig, ready to give the mound crust a really good poke. Her feet wide apart, she was debating where to start – at the top or at the bottom – when a shadow fell on the mound. Frowning, Shirin stood up. It was a tall man, with a huge turban on his head, fair suntanned skin, and a wiry moustache styled to fall to the sides of his face. She had seen men like him knocking at their apartment door in Islamabad, selling goods. This one also had a bag slung over his shoulders.

He smiled down at her; she gazed spellbound into his startling, liquid-blue eyes.

'What are you doing, my little girl?' the man asked in heavily accented Urdu.

Shirin blinked, not wanting to answer – small soft mouth fallen open, very much aware that he was standing too close. Her mother had warned her in the city not to talk to strangers. Nervously, she stepped back. The man's smile widened.

'Ah, little one, you want to play with the ants – let me help you.' He took the twig from her hand, 'Let's see what we can do.'

Shirin relaxed, watching him poke a very big hole in the crust. To her delight, almost immediately the ants began to scramble out. She giggled and he laughed.

'See … look at them. Now you do it …' Shirin let him guide her hand to poke another hole, his other hand resting lightly on her shoulders, his body leaning against hers from behind as he squatted down to her level.

*

Salma, the quiltmaker's daughter, was lying on the ground in the cramped space between the sturdy sugarcane shoots, the long sharp leaves digging into her back and scratching her arms. Eyes tightly closed, she waited, willing herself to shut out the pain; it was just a matter of time.

The blood was trickling down over the sugarcane shoots.

'Forgive me, Mother!' Feeling faint, a buzzing sound echoed in her ears. Then it was shattered by a startling scream and the words 'No! No!'

Salma sat up, heart thudding, listening. Thinking it was her imagination, she closed her eyes again, slumping against the sugarcane shoots, crushing them beneath her body.

Another piercing scream rent through the air. Salma sat up, alarmed. Staggering to her feet, her blood-soiled shawl caught on a stem was forgotten. Scratching her hands, she thrust her way out of the rows of sugarcane plants and stepped onto the village path.

Ahead of her, she saw a tall man pulling the landlord's screaming granddaughter behind him. And then, lifting her up, he threw her onto his shoulders and started to run down the path out of the village.

Salma screamed, startling the man in his tracks.

'Get your hands off her, you pig!' she called, running after him, her wrist leaking blood.

The man put Shirin down and sprinted off. Salma carried on shouting for help, hoping someone was around in the neighbouring fields to hear her.

'Help! Our daughter is being kidnapped!'

Traumatised, Shirin rose to her feet, body shaking with violent sobs. The man had told her he wanted to take her to see a *mela*, a fair. When she had politely refused, he had grabbed her arm making her scream as fear took hold of her, her mother's words of warning, that some men stole children, ringing in her head.

Reaching Shirin, Salma gave her a tight hug.

'You OK?'

'Auntie, your arm, it's bleeding!' Shirin was frightened of the gash and the stream of blood rushing out.

'Don't worry! Let's get you home.' Salma held her throbbing wrist against her chest, blood soaking into her *kameez*. Shirin let herself be pulled, but these hands Shirin trusted. And she was going in the right direction – back to the village.

Her own legs unsteady, Salma tightened her hold of the girl. Looking ahead, she thought fast. The potter's home was too far; she knew she would not make it there and so she stopped in the village square.

Salma ignored the young boys playing cricket, gawping at her bloody wrist, and the bearded Imam on his way home after leading the prayers in the mosque. There was no modesty *dupatta* or shawl around her body. The Imam quickly averted his gaze from the fulsome thrust of Salma's breasts straining through her thin cotton *kameez*. '*Besharm* woman!' he hissed under his breath. 'Has the quiltmaker's daughter really flipped this time? That she goes without any modesty covering, save a thin *kameez*!'

He had heard about her strange hiding jaunts in the sugar-cane fields. When a woman passer-by called her name, Salma ignored her and carried on walking, her only concern being the girl's safety.

At the *hevali* gates, she kept her fingertip pressed on the buzzer until a panting Begum, with Rasoola in tow, appeared.

'Hold on! What's the hurry, you silly girl? Look at you! What?' Begum exclaimed, stopping dead, her eyes on Salma's dripping wrist as she clutched tightly onto the terrified Shirin. What was going on?

'Please, take her home – she was being kidnapped.' Salma spoke so low that they could hardly hear her.

'What?' Aghast, both housekeepers echoed together.

Next minute, Salma was on the ground, in a heap at their feet.

'Oh my God! Rasoola, call the doctor! Call Ali! Look at this stupid woman – she's slit her wrist.' Pulling off her own shawl and tearing one end of it she wrapped it tightly around Salma's wrist. Begum did not care; showing the shape of her middle-aged breasts was the least of her problems.

'Take her inside,' she instructed Rasoola. 'And you, pet,' she turned to Shirin, 'come with me. I'm not letting you out of sight now until I hand you safely back to your mother.'

Begum thought fast. Master Arslan was at home. That was good, as he could take the girl. So much to do. They needed to let Salma's mother know. Child kidnapping, slit wrists, and a *goorie* bride at their door – what next?

'Fetch Master Arslan, Rasoola!' Begum called, glad to have the other housekeeper with her at this moment.

Shirin was now sobbing uncontrollably, looking at the woman who had saved her, with her closed eyes and bandaged wrist.

'What happened to her arm, Auntie Begum?' she asked meekly.

'Nothing, my princess, she cut it by accident …'

'She was in the sugarcane fields … she ran to help me when that man grabbed me!' Shirin hiccupped to a stop. Begum hugged her tight. The thought of losing her, being abused and sold by some man terrified her. Arslan came sprinting out of the *hevali* gates as soon as he heard.

'Master Arslan, please take this lovely girl back to her mother's home,' Begum instructed. Bemused, Arslan stood staring at the woman on the ground and his niece sobbing in Begum's arms.

Shirin slid back into Begum's arms, reluctant to go into the arms of another man, even if he had visited her mother.

'It's OK, my princess, I'll take you home myself! Master Arslan, please take Salma inside. I hope that her husband can take her away from this village.' She mouthed the words, 'The silly girl has slit her wrist … the doctor!'

'Why?' he asked. She shook her head before striding off with Shirin, her arm protectively draped around the girl's shoulders.

One street away her young companion timidly requested:

'Please don't tell Mummy about that bad man … she'll get angry. I disobeyed her – please, Auntie.'

'OK, but see that you now play inside the village. There are some wicked people in the world who are not kind to children.'

'Oh! I will, Auntie. I promise.'

Arslan waited for Rasoola to help him to pick up the semi-conscious woman, wanting to avoid having to touch her.

*

PART THREE

CHAPTER 20

The Friends

Massi Fiza panted into the goldsmith's lounge.

'Have you heard?'

Rukhsar frowned above the gem casket, the bead tweezers gripped between her fingers.

'What, Massi Fiza-ji?' she politely asked, hoping it would be worth it as her husband was waiting for the gemstones downstairs in his workshop.

'You won't believe this! In our village – kidnapping and slit wrists!'

'What?'

'Salma, that quiltmaker's daughter, tried to kill herself – slit her wrist and then ended up saving the landlord's granddaughter from a kidnapping. Just guess where she tried to kill herself? In the sugarcane field! Can you believe it?'

'What?' the frown was replaced by a speculative look.

'I'm now off to Zeinab's house to see how her daughter's doing – the doctor came just in time. I'll pop in later and let you know what's happened.'

'How do you know all this?'

'Rasoola, Begum's new helper at the *hevali*, told me when I returned the laundry. She always enjoys a good gossip. She's just like us, but she's mean and malicious, too!' she laughed. 'Well, there is no pretending we don't like a good gossip, is there?' Rukhsar giggled in agreement.

Massi Fiza panted out of the room, just as she had entered.

*

It was much later, after all her laundry work was finished, that Massi Fiza made it to the quiltmaker's house. Zeinab's humble courtyard and small veranda was crammed with women visitors, either perched on or hovering around the two portable *charpoys*. Salma's husband, urgently called from the city, stood in one corner, head bowed, arms folded across his chest. With lowered heads and behind the folds of their shawls numerous hushed female conversations were taking place. Whispering women, covertly signalling with their body language and active exchange of secret glances. This was an incredible moment for gossip-mongering, drama and speculation. Massi Fiza eagerly eavesdropped on her two friends and good customers.

'Will the silly girl pull through? First hiding in sugarcane plants and now trying to kill herself! What next? She's truly mad,' murmured the baker's wife. 'And they said she has a BA, huh! This is not how an educated woman behaves! She is sillier than the lot of us.' Her last sentence made the women around her frown. One uttered, 'Cheeky woman!'

The Gujjar's wife, hiding her mouth behind her hand, heartily agreed; she had stopped her own pregnant daughter-in-law from coming with her. After all, she could not take a risk with Salma's *perchanvah*. Had not the sweetmaker's daughter-in-law, Faiza, miscarried soon after hugging the 'unfortunate' Salma?

Skilfully sidling past the two women hovering in the doorway, Massi Fiza entered Salma's room, peeping over the shoulder of the village cobbler's wife.

Salma was lying on her bed, unconscious and breathing, her wrist now properly bandaged. Zeinab, sitting on the edge of the bed, was gently massaging her daughter's forehead. The young lady doctor from the local medical centre was just packing her medicine case when someone pushed Massi Fiza aside. Affronted and about to complain, the words died on her mouth as Zeinab leapt off the bed.

'Not done enough already! Come to see, have you?' she shouted.

Zeinab aggressively pushed Jennat Bibi, the sweetmaker's wife, who stumbled against her daughter-in-law, Faiza, and fell in the middle of the doorway with a thud.

'Ouch!' Jennat Bibi screeched in pain, having landed on her bottom on the concrete floor, unable to breathe. The women visitors, as well as the horrified doctor, were unable to believe their eyes.

Faiza bent down to help her up and the lady doctor hurried to Jennat Bibi's side, her dazed gaze swinging from one irate lady, the host, to the woman she had just pushed. Zeinab remained defiant.

'Sister Zeinab, what have you done?' the doctor asked.

'It's these women – they are responsible for the state my daughter is in. They made my Salma's life a real hell.'

'What?'

'This woman …' As she was about to poke Jennat Bibi on the shoulder, the doctor pulled her back, 'has been victimising my Salma! She made her go mad and want to kill herself.'

She spat at Faiza, 'And you, serpent of a friend, lied to protect yourself! See what you've done – Salma has cut her wrist and is on her deathbed! You two are responsible for this! If she dies, may all the curses of the world beget your home!'

Zeinab stepped out onto the veranda and jeeringly addressed all the women in her home, encompassing them in one ruthless glance, her finger pointing to them all. 'You are all hypocrites! You women have made my daughter's life a misery. The poor mite was already suffering from the loss of her babies – then you victimised her, by avoiding her and stopping her from entering your homes.'

'I don't understand,' the doctor interjected, looking bewildered and outraged. 'What's going on here? Are you saying …'

'This wicked woman blamed her daughter-in-law's miscarriage on my poor girl!' Zeinab interrupted. 'They have accused her of witchcraft, saying that her "evil shadow" made Faiza lose her baby.'

'What utter nonsense!' the doctor replied, shaking her head in disbelief. 'There's no such thing as a woman's evil shadow. This poor woman has miscarried because of a medical condition. Her womb is weak and unable to hold onto the foetus! What has her body got to do with other women's pregnancies? Can you women not understand that? Also is this not *shirk* and against the teaching of Islam?' The doctor's challenging gaze swung over the small crowd of women.

'What does she know?' someone muttered quietly, staring back unabashed, while others dropped their gaze in embarrassment.

The bricklayer's wife mumbled to her companion, 'Let's get out of here before Zeinab lays into me and pushes me out, too!'

Too late. As she rose to leave: 'Yes, it's women like Jennat Bibi and the bricklayer's wife who have slammed their doors in my daughter's face!' Zeinab screeched aloud from the doorway.

Her back smarting with heat, and too timid to retaliate in public, the bricklayer's wife hurried out of the door, followed closely by Massi Fiza. Outside in the lane, the bricklayer's wife turned round to see who was behind her and smiled.

'Just the person I wanted to see! Massi Fiza, are you going to the *hevali* for the laundry? If you are, please take me with you. I do so want to get a glimpse of the *goorie.*'

Massi Fiza cruelly giggled, 'Begum won't be very pleased if I keep bringing visitors with me to the *hevali*. She says that it's not a zoo, or that the *goorie* is not an animal on exhibition for us all to ogle. Anyway, I have already collected the laundry. Out of three women I took with me last time, only one was lucky – she took a glass of water to the *goorie.*'

'Oh. I would have loved to invite her to my house for dinner,' the woman preened, missing the disdainful smirk on Massi Fiza's face.

'She won't be visiting or having dinners at any humble people's homes.' Massi Fiza scoffed at the audacity of the bricklayer's wife in wanting to invite the Englishwoman into her house. 'Probably there will be a big party for Master Arslan's homecoming! You might be able to see her then,' she ended helpfully, relishing the wisdom of always remaining on good terms with everyone.

They started to walk back home together, as they lived in the same street.

*

Inside the quiltmaker's house, the doctor was in full flow

educating the women and trying to wean them away from superstitions that made them unwittingly cruel.

'This is a good example of a bad old wives' tale, ladies! Please listen. That poor young woman, lying on the bed, nearly died today. We don't know what drove her to it.'

'These women did!' was Zeinab's shrill answer.

'That might be true, but your daughter could be suffering from post-natal depression also. If you remember, she told me how low she was feeling the last time I saw you both in the medical centre,' the doctor hastened to remind Zeinab.

Jennat Bibi was now groaning aloud and trying to rise. The doctor leaned down to look at her.

'I had better check you over. Are you in a lot of pain?'

'Yes, you saw how this vindictive woman pushed me over! She's a witch with no manners – fancy pushing her guests? Have I pushed anyone in my house?'

'Manners? Get this woman out of here, Brother Javaid, before I do something else to her!' Zeinab heatedly instructed Jennat Bibi's husband who was standing nearby. He had followed his wife to the quiltmaker's house after he learned of the mishap with Salma and had watched the entire spectacle with a tight face.

'Come, Jennat Bibi, let's take you home.' Stiffly, her husband came to his wife's side. Everyone stared at the tall, dignified sweetmaker, often under his wife's thumb.

'Come, Faiza. Sister Zeinab is right. Neither of you two women should be welcome in this house. You have both caused enough damage as it is. I would be grateful if you, lady doctor, could come to our house and check my wife in case she has broken a bone or something.'

He turned to Zeinab. 'I'm so sorry about your daughter and I hope she recovers fully. I take responsibility for the behaviour of the two women in my family. And you ladies, I hope you have heard what the doctor said. There are no evil shadows – it's all in your mind. Listen to the doctor's medical logic, not to some of the rubbish that the *pir* has been feeding my wife.'

He guided his red-cheeked wife out of the courtyard. The women moved aside to let them pass.

'Please all go home,' Zeinab told the women. 'Thank you for coming, but I don't need you here. Go and see to your families and leave me to get on with looking after my daughter. *In'shallah*, with all your prayers, my Salma will get better.'

Thoroughly chastened, resentful and stiff-backed, the women filed out of Zeinab's courtyard.

'Well, I've never been so insulted in my life! I'm definitely not giving her my quilt to darn again!' muttered one of the women as soon as she stepped out into the lane.

CHAPTER 21

The Cousins

Laila and Ismail were in the valley, gazing up at the waterfall, where they used to bathe as children, running and skipping along the grassy bank of the stream.

'Is it true that you are married to an Englishwoman?' was the first thing that Laila asked, walking by his side along the path.

'Yes – but I'm not ashamed, nor have I any regrets, Laila! Save that I've hurt my family and Saher of course,' he felt obliged to add.

Laila stopped and looked at him for a moment.

'Can I ask what was wrong with our Saher?' Her condemnatory tone made Ismail bristle.

'Laila, I thought at least you would understand!' he accused, cheeks reddening, disappointed at her reaction. 'Can I be impertinent and ask you this question? Why didn't you marry the man you were promised to? Why the potter's son?'

Laila coloured at the way he had neatly turned the table on her.

'At the time, I thought it was for the best,' she replied sadly.

'Like you, I fell in love. You with someone from another class, I from another race – we couldn't help ourselves. Daniela, my wife, is a wonderful, lovely, sweet and highly principled woman, and has good moral values. She was also flesh and blood before me. Saher, on the other hand,' he shrugged, 'was just an image – so far away and inaccessible. In fact, I believe that your brother probably knows her better than I do – they are like twins, inseparable.'

'Yes, they've always been very close, and my brother dotes on her.'

'Yes, I noticed and, for my sins, he punched me for Saher's sake. I never meant to hurt anyone, especially her!'

'Neither of us meant to hurt anyone,' Laila wryly agreed, 'nevertheless, we have, by our selfish actions. Now that I have a daughter myself, I know what it must have been like for my parents. I wish you all the best with your Daniela and sincerely hope that it will prove the right choice. I have ended up sacrificing an awful lot, Ismail, but love alone is not enough … It's not a substitute for your family and their love. You see, everything has a rightful place in life.'

'Hey, hang on. You're becoming depressing. You and Jubail, is that his name? You've sacrificed a lot for one another, but you seem to have become embittered. You must never go down that path, Laila, otherwise you will have nothing left!' he earnestly advised.

'Then why don't you openly claim Daniela as your lawful wife and take her home with you? Begum tells me that she's still at my parents' house.'

Ismail was taken aback by the turn in their conversation and once again they fell into a long silence as they continued walking.

Shirin ran into the stream, shouting, 'It's cold, Mummy!'

Ismail and Laila sat down on two large boulders and watched her in silence.

'Yes, Laila,' Ismail said, 'you're perfectly right. I need to claim my wife openly and take her home. I've been a true, lousy git to the poor thing – and Daniela's pregnant, too.'

'You have already hurt our Saher, but please don't hurt your wife, too!'

'I know, but will my parents accept her?'

'Just throw yourself at their mercy. Don't abandon your home or your wife – for you have a right to both.'

'Well, well, our Laila is mouthing little pearls of wisdom.'

'They are not pearls, my dear brother, just little home truths that time has knocked into me. The door to my parents' home is now forever slammed shut to me. Don't let them slam the door in your face, too. I came for my brother's homecoming. I know that he'll come to see me in the city. My daughter is growing fast – I don't want her to learn about the *big house* … I want to protect her. Already she has begun to hate her grandfather, without realising who he actually is. Imagine what she'll think when she finds out? Her young innocent mind will not be able to cope with the rejection. Nor will she understand the damage that we, her parents, have done to her grandparents.'

'Oh, but that's terrible, Laila!' Ismail stood up, picking up a small pebble and throwing it in the stream. 'Please don't say that.'

'It's a fact, Ismail. My father passed by my daughter, ignoring her. Every year, I've sent photographs to my mother, via Begum, but I am told she locks them away in a drawer.' Her voice breaking, she openly wept.

'Cry, if that helps you, my sister,' he urged, distressed himself.

'It hurts so much, Ismail, when it happens to your own child. I was a coward. I should have come back the same night of my wedding. Win them over, my brother! Stay in their midst and when your child is born, place it in their laps, for they will not be able to shift it. I made a terrible mistake, and waited for them to come to me. I should have barged in and put my Shirin in their laps. Now, there is no other choice for me – but to bow out of my parents' life for good.'

'I'm so sorry …'

'Shall we go?' Laila was looking at her watch. 'I'm expecting Shirin's father's phone call.'

They walked back to the village in companionable silence, with Shirin hopping ahead of them.

*

From the rooftop gallery of the *hevali*, Daniela spotted her husband.

'That's my Ismail – with a woman! Is it his fiancée?' Her hand trembled with raw jealousy as she peered over the wrought-iron rooftop railings.

'I'm going!' she decided – not to the airport but to her in-laws' house. 'I haven't come all this way to lose my husband.' Ismail was going in one direction, the woman in another. It couldn't be his fiancée. Ismail's fiancée was trendy, wore fashionable clothes and didn't cover her hair. This woman was cloaked from head to foot in a large white garment. 'I'll show these racist village people and these landowners what a white woman is made of! Beastly of them to keep calling me *goorie* when I've got a proper name! And I thought my mum was bad! I guess they all have got it in their heads that I'm a tart who has slept around.'

Daniela crossed to the other side of the gallery and looked down into the central courtyard of the villa. She could hear male voices below.

*

Gulbahar was looking for her son and found him in the drawing room staring into space.

'What's the matter, Arslan?' she asked, forgetting to remove her *chappals* on the silk rug. She could tell by his flushed face that something was wrong.

'Nothing,' was his stiff response.

'Arslan, I know who you want to marry,' she teased, standing in front of her son, trying to catch his eye. 'You said the woman you love was a woman from our clan and that I would like her very much. I know who she is, Arslan.'

'Good! But I'm not marrying.' He startled his mother.

'What?' Disappointment smearing her face, Gulbahar was loath to let go of the topic. 'It's Saher, isn't it?'

He jerked away from his mother's grasp. 'Don't mention her name in front of me again, Mother.'

'But ...' Gulbahar stammered.

'No buts. Just ... just keep her away from me.' He strode out of the room, leaving his mother lost in thought.

'You can also hate those whom you love most.' She smiled as a sudden thought crossed her mind relating to her son's indignation. And Saher. How was the poor girl?

The phone on the coffee table rang, startling Gulbahar out of her reverie.

'Arslan?' Her daughter's timid voice floated across the line. Gulbahar held her breath. 'Arslan?' Laila repeated. 'Is that you?'

Gulbahar felt faint.

'Mother?' The voice asked after a pause.

Gulbahar's lips parted. 'Little fairy! *Chothi pari.*' The trembling husky words echoing down the line were greeted by a stunned silence. The words registered.

'Shirin, Shirin!' Gulbahar heard her daughter's excited shout and held onto the receiver. A few seconds later, a gruff, tear-ridden voice instructed, 'Shirin, please say *salaam!*'

'*Assalam alaikum!*' Shirin dutifully obliged. The two words of greeting gloriously fanned through Gulbahar's body, making the goose pimples on her skin stand on end.

'*Wa laikum salam*, my *pari*' Gulbahar softly greeted back. 'Beautiful little fairy!' she whispered, before her moist hand gently replaced the receiver.

At the other end, Shirin looked puzzled.

'What did the lady say?' Laila asked, eyes glittering with unshed tears.

'She called me a beautiful little fairy.'

Laila's heart dizzied to the heavens above, taking the phone from her daughter.

'Why, Mummy?' Shirin asked, intrigued.

Laila held onto the receiver, tears of joy openly gushing down her cheeks. 'You are a beautiful fairy! And a very special, beautiful lady said that to you.'

'Who?' Shirin innocently prompted.

Laila's mouth ached to spill the words 'your grandmother', but she ruthlessly stamped down on the urge. 'Just a nice lady, my darling,' she quietly offered instead.

Shirin returned to her game of hopscotch in the courtyard.

Heart thudding, Laila redialled the number and waited. It remained silent.

She cast her eyes over the shabby furniture: the oil-stained, moth-eaten, threadbare, cotton cover of the old armchair; the chipped, dressing-table mirror, draped with the potter's wife's old, crocheted tablecloth; the frayed, yellowy-blue curtains whose original colour she could never quite tell. Even the blue dye had made no difference. The nails precariously supporting the curtain rail were loose. Laila feared for her daughter's safety every time she tugged at them in the evening. She often recoiled at the disgusting spirals of cobwebs hanging around the ceiling cornices and in between the mesh frames of the door. The floor, with its missing cement patches, was a safety hazard for her daughter. Shirin had tripped twice already. Laila feared for her daughter's beautiful, pert little nose.

The potter's family, unable to afford a wardrobe, had lived out of suitcases. Clothes were neatly stacked in the two steel suitcases that had been part of the potter's wife's dowry. All the valuables, money and party clothes were stuffed in there. Jubail, as a university student, had his own suitcase, bought for him by Master Haider. Shirin's pile of pretty dresses was kept in a small basket beside the bed.

Laila was gazing at her world this evening through her mother's telescope. 'This is my humble world,' Laila cried. 'Thank you, Mother – it was so good to hear your voice again … Please forgive me for hurting you!' The ritual of self-flagellation had begun and she finished with her offering of a thanksgiving *nafl* prayer.

*

Daniela's case was packed and she turned to Arslan with a smile.

'I'm going to my husband! I've taken up enough of your wonderful family's hospitality and valuable time,' she explained. 'I've two choices: either to return to England or join Ismail.'

'Yes,' Arslan stammered, 'but his family have only just found out about you. Please give them time.'

'I am missing my husband and if I leave it any longer, I'm afraid I'll lose him entirely. What if they pressure him into marrying that fiancée of his?'

'They won't do that!' Arslan sharply informed her. 'I wouldn't let them. Very few Muslim men ever abandon their pregnant wives, and only in exceptional circumstances. Ismail is yours, and yours alone – believe me, Daniela.'

'Thank you,' she uttered softly, eyes filling up, anxiety still written all over her face.

'Please take me to my husband. I want to be under the same

roof as my Ismail! I'll put up with whatever his parents do to me!'

'Let destiny take its own course,' Arslan muttered aloud. 'OK, Daniela, I'll take you.'

'You will?' she exclaimed in delight. 'Thank you, Arslan!' And she rushed to plant a kiss on his cheek just as her hostess entered the room.

Daniela stepped away, red-cheeked.

'Mother, it's not what you think!' Arslan hastened to explain, trying to shake off his embarrassment. His mother attempted to form some words but failed. 'She's English, Mother, and comes from another culture. Kissing men and women on the cheeks is very normal for English people – this is her way of thanking me for our hospitality.'

'Thanking! *Besharm* people!' Outraged, his mother at last found her tongue. 'Kissing strange men! Is that normal behaviour?'

'Yes, there it is! And we've to accept and respect that way of life. Whatever you say, Mother, Daniela was only thanking me because I'm taking her to Ismail's house.' His flat tone didn't convince her, but the words did.

'Take her then! I don't want her under the same roof as you if this is the way she will behave, Arslan!' Now in an uncharitable mood, Gulbahar was eager to be rid of this unwanted, *besharm* female guest. She had lost her only daughter to a potter's son and she was not about to lose her only son to her nephew's cast-off! Wife or no wife!

'What did your mother say?' Daniela timidly asked, though astutely able to guess what they might be saying. Her hostess did not look her in the eye and Daniela knew she had deeply offended the older woman by kissing her son.

'Right, let's go, Daniela!'

'Thank you so much for your kind hospitality,' Daniela warmly offered in English to Gulbahar before picking up her handbag and adding, '*Shukria!*' in Urdu.

Gulbahar stood by the door, trying to smile, but her stiff face let her down.

As they crossed the courtyard, Begum came running out of the kitchen. Her mouth dropped open as she saw Daniela's case.

'Is she leaving, Master Arslan?'

'Yes, but only going to the next village, to Ismail's house, Begum.'

'Oh!' Begum closed her eyes in horror, imagining the drama likely to unfold in the other *hevali*.

*

Gulbahar had already phoned to warn her sister of the *goorie's* impending arrival. Mehreen collapsed on her bedroom armchair.

'Your English daughter-in-law is on her way, Liaquat-ji!' she whimpered bitterly through quivering lips.

'I'll let no foreign slut into this house!' Liaquat threw at his wife across the room, the contours of his face rigid with anger, nostrils flaring. Mehreen withered, mind ablaze. Heat flushed through her body, spiralling fast up her neck and into her face.

'How can you shut the door in her face? Imagine the scandal.'

'Your sister shut her door on the potter's son,' he jeeringly reminded her.

Mehreen's lips trembled with a desperate, silent prayer: 'Please, Allah Pak, save us! Why are you punishing us like this? What have we done to deserve such a fate?' The *hevali* was about to explode, and she had neither the strength nor the stomach for the explosion.

Liaquat, instead of showing empathy, lashed his wife with his angry eyes, demanding:

'Are you going to let her *pleat* feet step into the pure sanctity of our home?'

Numbed, Mehreen meekly stared back. She had no sharp quips to exchange, no points to score with her husband. In the car, it only took ten minutes from her sister's village to theirs. Allah Pak, the woman would be here any moment now! Who would open the door and let her in? Panic made her breathless, her body doubling over.

'Mehreen, you gave birth to one child only. See how that brat has repaid your obsessive love? He's made monkeys out of us.'

Mehreen hid her face in her lap, desperate to retaliate, but both words and strength had deserted her. The jibe, the aspersion on her fertility, the 'only one son' accusation galled her.

Aggressively pushing aside the armchair across the marble floor, Liaquat went out to the courtyard to wait for the foreign woman who had brought their world crashing down upon them. Behind him followed the clicking sounds of his wife's footsteps. Then she hastened back upstairs – panic-ridden.

'Cowardly woman!' he called after her.

CHAPTER 22

The Intruder

Liaquat heard the car doors slam. Heat rushing through his cheeks and shoulders stiffened, he stood tall against the marble pillar with his eyes fixed on the outside door.

Loud knocks thudded, then Arslan's clear voice. 'Auntie Mehreen!'

Liaquat sighed with relief; at least there was someone else with the woman.

Arslan gently thrust the door wide open with the weight of Daniela's suitcase.

'Daniela,' he called over his shoulder. 'Please come in!'

Heartbeat racing, a buzzing sound hammered in Liaquat's ears.

Daniela timidly stepped in, catching her first glimpse of her husband's home, the sunshine brutally beating a frenzied dance on the marble floor in the centre of the courtyard. By contrast, in two of its corners fruit trees cast their shadows, providing welcoming shade. Flowers were blooming everywhere in a rich array of bright colours. Climbing bougainvillea spiralled around the elegant alabaster pillars supporting the veranda roof. Huge earthenware pots of flowers circled the pillars. Two elegantly designed porcelain washbasins stood at each end of the courtyard. Doors painted in blue and cream with netted meshwork to keep out mosquitoes led to numerous rooms on the ground floor. Above the veranda was a gallery with its own set of rooms.

Daniela gazed in wonderment. It was just as Ismail described it, but even grander and more beautiful. Her eyes fell on the hostile face of the elderly man standing by a pillar and she experienced the urge to flee back to Arslan's home. Arslan read her mind and neatly stepped forward to block Daniela's view. He shot a hard, challenging look at his uncle. For some moments, the two men fenced with their eyes.

'Come, Daniela,' Arslan beckoned, with an encouraging smile, whispering in English, 'You've every right to be in this home.'

'You traitor! What are you doing?' Liaquat expressed his outrage at his wife's nephew.

Unperturbed, smiling firmly, Arslan repeated in English, 'Daniela, come! I'll take you to Ismail's room – it's here on the ground floor.'

He was now dragging the suitcase behind him over the marble floor, gaze still locked in a challenge with that of the older man.

Daniela timidly followed, peeping at the elderly man, knowing straight away he was her father-in-law. Liaquat watched helplessly, unable to speak her language.

Inside the large bedroom, Daniela gazed at the finely designed wooden wardrobe. The matching dressing table took up one third of one wall.

'Gosh, Ismail wasn't boasting when he talked about the splendour of his home – it's unbelievable!' She marvelled at the amount of marble everywhere in this house, and the bed – it was larger than the king-sized equivalent in England. The stunning wooden headboard encrusted with onyx reached halfway up the wall.

'Yes!' Arslan laughed, amused at her delight. 'Daniela, all three sisters, including my mother, are very wealthy women, and married equally wealthy men, constituting the wealthiest of families in the two neighbouring villages. They are mistresses of many acres of land. Of course not everyone in the village lives like this, or has the money to send their children to prestigious universities abroad.'

'Are you an only child, too, like Ismail?' Daniela, intrigued, wanted to know more about her husband's wealthy family.

'No …' Arslan replied tersely, in no mood to discuss his sister or her predicament, fearing that Daniela would not understand the complexities of the situation regarding his sister's elopement.

She would simply end up by saying what he had said as a child, 'So what, she has only got married.' Now, as an adult, he had revised certain ideas, and learned that some things had far deeper significance. The thirst for his sister and the ache to have her out of the potter's hovel and back in the *hevali* wouldn't leave him. Above all, he wanted to take his niece out horse riding. And Saher? He bitterly shook his head. It was time to call it a day on his childhood crush and adult passion for her.

'Right, Daniela, please make yourself comfortable. I'll stay here with you until Ismail returns.'

'Thanks.' She nervously smiled her gratitude, glad that she was not left alone in the building until her husband returned.

'I've got a battle on my hands, Arslan, haven't I? You saw the look on his father's face. He doesn't have to say a word!'

'Yes … There are challenging times ahead for you, but I'm sure that you are game for it,' Arslan teased.

'As long as I get to keep my Ismail, I'm ready for any battles.' Brave words uttered with little confidence.

'There'll be no battles, Daniela!' Arslan gently reassured her. 'Nothing will happen to you. Just try to understand how my uncle and aunt's world has been swept away – their plans, wishes, happiness – have all gone up in smoke with your appearance. They are reeling in shock. Forty-eight hours ago, you didn't exist in their lives. Think what it must be like for them?'

'Yes, Arslan, I can understand!' Daniela sharply retaliated, on the defensive. 'But what about me – to be abandoned by my husband, and then find out he has a fiancée waiting for him.'

'Everyone is suffering. Do you know how much anguish there is in all three households as a result of Ismail's cowardice? If only he had told his parents about you before coming here.'

'Tell me, Arslan, do you love Ismail's fiancée?' she enquired, her eyes fixed on his face.

Shocked by her question, he paused before replying, 'Whether or not I love her is irrelevant at the moment, Daniela, for she'll have nothing to do with me. She loathes me and has insulted me in no uncertain terms. I don't think I could ever marry her now. I'll probably go back to the States.'

'Don't do anything silly – see what my rash actions have resulted in!'

'No, Daniela. Eventually, his family would have discovered your existence. Here, let me get you a drink.' Her pregnancy had him worried about the effect of the heat on her.

He left to get water for her. Soon afterwards, the door was thrust open and Ismail entered – husband and wife stared at one another.

'What are you doing here?' Ismail was the first to recover, his head spinning with crazy images, experiencing the weird sensation of having his wife in his Pakistani home, while shying away from the condemnation in her eyes.

'Are you going to own up to everyone that I'm your wife? Or will you go on running from here, too?' Daniela accused.

'Yes and no!' he snapped back. 'You've caused enough damage. Two sisters are now at each other's throats! Satisfied?' In a foul mood, he wanted her to understand the critical situation in the sisters' households.

'And whose fault is that, tell me?' Daniela shouted, stung by his words.

'Shut up, don't yell!'

'I'll yell as loud and as much as I want!' And striding to his side, she slapped him hard across his cheek and looked down at her throbbing hand.

'Feel better now?' he jeered. 'I suppose I deserved it.' His arm reached for her waist from behind – she pushed it away.

'No, I don't feel any better!' Daniela taunted back. 'This trip is a nightmare. I'm in a country where nobody wants me, and where there is already another woman in your life! Waiting to wed you! How do you think that I should behave, my loving husband? Any guesses? My beastly husband then abandons me and a kindly stranger ends up taking care of me. Is this the holiday of a lifetime that I had impulsively imagined?'

'I never invited you …' he coldly reminded her. 'It was your stupid plan that has brought all of this on! I was going to tell them in my own time.'

'When? In 25 years' time?'

'No, during this visit! I'm going to be a father, remember? My parents needed to know that!'

Anger sapped out of her, Daniela sat down heavily on the bed.

'I have lost control over my life. Everyone hates me. My cousin nearly beat me up – it's been quite a picnic for me, hasn't it?'

'Come here, you big oaf!' She held out her arms to him.

He fell into them, revelling in the feel of her warm body around him. They held onto each other for a long time.

'I'm so sorry, Daniela, for everything!' he apologised, nuzzling his face against her throat.

'It's OK. As long as you don't desert me and marry your cousin. I'm fine now.'

'No chance of that – I love you too much. Even if I wanted to, Arslan has barred me for life from having anything to do with Saher.'

'Good. She's very pretty, isn't she?' Daniela could not help adding.

'Yes, but not as sexy as you! Especially with this pregnancy.'

Daniela glowed upon hearing those words. Snuggling down on the soft, feathery pillow, she pulled his head against her breasts.

'Can you hear my heartbeat?' she giggled.

'Yes, I can.'

'Well, imagine what it must have been doing to our baby? It hasn't been a picnic for me, either, you know, being surrounded by hostile people and with whom I could not communicate. It's been terrible!' Tears came flooding back.

Ismail raised his face. 'I know, my darling. Cheer up now and smile.' He felt very contrite. 'You must be hungry – can I get you something to eat or drink?'

'Arslan has gone to get me something.'

A few moments later there was a knock on the bedroom door. Ismail stood up. Daniela quickly raised herself up.

Arslan entered carrying a bottle of Coke and a glass on a tray. Ismail avoided eye contact with his cousin, a reddish hue smearing his cheeks.

'I'm glad to see you, Ismail. Now, look after your wife and

protect her!' Arslan sarcastically instructed in Urdu. Daniela looked from one to the other. 'You will be all right, Daniela, now that your husband is here,' he explained in English.

'Thanks, Arslan, for everything you have done for me.'

'My pleasure. But please don't be too hard on my uncle and aunt. They are still in a state of shock. They will not bite, nor are they vindictive people. Try and keep a low profile for a little while. You never know, they may well begin to like you.'

A nervous laugh shuddered through her body, recalling the hostile look in Ismail's father's eyes as she had passed him in the courtyard.

'I hope so, Arslan.' She wistfully looked down. 'Especially as I am competing with your cousin, whom your whole family adores. I have, apparently, become the villain of this drama.'

'You are not a villain, but a beautiful, sweet and gentle woman,' Arslan generously added.

They all laughed.

Arslan quietly let himself out of the *hevali*. He was glad that his uncle and aunt were nowhere to be seen.

*

Upstairs Mehreen sat stunned, heart thudding, fingers stuffed in her ears. 'Can you hear them laughing, Liaquat?' Hysteria coursed through her body.

Liaquat Ali was lying in bed. 'You'll hear more than their laughter, Mehreen!' was his bitter reply.

'This is my home!' she mourned. 'I feel as if I am living in a stranger's house? What are we going to do?'

'Ignore them, Mehreen!' Her husband tossed onto the other side, facing the wall.

'Ignore them? Has our son no shame? He has not even bothered to come up and see us!'

'Well, there is only one course of action!'

'What?'

'It's our house! Why are we hiding in our room?' Liaquat Ali sat bolt upright. 'Come, let's go down. I'm hungry!'

'You're hungry!' Mehreen threw an incredulous look at him.

'Yes. I know we are upset, but my stomach isn't, Mehreen! It needs feeding.'

'But Rasoola has gone, remember. Who will do the cooking?'

'You!'

'What?' She blinked.

'Yes, Mehreen, until we find another housekeeper. We are not going to starve, are we? You don't have to meet the *goorie*. You can turn your face the other way if you pass. Remember, she's the intruder – not us! This is our house!'

'Liaquat-ji, do you think that they are really married?

'What?'

'What if … What if they aren't?'

'Don't be silly.'

'Think, Liaquat Sahib …' A nervous look smeared her face.

'Spell it out, woman!' He was now quite agitated.

'I don't want any *haram* being committed in our house. What if they have not done the *nikkah* ceremony? Allah Pak, protect us from *haram*.'

Liaquat's face creased with shock and disgust. His son had claimed that he had married the woman. They had to accept his word for it.

Liaquat's firm tread had disappeared, his posture bent. Mehreen's hands felt clammy on the handrail, timidly following her husband down the stairs. What if? Mehreen was gripped by a panic attack.

'I don't want to go near the kitchen!' she whimpered. His angry glare forced her to explain. 'I can't pass their room, Liaquat-ji – please believe me! I can't do it!'

Her husband was staring at the window in the far corner of the courtyard. What were they doing inside? Liaquat Ali suddenly experienced the urge to take flight himself and he steered his wife round in the other direction. Hunger forgotten. Mehreen was right – they could not face them yet.

'Let's go to Rani's!' he instructed.

'Rani's?' Mehreen croaked, wondering if her husband had gone mad. That was the last place she wanted to visit. 'Out of the frying pan into the fire!' she bitterly commented.

'Mehreen, we have to talk to your poor sister! Imagine our poor dear Saher! They need us,' he explained sadly. From her childhood, Saher had become Liaquat Ali's darling little daughter. The thought of having lost her devastated him.

Hatred surged through him again, imagining his son lying in the arms of the Englishwoman. He shuddered, nausea spilling through him – that woman had soiled their *zemin*, their home.

'Come, Mehreen,' he commanded, pulling his wife behind him.

'No, my husband, don't do anything stupid!' Mehreen panicked, catching a rebellious glint in her husband's eyes. 'Ismail is our only child! I can't lose him!' she pleaded, looking back at her son's room.

'Look, the door's opening! Go!' Panicking, she pulled her husband out of the door – fleeing.

'Yes, better go before I do something that I might later regret!' Liaquat Ali muttered, banging the door of the *hevali* shut behind him.

Disconcerted by his parents' departure, Ismail returned to his room. Daniela had to be fed and there was no cook in the house.

'Daniela, there's no one at home at the moment,' he sheepishly informed her. 'I'm sure we can rustle up something to eat between us.'

Warily, Daniela crossed the courtyard, looking from right to left, expecting his parents to appear.

'Relax, Daniela!' Ismail reassured her, putting his arm around her shoulder. 'At the moment, we only have an old retainer and he's out shopping.'

'Your villa is so big, Ismail.' She was gazing up at the top gallery circling the courtyard. 'Our three-bedroom semi back in England is no match for this place. Now, I can see why you have been so keen for us to build a conservatory. This courtyard is larger than our entire house and rear garden put together. Look at all this marble! The place is slabbed with it! Back at home all the marble we can boast of is our ashtray!'

'Marble is cheaper and more popular here than in the UK. The wealthy families use it in abundance in their homes, for everything, from pillars and staircases to bathrooms and balustrades on the rooftop floors. You've only seen the courtyard – there is an entire floor upstairs and a conservatory-like garden at the top. And at least three acres of land belonging to my mother which is annexed to our home – it was offered to her as part of her dowry by her father.'

'Does everyone live like this?' Daniela was truly awed. 'I've stayed in two houses and both are palatial.'

'Most wealthy people live like this, but of course there are many humble dwellings like the small two-bedroom terrace houses back home in England.'

'Ha! I love the way that you say "back home"!'

'Well, of course! It's our home, isn't it?'

'I know but what about this place? Do you feel more at home here?'

'Actually, I don't. Home is where you live your daily life, and mine is with you in our cosy semi in the UK, with our nice warm rugs on the floor!'

'So you would not exchange this marble floor for our humble kitchen tiles?'

'Not even our worn-out Chinese rug in the lounge,' he giggled, hugging her in a tight embrace. 'I'm beginning to miss our home already.'

'But this is your home, too.' Daniela was keen to pursue this topic, trying to gauge his loyalties. The issue of identity suddenly seemed very important to her. Where did her husband truly belong? Here or back in England – the place he called 'home'.

'Yes, but I don't feel very much at home here at the moment. And you know the reasons, too!' he reminded her, disgruntled, changing the topic. 'Would you like to see the rest of the house?'

'Can I?'

Caressing her cheek, he murmured, 'Remember it's our home, too. And I am the only heir – unless of course they now decide to disinherit me,' he teased.

Dismayed, she asked, 'Would they really do that, Ismail?'

He shrugged, his eyes dull. The storm he had unleashed had to be dealt with and he wasn't sure which way it was heading.

'Come, Daniela. And remember, you are not an intruder!'
Smiling, she ran after him – afraid and yet eager to take a tour of
her husband's home.

CHAPTER 23

The Sisters

Mehreen and Liaquat stood awkwardly in the courtyard of Rani's house, waiting to be welcomed, their *salaams* to be heard.

In both their heads the fearful thought hammered – how would Saher react to them? Their eyes automatically filled when she materialised from the drawing room. A brave but poignant smile played on her face.

Mehreen rushed to Saher's side and, grasping her arm tightly, she openly wept on her shoulders. Standing woodenly in Mehreen's arms, Saher was happy to indulge her aunt. Tears and tantrums were her Aunt Mehreen's domain. Liaquat patted Saher on her head, eyes sad and gentle in their pleading, tears also openly flowing.

'We are so sorry! How will you ever forgive us, Saher? On our honour and as Allah Pak is our witness, we didn't know anything about what our scoundrel of a son has done.'

'No, we didn't!' Mehreen chimed between sobs over her niece's shoulder.

Across the courtyard, Rani watched with cynical eyes from the window of her dining room.

'We've been made strangers in our own home, Saher. It's a nightmare,' Mehreen explained, wailing in a piteous tone.

'I'm so sorry, Auntie and Uncle, but please don't worry on my behalf. Believe me, I am all right,' Saher hastened to reassure them. 'These things happen, you know; perhaps I was never destined to cross your threshold as your son's bride,' she ended, looking down at the floor.

'Another woman has forced herself into our lives! We are helpless, my dear,' Liaquat added bitterly. 'Where's your mother?'

'Mother didn't know about the *goorie*. I told her!'

'You mean that when she visited us, she had no idea?' Liaquat felt faint.

'No, I didn't!' Rani's strident voice hit them from behind. Hearts thumping, they turned to face her.

Mehreen shifted from her niece's shoulder, unable to utter a word. It was left to her husband to enter into a dialogue with a sister who had always been difficult, but today had every reason to be.

'We're sorry, Sister Rani, we really had no idea! Please believe us!' he pleaded.

'Of course not!' The sarcasm was not lost on them. Rani's eyes were gleaming with hatred, ignoring her daughter's signal not to make a scene. On the contrary, she intended doing exactly that; it was her right to spill out her poison.

'So you've both come to commiserate and have the cheek, the *chal*, to pretend that you didn't know. You expect me to pardon you! How wonderfully easy it would be for you to wriggle off the hook of blame.'

Deeply offended, and hating her sister for her acid tongue, Mehreen burst into a fresh bout of tears again. 'Rani, we are suffering, too!'

'Yes, I know!' The voice had hardened. 'The difference is that your son caused it and is married, whilst my daughter has been dumped and left humiliated. Now tell me which situation is worse, my dearest sister? Yours or mine?' she jeered.

'I don't know if that rascal is married or not.' In her self-pity, Mehreen was sobbing out her own anguish. 'A strange woman has hijacked our lives.'

Dry-eyed, Rani sized her sister up and down, mouth curled in contempt.

'Mehreen, my darling, spoilt sister, if you have come to me looking for sympathy, you have come to the wrong place. This is not your beloved Gulbahar's home, but one that has been wrecked by your brat of a son. Your lousy upbringing spoilt him!'

'Rani, you're cruel' Mehreen wailed.

'I'm cruel, you say?' Rani glared her loathing straight into her sister's frightened eyes. 'Has your scoundrel of a son not been cruel to my daughter?' The words were like a whiplash.

'Mother! Please!' Saher diplomatically stepped in, horrified at the downward spiral in the sisters' relationship, and gently pulled her mother back. Liaquat, on cue, similarly pulled Mehreen aside, the image of them exchanging heated slaps at an Eid party not too far off. The sisters had slapped each other hard, much to the horror of their family members.

'I think, Mehreen, it is best that we return home, my dear,' Liaquat quietly advised.

'We're very sorry, Sister Rani.' Though shocked and dismayed by his sister-in-law's hostility, he pardoned her, empathising with her suffering and predicament. 'Mehreen, let's go! Saher, please forgive us. If anything was in our hands, do you think we would have let all of this happen to you, my dear?' His hand momentarily rested on Saher's bare head – a solid, comforting hand. She really liked this uncle and had longed to spend many years in his company. Alas, it was not to be.

'Your mother has every right to blame us. Nothing can compare with what she is experiencing … But do you know how much it has hurt us, too? Parents become such vulnerable creatures when their children grow up … and our child has betrayed us in a terrible way. If only we had another son, then I would have married you off to him, Saher, just to keep you with us!'

Saher was now openly crying, touched by his words; he had always cared about her welfare.

'It's all right, Uncle. I know how much you respect and love me. Please don't mind Mother. She's just upset, that's all.'

'She does mean it, Saher, but we don't mind, do we, Mehreen? Let's go.' With Rani's mouth open, ready to blast them with another bitter comment, he steered his wife firmly out of the courtyard. He had no wish to hear more. Respect for Rani had now reached zero. In some ways, she was worse than his wife, with her daggers always drawn. He wondered how two sisters could hate each other so much. Gulbahar was so different. If only … he sighed, turning to Mehreen. Today, his mission was to protect his vulnerable wife.

Shooting an aggrieved look at her sister, Mehreen followed her husband.

'Why does Rani hate me so much? Why is she taking it out on us? We did not bring the *goorie* home. It's not fair,' she muttered.

They stood outside Rani's *hevali*, both experiencing a strange reluctance to return home. The *adhan* from the central mosque's minaret calling the faithful to prayers reminded Liaquat that he had missed his earlier prayers.

'Wait in the car, Mehreen, whilst I join the prayer congregation in the mosque.'

*

In the car, Mehreen pulled her shawl lower over her forehead and shed bitter tears. When would she wake up from this nightmare? The wedding had to be called off. Explanations needed to be given to the gossiping mouths.

'Ismail, I wish you were never born!' she cried aloud, peering out of the car window at the village at work – its routine calmly dictated by the cycle of rural life.

There was a tractor tilling the soil, making grey parallel lines in the field. Further along the road, laden with sugarcane plants, a truck was leaving the village, billowing out clouds of dry dust in its wake. Mehreen saw Bina, the rubbish lady. Her shawl tied round her head and *shalwar* pulled up to her ankles, Bina, squatting on her heels was energetically shaping another cow-dung cake between her palms before rising to slap it on the wall of the school. The village school committee had kindly granted her a small portion of the back wall for her cow-dung cakes. This was in appreciation of her work as the school cleaner and keeping the area around the school free of any animal droppings. She had already done her rounds of carrying baskets of rubbish out of many homes. Into one of her baskets, she had swept the streets of all the animal droppings and waste. She very rarely threw it away on the rubbish tip. It went either on the fields as manure or on the school wall for fuel. The sun would dry the cow-dung cakes within two days, ready to be used for the cooking fire. Bina supplemented her meagre income by selling them to the poorer families who, like herself, could not afford gas, wood or oil for their cooking.

A herd of about 30 black milk buffaloes, their lower bellies coated with mud, stood in the far field, languidly soaking up the sunshine before being herded back into the shade of the farmhouses.

Over on the other side of the school playground, lively schoolboys in their crisp white shirts and black shorts were playing cricket. Teenage girls from the girls' school, dressed in their demure blue and white starched uniforms with matching white chiffon *dupattas* draped across their chests or over their heads, walked in groups of twos and threes on their way home. They were either hugging their bundles of books to their chests, or carrying them in holdalls slung over their shoulders, their heads bent, chattering away.

'Ah, what it was like to be a schoolgirl,' Mehreen mused, remembering her own time at the convent school the three sisters had attended in the city. The village school dismissed as not being good enough for the education of his daughters, their father had a chauffeur-driven car ready to bring his daughters to and from the city.

Mehreen could not help noticing one girl hanging out on the fringes of the group, looking decidedly sulky. 'Just like our Rani!' she smiled wryly. It had always happened that way with them. Gulbahar would be with Mehreen, chatting away, while Rani would deliberately hang back – moody and miserable. They could never make out why she behaved like that. Nobody had. She always held back. Her scowling face not only distanced her sisters, but also put other schoolgirls off. Her punishment was that she was left to herself, to wallow in her own misery.

Rehmat Ali, the vegetable man, aged before his time, pushed his wooden cart of fresh fruit and vegetables carefully displayed in raffia baskets. He was halfway through his door-to-door round, keen to sell to those who could not be bothered to go to the shops or the bazaar in the nearby town. Mehreen had no idea where Rasoola bought their vegetables. Was it with the meat from town or were they from their local general store?

'This is our very small world that we have happily embraced,' she thought. 'Yet, we sisters have cut ourselves off from the rest of the village. We've no idea what's going on in the nearest home and have nothing in common with our neighbours, who often live poverty-ridden lives.'

Their wealth and status divided them from their neighbours, so very few friendships were cultivated within the village. Most of their personal friends – other landowners, politicians and lawyers – were from other villages or towns.

'Our children have gone to other worlds, Arslan to America, while my son went to England, bringing back their foreign worlds and customs into our lives. Is that what we deserve? My Ismail has brought home a foreign bride and made me a laughing stock!' Bitterness lapped through Mehreen's body again.

Another car with one of Rani's friends from the city drove up outside the gates. Fearful of being spotted and forced to enter into inane conversation Mehreen ducked her head. Now, surely, all of Rani's friends and the local village folk would be aware that Saher had been jilted and there would be plenty of gossip-mongering and commiserating. As the local saying went: 'One's daughter is everyone's daughter. Everyone's honour.' And Saher was a daughter they were immensely proud of, looked up to and consulted on all legal matters. Above all, she was the daughter of Mistress Rani – the widow they respected highly and who had won over their hearts and minds with her generosity, despite her unsmiling face.

She was kind, and quietly saw to all the needs of the five village widows and their offspring – from the weekly flour ration, to the dowry and the wedding dinners she sponsored. Similarly, she had donated a portion of her land for the village school. The funeral dinners for the village poor were mostly taken care of by Rani. As the village Imam said, she did 'grand' charitable things, but did them with dignity and deliberately kept a low profile. She never made a show of it, always quietly tucking crisp notes into the hands of the poor visiting her home.

CHAPTER 24

The Meeting

Rasoola was in a blazingly angry mood and very keen to share it with her companion. 'Begum, this set-up suits you, but I am being strangled alive under this bondage of slavery. Thanks to Master Ismail bringing home a foreign wife, I've escaped from a life of servility! I've decided that I will not work for anybody, in *any household,* from now on.'

'What?' Begum cried, thinking that the arrogant, sharp-tongued Rasoola had lost her head.

'Only in the mosque. There no one will boss me … Of course I will be offering my services to Allah Pak. However, not in this village mosque as everyone knows me here. I'm off to the city once I've saved enough. I intend finding proper paid work in a factory and renting my own living accommodation.'

'At your age?'

'Me … I am only in my late forties.'

'Well, it's not that young!' Begum scoffed.

'I want to be mistress of my own destiny. Begum, we humble people also have a right, don't we? Why is it our lives are chained to the households of the rich, where even our breathing is being controlled by our masters? Mehreen suffocated me.'

Begum gawped, unable to understand how someone like Rasoola could think like this. Her view of the world was so different.

'Stop exaggerating,' she replied dismissively. 'But I wish you luck, my friend, if you are bent on "escaping" this so-called rotten life. I'll not forsake you … if you ever need anything, you'll always be welcome here. Listen, I have an idea. Why don't you stay a few more days and work in Mistress Gulbahar's household? You like Mistress Gulbahar, don't you? And I will swap by going to work in Mistress Mehreen's home. They desperately need someone till Ismail goes back. I'm sure Mistress Gulbahar won't mind. I'll have a word with her right away.'

'OK, that's great. But what about when Mistress Mehreen comes to Mistress Gulbahar's household – what do I do? Disappear into thin air?' she scoffed. Had Begum not thought of that?

'We'll get you a wig and a mask!' They both giggled, their wiry bodies shaking.

'What about the rest of me? Drape a sack around me?'

'We'll have to mummify you all over to hide your skinny waistline.' They carried on giggling loudly, not caring that Begum's husband could hear them. In the bedroom, lying on his bed, Ali grunted. Fuming, he was bent on getting rid of Rasoola as soon as possible! He had heard everything. The wicked woman was a terrible influence on his kind, loyal, but very gullible wife. Rasoola both abused and betrayed her masters. The young Mistress Laila had manipulated his poor wife and look where it got everyone. Now it was Rasoola who had his wife under her skinny thumb.

The cracking sound of monkey nuts had begun again. It looked as if the two women on their portable beds on the veranda were bent on finishing every single darned monkey nut from the two-kilo bag in one night! They were both mad. Did they not want to sleep? They had to get up early in the morning. Master Haider was entertaining an up-and-coming politician and his wife from Islamabad.

'And if they dare to cough later after this gorging on the nuts, I'll throttle them both with their shawls. But which one first? Perhaps my wife, for letting that wicked woman into our home!'

*

Heart thumping, Mehreen stood outside her son's bedroom listening for any sounds. Liaquat had already gone to bed. Hand trembling she turned the handle, took a deep breath, and pushed the door open. Daniela, on seeing the older woman, immediately guessed her to be her mother-in-law. Mehreen's eyes fell on the woman who had 'stolen' their son.

Daniela's gaze was the first to fall, pulling her bare legs under her on the bed as her nightgown only reached above her knees.

'*Assalam alaikum,*' Daniela shyly offered.

The Muslim greeting from the *goorie's* mouth startled Mehreen, her head reeling. Eyes closed, she tried to block out the woman in front of her. Daniela sat up, assessing the older woman. There was no smile on her face but neither was there hostility. Only the look of someone lost. Mehreen opened her eyes and could not help marvelling at Daniela's very short, shiny, golden hair under the light.

She did not become aware of her son's entrance until he stood beside her.

'I'm glad, Mother, that you've met my wife,' Ismail sheepishly offered.

Switching a dull gaze on her son, Mehreen left the room, unable to enter into a discussion with him yet. Ismail raised his arms in defeat. Daniela looked away in understanding.

'Glad that we've got that over and done with. You've now met both my parents,' Ismail offered lightly.

Daniela shook her head, unable to stem the tears from falling on her hands.

'Daniela! What's wrong?' Ismail was beside her, squatting on the floor.

'Your mother hates me, Ismail!'

'No, she doesn't. She's just in a state of shock.' He hotly defended his mother.

'I know!' Daniela wiped her cheeks with the back of her hand. 'I wish to God I'd never come!'

'A bit late now, gorgeous, is it not?' Ismail teased. 'It's OK! Cry if you want to!' he offered, sitting beside her on the bed.

Out in the courtyard, on the bottom step of the staircase, Mehreen leaned her head heavily against the balustrade. A dull ache spread through her body.

'Allah Pak, help us all! The nightmare is endless,' Mehreen muttered, shuddering.

She heard footsteps but didn't bother getting up.

'Mehreen?' Liaquat was worried on seeing his wife's posture and put his arm protectively around her. 'Come, Mehreen!' he gently urged.

Blindly, she followed him up the stairs.

'There's *haram* taking place in our household, Liaquat-ji, and we are helpless to prevent it. Our son is sleeping with a woman, who might not be his wife!' she murmured.

'They are legally married, Mehreen, please don't say such things! Our son wouldn't do that!'

'Would he not?' she rasped, panting. Liaquat was shaking his head. Their son couldn't possibly be living openly in sin with a woman. Cohabiting with a woman outside of marriage – surely their son had not crossed parameters of such cultural and religious importance and etiquette?

He aggressively dismissed his wife's fear. 'Don't ever utter such nonsense again, Mehreen!'

Downstairs, Daniela stared around her new room. It was past midnight and she couldn't sleep and needed fresh air. The omelette Ismail had made was proving to be too spicy for her. A chilli lover she was, but now pregnant, she felt everything heaving inside.

'Ismail, I feel sick. I need fresh air.' She tried to nudge him awake but he was sound asleep.

Out on the veranda, the dark shadows of the pillars strewn across the moonlit courtyard intimidated her. Padding barefooted across the cool marble floor, Daniela reached the sink and threw her head over it, emptying out her stomach.

Her mother-in-law, unable to sleep, had happened to be looking down into the central courtyard from the rooftop gallery and had seen her. Bent over the basin with another stomach spasm, Daniela was about to go back to her room when she saw the shadowy figure of her mother-in-law standing a few feet away. The two women stared at each other. Mehreen noted how Daniela held her arm tight across her waist.

Eyes widening, Mehreen leaned against the marble pillar. Softly padding across the courtyard and reaching her room,

Daniela closed the door firmly behind her. It was a long time before she was able to sleep. When she next opened her eyes, the village cocks had merrily begun their morning crowing ritual, almost as if they were competing with each other. This was soon followed by the sound of the *adhan* from the local mosque.

She whispered behind her husband's shoulder, 'Ismail, please don't wake me up. I haven't slept a wink all night.' Smiling, Ismail hugged her closer.

'You can sleep all day, my darling, but that is if you don't want to go sightseeing in Islamabad,' he whispered, nuzzling his face in her neck.

'Oh! How wonderful!' was Daniela's answer. 'Give me a couple of hours then!'

'OK, lazybones … You'll get to see all the sights in the next couple of days.'

CHAPTER 25

The Party

Horrified, Laila watched her daughter turn the corner with the musicians heading for her father's *hevali*.

'Shirin, come back.' Panicking and lifting up the hem of her *shalwar*, Laila ran after her daughter, beseeching her Allah Pak above the clear blue sky to come to her aid. For he now held her fate in his hands. Her daughter had disappeared straight into the crowd of men. Laila leaned against the mud-baked wall of the woodcutter's house and held up her face to the beaming hot rays of the sun.

Behind her closed eyelids, images of the past plagued. Renowned for his generosity, her father hosted big celebratory parties, like on the day of her brother's birth, the *haqiqa* party, to which the whole village had been invited. Her aunties, Mehreen and Rani, accompanied by other women, had danced to their hearts' content till their legs collapsed under them, inside the inner courtyard, swaying to loud music, away from the men's lewd gazes. The male guests, too, had enthusiastically rejoiced with several *bhangra* dances to the loud beating of the drums in the *hevali's* outer courtyard, with the crowd spilling out into the village lanes. Not only that, in every home some form of celebration had taken place; for their landlord was blessed at last with a son after many years of waiting. Everyone wholeheartedly shared in his joy.

Laila could not get enough of cuddling her young brother and holding his face against her cheek and running down to Begum for his feeds when he refused to suck his mother's breast. The two aunties also fought for time to demonstrate their affection for their longed-for nephew. Both with young children of their own, they had stayed for over two weeks to help look after their sister, the new baby and all the guests who constantly streamed in to congratulate the family. Many relatives stayed for days, lingering on to enjoy the festive atmosphere and the marvellous feasts on offer. Rani was often late in breastfeeding her own young daughter, Saher, as she supervised the feasts served in the dining rooms on her sister's behalf.

The crushing ache for her parents' home leapt and then died a quick death. 'It was the past – I have to let go of it,' Laila mourned.

The loud drumming of the *dhols* and the music of the Scottish bagpipes sounded the same as on the day of her brother's *haqiqa* party. The musicians had played tirelessly all day, their faces lit with joy for the popular *zemindar*, their aching hands and limbs forgotten. Master Haider, in return, thanked them by lavishing expensive gifts on them.

Today's celebration marked Aslan's homecoming; it had been a long time since the *hevali* sounded with the celebratory beat of the drums. Sadly, the villagers mourned that their landlord had been robbed of the biggest celebration of all – his beloved daughter's wedding.

They also felt sorry for Chaudharani Gulbahar for not giving birth to any other children. 'What it all shows,' Rasoola had cattily twittered to her friend, 'is that all the bags of money notes in the world, or dozens of gold bangles on your wrists can't buy you fertility or furnish your womb with children. That's a blessing indeed, my friend, that only Allah Pak can bestow on us.'

Did Allah Pak deliberately overlook others? The village women shook their heads. The baker's wife could not stop herself from voicing aloud her thoughts and commiserating, 'None of the three sisters is blessed with many children. Rani has just one daughter, but of course she was a widow, so that accounted for it. Mehreen has only one son and Gulbahar one son and one daughter. Between the three of them only four children. They are indeed impoverished in numbers, though there are so many rooms in their homes.'

'Well, they could not compete with Khanum Bibi with her brood of eight and still happy to go on adding, boasting philosophically, "If Allah Pak has blessed me in this way, why should I turn away his blessing?" Can you believe it, sisters! Is the woman mad or merely witless?' The women agreed unanimously that Khanum Bibi was utterly 'witless'.

'She's also cruelly skilful in delegating the childcare to her three teenage daughters. The poor girls have lost their own childhood – they've been propping babies on their hips and changing nappies since they were seven. And what about when all the kids grow into adults, ready for marriage? Has that idea never dawned on her? Or would she delegate that task to others, too? She nearly died during the seventh birth – or was it the eighth, I can't quite remember,' the baker's wife bitchily continued.

'Perhaps with the active breeding she has no brain cells left,' gossiped the greengrocer's wife, who prided herself on having a perfect family of two sons and two daughters; sons were needed for looking after the parents, but daughters were a *must* for household chores.

Quite a few of the women were still openly speculating on the fertility status of the three land-owning sisters. With so much wealth why did they not seek medical help abroad? Was it the sisters or their spouses who were infertile? Yet, all three? Surely that couldn't be right. It must be the sisters themselves! Especially Mehreen, the pompous one. Heads had unanimously nodded.

'No woman wishes to be infertile!' Begum angrily cut short the women's malicious gossiping. They had all forgotten that she, too, was childless. 'It's all in Allah Pak's hands! And don't forget fertility is not guaranteed for life – either for yourself or your daughters. I, too, have no children. You've not commented on my fertility status! Do you think I did not want any? Mean women! So shut up, the lot of you! Bitching about the very household that is feeding you!'

A loyal servant and a personal friend of Mistress Gulbahar, Begum found it very painful to listen to their spiteful chit-chat and was especially cross with Rasoola for starting it all off. She let her know it with a mighty scowl.

Seething, the women shut up, pursing their mouths and exchanging hate-filled, heated glances. Why was Begum always championing her mistress? What was wrong with her? Did she not enjoy a bit of harmless gossip?

As soon as Begum had left the room, it was their cue to happily begin again. After all, they had to entertain themselves. This time the gossip hinged on Mehreen, the most reviled of the three landladies! It was the master tailor's wife who started the ball rolling. For she was thoroughly fed up with Sahiba Mehreen's complaints about her dressmaking skills, in particular with the positioning of the darts and zips on her dresses!

'With all her snooty airs and graces, just look where it has got her as a woman – she has lost her only son to a foreign woman! On that subject, tell me, ladies, why do all these rich folks, *waderas*, want to send their children abroad, when they have all the worldly goods they need at home? The sisters have had their fair share of family calamities, haven't they? From Laila's marriage to the potter's son, to Ismail bringing home an English bride and to Saher being jilted by her cousin.'

They all chuckled under their breath, afraid of another one of Begum's scoldings raining down on them. They still had to be fed by her. 'Now where have Mehreen's airs and graces disappeared to? If one overreaches, Allah Pak, let me tell you, has a delicious way of dropping us down to earth. Well, our almighty Mistress Mehreen's ego has been badly bruised, by the look of things!' The tailor's wife stopped, seeing Begum reappear in the marquee with a tray of drinks. The women enjoyed another bout of sniggers before reaching for the glasses of cool home-made sherbet.

CHAPTER 26

The Jealousy

Mehreen was sitting on her bed, debating whether to attend her nephew's celebration party.

'There'll be so many people there, practically the whole village. I can't face them, Liaquat-ji!' she pleaded, desperate to be spared the public ordeal of meeting people. Surely her husband could not be so cruel as to force her to go.

'Mehreen, we cannot, and will not hide from the outside world because of this foreign woman!' he calmly informed her through gritted teeth. 'You'll have to be strong, my dear. I know that it's difficult, but you'll have to face the world sometime. Imagine what it has been like for your beloved Gulbahar with Laila's elopement. Do you not recall her suffering? It is a really challenging time for her now with Laila back in the village. You've always been so caught up with your own life that you leave absolutely no time for others!' He tried hard to disguise his sarcasm, but she heard it distinctly. Jealousy always made her ears sharper.

'I beg your pardon!' Mehreen squeaked in indignation, unable to believe that her husband could be so cruel to her, especially at a time like this. 'Are you telling me or suggesting that I'm a very selfish person, who has no time for others?'

'No!' He tried to calm her: 'I'm just reminding you what it has been like for others in crisis.'

'I know jolly well what it has been like for my sister, Liaquat!' Her fiery eyes scorched him, omitting the 'ji' to his name.

'Mehreen, I'm just pointing out to you that your sister is suffering, too … She has paid a costly price for it – with her heart!

Laila destroyed her health. In fact, my own heart aches for your dear sister.'

'I know your heart aches for her. Sometimes I wonder if you married the wrong sister!' Mehreen burst out, unable to hold back the bitter words or stop the vicious pangs of jealousy tearing at her. 'You'd rather have married Gulbahar, wouldn't you?' Her voice was now dangerously calm, as the ugly secret carried inside for so long slipped out in the open.

'What?' Liaquat scanned his wife's face, taken aback.

'You don't want me. It's her – Gulbahar – who sits on the throne of your heart! You're always going on about her!'

'I … I …' Lost for words, the colour had drained out of Liaquat's face.

'Well?' she challenged, mouth contemptuously curved at the corners.

'What a terrible thing to say, but I'll forgive you!'

'Forgive me? How grand of you, my dear husband! But it doesn't take away the horrible thought in my head that you desire my sister!'

'For goodness sake, woman, shut up!' he shouted, thoroughly livid, his voice raw. 'Are you mad?'

Mehreen was drowning in a flood of jealousy. All along, she had suspected that her husband had lost interest in her. But there was always a special light in his eyes and a softening of the face when he spoke about or to Gulbahar. And surely that could not be mere brotherly admiration? Heart sinking, her knowing eyes were agonisingly sketching a concrete picture in her head. It wasn't her imagination playing tricks on her. A slow tide of colour crept up her husband's neck under her feverish gaze.

Sickened, she turned away. She had her answer – at last.

'Mehreen,' he paused, then changed the subject. 'Mehreen, are you going to the celebrations or not?'

'Yes!' she replied flatly, eager to be rid of him. She remained standing with her eyes closed. Somehow the *goorie*, the unwanted guest in her home, no longer posed as great a threat to her world as her own eldest sister.

*

Liaquat had waited long enough; the matter of the *goorie* had not been sorted out yet. Entering their bedroom, he hovered behind Mehreen, experiencing a strange awkwardness.

'Mehreen, no matter what our son has done, we still have to face the world.' He waited for her to say something, but only silence greeted him.

'At least our son is not dead!'

'How dare you!' Mehreen sprang into life, shoving his arm away from her shoulder, panting.

'See how you react when it comes to his well-being. Tell me what's wrong,' he asked tenderly.

'Nothing!' she whispered. In her head the words 'You and Gulbahar' hammered. 'What about *her* – the *goorie*? I mean, shall we take her, too?'

'Do what you want!' was his parting shot. She was left staring at the closed door, a stranger in her own home.

*

In the party crowd, Shirin peered from behind the man with the big chest, her hand brushing his arm. He stiffened, looked down, and then a wicked look flashed across his face. He winked at his friend, the village butcher, standing beside him. Shirin was eagerly peeping through the gap between the two burly, sweaty bodies and missed the wink.

Wow, to have in their midst the landlord's granddaughter. The man with the big chest smiled with pure malice. A golden opportunity, not to be missed, had danced straight into his fat palms and he wasn't about to let it go to waste! Fixing a smiling mask on his face, he kindly proffered his chubby, roughened hand to Shirin.

'Want to get a better view, my little one? Let's get you in front.'

Shirin eagerly nodded, craning her neck to see his face. The look on his face troubled her somewhat, but she reluctantly took the man's hand, hating its warm grasp. She looked over her shoulder, wishing all of a sudden that her mother was there, too, as the big-chested man aggressively pushed through the crowd. Shirin shielded her face from the male bodies with her small hand. Then she was in the front – facing the two marquees outside her grandfather's *hevali*.

Led by their jockeys, three horses cantered around in the open ground in front of the rows of chairs set out for Haider's relatives. There were six grand-looking chairs with padded seats and tall backs, all vacant at the moment.

Shirin began to watch with interest, her eyes on the horse and rider.

*

Gulbahar remained in her room; her son's homecoming party no longer mattered, only the vision of the departing figure of the little fairy from the *hevali* gates, after catching a glimpse of her grandfather.

She heard Mehreen's raised voice in her room. Through the dense fog in her head, Gulbahar waded back to reality.

But the image still beckoned of the beautiful fairy striding away; head and chin held high, a small figure in a white cotton frock, the bouncy auburn curls swinging and glinting in the sun. It was the pert little mouth, the soft lips pursed tight, that captivated the anxious audience.

Gulbahar recalled the stunned look on Shirin's face the moment her eyes had fallen on her grandfather. Her uncle's downstretched arms, ready to pluck her up for a ride, were totally forgotten. In front of a stunned crowd of guests, she had left the side of the big-chested man and had walked up to one horse, looking up at the rider, and not realising that it was her own uncle, had innocently asked:

'Can I have a ride on your horse, please?' Those who could hear, including her grandparents seated in the front row, caught their breath and gasped. Everybody wondered what would happen next.

Arslan was totally taken aback, but a smile of delight washed over his face and he leaned down to pick her up, arms aching to fold her in a warm grasp. Then, Shirin heard a cough and swept round to locate it.

She was startled to see that it was the older man with the reddish hair and cold blue eyes. Shirin paled; she was at the party of that horrible man who had made her fall. Arslan watched in a daze as his niece slipped away through the crowd and out of sight, leaving over a hundred pairs of eyes staring after her and at each other.

'How could you, Gulbahar?' her sister's accusing tone frightened Gulbahar – the eyes glowing, the body aggressively poised beside the bed.

'Why have you disturbed me?' Gulbahar wanted to shout. But her mouth wouldn't open.

'How could you, Gulbahar?' the irate sister repeated. Gulbahar had never before glimpsed such fury in her sister's face.

'What's the matter, Mehreen?' Gulbahar quietly uttered, still fighting the ache inside her for the fairy.

'How could you?' Mehreen spluttered for the third time. 'How could you take on Rasoola, after what she has done?'

Gulbahar's eyes widened.

'What? Is that all?' The fog in her head was dashed away. Sitting up, Gulbahar composed her features. There was a lot going on behind her sister's dark fury-ridden pupils and burning cheeks.

'I'm sorry!' she softly offered. Diplomacy was the best option with this sister.

'Is that all you can say?' Mehreen screeched. Gulbahar's eyes traced the planes of her sister's face. This did not sound like Mehreen's normal tantrum. And Gulbahar didn't have long to speculate.

'I hate you!' Mehreen pelted her sister with her venom.

Gulbahar's body shot up straight, heart thudding.

'Mehreen!' she quailed, nervously tugging at the end of her *chador* lying over her pillow.

'I'm sorry,' Gulbahar tried again. But Mehreen was ruthlessly bent on punishing her.

'I hate you!' she lashed.

Her eldest sister, her protector all her life and who had even made an enemy of her middle sister on Mehreen's behalf, was utterly devastated. Tears of self-pity blurred her vision.

'Give me back my husband, Gulbahar!' The agonised words electrified her sister, trying to grapple with their meaning. What was her spoilt sister saying?

Through parched lips, she uttered, 'Mehreen, I know you are upset about Rasoola, but what rubbish did you just utter now?'

'Return my husband to me!' Mehreen repeated. No fury this time, only misery.

Gulbahar reached forward and slapped her sister straight across her cheek. Stepping back and cradling her smarting red cheek, Mehreen slid down into her sister's armchair, eyes downcast.

'Liaquat likes you! It's you he really wants!'

Gulbahar's ears burned, eyes aggrieved. Even her daughter's elopement had not wounded her as much as her sister's accusation.

'Do you realise what you are saying?' Gulbahar hissed in despair. 'How dare you sully my ears with your wickedness! Have you actually flipped, Mehreen?'

But her sister was beyond caring, the words just fell out of her mouth.

'He has always loved you, Gulbahar!'

'Mehreen, stop!' Gulbahar shouted, striding across the room, wanting to get as far away as possible from the dirty swamp of Mehreen's twisted imagination.

On unsteady legs, Gulbahar fled to the fresh air – to the sanctuary of their rooftop gallery.

CHAPTER 27

The Falling Out

Massi Fiza was in a mighty hurry to reach her friend, Rukhsar, with the news about the *goorie* in a *shalwar kameez* and the drama of Shirin angrily striding out of her grandfather's *hevali*, leaving her grandparents and the guests wide-eyed and open-mouthed. The *goorie* was accompanied by her infamous husband, who had brought catastrophe to three households. She was dressed in a turquoise *shalwar kameez* suit, her legs discreetly covered, and a matching taffeta *dupatta* draped over her head. Apart from her fair freckled face and her golden fringe, she looked every bit a *desi* woman.

'She indeed made a spectacle. They had come out, in the open ground, just as Mistress Gulbahar had walked back into the *hevali* after seeing her granddaughter dramatically leave. Arslan had got off his horse and stormed into the house. Master Haider then went inside, too, his mouth tightly pursed.'

'It was a quite a do, Rukhsar-ji. You should have been there,' Massi Fiza expanded, her eyes lingering on the necklace box lying on the cushion in front of her. Rukhsar gave her full attention to Massi Fiza. 'Oh, I wish I was there.'

'Well, why you don't come along? The party is still in full swing. You've been invited like everyone else in the village, and the meal has not been served yet. Begum boasts that there will be so much to eat and plenty of meat.'

Rukhsar looked at her friend in disdain, 'Oh, what do I care about meat,' she loftily informed her neighbour. 'My husband through his hard work has ensured that meat is served twice a day in this household. So, Massi Fiza-ji, these landowners' feasts mean nothing to us. Our palates do not salivate for Haider-ji's dinner feasts!'

Embarrassed and feeling well-rebuked, Massi Fiza reddened down to her scrawny neck, and was quick to defend her own diet and station in life. 'We don't all roll in gold, my friend, or have the means to enjoy meat even once a day. Do you know how much red meat costs? Some folks like us have to depend on rich folk's parties for a lavish meal.'

The sarcasm was not lost on her friend. Eyeing a bristling Massi Fiza with her mouth angrily pursed into a fine line, Rukhsar laughed aloud. 'Sorry, I did not mean to offend you. Let me go and fetch my shawl from the other room. I can't be bothered to change these clothes. They'll have to do, but I do need a special *chador* to match this suit.'

Forgetting her necklace set on the cushion cover, Rukhsar walked out. Massi Fiza was taken aback by this strange occurrence. For the first time in her life, Rukhsar had left her valued property lying unguarded. And Massi Fiza was all alone with it.

And the butcher's daughter's five *tholas* worth of necklace sparkled mischievously in front of Massi Fiza's eyes. Massi Fiza stared in utter fascination. The sound of running feet made her quickly snatch her gaze and, straightening up, she leaned her body far back in an effort to distance herself from the gold.

Rukhsar dashed in, breathing ragged, the shawl in one hand, anxious eyes falling straight onto the cushion cover with the gold necklace.

Massi Fiza was mortally wounded; blood rushed through her brown-pigmented cheeks.

'Your gold is still here, Rukhsar. Not walked off into my *kurtha* pocket!' she stiffly informed her dear friend, feeling utterly betrayed.

Rukhsar neatly crimsoned. After an embarrassing pause, she picked up the necklace and muttered, 'I'll see you downstairs in two minutes. I've one or two things to sort out here.'

Deeply affronted, Massi Fiza was already out of the door, leaving her friend to hide her jewellery. Calling her youngest daughter to lock the necklace set in their safe, Rukhsar knew she owed her friend an apology, but hoped nevertheless that Massi Fiza would understand. Gold was such a temptation; even saints were said to be tempted by it, and siblings fought over it. Therefore what was to stop her humble *paisa*-earning neighbour from grabbing it, Rukhsar reasoned with herself.

Later, as they walked side by side in the village lanes, Rukhsar diplomatically ignored her friend's tight-lipped silence and hostile manner, not wanting to mar this rare occasion of her leaving her home to attend a party. The real reason was, of course, to catch a glimpse of the *goorie* wearing a *desi shalwar kameez* and that was why she decided to honour Master Haider's son's homecoming party with her presence.

At the entrance of the marquee, the friends stiffly parted company. Massi Fiza eagerly went searching for Rasoola, for news of all the latest goings-on in the *hevali*. Discreet and faithful, Begum would never utter a word against the family she worked for, unlike Rasoola who had no scruples whatsoever in parting with any information.

Rukhsar, with a dignified step, reached the side of Bano, the tailor master's wife. There were plenty of suits to be stitched for her daughter's wedding trousseau. A warm conversation with the wife always helped; quite a few rupees would be saved. Didn't the other village women try the same approach with her by cultivating her friendship for the sake of a few rupees on the gold items?

Massi Fiza, still bristling and highly indignant, kept her back firmly turned to her neighbour, whom she could no longer call a 'friend', let alone a 'sister'.

'She thinks I'm a thief! That I would actually run away with their gold!' Massi Fiza was mortally aggrieved.

CHAPTER 28

The Departure

Laila gave up, sitting down in the courtyard, ready to vent her misery in an outburst of tears, but concern for her daughter stopped her from doing so. She tried again.

'Shirin, we're leaving! Do you hear me?' Laila's belligerent voice had little impact on her daughter's rigid figure. 'Shirin, we've been here for nearly two weeks. Your father misses us. Don't you feel sorry for him? We've got to go back to Islamabad.'

'But, Mummy, you said we were going to stay longer! Begum said she was going to bring me *jallabies*.'

'We can buy *jallabies* on the way!' Laila hardened, not wanting her daughter to eat even a morsel from her father's home.

Fuelled by rage, Laila flew around the two rooms, collecting her belongings, in no mood to tolerate her daughter's tantrum. Even if she had to drag Shirin physically she would do so. For today was her last journey. In resignation, her eyes skipped bitterly over the humble contents of the small living-cum-bedroom. Her husband could do what he wanted with this place but she would never return.

'Shirin!' The firm voice had her daughter scrambling down the stairs with a sulky pout. A glimpse of her mother's eyes sobered Shirin immediately.

Swallowing a sob, she offered, 'I'm sorry, Mama.' Flinging her arms wide around her mother's body, she cried, 'Let's go! I don't like it here, either … you're always crying here, Mama, and I hate that beastly old man living in the big house!'

Putting her hand in her mother's grasp, Shirin pulled her towards the door.

'Wait! We must sweep up the dust from the floors before we leave.'

'All right, Mama,' Shirin shrugged, wondering why her mother bothered tidying up such a shabby place, and they were leaving anyway.

*

The flies were buzzing around her face, but Gulbahar ignored them, leaning her head against the tiled wall.

'Mother?' Arslan stood behind her chair.

Her sister's words 'Return my husband to me' were raging through her head.

'Mother, are you OK?'

'No, Arslan, I'm not OK!' Her agonised reply startled her son.

'My world is falling apart. The people I've loved have all betrayed me. My Laila destroyed us and today her daughter shunned us. An hour ago my sister, whom I doted on all my life, struck a blade through me.'

'What? Auntie Rani?'

'No.' Gulbahar collected her wits about her, shaking her head. She must not, could not repeat any of the vile stuff her sister had uttered to her son. At the moment, she could not forgive her sister for this, but one thing was certain, she had to get to the bottom of the matter.

Arslan was now looking over the rooftop railings, his eyes on the two figures in the village lane. In despair, he watched Laila dragging a large suitcase with one hand whilst holding onto her daughter with the other. That young, beautiful thing was weighed down with a bulging rucksack over her shoulders. An agonised cry ripped through him, startling his mother.

'Look, Mother, there they go! Well done, you have driven them away! That's what you and Father wanted, wasn't it?' He clapped his hands in mockery, mouth twisted. On shaking legs, Gulbahar got up to see, to make sense of his words.

The two figures in the distance elicited a cry of anguish, nearly choking her. Yes, they had driven them away. And paradoxically, the beautiful fairy, the little *pari*, had punished them. Not only had she fled from their *hevali*, but was now fast striding out of their lives; turning her back on them – without even knowing who they were.

Gulbahar's eyes could take no more and she sidled away from her son's side. He watched until his sister reached the bus stop on the main GT trunk road.

'Laila, the landlord's daughter, waiting to catch a local bus in a queue of common people. Mother, that's what one calls life's poignant incongruities,' Arslan cynically mused.

A man was helping them with their luggage onto the bus. No manservant or brother to accompany them – just a kind stranger coming to their aid. Arslan stood lost in thought, as questions raged through him: 'Who am I? Which world do I belong to? To America or this country? What sort of man have I become to let a beloved sister walk out of our lives?'

'A coward – losing his faculties,' his mind retaliated. 'I've got to get out of here!'

Down below in the men's marquee the party drums and the *bhangra* dancing were in full swing. His father would have to entertain, but he, Arslan, had no intention of going anywhere near that marquee today.

*

The bus skilfully wove down the mountainside. Shirin's English nursery song 'Baa, baa, black sheep, have you any wool?' echoed inside the crowded vehicle. The passengers did not understand the English song but most smiled or praised the pretty little girl. Laila did neither; her *chador* was pulled firmly up to her chin, her face pressed against the bus window as she gazed out at the rugged terrain. Laila wanted to wail aloud.

'All come to nothing! Ten years of heartache …' she bitterly mourned. Her parents' hearts of stone were not melted.

'Mummy, you are crying again!' Shirin loudly accused, causing the elderly, burka-clad woman sitting behind them to peer over Laila's shoulder and ask softly, 'My dear, are you all right?' Laila paused and then replied, 'I'm sad at parting from my loved ones.'

'Are you going far?' the woman persisted, staring at Shirin's dress and looks. This was no ordinary village child.

'This is my last journey,' Laila determinedly told the kind but nosey lady.

'Mummy?' Shirin was horrified. 'But Massi Fiza still has my best pink frock with her washing!'

'Daddy will buy you dozens,' Laila assured her, a wry smile crossing her face. Finally, she had chosen her husband over her parents, but she would never give up on her brother.

'Mummy?' Shirin questioned, her small, chubby hand touching her mother's wet cheek.

Laila hurriedly wiped her face, eyes shining with pleasure. God had indeed blessed her; she would provide her daughter with all the support she needed and allow her to marry whomever she pleased. All people were equal in her mind; there were no boundaries – only the prejudice and human arrogance that created them. She pulled her daughter close, hugging her.

'Daddy will be waiting with a bag of delicious *jalebis*, my princess.'

Peeved, Shirin declared, 'But I wanted Begum's hot *jalebis* from the party. You didn't let me have any!'

'Quite a greedy girl, aren't you, my darling?' Laughing, they both looked out at the beautiful view of the valley below, as the bus continued to snake down the pass.

*

'Gulbahar.' Haider saw his wife huddled against the headboard, face hidden behind her *chador*. Begum's *chappals* clicked behind him, forcing him to signal with his hand for her to retreat. Immediately obeying, Begum's eyes remained on her mistress as she left.

Touching his wife's face, Haider asked with marked concern in his voice, 'What's wrong, my *jaan* – my life?'

Mehreen's awful words were still stinging Gulbahar's ears, words that she could not share with her Haider.

The ceiling fan was purring away; down in the courtyard the muffled voices of the relatives and guests could be heard. Inside the room, heavy silence reigned.

'Does she hate me so much that she won't talk to me now?' Haider wondered.

'It was not my fault that the girl walked out. Gulbahar, what could I do?' The defensive tone had little impact on his wife. Her gaze remained fixed on the appliqué pattern of the quilt cover, the silence stifling them both.

'Please say something, Gulbahar,' Haider gently urged.

At last his wife's lips parted. He barely heard her whisper, 'Everything I loved, I have lost. I trust no one.'

Indignant, Haider quickly added, 'I'm here. Your son is still here.' Gulbahar raised her bleak eyes. 'A sister I doted on has now become my enemy. Where did I go wrong, Haider-ji?' Her 'Haider-ji' merely blinked, taken aback by her question. This was not what he was expecting.

'Who?' he asked, his body language now aggressive, resentment flushing through him. His poor wife had spent half of her life caring for her sisters' welfare. He waited.

Gulbahar's eyes were squeezed shut, unable to repeat Mehreen's ugly words, but the hurt and bitterness burst forth, startling her beloved husband.

'The one I protected all my life, whilst alienating the other, has now become my mortal enemy … She hates me so much, Haider-ji.'

'Who? Rani?'

'No! Mehreen!' The anguish shuddered through her in the cool room.

'Mehreen?' Haider echoed, bristling with hatred for that sister, his fists tight. 'What has she done now?'

Mehreen always brought out the worst in him. Her petulant and childish manner utterly angered him, making him resent the hours his wife had ploughed into this sister's welfare in the early years of their marriage. Later, to save Mehreen's marriage, Gulbahar had unwittingly established a routine of regular visits to Mehreen's household. As many as three times a week! Gulbahar alone was responsible for Mehreen having successfully reached middle age with her marriage still intact.

'This is my orphaned sister. Please give her another chance,' she had fervently appealed to Liaquat so many times. And Liaquat would invariably give in, lost, no doubt, in the look of pure gratitude etched on Gulbahar's face.

Gulbahar, in short, had become Mehreen's surrogate mother, father and older sister all rolled into one. Haider secretly considered Mehreen not just a 'spoilt halfwit', but a very clever 'manipulator'. And one who knew precisely how to pull at her sister's heart strings. At times, he had felt like throttling her, for that is what he would have done if he had been her husband. How Liaquat coped with such a wife was a mystery to Haider. Perhaps he, too, like Gulbahar, was jointly responsible for what Mehreen had become; for both had generously indulged her.

Not Haider! He had kept well away from her since her full-blown tantrum after he had told her what he really thought of her. 'Your husband might put up with your childish manner but I'll not! Behave yourself, you silly, good-for-nothing woman!' he had thundered at her. Mehreen had treated him to a scandalised stare and never forgave him for that cruel remark. A chilling distance had reigned between them ever since. Haider happily welcomed this arrangement. As long as his wife kept that sister away from him, she could do what she liked. His sweet gullible Gulbahar, however, would never allow a single soul to utter anything against her *ladli* Mehreen.

So what was it, Haider asked himself, that Mehreen had done today, to bring this mother-like figure, this loyal sister, to feel so utterly betrayed and wounded? There might be a silver lining in this matter, Haider chuckled to himself. Perhaps, at last, his wife would see sense and wash her hands of her spoilt sister.

'Please, Gulbahar, tell me!' he urged, caressing her cheek. It was his gentle, coaxing tone that was Gulbahar's undoing. Her anguish spilled out, drowning them both.

'She said, "Leave my husband alone!"' As soon as the words left her mouth Gulbahar froze, wanting to shield herself from her husband's gaze. What had she done? Colour flushed through her cheeks, a testimony of her shame.

At last Gulbahar peeped at his face, trying to gauge his

reaction. Her Haider-ji merely looked bemused. Surely he had understood what Mehreen meant?

Haider did understand. What he didn't believe was what she was saying. His wife was the purest woman on earth. Therefore what was the crazy sister trying to imply? Deeply interested, his eyes swept over Gulbahar's coloured cheeks and nervous gaze.

'Your sister is a strange creature – I don't know what silly remarks she has made, but please don't be distressed by them, my beautiful wife.' Gulbahar nearly wept at his kindness and sensitive words. Cheeks still stinging with the heat of shame, she raised her eyes to examine her husband's face. Her heart soared in joy, but she could not take any chances; she had to make sure that he fully appreciated the gravity of Mehreen's wicked words.

'She meant it, Haider-ji, she thinks … she thinks …' she stuttered, unable to go on.

'Go on, Gulbahar, say it, please!' he coaxed. The words, however, would not be uttered. She tried again.

'She thinks Brother Liaquat likes me more than her …' Gulbahar's voice trailed away; she was now trembling under the full weight of her husband's scrutiny.

He was silent for a long time, realising that this was not as clear-cut a situation as he had assumed. Perhaps Mehreen was not so stupid, after all. His wife's lowered gaze told its own story. Tiny messengers of unease were shooting across his brain. How many times had he seen Liaquat in his wife's company? The laughter he had heard, the sense of rapport and intimacy between them. Had his unwitting and innocent wife been stolen under his very gaze?

Haider shook his head ruthlessly, dismissing the mean, ugly thoughts that were unworthy of him. How could he let his train of thought sully his pure wife who was rarely in the company of strange men!

'Gulbahar, what do you think?' he gently prompted, noting the shape and thickness of her eyebrows. His darling wife was already distressed. 'Tell me, Gulbahar, do Mehreen's nonsensical words have any ounce of sense or substance in them? Or has she simply become crazed?'

'I don't know!' Gulbahar truthfully replied. There was no doubt Liaquat liked, respected and paid homage to her, but surely not in that way!

'Almighty Allah Pak!' Her husband's cold voice cut her off from her thoughts. He snorted, 'Then I suggest you find out. Tell him what his wife has said. Also, challenge her. Put the record straight. If she's wrong, that is it.'

Gulbahar's eyes fled to her husband's face. 'What are you saying?' She paled. 'How could I possibly ask him that?'

'What is the alternative? To get involved in an argument with Mehreen? Do you want me to ask Liaquat, "Are you in love with my wife?"' The voice was icily cutting. Colour again flooded Gulbahar's face, richly flushing down her neck. In shame, she hung her head.

Haider slid off the bed. She had to ask, clawing desperately at straws, 'Haider-ji, you yourself … don't have any doubts, do you?' He stopped halfway across the room, his back to her. 'No, I have none, my *jaan*, but Mehreen does. I know my wife, but does Mehreen know her husband? I suggest you ask him what he feels for you!' he finished dismissively. The door shut firmly behind him.

'I hate you, Mehreen, for what you've done! At my age! A grandmother! How *besharm* you are to suggest such a terrible thing. You are crazy, Mehreen, to be jealous of your own sister!' Gulbahar cried.

She closed her eyes in horror at the images that her husband's words had conjured. That Liaquat loved her. Unforgivable! How could she possibly look him in the eye again? He was like a brother to her. How could Mehreen and Haider say such things?

The door opened. Gulbahar lifted her head. Begum was hovering near the door, anxiously waiting for some signal. Gulbahar turned her face the other way and slid down into her bed. This was a matter she couldn't possibly repeat to anyone, not even to her housekeeper. Dismayed, Begum stayed for a few more seconds, then reluctantly withdrew. Master Arslan's homecoming party had turned into a disaster with virtually no one hosting it. The prince, on whose behalf the village was eating half of the land's revenue, had angrily ridden out on a horse into the fields.

Haider-ji had disappeared into his office. And Mistress Gulba-har was lying in bed, in the middle of the day, while the *hevali* was filled with guests.

Begum dutifully shrugged her shoulders; it looked as if both she and Rasoola were to take care of everything. Ali could look after the male guests, whilst they saw to the women. What were faithful servants for if they didn't support you in your hour of need? She just prayed that Mehreen, who was outside in the women's marquee, didn't spot Rasoola at any time. That would be disastrous and there was still the question of the *goorie*, who was here in the *hevali* somewhere, and in all likelihood would keep the women guests agog with excitement at her presence. For apparently everybody was anxious to catch a glimpse of the first European woman in their midst and one who had scan-dalously stolen one of their countrymen from a fiancée. Begum smiled wryly – imagining all the women making a beeline for the white woman.

CHAPTER 29

The European

'The *goorie* is here!' The excited chant of the bricklayer's wife had everyone's necks craning towards the opening of the marquee.

'Where?' spluttered the baker's wife over her bottle of Mirinda drink, swivelling her sagging, heavily pleated neck, and swinging the large *chumkay* earrings weighing down her small ears. The baker had generously deposited three wads of crispy notes into the goldsmith's hands. So it was very appropriate that his wife had the opportunity to display their worth and by extension her husband's wealth.

'I can't see her!' she groaned in frustration, eager to set her eyes on a real white person, a European. 'There she is! Can't you see her?' the bricklayer's wife proudly pointed out. 'Dressed in green and with her head covered!' she cried out in awe.

'Where? You're having me on!' The baker's wife excitedly scrutinised her friend's face for telltale signs, for she was known for playing pranks on her friends. Her eyes followed the bricklayer's wife's index finger.

'Ah, yes,' she sighed in wonder, taking her fill of the white woman.

'My God, she's covered her head! No wonder I didn't spot her. And she's wearing a *shalwar kameez* suit! Doesn't she look absolutely gorgeous?' Respect for the foreign woman dressed in local clothes beamed on her face; this woman from another land had made an effort to fit into their society. She could now almost pass for a native. The bricklayer's wife sat back in her chair and let her eyes follow the *goorie* down the aisle of the marquee.

At the back of her mind was the smug thought of their *tandoor* supplying the *chappatis* to Mistress Gulbahar's household in the summer. So it was very apt for her to cultivate the friendship of the landlady with the 'white' daughter-in-law. A visit or two to that household was definitely merited in the next few days.

*

Daniela, the centre of attention, found herself hemmed in by an excited entourage of women burgeoning in size by her side. Some were openly staring while others were grinning. Her cheekbones aching from the forced smiles, she shyly greeted them with '*salaam*' and was glad to slide down onto the seat next to a woman who blushed with delight, looking down at her hands.

Daniela was very conscious of her appearance in her mother-in-law's suit, a couple of sizes too large. Keen to blend in, she had expressed her desire via her husband to wear the local dress and her mother-in-law had quickly obliged by handing her one of her own best, heavily embroidered suits. Above all, she desperately wanted to speak the local language, join in their conversation and thereby bond with them. Two or three simple sentences with a strange accent didn't go very far. Her chiffon *dupatta* was slipping off her head again.

'Allah Pak, her hair is shining like gold … and so short!' whispered the baker's wife to Massi Fiza, hovering three steps behind her. Massi Fiza assented, coldly muttering, 'I told you, didn't I? I was the first one to catch a glimpse of her and not just her head, but her bare white legs, too! Oh, they were so white! She covered them up after the first day.'

Massi Fiza abruptly stopped, remembering saying the same words to her neighbour. Still very much smarting from the insult, she now regretted both the service and the friendship she had offered to the goldsmith's family. It was she, Massi Fiza, who provided a more valuable service than Rukhsar twice over. After all, she was not running up to their chamber every day for jewellery repairs. The extra dollops of detergent she had scooped into the buckets of water for those fussy girls' delicates, all those chiffons, the painstaking ironing of laces and shawl trims afterwards – all literally for free.

And, of course, her role as the village news lady, the 'village radio' as Jennat Bibi cattily called her, was simply indispensable. Forever tied to her upper chamber and guarding her husband's stock of gold, Rukhsar had no idea about what was going on in the village. She, Massi Fiza, despite her physically hard, but honest work, had more fun in life than her neighbour, for she got to visit all the homes, walk down the streets and breathe the fresh clear air in the open fields. And her two sons working in the nearest town had promised her that when they had saved enough money, they would build her a bigger house, with at least three good-sized bedrooms. That was her special dream. But her youngest one was busy squandering her hard-earned money gambling. Now, she didn't know where he was, and she was worried sick. The word 'Taliban' kept hammering in her head. She prayed and prayed for her sons' welfare at the Friday *Juma* prayers, the only time she entered the village mosque in her clean crisp white clothes and Kashmir shawl.

'Ah well, I'm not the only one with lousy offspring!' she consoled herself. 'Look at poor Mistress Mehreen whose son has brought home a *tofa*, a white woman, now sitting decked in clothes that look so odd on her. Not at all elegant.'

'Their' Saher would never go near those clothes. That successful lawyer woman was universally known in the village as 'the stylish one'. And where was Mistress Saher anyway? That was a question that ran through many heads. Life was indeed strange. The two villages had been preparing for a big wedding and what did they get instead? A foreign woman in their midst, reputedly the wife of the man who was supposed to be getting married.

'Oh!' An excited, four-year-old girl in a pink frilly frock dashed past Massi Fiza's legs and bounded straight against Daniela, startling her and those around her.

The flushed, panting young mother reached Daniela's side just as she was lifting the girl onto her lap. The child innocently stared up at the woman's smiling face.

'*Hello! Ap ka nam kiya hai?*' Shyly Daniela asked the girl's name. Electric silence gripped the women guests. The white woman had actually spoken Urdu! Unbelievable! Awestruck, some of the women stared in wonder. The blushing mother stood happily smiling over Daniela's shoulder.

'*Iss ka nam Firoza ha,*' she shyly informed Daniela.

'Her name is Firoza,' she repeated in clear English, her heaven-sent opportunity to show off to her fellow village women her competence in the language of the *Engrez*, the rulers of India. And this in turn indicated her high level of education – up to a BA – fourteen classes successfully passed, and English being her favourite subject.

Daniela beamed at the woman. '*Acha, bohot khub hai*, what a lovely name!' Daniela tried some of the phrases she had learned from Mrs Sheikh, their school dinnertime supervisor, her heart racing at the reaction she was eliciting from the women. She introduced herself, 'My name is Daniela … Ismail's wife.'

The mother smugly nodded her head, heat rushing into her cheeks with pride as she slyly pulled a chair next to Daniela. The baker's wife and Massi Fiza grimaced enviously, exchanging a pointed look. That '*fourteenth jamaat*' upstart daughter of the milkwoman had cleverly managed to ingratiate herself with the white woman by showing off some words of *Engrezi* she had picked up at college! They could bet with their lives that she would not be vacating her chair for anyone!

'In fact she'll be glued to that seat as long as the *goorie* remains by her side! See if I am proved wrong,' Massi Fiza challenged her companion. 'If only we, too, knew some words of *Engrezi*.' Massi Fiza was already in the thralls of a fantasy in which she was having a personal conversation with the *goorie* and in English.

'Oh, goodness me, look behind you! We are blessed, ladies, with a real drama today!' the baker's wife whispered loudly into Massi Fiza's ears, swivelling her plump neck round to follow the direction of Massi Fiza's eyebrows, pointing to the marquee entrance where Mistress Rani and her daughter stood.

'They are here!' Massi Fiza marvelled, her head automatically turning to the *goorie*. Daniela was busy with the little girl on her lap, and so did not see Saher coming to stand next to her. It was only as she heard the familiar, impeccably clear tone of Ismail's fiancée that she glanced up, the goose pimples standing up on her arms.

'Hello, I hope all these women have not been bothering you?' Saher politely asked of the woman who had turned her world upside down.

The little girl was forgotten, the smile whipped away. Noting the stylish cut of Saher's suit, Daniela felt frumpy in her mother-in-law's oversized *shalwar kameez*. Also, she could not help admiring the immaculate make-up, the lip liner accentuating the shape of the full, soft mouth. Daniela carried on staring, forgetting her own appeal once again. Dressed as a native, her Western beauty shone through. A touch of lip gloss was all she had on but the translucent glow of healthy cheeks and freckles made her look amazingly alive.

Whilst the two women were locked in admiring one another, Rani hovered stiffly behind her daughter, taking her first glimpse of the woman who had 'stolen' her daughter's world from her. And Rani made no effort to hide her personal loathing of the 'robber'!

'Let the village women see! I couldn't care less!' Her cheeks flamed, unable to fathom her daughter's idiotic behaviour in talking to 'that woman'. When she could stand it no longer, she poked a finger in her daughter's back. Saher gave her mother a steady, cool stare, signalling her message: 'There's already a *tamasha* in the making, Mother, please don't add to the drama yourself. The village women are having a wonderful time in comparing us two women. Don't you add to their fun, please.'

Indeed, the women assembled in Master Haider's marquee were charmed by Daniela, who provided a feast for their eyes; their roving eyes comparing the 'foreign' woman to their countrywoman! Strangely, Daniela, the *goorie*, appeared more *desi* than Saher. In their eyes that *vaqil* – lawyer lady – had never been the epitome of a village woman. She lived a different life-style; spending her nights at home and her days in a plush office in a large city. Dressed in crisp, smart outfits, designed by the best tailors in the city, Mistress Saher had never stooped to enter the door of their humble tailor mistress, Zeban.

Of another class, wealthy and with an excellent education, she was aloof in every way and never mixed properly with the semi-literate village women. They only caught rare glimpses of her, in her car mainly, as she visited her Aunt Gulbahar, or when she used to walk around in the fields in her teenage years with Arslan. They knew for sure that Saher would be snapped up by some city tycoon.

Daniela gently placed the child on the ground. 'She looks lovely in her frock!'

'Thank you!' the girl's mother gushed. Daniela drew the little girl closer and then, startling everyone, including the little girl herself, kissed her on the cheek. Her mother swooned up to seventh heaven, and the envious women around her with children of their own could take no more.

Saher looked on with mixed feelings, not quite sure what to make of a gesture that had electrified the crowd around them. It would never have occurred to her to go around planting kisses on strange children's faces. But this was a *goorie*. Perhaps that was what they did back home. She couldn't help, however, voicing a cynical remark to their foreign guest. 'You have made the mother's day. Look, the poor woman – she's blushing all over with delight.'

Daniela reddened. 'Oh, did I? I could not help it … I love children. I work with young children, you see, and I am now expecting …'

She abruptly stopped, praying that Ismail's fiancée didn't understand what she had been about to utter. How cruel under the circumstances.

An awkward pause led to Saher helpfully stepping in and asking, 'Where's Auntie Mehreen?'

'She was here with me and then I don't know where she went.'

Pity overwhelmed Saher. 'Shall I take you inside the house, Daniela? This marquee is only for the village guests – family members are expected to go inside the *hevali*.'

'Oh.' Daniela glanced up at the older woman menacingly hovering behind, knowing for sure it was Saher's mother, taken aback by the look of naked hatred on the woman's face. With trepidation Daniela asked Saher, 'Are you sure it's all right for me to go inside? I don't want to cause discomfort amongst your relatives.'

The thought of sitting next to Saher's glaring mother made her shudder. Disconcerted by the remark, Saher smiled warmly and held out her hand to her *sokan*, distressing her mother and shocking the other women guests in the marquee.

Massi Fiza's eyes widened, shooting a look at her friend, Rukhsar.

'Daniela,' Saher beckoned, voice firm. 'As Ismail's wife you are now a family member and deserve to be in a better place than here. Come!'

Blushing, Daniela got up, her hand held in Saher's grasp. Eyes filling up, she mumbled her gratitude to the woman whose world she had unwittingly toppled.

'Thank you, I would like to go inside.' She pulled the flimsy *dupatta* back on her head, but it stubbornly slipped down again. Saher gently offered, 'Don't worry, Daniela, about covering your head. Nobody expects you to. See, my head is bare!' Daniela happily let the chiffon fabric slip to her shoulders. Saher's appraising eyes swept over the Englishwoman's layers of fine soft hair, the smile momentarily slipping from her face as the thought echoed in her head, 'That's what Ismail fell for!' Elegant body poised and held straight as in court, Saher led Daniela out of the marquee. Skilfully winding their way through rows of tables and chairs, both were acutely aware of the spectacle they made, walking hand-in-hand with Saher's glowering mother in tow.

*

The women guests left behind had mixed feelings; some admired Saher for her noble heart.

'Fancy offering your hand to the very woman who has taken your man!' the baker's wife slyly twittered. 'What do you say, ladies, isn't our lawyer lady generous?'

'But then as a *vakil*, she knows how to save her face!' drily quipped the bricklayer's married daughter, who had eagerly extended her stay in the village just to attend Master Haider's party. She had secretly made sure of coinciding her visit with the arrival of Master Arslan from America. Such a good-looking young man and she was not quite over her teenage crush on him yet. Not that he had ever paid her any attention. 'In his eyes we are just the gauche, village girls!' she had bitterly reminded herself.

'Yes, you are right, dear,' the milkwoman eagerly agreed with the bricklayer's daughter as she sat at the same table.

'How is it possible for any woman to treat another *sokan* like that? Well, if it had been me in Saher's place, I tell you that the *goorie* would have lost a handful of that short golden crop!' The baker's wife laughed aloud at the scene in her head, of soft silky tufts of golden hair coming away in her hand. In reality, she knew she could never carry out such a deed.

She pulled herself up short from her thoughts, spotting half of a bowl of meat disappear before her very eyes. Bali, the greedy bricklayer's wife, had skilfully scooped up all the lean chunks of meat in the *shorba* curry, leaving but pieces of bone and gristle. With the equally greedy Resham, the baker's daughter-in-law, poised to dip into the bowl, there would be no scrap of meat left; or only the bony ones miserably swimming in the reddish, chilli meat soup. Did they have no manners or concern for other people?

Raising her hand, its fingers studded with four rings, she signalled down the aisle to the waiter serving them. As the wiry young man sidled to her table, she grabbed one bowl of meat. Not to be outdone by the other women's greed, she spooned away four of the best chunks of meat onto her plate, telling herself philosophically, 'If they are all eating heartily, why shouldn't I?' After all, meat was what most of them looked forward to at such parties. And it came in abundance at Master Haider's party, A very generous man he was; he had dozens of *daigs* of meat cooked.

Next, her eager eyes were scanning the table for the trays of rice and roast meat. Did that daughter of Hafiz not think of passing the tray of roast meat around? Now, the milkwoman was reaching for it. Good. Then she began to count in her head. If everyone on this table plucked two pieces of roast chicken, what would be left by the time it reached her? Her face fell. Just then, the other waiter leaned over her shoulder and placed a tray of steaming roast chicken in front of her, nearly hitting her hand as she reached to pick two pieces, already able to taste the succulent meat juices even before she had placed a morsel of it in her mouth. Their village chefs were the best in the land, their landlord host made sure of that.

With her plate full, the baker's wife happily settled back in her seat to enjoy the feast. This was the best part of any party, especially when there was no obligation whatsoever to offer presents or money garlands.

Meanwhile, things weren't quite right in the outer courtyard. The news of Haider Sahib's granddaughter snubbing the family by strolling out of the *hevali* upon seeing him had begun to circulate around the women's marquee. And now rumour had it that mother and daughter had left the village.

'*Bechari* Laila came to celebrate her brother's homecoming and did not even peep at the party and now she's gone, poor mite!' mumbled Massi Fiza. The sweetmaker's wife had come off the same bus that Haider's daughter had taken. Jennat Bibi had been to consult her *pir* again. This time to get a new 'good luck' *tweez* containing a special prayer for her daughter-in-law to conceive again.

'Is it not a sad state of affairs with these *big* people,' the milk-woman loudly tutted, whilst spooning a dollop of rice pudding into her mouth. 'You just don't know what's happening inside these marble-slabbed *mahals,* with their posh roof galleries.'

The baker's wife passed the tray of roast meat to the goldsmith's wife. Rukhsar stared down at it, contemplated it for a few seconds, then pushed the tray aside, eliciting a strange look from the woman sitting beside her as she slipped two pieces onto her plate. What was wrong with the goldsmith's wife's stomach?

Massi Fiza snorted, covertly keeping her eyes on Rukhsar's plate from across the table. What was her neighbour trying to prove by loftily snubbing the meat? Perhaps they did have meat twice a day in the goldsmith's house!

CHAPTER 30

The Adoration

Someone was in the room and, thinking it was Begum, Gulbahar remained with her back to the door.

'You wanted to see me, Gulbahar.'

Liaquat's cool voice had her sharply turning round and she noticed immediately that he didn't address her with the customary title of 'sister'. Now that she came to think of it, he very rarely had, or perhaps only in the early days of his marriage. Afterwards, he had addressed her by her forename. Today, she wished that he had used the conventional term 'sister' and regretted her impulse in calling him upstairs.

The tall man hovering in the middle of the room was intruding into her and Haider's intimate world; and here she was in bed. Heat rushed into her cheeks. Liaquat was a *ghair mard*, with no right to enter her personal space. Then she brutally reminded herself that this was her brother-in-law, a close friend. Not some stranger. He had been in this room so many times; it was natural for all her family members to enter the bedroom. 'So why am I behaving so idiotically?' she chided herself.

All of a sudden hatred rushed through her. But for whom? Mehreen, for soiling her world? Or for the man standing in front of her who now made her feel so self-conscious. Both had in equal measure spoilt her *pak* world, her pure world. Nervously, she draped her *chador* around her shoulders and over her head, discreetly tucking the stray strands of wavy grey hair under the soft cotton lawn fabric, and dropping its loose folds over her chest.

Venturing to look him directly in the eyes she immediately

dropped her gaze; the heat of shame flooded her body under the sheet.

'All those hours I spent enjoying this man's company. He was always there to lend a listening ear and offer me moral support, especially after Laila's elopement.'

Just as she had always been there for Mehreen, Liaquat had been there for her.

Blind! BLIND!

Adoration!

No attempt was made at masking it. It was there in the coal-black eyes; only her sister's anguish had now made her see it. Gulbahar rose tall out of her misery, in command once more. No matter how painful, she would protect her vulnerable sister. A dignified way had to be found to deal with the matter and salvage what she could from this ugly scenario.

'Yes, I did, *Brother* Liaquat,' she affirmed, laying particular stress on the word 'brother'. 'Please sit down.' Inside she was debating fast.

He waited. Wondering. Was it some errand for the party? Perhaps to supervise the cooks in the kitchen area. Gulbahar, trusting his skill in managing catering staff, normally delegated this task to him.

'Brother Liaquat.' A reddish hue ran through Liaquat's olive cheeks. The twice-repeated word 'brother' was not lost on him. Slightly perturbed, he continued smiling but knew something wasn't quite right. His eyes widened, becoming alert to Gulbahar's body language and demeanour; the way she had tightly cloaked herself with her *chador*, the manner in which her eyes kept wandering off.

Mehreen!

'Sister Gulbahar, is everything all right?' he finally asked, quickly adopting the conventional form of address. Gulbahar's body relaxed, thankful for his sensitivity. Raising her head, she was able to look him squarely in the eyes now. His use of the word 'sister' had established conventional parameters of communication for them.

'No! Brother Liaquat.' Her tone was cool, eyes drifting away again. 'Especially not according to Mehreen.'

It was Mehreen!

'It has been a tough time for Mehreen, Sister Gulbahar, with the *goorie's* arrival and Rani's animosity,' he rushed to explain, sighing in relief, his body relaxing.

'Yes, it's been tough for our poor Mehreen … The world has not been very kind to her lately, has it? She seems to be cut adrift – from everyone, from you, her husband, her sisters, her son and all the way down to her servants.'

'I know!' he heartily agreed, smiling.

A pause.

'You and I have not helped matters.' The voice was dipped so low, he barely heard her.

'What do you mean?' He moistened his lower lip.

'My sister is very unhappy – in her marriage … I mean, at the moment.'

'You mean in her son's relationship with the *goorie*?' he coldly questioned.

'No! In her relationship with you!' She stopped, eyes squarely meeting his again, letting him mull over her words.

'I don't understand,' he uttered finally after a long silence, gaze lowered.

'I see.' She chose her next words with care, wondering how she could communicate with Liaquat without hurting him or embarrassing them both.

'Perhaps you don't understand your wife well enough or are unfamiliar with the crazy ideas locked in her head.'

Liaquat paled. It was to do with the subject his wife had broached with him earlier.

She waited.

'Mehreen is a foolish woman! We both know it,' was his defiant reminder, a reddish hue now chasing down his neck. Gulbahar looked away.

'Yes, my sister is foolish at times.' Voice raised, face flushed, Gulbahar came to her sister's defence. 'But perhaps she has reason to entertain such ideas … Tell me, Brother Liaquat, are they all fiction, part of her imagination? Is she just being paranoid or has she jumped to some sort of semi-accurate conclusion? Liaquat-ji, as you well know, I love Mehreen more than my life itself at times. Therefore, I would never do anything to hurt her knowingly or unwittingly, but would always want to protect her, as I've been doing all my life. A vulnerable creature, little things make our Mehreen jealous and insecure in herself. At this moment in time she feels threatened by the apparent respect you have for me and the close friendship we have shared over time as brother- and sister-in-law. I know you respect me very much and I am truly honoured by that, but it hasn't helped my poor sister. Has it?

'I know Mehreen remains a challenge for you – she's not the easiest of people to live with. As we don't have a brother our-selves, Rani and I have always regarded you as such. I truly value your friendship, Brother Liaquat. You've been such a pillar of support to me after Laila's elopement, but we remain, in the eyes of Allah Pak and of the world, a brother and sister. There can never ever be any other form of friendship between us.

'I'm sorry to say that life doesn't always offer us everything we want or give us the choice of people we want in our lives. On the contrary, we should make the most of what we have and hold onto it and protect it. Therefore, we must rid Mehreen of these harmful ideas of hers. No doubt you've been a wonderful husband to Mehreen by indulging her every whim and support-ing her throughout. Go on doing that. Spend more time with her.

'Again, I thank you from the bottom of my heart for the support you gave to me in the years after Laila's marriage. More than my own two sisters! However, things are now much better. Please don't overburden yourself on my account – I have a son and a husband there for me.

'Just make Mehreen feel incredibly special – that would please me enormously!' Gulbahar breathlessly ended her long speech, assessing his reaction. He had let her talk uninterrupted, noting the beseeching look in her eyes, the unspoken words, 'If you harbour any feelings for me, then do this for me.'

He continued to stare at her, bemused by her words. She had said everything and he had been put firmly in his place. He sadly accepted the wisdom of her words but he wouldn't leave without making his feelings known. That was his right as a human being.

'Why couldn't Mehreen have been more like you, Gulbahar?' He could not disguise his longing.

Colouring, Gulbahar dropped her gaze, but felt it pertinent to add with a nervous laugh, 'Brother Liaquat, you may not like me very much if you truly knew everything about me.'

Smiling wryly, he honourably let the matter rest. His eyes, however, revealed what he truly felt: 'For me you'll always remain the perfect woman.'

Formal and correct as always in his bearing, with a nod he strode out. Sadly, he knew that she would never confide in him nor seek his company again. Outside her room, on the balcony, he stood lost in thought. Where did one trespass onto the boundary of what was right and what wasn't? How far was it socially and morally acceptable to enjoy the company of one's sister-in-law, before it entered the red zone? Had he already, so unwittingly, entered that dangerous zone? If so, how long ago was that – a decade?

He shuddered, uttering aloud, 'The things we do!' as he went down into the central courtyard. For the last few years, he had visited Gulbahar's home almost twice a week – on some errand or other. In his heart of hearts he knew it was a pretext to spend some enjoyable and intellectual moments in her company. She was an extremely witty woman and they shared a love of poetry, reciting Rumi, Ghalib and Faiz Ahmed Faiz to each other. Mehreen, on the contrary, did not even know which century Ghalib lived in and often scoffed at her husband's reading habits.

Haider was in conversation with Begum under the veranda. Quietly and not wanting to draw attention to himself, Liaquat passed them by and returned to the men's marquee where dinner was being served; but he had no appetite for food.

*

Upstairs in the *hevali*, Gulbahar tucked the quilt cover closer around her body. How naïve and blind she had been for so long, in not recognising what was staring her in the face – Liaquat's attraction for her.

'Strict parameters of behaviour must now be in place! I have compromised my female modesty with Liaquat. No *ghair mard* will ever pass through my bedroom door,' she vowed to herself.

She was the one who hastily drew back from the sight of other men, keeping behind doors in semi-purdah. Haider adored her modest, shy ways, immensely pleased with her. Distressed at the thought, she cried '*Haram*! *Haram*!' Only her sister's shocking words had alerted her to the 'immoral' path that she had unwittingly taken.

'Allah Pak, I love my husband and am a pure woman in my heart, soul and body. Please forgive me!' Gulbahar closed her eyes, beseeching her Lord's forgiveness.

Downstairs, Haider had out of the corner of his eye noticed Liaquat pass by. After instructing Begum about the distribution of sweets to the guests, he strode up the stairs to their bedroom.

＊

His wife was lying down. Gulbahar heard the firm footsteps and waited with trepidation for Haider to say something. Pulling his legs up, he sat beside her, looking down at her. She turned, her nervous eyes scanning his face, seeking any telltale signs of what he was thinking. He had no intention of helping her; they both knew Liaquat had been up here.

'Brother Liaquat harbours no feelings for me, save that of sisterly respect.' How true that was she didn't care, but it was the answer that she was going to give her husband.

'Good,' was Haider's quiet reply, tenderly looking down at his wife and then, leaning forward, he kissed her firmly on the mouth and slipped off the bed. The matter was closed. Gulbahar stared after him, confused and relieved, yet still uneasy that her husband wasn't going to discuss it further. That was it.

Next it was Mehreen.

CHAPTER 31

The Wooing

'Oh, God, what have I done! And why did you tell him, Gulbahar?' Mehreen was shaking as the full horror of the situation dawned on her. Her inner demons had now smothered two families. The thought of the contempt in Haider Sahib's eyes had her writhing in horror. He already held a low opinion of her, but this ... She wanted to flee.

'I think it'll be best if I don't show my face for some time to my brother-in-law. Please pass on my apologies and beg his forgiveness.'

Gulbahar laughed. 'Don't worry, Mehreen, he won't eat you.'

'But he'll freeze me with his icy blue eyes and frosty manner,' her sister was quick to respond.

Their laughter rippled around them in the starry night up on the rooftop gallery where they had more privacy; the guests were still in the *hevali*.

Mehreen was about to move away when Gulbahar, on impulse, pulled her back and kissed her hard on the cheek. 'I love you so much, my sister – never let anything stupid ever come between us again.'

'I love you, too, *baji jaan*. That is why I couldn't rest tonight without asking for your forgiveness. Please say you've forgiven me!'

'Yes, I have, as always!' Gulbahar felt light-headed. 'Thank you, Mehreen, for coming to make amends. Now, go home to your husband. If you cherish that well of marital bliss then guard it and treasure it.'

'I know. Goodnight,' Mehreen called from the top step,

fervently praying that she could sneak out without meeting her brother-in-law. When she reached the central courtyard, the first person she saw was Rasoola, her housekeeper, hovering near one of the pillars. Mehreen froze, but strangely felt no anger, passing the 'wretched woman' without a word or any ill thoughts. Rasoola did not matter any more; she could work wherever she wanted. What mattered was that she had her sister back!

Next, she had to woo back her husband.

*

Liaquat was sleeping under the veranda on a portable bed. Mehreen touched his foot, startling him awake. Steadily holding his gaze, she beseeched, 'You'll be cold here – please come upstairs.'

She was about to touch her husband's hand when their son's bedroom door opened. Mehreen froze, watching Daniela step out, her body swathed in a long creamy gown.

Daniela, too, was startled to see Ismail's father lying on the veranda, just a few yards from their door. Why was he there? Spying on them?

Struck by another attack of nausea, Daniela ran into the courtyard for fresh air and stood next to the basin, hanging her head over it, her gown billowing out from behind.

In the shadows of the pillars on the veranda, husband and wife exchanged a quick glance. Mehreen knew about the pregnancy, but Liaquat didn't.

'Our son is soon to be a father,' she announced softly, half smiling, deciding to break the news to him, nervously scanning his face to assess his reaction. Liaquat's eyes widened, his body tense. For Mehreen, the impact of the *goorie*'s entrance into their lives had lessened, paling in comparison beside the demons of her jealousy. She had a crisis to deal with much nearer home – with her husband. It was imperative that it was resolved without delay. Boldly, she began:

'If I've made an utter fool of myself and, as a "foolish" woman, have said some "foolish" things, then is it not right for you, as a

person of intelligence and generosity, to overlook such foolish-
ness? Please, come upstairs! We've enough to deal with, than to
be divided ourselves,' she urged, watching Daniela, head down,
glide back to the bedroom.

Mehreen turned to her husband and was disappointed by
the look on his face, reminiscent of that of a sulky child. With
dignity, she spun round and headed for the stairs. At the top her
step faltered.

No sound. No step followed.

With a heavy gait, she walked into her bedroom. In the
morning when she came down both her husband and the portable bed were gone. Listlessly, Mehreen stood in the courtyard,
listening to the jolly cawing of the crows. Blind panic swept in.
There was no servant to help around the house. If her son left
his foreign wife alone with her she could not communicate. And
her husband no longer loved her.

'I wasn't imagining it. I'm sure that Liaquat feels something
for my sister. I know I am naïve but perhaps not so naïve to
notice that twinkle in his eyes when he speaks to Gulbahar.'

In her heart of hearts Mehreen craved respect. Both Gulbahar and Liaquat spoiled her by smothering her with love but
accorded her little respect. If a single saucer of a tea set was
broken or chipped her husband would good-naturedly rush
to buy her another – a better one. If a servant made her cross,
he would anticipate her tantrum and quickly sack them. If she
quarrelled with Rani, he would intervene, eager to smooth
things over, neatly separating the two. Yet he never created an
opportunity for reconciliation.

Gulbahar was her childhood guardian; Liaquat became her
adult protector. She virtually slid from one set of protective
arms into another – ironically chafing in both. The local village
women, even the illiterate ones, held her in contempt, exchanging gossipy titbits about her. All the horrible things they said
about her, such as, 'Mistress Mehreen is spoiled, utterly selfish
and cruel to her servants' had never bothered her before, but
today she felt raw with the pain.

Tearful and wallowing in self-pity, Mehreen headed for the

kitchen. Was she not blessed with good hands? Could she not get something ready for her family's breakfast? Stepping barefooted on the cool tiled floor, she pulled up her *shalwar* and tucked it around her waist. It was a long time since she had got her hands messy with sticky dough. Slapping a *paratha* on the hot *tava* pan, she nearly scorched her finger on the buttery surface, wryly smiling at the shape – a cross between a circle and a square – and telling herself that it was nearly 25 years since she had made a *chappati*. In her father's home, there were always the servants or Sister Gulbahar. *Tava* and Mehreen never quite got acquainted. And nobody minded. Plucking the half-burned *paratha* off the pan, Mehreen reddened in embarrassment. 'Am I such a hopeless woman that I've never learned how to cook properly?'

She persevered and managed to produce a small pile of *parathas*. A funny thought struck her: 'Will the *goorie* know what a *paratha* is?'

Putting eggs to boil, Mehreen began looking in the large glass cabinet. 'If Rasoola has broken them all, I'll wring her neck!' Then she laughed aloud, spotting the dainty china egg cups with pink roses. All this rage for an egg cup!

With the breakfast tray propped on her arms, Mehreen wedged open her son's bedroom door with her bare foot. She couldn't tell who was more surprised, her son or the '*goorie*' in her nightgown scrambling to sit up on her bed. Ismail stood in front of the wardrobe mirror, brushing his wet hair.

Greeting them with '*salaam*' Mehreen shyly informed her son, 'I've made you both breakfast. I'm not sure whether she likes our *parathas*, but there is a boiled egg, too, and some cereal.' Her son rushed to take the tray off her, seeing her grimace with twinges of back-pain. 'No wonder Rasoola always complained of a constant back problem,' Mehreen silently echoed in her head.

Mehreen was awash with guilt. Mentally she was already buying lighter trays to replace the heavy steel ones. Moreover, she would employ a young man who would do chores like carrying the trays across the *hevali*.

'Her name is Daniela, Mother,' Ismail gently reminded her, placing the tray on the table. Mehreen blushed.

Daniela was smiling shyly at her mother-in-law. Mehreen stretched her mouth apart, but there was nothing to smile about this morning. Only the grooves at the sides of her mouth spread slightly.

'Mother, sit down and join us for breakfast,' he gently urged. 'Thank you for all this, but we could have made it ourselves.'

'What, make *parathas!*'

'Yes, Mum. I can cook – learned it in London … whilst doing a short stint at an Indian restaurant in Hackney. I have taught Daniela how to make all our Pakistani dishes.'

'I … I …' Mehreen stammered, watching Daniela leave for the bathroom, her eyes on the full-length silk gown. Her son followed her gaze.

'Mother, Daniela is a very nice woman – I adore her. Please learn to accept her presence in my life. And I've some news for you – we are expecting our first baby! The doctor told us it's going to be a boy. I'll not abandon her or give her up. Do you hear me, Mother? You must get used to the situation!'

Mehreen dumbly nodded. In her head, she was gasping at the picture of a small golden-haired little boy. All of a sudden, she recalled her sister, separated for ten years from the beautiful fairy, as she called her granddaughter, Shirin. Were they going to do this to her grandson?

'No!' she screamed in her head. She would not suffer that ache. No matter if the child was of mixed-race heritage; he was still her flesh and blood, too. Her shoulders straightened, and looking her son in the eye, Mehreen spoke aloud her thoughts: 'I know your wife is pregnant and I don't expect you to desert her, for that would be inhumane, and against the teaching of our faith. Pregnant women, above all, should be protected and supported by their husbands and families. But please tell me that you have actually married her – I mean a *nikkah*, my son?' She had to ask, unable to cope with the thought of a *haram*, an illegitimate birth, in their household.

Ismail shook his head, exasperated. 'Why won't you believe me, Mother? The child is *halal* in everyway. The *nikkah* was performed in a London mosque with two witnesses. I have a certificate to prove it, but it's in Liverpool.' His earnest words touched her. Walking up to him, she kissed him on his forehead. 'I believe you, my son.' It was at that moment that Daniela returned. Eyes pricking with tears, she was afraid to trespass into the mother and son's intimacy.

Mehreen caught the uncertain look in her daughter-in-law's eyes. Something tugged sharply at her and, obeying that primitive impulse, she floated to her daughter-in-law's side.

Then, placing her hands on Daniela's shoulders, she gently kissed her on the cheek. Dropping the cosmetic bag, Daniela, stunned, lifted her arms to clasp the other woman in a tight embrace. Now it was Mehreen's turn to be shocked, finding her face pressed against the cool, silky fabric of Daniela's gown. Ismail looked on, his eyes sparkling.

Both women wept on the other's shoulder, but for different reasons: Mehreen for the trauma of the last few days, and Daniela in pure gratitude for the embrace and the human warmth she received from the woman she feared would never accept her.

'Well, are you women going to carry on like this? The *parathas* are getting cold.' Ismail first spoke in English, before translating it into Urdu for his mother's sake.

Daniela and Mehreen shyly shifted apart. Mehreen's eyes were the first to fall, unable to make sense of her own behaviour. Her son, however, had the look of a man who had conquered Mount Everest.

*

From the veranda outside she heard their laughter. Her son was speaking in *Engrezi* again. All she could make out were the words 'Daniela' and 'Mother'.

Mehreen walked across her courtyard, a light-headed woman. Liaquat would be dealt with later but first she would visit her elder sister again. Gulbahar had lost her daughter and her granddaughter. She, Mehreen, wasn't prepared to lose her only son and grandson. If a foreign woman was acceptable to her, Mehreen mused, could her sister not accept a fellow national, from her own village, as her son-in-law?

CHAPTER 32

The Rivals

After a walk through the village, Saher and Daniela were taking a leisurely stroll along the pebbly stream down below in the valley. Saher had brought a designer *shalwar kameez* outfit for Daniela as a gift, making Mehreen shed more tears. Daniela had excitedly got into it straight away; happy that she was now able to blend in with the people around her, and equally happily had accepted Saher's offer of a ride out together in the evening.

'You look wonderful in this outfit, Daniela,' Saher enthused, without explaining that she had had it especially designed and stitched within hours by her own exclusive city tailor. Ismail had humbly looked on, grateful to Saher, marvelling at her ability to forgive so easily. 'This is the woman I've let down, and how nobly she treats my wife,' he mused.

He had deliberately remained behind, in the car, letting them carve out a tentative relationship, as they walked along the stream side by side.

'The last 30 years have emptied some of these villages of their menfolk to the cities or abroad,' Saher informed Daniela in reply to her question as to why there were so few young men around.

'There's nothing here in the village, apart from agriculture, to keep young, educated men fulfilled, employed and happy. Inevitably they begin to drift away, seeking a better life, nagging their families to send them abroad, being egged on by peers and friends. Many have migrated to the Middle East for work, to places like Dubai, Qatar, Doha and Saudi Arabia, as well as the USA and Europe. One has gone to South Africa, Durban, I think. Many families have borne terrible hardships in raising the funds to send their men off – borrowing money, selling land and gold jewellery – sometimes through illegal channels. Often they become victims of exploitation. Many die along the way, tragically killed in different circumstances.

'These are men, often groomed as "princes" in their homes, with little knowledge or experience of any work; they are then thrust out in a big foreign world, and have to mature overnight. And from abroad, that is if they manage to find work, they send money back home to support their families. They return as different men, often sunburned beyond recognition, those working in the Middle East for instance, and with a worldly-wise look about them. Life is never quite the same, and they struggle to come to terms with living two lives, torn between two countries and two cultures. I'm sure you see this pattern of migration in Britain.'

Daniela nodded, letting Saher continue, finding the topic of immense interest.

'It's a global predicament, but a very sad one, too. It leads to broken families, and heartache and misery unleashed by years of separation from loved ones. Yet, ironically, the whole process is palatable to all back home, sweetened as it is by the material wealth it brings. The remittances sent back keep everyone happy, transforming people's lives overnight, effectively keeping a mother's and a wife's nostalgic tears and sighs at bay.

'What about the children? Surely they must be affected by all of this?'

'Of course! The fathers become strangers to their offspring and the children get used to life without a father's presence in the home, relying instead on other male relatives. On the other hand, poverty is hard to cope with, Daniela.'

'You are right, it's a global malaise affecting the whole world. Women and children do end up paying a costly price. I often wonder how some refugee families or spouses of asylum seekers in the UK are coping back home. I would hate to be separated from my Ismail. My father's family migrated from Ireland – that's an island near to England, so I am half Irish.'

Saher gently but drily reminded the other woman, 'Women

here have little choice but to grin and bear it. What would you rather have, a husband by your side or a better standard of living for your children? Materially, they all benefit. If you were to peep inside one of those homes, the places are often stacked with all sorts of modern electrical appliances. There is a special rural delight in collecting them – from blenders to chest freezers and curling tongs. The irony is that the electricity here is often unreliable, and therefore half of those items are never used or go bust over time.'

'Do these families change in other ways, apart from materially?' Daniela asked.

'Money often gives these families from humble roots not only a new lease of life but also accords them increased influence and popularity – a higher status in the village. For instance, helping their children to go to special schools. People often borrow things or money from them. Often their behaviour changes; there are new social set-ups. There are those landowning families, like ours, where the wealth has been passed down from generation to generation, rather than from abroad. Then there is the local tailor, who has dispensed with his stitching trade and replaced it with more lucrative work like arranging visas for people to travel abroad.'

'Really!' Daniela marvelled.

'Yes, really!' Saher laughed aloud at the expression on the Englishwoman's face. 'As the saying goes, "money speaks". Well, here it definitely speaks loudly … and often through the number of Jeeps owned by a family. That said, I don't own one!'

They enjoyed another hearty gale of laughter. 'What about yourself? Why do you still live in the village, if you don't mind me asking? Aren't you a successful lawyer?' Daniela ventured.

'I work in the nearby city but I commute there on a daily basis. I live here for my mother's sake. Our home, the land, is here. I am the sole heiress. Your husband is a very wealthy man, do you know, Daniela? At the moment his mother owns more land than us, and she gains greater returns from it. We had to sell some of ours to build a local school and another house in the city for me, in case I decided to settle there.'

'Have you ever stayed there?'

'No, I have someone looking after it. I like to get back to the village at the end of the day, preferring the tranquillity of the rural world and our *hevali*, and I'm glad to leave behind the hustle and bustle of a large city. Sometimes, however, I find the two worlds so different, and am unable to identify with either. Just to give you an example: I eat everything from the village, but wear and buy everything else from the city, for there are hardly any decent shops here. I love living here because I grew up here.'

'What about when you marry?' Daniela couldn't help asking. Saher stopped in mid-track, looking down at the small stone she was treading on.

'I don't know,' she replied, eyes still lowered. 'Obviously, the original plan was that I would leave for the UK. Now, I am committed to staying on and if I marry someone, there is a high chance of that happening in the city, since there is no one suitable for me in this village.'

'Would you consider marrying someone from abroad?'

'No!' The answer was emphatic, surprising them both.

'For my mother's sake,' Saher hastened to explain. 'With Ismail out of the picture, I would always want to remain near her. My mother is a very lonely, troubled woman. She never quite fitted in with her two sisters – always the odd one out of the three. And I know that something in the past has gone wrong for her. I've become very protective of her lately. She lost my father in her early twenties, after just five years of marriage. She never remarried, though I understood there was a chance of her marrying someone once, but she turned him down and instead withdrew into herself.'

'Tell me about your family, Daniela. Do you have a mother?' Saher neatly changed the subject, blushingly aware that she had shared too much about herself, including details about her mother.

There was a pregnant pause before Daniela answered with a nervous laugh.

'Yes, I do, but unlike you, I'm not very close to mine, I'm afraid. In fact, we've drifted apart since my marriage. My mother could not handle my marrying a man from another race. I'm closer to my dad – Dave. He's really nice and I love him very much. I, too, am the only child – don't ask me why!'

'I see!' Saher had picked up the dullness of the tone and decided not to pry. Daniela had spotted Arslan walking towards them.

'Hi!' she shouted, waving her hand.

Saher scowled. Smiling, Daniela waited for Arslan.

'I'm walking further down the stream to bathe my feet,' Saher explained in a low voice. Arslan heard, noting her retreating figure. So he switched his full attention to Daniela.

'Hi, Daniela. Looks as if you are enjoying this wonderful cool breeze and the company of my equally "wonderful" cousin, who, as you can see for yourself, has hastened off upon seeing me.'

Daniela's eyes sparkled with mischief.

'I wonder why that is so?' she teased. Arslan coloured and changed the subject.

'Your "loving" husband is waiting to take you to a nearby city, Attock, for some shopping. He's now trying his very best, you know, to make it up to you.'

'Yes, he is.'

'Good! So his penance is to empty all the bazaars for you. If I were you, I'd buy the lot just to punish him for what he did at the airport!' They both laughed aloud, making Saher, now in the distance, stare back at them, her face still tight.

'I don't want to empty the bazaars – I just want his parents to like me,' she said with a sad appeal in her voice. Arslan sobered. 'They'll like you – they do like you!' he kindly amended.

'His mother is really nice. Do you know she made us break-fast this morning, hugged and kissed me? His father, though, still has that fierce look in his eyes … it frightens me.' Daniela was reluctant to expand. 'I had better go. Ismail is waiting.'

'I'll take Saher home in my car. You go.'

He waved her off and then strode down the hillside, his train-ers slipping over the polished stones.

CHAPTER 33

The Lovers

Saher was perched on her favourite boulder, the one she used to sit on as a child, dangling her feet in the water that rushed down from the glacier in the mountain, humming to herself.

'Feels good, doesn't it? I think I'll join you.'

She glanced up, disconcerted, but Arslan was already untying his shoelaces. Before she knew it, he was plodding barefooted over the pebbles and into a foot-deep stream, jeans tucked at the knees.

She pulled her feet out of the water. 'Wow, it's cold!' he cried, standing in front of her.

'Here, let me do it.' Before she could stop him, he was mopping the grainy sand off her foot.

'Let go!' Saher tried to pull her feet away.

'How long will you keep up this aggression with me, Saher?'

'Aggression!' she shouted angrily, standing up, not caring that her feet were back in the water again.

'Leave me alone!' she cried, tearful.

He stepped back, mentally withdrawing. 'Fine,' he coldly replied. 'I'm only offering you a lift home. Daniela and Ismail have gone shopping in Rawalpindi and Attock. If you want to walk back to the village, that's up to you!'

He waded out of the water and hurriedly brushed his feet on the warm tufts of grass. Saher watched him stride up the hill; following him, but keeping a strategic distance between them.

Arslan waited in the car, staring ahead. When she got into the back, he drove off, the silence between them only broken outside her home: 'You'll be happy to know, Saher, that I'm leaving soon.'

If she was taken aback she didn't show it; instead, she got out of the car and entered her home without a backward glance.

Arslan wrenched the car into action but did not drive away. The bleak thought hammered: 'My sister and lovely niece have gone. My parents will never change! The woman I have loved since childhood won't even speak to me now. Only Begum remains, but she's a servant. There's nothing here for me. This is not where I belong.'

He stared out of his windscreen at the orange orchards circling Saher's village. All of a sudden, he recalled that poignant moment at the age of twelve – that kiss, and how, red-cheeked, he had fled from the room. The childhood rapport vanished.

In her late teens, Saher never suspected that the cousin she doted on was passionately in love with her. No other members of the clan suspected anything, either. Only her mother sensed something; uneasy at their close relationship, hating the open fondness her daughter demonstrated in front of everyone towards Arslan. They were growing into young adults – did her foolish daughter not realise that she could end up compromising herself and her *izzat*?

Arslan always hid his feelings well from everyone, including from the woman who was beginning to make his life wretched by dismissing his feelings for her. It cost him dearly. Whilst he was in the USA completing his degree course, he received a cruel blow, learning that she had become engaged to their cousin, Ismail. It forced him to cage himself in a cloak of silence.

Arslan sighed; it was time to move on. Childhood crushes were one thing, but adult realism another matter. He recalled poor Suzanna, his university peer, who had fallen for him from the first semester and, by God, she was persistent, but it was Saher he craved.

He shook his head. Perhaps he was a lost cause, a product of one country, yet now standing on its soil as a virtual stranger. Even the woman he had pined for all these years had deserted him. Perhaps he, like Ismail, was destined to lie in a foreign woman's arms.

Then, miraculously, the gates opened and Saher appeared,

surprised to see him still there. Opening his car door, she asked accusingly, 'Why are you still here?' He startled her by grasping her wrist.

'Don't go!' The look in his eyes made her sit beside him. 'Promise me, you won't leave the car until I've finished speaking,' he urged. She stared out of the windscreen in silence. In front of them, little boys, still in their uniforms and with excited faces, were playing cricket in the open ground outside the primary school.

'Do you know what I was thinking about as I sat here after you left?'

Saher shook her head. 'About the time I first kissed you!' Her head swung round, eyes standing large in her face. Breathing ragged.

'What?'

'Don't worry. You don't know … It was such a long time ago, when we were young, done on impulse.'

'When?' She could barely get the word out of her mouth.

'Just after Laila left home. We had been playing chess and I left the room. While I was out you fell asleep on my bed. I stood staring at you, unable to help myself, Saher. I had this strange impulse to touch you – to brush your soft, pink lips with mine. Before I could stop myself I had kissed you – so quick and wonderful. Then I fled the room, shocked at what I had done and afraid that you would wake up and be angry with me. Amazingly, you slept on, dead to the world and although I was quite young, I believe that it was from that moment that my attraction for you began.

'My relationship with you was never quite the same after that. I wanted to kiss you again and again! It was wrong, I know. Please don't look so horrified.'

'How could you?' Saher at last found her voice.

Arslan was in a punishing mood and continued, 'Do you remember that moment when I went to your house just before going to the airport and planted a quick kiss on your cheek, but as you turned I touched the side of your mouth. We were both startled by this accidental contact and although I soon flew out of the room, I've never forgotten the moment. It has stayed with me for years. The passion became a nightmarish ache when I found out that you had got engaged – ready to become another man's wife.

'The rest you know. When Daniela turned up, I felt betrayed on your behalf and wanted to kill Ismail. I want you to understand that my feelings for you have been there for over a decade. It's not what you think … that I'm just feeling sorry for you. It's my *kismet*, I guess, that you are not fated to be my bride and that, maddeningly, you've always thought of me as a brother. I'm leaving tomorrow. I'm now surrendering myself to my fate. Just as I respect your thoughts and feelings on this matter, please learn to respect mine. One cannot stop falling in love. It just happens, Saher, capturing and imprisoning you. But I can't expect the same to happen to you and even if it did, it may well be for someone else.

'My feelings for you may dull with time. Who knows? Perhaps I'll meet another woman who will mean a lot to me, but I don't want to leave with this rift hanging between us. If you don't like what I've said, I'm truly sorry, but let's part as friends, at least. Thank you for listening, Saher. I'll never speak on this subject to you again. You are a free woman and I have no hold over you. I just hope that you will not hate me or forget the wonderful and tender moments of our shared childhood.'

He stopped and waited. When no response was forthcoming, he bleakly finished, 'Allah Hafiz, Saher,' and reached forward to open the Jeep door to let her out.

*

As if in a dream Saher walked away, hearing the vehicle crunch into action. At the gates of her home, she put her hand to her flushed cheeks. 'I must wash my face, otherwise Mother's prying eyes will draw their own conclusion.'

If she had any doubts before about Arslan, now she had none. For he had truly spoilt their relationship; soiling her pure, inno-cent affection for him.

Angrily she chided herself: 'How naive I was. The telltale

signs were everywhere and I just ignored them. Arslan, you were supposed to be my brother,' she mourned aloud, but the words didn't quite ring true.

CHAPTER 34

The Row

In the goldsmith's household, the washing had become a nightmare.

'Mother, the pile of dirty laundry is now an ugly mountain in the veranda. Is Massi Fiza OK, she's not been here for the last two days?' Rukhsar's eldest daughter, Shabnum, enquired. Her mother was busy threading six tiny seed pearls into place in a *natli* and didn't want to be disturbed. Her daughter, however, remained stubbornly by her shoulder. So Rukhsar had no choice but to put the necklace gently back on the velvet cushion and give her daughter an angry stare.

'No, Shabnum, she's not ill!' was her brusque answer.

'Then where is she? Shall I take a load down to her?'

'No, you can't!' Rukhsar sharply admonished, startling her daughter. 'Just wait, Massi Fiza will come up for it – she must be busy on her rounds.'

'But, Mum, we can't wait!'

'Well, why don't you girls get on with it then!' was the caustic answer. 'Sturdy girls, aren't you, stronger than poor, bony Massi Fiza anyway. There's a good washing machine in our house. What's the problem? Has Allah Pak not blessed you girls with hands?'

'What?' her middle daughter, who had joined them, exclaimed. Helping the maid with the cooking was fine but washing heavy bedlinen, and by hand – ugh!

Their mother was now trespassing over the line of what was possible for her college-educated daughters with their manicured nails! Rukhsar laughed aloud at her daughters' expressions. Washing had never been their favourite pastime.

'Ruhi, when the dinner is ready, send Auntie Fiza a plateful of meat, with at least two chunks of lean meat, remember.'

Her daughter's neatly maintained, arched eyebrows had shot up. What was going on? First, their mother told them to do their own washing and then asked Ruhi to take the laundrywoman a bowlful of meat.

'Mother, is everything all right between you two?' Shabnum prompted. She had picked up the angry vibes from her mother and also noted that their neighbour had not popped upstairs for two days now. When spotted in the street from their window, Massi Fiza had merely looked away. How strange!

'No, my "perceptive" daughter, we're not on speaking terms with "your" Massi Fiza,' Rukhsar reluctantly owned up.

'What, how?' Her daughter was flabbergasted.

'I seem to have offended the silly woman. At Master Haider's son's party, Massi Fiza not only kept well away from me but also threw me daggers of hatred across the dinner table.'

'Oh dear,' Shabnum commiserated, cheeks plumped with laughter. 'I really can't imagine Auntie Fiza giving anyone dagger eyes – but what did you do to elicit such a reaction?'

'I left a necklace outside on the cushion, whilst she was in the room. When I came back, Massi Fiza was staring at it and I put it away. The crazy woman was offended, thinking that I thought she was going to steal it. That's what it's all about. I gather that's the reason why she has not collected our laundry, either. It's her way of punishing me, girls, I guess,' she ended sheepishly.

'Oh dear!' Her daughter was exasperated. 'Now we are all being punished, Mother, for your actions. If Massi Fiza won't do our washing, you'd better find another laundrywoman! For none of us girls will touch it. We don't mind little items, but not white linen sheets. So if you think a plate of meat will bring Massi Fiza round, then please, Mum, send her two platefuls. Better still, I'll send her the whole pot!'

Rukhsar laughed aloud at their biting sarcasm, getting up to stretch her legs and plump neck, which was becoming more rounded with her bent posture. 'Now, now, girls, don't get carried away. Just three pieces of meat will do.' Her eldest daughter had already dashed into the kitchen.

The plate of meat, however, was returned to the goldsmith's household untouched soon afterwards. With gaping mouths, the two daughters waited for their mother to come out of the bathroom after doing her *wudu* for the prayers.

'Massi Fiza doesn't want it … she said she had some meat last night,' Ruhi informed her.

Rukhsar was livid at the snub, eyes darkening, but controlled herself in front of her daughters.

Later, during the painstaking task of threading some more pearly beads into a gold and ruby *kara,* Rukhsar's mind kept straying to her friend. Apart from the laundry, Massi Fiza was indispensable in so many other ways, too. Without her presence, life would become infinitely dull. It was time to patch up, but she was in no hurry – Rukhsar sat back on her cushions.

In the end, it was that very afternoon, thanks to her aggressive daughters, that she was forced to do her grovelling. With the sharp rays of the afternoon sun beating down on her head, Rukhsar found herself shyly knocking on her neighbour's door, her creamy face pink with embarrassment. The ugly mound of washing littering their veranda had her abandoning her task there and then. The girls were still moaning about their broken nails and twisted wrists after washing just a few items. All three of them had tried to tackle the mound, which resulted in a hearty squabble as to who had done the most and whose hands were in the worst condition. There was only one pair of washing gloves in the house and those only fitted Shabnum's big hands, leaving the other two fuming.

'This is like a laundry house, you messy girls! Clothes everywhere!' Rukhsar grimaced at the different piles of clothes, bringing back memories of the communal washing days of her youth. Unlike her pampered daughters, she and her sister had to do all of the housework, including the washing. Only the men's clothes were sent to the local *dhobi ghat.* The bedding, regarded as a nightmare, was always done at home, often taking a whole day. Her generation had learned to take it all in their stride and with good grace and humour. On top of that, there were always so many guests to cope with; the cooking, the serving and the laying of the bedding to sort out.

'What a different world it was then!' Rukhsar mused. Her 'educated' daughters on the other hand had become too spoiled to even rinse their flimsy chiffon *dupattas*. The only things they deigned to wash themselves were their undergarments.

Rukhsar sighed. She and her husband had only themselves to blame for pampering their daughters too much.

*

Standing in the village lane, Rukhsar pondered on the fact that she had not visited Massi Fiza's home for three years, whereas the latter had climbed up to their top floor every day.

Rukhsar pushed the door open. Pride had to be dispensed with. A strong blast of the soapy smell from the basin of hot water bubbling away on Massi Fiza's portable cooker hit Rukhsar. Crouching over it, Massi Fiza was dipping a bedding sheet in the boiling water with a washing ladle.

Rukhsar crushed the urge to squeeze her pretty, pert nose tight with her fingers. The stench of wet washing and detergent making her swoon, she mentally chided herself that this was a wash-house, after all. What else did she expect? This was tough living. Washing couldn't be compared to the dainty task of threading beads and pearls into necklaces. Both of them did jobs which helped their families, but poor Massi Fiza did the back-breaking one, Rukhsar commiserated, watching her friend haul a dripping sheet out of the wide steel bucket and slop it down into an empty plastic basin. Her daughters had complained about their wrists, but what about poor Massi Fiza's? 'She does all this work to support her two good-for-nothing sons, who've abandoned her, and are ashamed of their mother's work.'

'Hello, Fiza-ji,' Rukhsar shyly greeted her friend, eyes tearful from the detergent fumes.

Massi Fiza was partially hidden behind the mist of steamy water on the boil. Glancing up from her squatting position, she was taken aback by her friend's appearance and nearly dropped the laundry ladle into the pot of hot soapy water. She was trying to recall the last time she had seen her friend on her doorstep; it was when she had nearly died of typhoid fever.

Massi Fiza automatically stiffened, and Rukhsar sensed it across the few feet separating them.

'I've not seen you for three days, Massi Fiza. Is everything all right?' Rukhsar politely began, trying hard to smile, but failing.

'Everything is fine,' was Massi Fiza's curt reply, averting her gaze. 'It's the laundry that brings you here, isn't it?' she taunted.

'No, Massi Fiza,' Rukhsar glibly lied, nevertheless colouring and dropping her gaze. 'I wanted to see how you were.'

'Well, as you can see, I'm fine – just as your daughter saw me when she came with a bowl of *meat*. No need for charity from your household, Rukhsar. I can afford meat, too!'

'Glad to hear it,' Rukhsar stiffly returned, taken aback by her friend's rude tone and manner. 'Can we go inside and talk?'

'No, we can't! There is a mound of washing to do, as you can see!' The belligerent tone deeply offended her neighbour who struggled to remain calm.

'OK, I wish you a good day then. Allah Hafiz.' Rukhsar coolly bid goodbye, her hand on the door handle.

'If it's your washing that has brought you down to *grace* my courtyard after *three years* then send Ruhi down with it, for I'll not step foot on your premises. Massi Fiza is no thief!'

'Of course you are not a thief!' Rukhsar angrily replied, red-faced. 'It's all in your head, you silly woman – *befakuf*! As to our washing, it's about time we relieved you of its burden!' Her biting sarcasm was not lost on the laundrywoman. 'You've mountains of other people's dirty washing as it is. Good day to you!' Heart drumming, Rukhsar slammed the door shut, thinking ahead.

Once upstairs in her lounge, it was the baker's wife who enjoyed her long-winded conversation over the phone, before the subject of laundry was discreetly brought up.

*

In her small courtyard, a grinning Massi Fiza congratulated herself on her performance, and the handling of the arrogant goldmistress. 'Who does that madam think she is?' she fumed, as she slopped the butcher's blood-stained *kurtha* hard on her wooden washing slab.

Before the day ended the goldmistress's washing was being ceremoniously carted off to the village's other *mala* – to Massi Fiza's rival, Mahmood's *dhobi ghat*. A brisk and thriving laundry business, with the facilities of a proper factory washroom and a score of young men and women employees, Mahmood enjoyed a good lifestyle. His second safe, hidden in his wife's trousseau suitcase, was always stacked with crispy notes.

When Mahmood realised whose washing had entered his big washroom, the wiry *dhobi*'s chest swelled with pride.

With six women to support, including three daughters-in-law, it was great to be patronised by the goldsmith's household. He quickly instructed his supervisor to take special care with this washing, for he had plenty of jewellery to be designed for his youngest daughter's wedding. That Massi Fiza woman had monopolised all the laundry from that street. And not only that, she delighted in openly taunting him every time they met. Good-natured, he ignored it all, feeling sorry for her, whilst marvelling at how she managed the gruelling work all by herself in the pokey area around her courtyard and still had time to go gadding about the village in search of gossip.

As he personally mixed the starch solution for the goldsmith's white cotton clothes, determined to please his new clients, he speculated as to why the washing had walked up to his door. Dollops of starch went a long way, he had learned early on in his washing career.

'Massi Fiza, sneer as much as you want, but we are now in your neighbourhood! We may well take the orders from your other wealthy neighbours – the migrant's home,' he laughed, taking out three boxes of soap powder for the goldsmith's daughters' delicate fabrics.

Massi Fiza waited in vain for two days for the washing to land in her courtyard from the house next door. It was only as she spotted Mahmood's son gaily speeding down the street on his motorcycle, carrying a parcel of freshly-pressed clothes into the goldsmith's house, whistling a merry tune and winking at her, that it dawned on poor Massi Fiza that her plan had backfired; her pride had cost her in business.

She had overlooked the fact that people could not cope with mountains of dirty laundry littering the place. Rukhsar had apparently dealt with the problem with alacrity, to the benefit of Massi Fiza's rival!

'So be it, Rukhsar!' Massi Fiza raged. 'At least I'll not be badgered by your spoilt daughters' requests to stitch stupid buttons and zips, and tighten their seams in the middle of the night! All that *nakhra,* all that fuss I had to put up with.'

In fact Massi Fiza felt as if a ton of bricks was lifted from her back. Those fashionable young madams had taken her for granted. Money-wise there was plenty of work elsewhere. The only thing she would miss was the coffee the girls plied her with and the conversations with their mother.

'Never mind, all the villagers are my friends,' Massi Fiza happily reassured herself. Begum, from Haider Sahib's household, was like a sister to her, so kind. The baker's wife was also a close friend. At least in the baker's house she did not have to be on guard. Surely the baker's wife wouldn't expect her to steal *naan* breads or *khathaie* biscuits. In fact, come to think of it, the baker's wife was a good option for a new friendship, with the added bonus that she would be getting free *chappatis* every day.

Yes, that is what she would do; have a special agreement with the baker's wife, that in exchange for two *chappatis* a day she would wash a suit each day for her, and if by any chance she decided to offer her some curry, too, that would mean she would no longer need to cook for herself. On second thoughts, she would wash her three suits. It couldn't be fairer than that, could it? The baker's wife would certainly love the idea. They had plenty of food, with pots of curries being cooked every day for their large family and three grandchildren. Money and meat was in abundance in that household, too!

'Rukhsar, you and I have truly parted company today,' Massi Fiza defiantly told herself that night after depositing the washed clothes back to the baker's home and in exchange had enjoyed a hearty meal, sitting at the eight-seater dining table that their eldest daughter-in-law had brought with her to that house as part of her dowry. They had even offered her a full plate of tomato and onion salad!

Massi Fiza felt so good about this venture that she decided to offer employment to Rasoola, as a gesture of goodwill for not having a permanent post since she left Mistress Mehreen's home. That arrogant housekeeper, however, flatly turned the offer down, a look of utter disgust smeared on her face: 'I'm made for better things than washing other people's dirty linen.'

Stung, Massi Fiza had quickly rounded on the woman: 'You scour other people's pots, which touch their lips. I just dip clothes in hot water, pound and rinse them.'

'I'd rather go back to Mehreen's household than work on other people's laundry.' Rasoola sneered. The cheek of the woman to offer dirty laundry as work for her!

Bristling, Massi Fiza deposited a pile of washed and pressed clothes to Begum with Master Arslan's starched shirt right at the bottom. She was still cursing herself as to how she managed to do it, but the cerise *dupatta* belonging to the bricklayer's daughter had ran into Master Arslan's immaculate white shirt which she had just washed. Even bleaching had not helped. She just prayed that she would get away with it and Master Arslan wouldn't make a fuss.

CHAPTER 35

The Housekeepers

'Then why don't you?' Begum had teased Rasoola later.

'What, work for Massi Fiza? Are you kidding?'

'No, I meant go back to Mistress Mehreen's house as you suggested in the heat of the moment. Mistress Mehreen is desperate for someone and is even doing the cooking herself now!'

'What? Go back to that monster! She'll eat me alive after what I did!'

'I don't think she will, but anyway it's a thought. I've been entrusted to supply a housekeeper for her, especially with the *goorie* there. I feel very sorry for the poor woman. In fact Mistress Gulbahar was worried about her sister's welfare. She has had a rough time lately, hasn't she?'

'Well, whose fault was it?' Rasoola cattily snapped. 'Hers!' She had no goodwill or patience to spare for Mistress Mehreen. It was better that their paths never crossed again. In fact she wanted to leave the village very soon. For she was getting fed up with Ali and his dark scowls when he looked at her. Furthermore, she was fed up with her nit comb and jar of Tibet cream going missing from the niche in the veranda wall. Twice her sticks of mouth *sak* had been discarded in the rubbish, and she had to listen to him complaining about the orangey stain around the sink bowl after she had brushed her teeth with them. At times, Ali, as her host, was barely civil to her. 'Some would call it pure rudeness!' she told herself, quite hurt.

Good old Begum, however, was a great chum, and had not changed one bit. They still enjoyed their nightly bouts of giggles as they exchanged tidbits of gossip, at times choking on their usual treat of monkey nuts.

In Ali's view, however, Rasoola had overstayed her welcome – and by a long shot. Ali stopped buying meat and he and Begum began taking their evening meals at Mistress Gulbahar's. As for the monkey nuts that she loved to munch on at night, the fifth bag had not been replaced. Ali said it was because of their chesty coughs. To his credit, the only thing he had not done was to tell her to her face to leave, otherwise, he had made his feelings very clear.

In his eyes, she was either dense, or just foolishly stubborn; Ali secretly believed it was the latter. For she had ignored all his signals with a wide speculative grin, meaning that she would only leave when it suited her or when he told her to.

Tonight, after talking to Massi Fiza and Begum, Rasoola knew it was time to move on, to seek new pastures – time for action. After all, she was cut out for a better future than as Begum's assistant, always at her beck and call. How she loathed that title, having enjoyed over ten years as a housekeeper.

And it was action that she took.

*

Rasoola arrived at Mistress Rani's *hevali* first thing in the morning, just after the lawyer woman had zoomed off in her shiny blue car to the city. Rani's manservant loftily informed her that the mistress was around somewhere.

Still sulking, Rasoola stayed in the air-conditioned kitchen with the cook, sipping the promised cool drink. Rani, who happened to pass through the veranda, spotted her and grimaced. Both women had a lot in common, in particular their morose manner. As a result, they disliked each other.

'Rasoola, what are you doing here?'

'Looking for work!' Rasoola tartly returned, surprising the other woman.

'Right, you can start here by helping us with some errands around the house, cooking and shopping.' Rasoola was so taken aback by the immediate offer that her mouth fell open. Then she smiled, eagerly rising to her feet. 'Yes, I'll happily do that. Can I start today?'

Rani was equally nonplussed.

'Shouldn't you explain to my sister, your previous employer, what you are doing?' Rasoola's face immediately fell, brown cheeks flagged red.

''Course I will.'

'OK, when you've done that, then you can start.' She was about to turn away, but added, 'And one more thing, if you're going to work in this household, I suggest that you mend your ways. I'll not tolerate you gossiping. I'm not Mehreen. If I find out that you have leaked any tales from this home, you'll have me to deal with. I don't throw tantrums like my sister – I've a different manner of dealing with people like you. See that you don't find out what it's like.' Rasoola nodded mutely. Then found her tongue.

'Yes, of course, Mistress Rani. You should expect nothing but loyalty and hard work from me.'

'Good. I'll see you later.' They parted company, both tight-faced.

*

Rasoola departed soon afterwards, having quickly decided there and then that, of the three, Rani was the worst sister to work for. Even bossy Mehreen, amazingly, appeared in a better light. There was something chilling about the very-quiet middle sister. Rasoola was in no hurry to lead a cowed life under the ever-watchful eye of her gloomy new employer, whose mouth hardly ever lifted in a smile. Also, she was no pet-lover. The sight of a pigeons' cage and their droppings had her face twisted in disgust. 'I'll jump into a well rather than clear away pigeon droppings in Mistress Rani's home. Ugh!' As she was leaving, the fierce dog tied to the front gate nearly bit her calf.

By the time Rasoola reached Mistress Gulbahar's house, after a bumpy ride in the village rickshaw, the weirdest thought went through her head; that she actually missed Mehreen's home and the role and status she enjoyed there. Mistress Gulbahar was wonderful, but in that famous household Rasoola was a mere temp, whilst Mistress Gulbahar's own favourite housekeeper Begum was the 'madam'.

Apart from her shouting and occasional tantrums, especially if her beloved china got broken, on the whole, Mistress Mehreen left her well alone to get on with her work, and hardly supervised her. Mistress Gulbahar, on the other hand, was always in and out of the kitchen – keeping an eye on everything. And she could just imagine Mistress Rani, with her eagle eyes, standing over her shoulders dictating every task. Moreover, she loved inheriting Mistress Mehreen's cast-offs, often new outfits.

As she helped Begum to prepare the evening meal, Rasoola realised it was time for her to grovel at Mistress Mehreen's feet. With a sigh, she wryly shared her plan with Begum: 'Strange what changing circumstances do to you – bring you around full circle!'

The latter was delighted, exclaiming, 'That's right, silly woman.'

That very night, Begum visited Mistress Mehreen and begged her to take Rasoola back in her household. Stunned, Mehreen managed to keep her face straight, though inside her heart was singing, having learned the lesson well that 'even a good-for-nothing servant' was better than having to manage her home on her own. And she had owned up to the truth that Rasoola was indeed a very efficient housekeeper.

Her body stiffened all the same; the image of the wretched woman nervously set her pulse racing. It was Rasoola, the witch, who had brought her the bad tidings regarding her son. Mehreen had her honour and *shan* to see to, and found it pertinent to remind Begum to 'instruct' Rasoola not only to beg for *mafi*, forgiveness, but also to keep out of her way when she returned – for she didn't relish looking Rasoola in the face, not yet anyway.

'Perhaps things will get better as time goes on, Begum, but for the moment I'll let her work on a trial basis only,' Mehreen added firmly.

'Thank you, Mehreen-ji. I'll bring her in straight away. In fact …' Begum looked sheepish, 'she's waiting outside the gate now.'

Mehreen panicked, her cheeks flaming; she hadn't bargained for this sudden meeting with that *charail*, that wicked witch.

When they met, Mehreen looked anywhere but at Rasoola, while the latter kept her eyes down.

'Go!' Mehreen's curtly commanded. 'You know where everything is. See to the needs of my son and his foreign bride, whose arrival you so *graciously* announced to us a few days ago.' The tongue-in-cheek quip had Rasoola blushing hard.

'Daniela, my daughter-in-law, by the way, likes curries but not very hot food. So you need to prepare a special menu for her on a daily basis, do you understand?' From the corner of her eyes she observed Rasoola nodding her head and then disappearing into the kitchen. 'Yes, Sahiba-ji,' she had muttered – her body language unusually subservient.

Inside, Mehreen felt relief at throwing the reins of her household back to Rasoola. She could now concentrate on working her 'womanly magic' on her stubborn husband, who still refused to hold a proper conversation with her.

'How strange life is!' Rasoola happily turned on her mattress in the servants' quarters. The thought of Ali having his wife all to himself again made her giggle. She still had to go back for her stuff. 'But Ali won't be pressing me to stay, I'm sure of that!' Rasoola snorted in the darkness. Then she sobered, caustically reminding herself that despite his manner, he was a good soul and a generous host; not only had he put up with her for many days but he had quietly indulged her, too, especially with bags of monkey nuts and village *rewarian* sweets.

So she couldn't possibly hold anything against him. On the contrary, she had gained two trusted friends and owed a lot to Begum. From now on, she would not resent her, but defer to her judgement and learn from her. 'That's as long as Begum doesn't interfere too much in this home,' Rasoola added.

*

'What are you telling me, Begum? That your friend has actually left?' Ali raised his eyebrows in disbelief, creasing his high forehead with four distinct lines. 'You're teasing me!'

Begum chuckled.

'Believe it or not but she's gone, and you won't guess where?'

'To the nearest town, as she boasted.'

'No, she's still in rural surroundings. Go on, have another guess, Ali.'

'I haven't got time for guessing games, Begum – too tired. I've been carting sacks of rice! My back is shattered.'

He leaned affectionately towards her in bed. At last, they had the place to themselves.

'I hope the new government sorts out the price of food. Do you know how expensive those bags of rice were? As for flour – what poor soul is going to be able to feed his family? These politicians, no matter who they are, they only care about their own hides and their personal squabbles and vendettas. That's what they're good at. Who cares about the food on our plates? They are millionaires! Their wealth is stashed away in overseas banks. Who cares for the poor? Let me sleep, Begum.'

'Sleep then! I didn't ask you for a lecture on politics,' Begum retorted and then rushed to explain. 'Just let me tell you where Rasoola has gone – back to Mistress Mehreen's household!'

'What?' he cried, sitting poker straight in bed and giving her his undivided attention. 'Well! Miracle of miracles! *Kamal hai*!'

'It's a miracle indeed, Ali! I'm so glad. Mistress Mehreen has got her housekeeper back.'

'Good riddance!' Ali exclaimed, lying down, a smug smile on his face. 'We can now have our home back.' He sat up again, 'And don't you dare pick up any other unwanted guests! I'm sure you're fed up of sleeping on the veranda – just to keep that stupid woman company.'

'Not that you missed me much!' Begum tartly reminded him. He grinned, showing the gap in his front teeth where he had broken one biting a hard sugarcane.

'Do I have to spell it out for you?'

'Yes. Occasionally.'

'All right, I'll do it tomorrow, especially after you've made me a wonderful *paratha*?' Smiling, he snuggled down under his sheet, pulling it over his head, too tired to engage in any intimate matters, physical or otherwise.

The next minute his head had popped out. 'And tell that wretched woman to take her damn stuff away – especially that nit comb of hers. If I find out you have got nits from her you are not coming anywhere near me!'

'Don't be mean, Ali, I've no nits – nor does poor Rasoola! The comb is only to keep her hair ultra clean. She's obsessive about her personal hygiene. I've checked her hair myself, not a single egg did I spot. Not only does she wash it with *lassi* milk, but she buys the best brand of shampoo, and often massages her scalp with real egg yolks. I know you don't like her. You wicked man! You threw away her new stick of *sak*, but she made no fuss about it, did she? So don't be so mean, Ali.'

'I'm not mean! That silly woman has cost us a packet in hair oils, shampoo, monkey nuts and of course meat!'

'Ali, stop counting your *paisas*, please. You know both our families pride themselves on their hospitality.'

'OK, but she'd better stay where she is … I'm not letting her crawl back into our house again! Do you understand, Begum?'

'I understand, Ali. Go to sleep!' Begum sweetly agreed, chuckling at the defiant look in her husband's eye. Rasoola really did get on her husband's nerves.

*

Rasoola had every reason to stay put in her *old kingdom* as she now fondly referred to it. Coupled with a new heart and focus, she was viewing her hitherto 'burdensome' working domain with a new pair of eyes. She shuddered at the thought of Mistress Gulbahar's household where there were always guests coming and going, all needing to be fed and looked after – but Begum, a kindly devoted soul, took it all in her stride. Here in Mistress Mehreen's home there was the *goorie*, but Rasoola loved looking at her and Ismail. The couple were out most of the time sightseeing anyway, including visiting the beautiful hill station of Murree.

Rasoola nervously hovered outside Mehreen's room recalling

the last time she had taken her a glass of milk and shattered her mistress's world by blurting out the news of her son's secret marriage. It was time to make amends, no matter how painful. After a timid knock she entered, shocked to see her mistress with wet cheeks and evasive eyes. Mehreen hastily mopped her face with a tissue and stiffly turned to look at her housekeeper.

'Sahiba-ji,' Rasoola stammered, unable to lift her eyes, distressed on her mistress's behalf, 'can I get you an aspirin? That's if you're having a headache.'

Mehreen coolly answered, 'I'm fine, Rasoola, just put the glass of milk on that table.'

Rasoola did as instructed and then abjectly apologised. 'I'm sorry, Mistress Mehreen. From today, I'll work hard and make amends for that terrible day when I upset you.'

Touched, Mehreen found her lips forming the generous words, 'Thank you, Rasoola. I'm very glad you're back.'

Flushed and triumphant, Rasoola kept her back to her mistress.

'And Rasoola, don't carry those heavy trays. I've ordered some lighter ones – better for your back. From now on Riaz will do all the heavy carrying.'

Surprised, Rasoola stood there with only the sound of the air conditioner breaking the silence. 'Yes, Mistress, thank you!' she whispered before leaving.

Overwhelmed, she stood panting outside in the corridor. Master Liaquat was coming down the corridor. About to pass him, she whispered, 'I found Mistress Mehreen crying, Master.'

Liaquat heard but did not bother with a response; instead he entered another room down the corridor. Rasoola returned downstairs wondering whether she should go to the *goorie* and Ismail – to offer them almond milk drinks. 'It's so exciting having a woman who looks so different, speaks another language and has come from another country *and* is staying in the same house as me! How blessed I am,' Rasoola congratulated herself.

Upstairs, Mehreen debated on whether to drink the glass of milk or not as her doctor had advised her to cut down on dairy products and sugar to reduce her weight. She reluctantly reached for the glass of milk, unable to insult Rasoola by not drinking it. Her appetite was gone after four failed attempts to win back her husband. Today, he had rebuffed her smiles and her efforts at humouring him, by ignoring her and childishly walking out of the room. As for Rani, Mehreen had stopped worrying about her. Life was bleak, all around.

Ironically the only happy couple appeared to be her son and his foreign wife; they had spent another enjoyable day visiting the famous Khyber Pass in the mountains. Mehreen had tried to stop them because of the fighting with the Taliban in the mountains and was on edge all day, but she needn't have worried. Daniela had returned with glowing pink cheeks, eyes sparkling.

Mehreen pulled off her *chador*, ready for bed; she couldn't be bothered with the ritual of cleansing and toning her face today.

The bedroom door opened. Was it Rasoola or …? She waited, heart beating, carrying on with the task of removing the gold *karas* from her arm. She sighed, then on hearing the sound of the duvet cover, rebellion surfaced – did her husband miss his bed or her company? The proud Mehreen got out of bed and stood up to her full five feet and five inches, offering her husband the entire bed! Plucking up her pillow she strode out of the room.

Once in the guest bedroom, she made a mental note to get back to her own room early in the morning. The last thing she wanted was Rasoola gossiping about their sleeping arrangements.

The door opened. Mehreen was surprised to see her husband and shot him a challenging look. Barefooted, he crossed the cool marble floor to the bed and half smiling, he lifted the bed cover and got in beside her, ignoring her angry look.

'It's not this bed I want, but my wife.'

Colour swept high in Mehreen's cheeks. She slid to the other side of the bed, leaving an ominous space between them, and stared stonily up at the ceiling. Inside, bitterness raged. For four days he had rebuffed her, treating her with contempt, so much so that she had begun to despise herself.

So when he reached to pull her into his arms, her legs automatically sidled away, mind screaming, 'No, I'll not let him touch me!'

This rift had to be talked through, otherwise it would gnaw away at their marriage. She had to know what he thought of her and he had to face the truth that she truly did have reason for her jealousy.

Teeth gritted, he was out of the bed and out of the room. Stunned by his reaction, Mehreen turned over onto her side and wept.

CHAPTER 36

The Sisters

It was a strange night. Mehreen may have lost respect for her husband, but she had regained her long-lost respect for herself, telling herself sharply, 'I'm now a grown-up! I don't need my husband as a lever any more.'

Next morning, not relishing her husband's company if he was unable to love her as he should, Mehreen walked out of her home with a suitcase; a tall, proud figure, feeling emboldened to even take on her sister Rani. Rasoola immediately noticed her mistress's poise – Mehreen's body language and demeanour shouted one word: 'confidence.' A gentle smile tugging at her mouth was also highly unusual.

Mehreen wanted to put into practice her new-found independence; had not their Rani managed her land, house and servants all by herself since the age of 24? Why should she, a mature woman, not be able to cope with the simple tasks of daily living? 'How and why did I become so dependant on my husband and sister?' Mehreen bitterly mocked herself, instructing her chauffeur to drive her to Rani's village, ready to brave her sister's company. This would be her ultimate test.

Stepping on the gravel of Rani's driveway, it occurred to Mehreen that she couldn't remember the last time she had visited her sister alone. Perhaps everything whittled down to her continuing guilt for her childish spitefulness in spoiling Rani's bridal dress so long ago, an incident that had cut them off. Even Ismail and Saher's engagement had been initiated by her husband and Gulbahar – both equally fond of Saher. For the thought of Rani as her *qurmani*, didn't entirely fill Mehreen's heart with joy. Now she had a foreign *qurmani*, Daniela's mother. God knew what she was like!

Well, if today Rani wished to vent her rage for Ismail's cruel actions, then so be it. Poor Rani had every right to do so. Smiling, and feeling more cheerful than normal, Mehreen entered her sister's house, her head held unnaturally high.

*

Inside Rani's *hevali*, Mehreen was disappointed to learn that her sister was out shopping in town with her daughter. Mehreen instructed her driver to take the basket of fruit into Rani's kitchen and to return home.

She couldn't quite remember having stayed a single night in Rani's home; nor, for that matter, had Rani ever spent a night at Mehreen's. An unwritten rule had been mutually established; simply to avoid the other's company.

'Today, there'll be no squabbles,' Mehreen smiled to herself. 'Even if Rani does her worst!' she vowed.

Rani returned late, hot and bothered from a long day of hunting for silk carpets for the newly furbished TV room in Islamabad. When her eyes fell on her younger sister sitting in the cool breeze on the roof terrace gallery, sipping milk soda, Rani blinked in disbelief, face paling. Mehreen had made herself at home and had asked her sister's cook to make peas pilau for her supper and to serve it on the rooftop so that she could enjoy the evening breeze.

Rani dispensed with politeness, 'What are you doing here?' This was the sister she loathed. 'Quarrelled with your husband?' she bluntly asked.

'No!' Red-cheeked, Mehreen glibly lied, indignant at her sister's question. 'Can't I come and stay here for a night?'

'A night!' Rani's mouth fell open.

Then a strange thing happened. For the first time in her life, she had the instinct of the protective, older sister.

'Are you OK? You haven't abandoned your home, have you?' she asked with an urgency in her voice, surprising her sister.

'God forbid! No!' Mehreen hotly denied, slipping off the

charpoy. Touched by her concern, Mehreen pulled Rani into her arms. 'If you don't want me to stay, I can go back.' Not at all flummoxed by her sister's stiff figure she hugged her even tighter. Disconcerted, Rani stepped out of her sister's arms, asking instead, 'Have you eaten?'

'Of course! I instructed your Jamila what to cook for our evening meal. The witch kept on badgering me as to what I liked to eat. As well as pilau rice she has also made me a steamy, syrupy halva, the way I really like it. She certainly is a great cook.'

'Yes,' Rani acknowledged, face still tight. 'I'll let Saher know you're here.' She looked at the portable bed. 'Is that bed all right for you, Mehreen?'

'Yes, it's very comfortable. It reminds me of the time we all used to sleep together on the rooftop as young girls.' Traces of childish excitement threaded her voice.

Rani was on her way down the marble stairs. 'Yes,' she muttered.

'Rani, can I sleep near you? Like old times.' She looked embarrassed. Completely taken aback by the request, Rani didn't know what to say.

'Yes, whatever,' she answered flatly.

Mehreen was still baffled. Did she imagine it or did she actually see Rani's eyes fill?

Stoically, she turned her gaze to the fields circling the village, knowing life would never be the same again. This visit to her sister's went beyond sleeping in her sister's home; it was a matter of wooing loved ones and building bridges, especially after burning an important one with her eldest sister, the 'bridger' of all things in her life.

Mehreen began to fan her neckline with the raffia hand fan.

*

In Master Haider's *hevali*, Begum informed Saher that her Aunt Gulbahar was upstairs in her bedroom. Afraid of coming across Arslan, Saher hovered beside the pillar under the birdcage. Mithu, allowed out for exercise, was busy hopping on Begum's washing line. Disgusted, Saher tried to shoo him off, knowing

Begum would not cherish having her tea towels soiled with parrakeet droppings.

Firm masculine steps sprinting down the marble stairs prompted her to step behind the tall ivy plant circling the colonnade. Arslan caught sight of her, smiled and then strode into his room. Saher hurried up to her aunt's room.

Gulbahar was sitting on an armchair, wiping her cheeks, attempting to smile at her niece. Saher stood against the door, dismayed by her aunt's distress.

'He's leaving, Saher!' her aunt wailed.

'Who?'

'Arslan!'

*

Unhappily, Mehreen stared down at the peach and turquoise silk carpet her sister had ordered for her daughter's wedding reception party. All the rooms in the villa had been lavishly refurbished, no cost spared. Only the new carpet for the TV room remained to be purchased. 'I want the house to be in a splendid state before the arrival of our wedding guests,' Rani had commented with pride to her daughter.

'Go on,' she now prompted. 'Why have you stopped?'

Mehreen shook her head, more tears trickling down her cheeks and onto the cushion she was resting her head on.

Rani was dazed. This was no play-acting.

'Why does your husband hate you, Mehreen?' Rani had never used such a gentle tone. Between loud sobs, Mehreen wailed, ashamed, 'My Liaquat-ji despises me! He prefers Gulbahar – the epitome of an ideal wife. He treats me like a child ... shows no respect for me whatsoever. And since I said something horrible to him, he really has no time for me. I've ruined everything – even had an argument with Gulbahar. I'm sure she hates me, though she says she has forgiven me.'

Stunned into silence and sensing her sister's wretchedness, Rani pulled her into her arms.

'Don't be silly. How can our Gulbahar ever hate you – her adorable babe?' No trace of sarcasm this time.

'But she does, after I said something stupid.'

'Hush, you're not stupid, Mehreen!' Rani gently coaxed, hugging her little sister even tighter; the one she had envied for nearly two thirds of her life, now a pitiable bundle of misery and insecurity.

Rani surprised both of them with the words leaving her lips.

'You're beautiful! Not stupid. Of course Liaquat Sahib doesn't hate you! You must have annoyed him as you always do. Don't look so aggrieved – you know what you are like and, of course, our Gulbahar doesn't hate you. She's like a mother to us. How can a mother hate her children for long? And for that matter, I don't hate you, either. So what if that selfish son of yours has married someone else – it was fated to happen. My Saher will find another husband. Do you hear me, Mehreen?'

Mehreen dumbly nodded, her head still pressed against her sister's shoulder. Smoothing away wet strands from Mehreen's face, Rani kissed her sister's forehead.

Mehreen's body heaved with fresh weeping.

'You're so kind, Rani!' she muttered through broken sobs. 'And I'm so selfish.'

Rani's own eyes were full of water.

'Hush, don't say that. You were young, Mehreen, and the most affected by our mother's death – no more crying now!'

*

Saher returned home and upon entering the drawing room she couldn't quite believe the scene facing her – her mother massaging her younger aunt's feet, a woman she had despised virtually all her life.

'Is Auntie all right?'

'Just tired. She'll stay with us for some time, Saher ... our care and support,' Rani quietly informed her daughter, gaze lowered, reluctant to explain further.

Later, whilst coaxing her sister to eat some fruit, Rani discovered the truth as to why her elder sister was so protective of her younger one. Rani forgave her older sister. Was she now not doing exactly the same as Gulbahar had been doing for over three decades? Rani protectively pressed her sister's body against her own and lovingly whispered, 'You're sleeping in my room tonight, so that I can keep an eye on you, Mehreen.'

'You are so kind today, Rani, but I'm always afraid of you,' Mehreen sniffed loudly followed by nervous laughter.

'Why, Mehreen?' Rani answered after a long pause. 'Am I some sort of a monster? I am your sister, aren't I, for God's sake?'

'Yes,' Mehreen quickly responded, with an accelerating heartbeat, neither wanting to rake up their past nor to take a step back.

Later, her last words before her eyes closed were, 'You're so kind, Rani – I love you.'

Rani lifted her head, staring into the darkness across the beds as her eyes filled up again. 'My poor sister was crying out for love and respect, and I've withheld both. Why have I allowed myself to be alienated for so long from my two sisters?' the words ran around in her head.

Mehreen, unburdened, blissfully slept on. Rani could not; like many a night her thoughts were with Rashid again. Angrily she brushed her wet cheeks. It was her own doing.

She knew that the first thing she would do the following day would be to visit her brother-in-law. And the words she would hurl at him! A cynical smile crossed her face in the darkness. Liaquat Ali was always the go-between for the two sisters. The next day Rani would take on that role.

∗

'You've given my poor sister a nervous breakdown!' Rani declared to her brother-in-law, Liaquat, going straight to the point; no frills or dressing it up or wasting words on greetings! 'How could you do it?'

Liaquat had baulked, believing neither his eyes nor his ears. It was this sister and her wrath he had carefully protected his wife from for over 25 years. Now, overnight, she had become his wife's gallant champion!

Colour drained from his cheeks. Loathing his wife, he looked away from Rani's all-knowing eyes. 'She has blabbed everything to this sister, too!' he silently groaned.

Rani watched with interest the angry tide of colour sweeping up his throat, reading its shade and the meaning behind it before carefully looking away. There was definitely something here, but she was reluctant to tread on the marital minefield.

With dignity and added warmth, she made her point.

'Whatever your disagreement, Brother Liaquat, only you and Mehreen know the details, for she has not said much, but simply weeps all the time and says you hate her and don't respect her. So I've decided that until she has regained her normal bearing, I'll look after her for a few days.'

He was going to mention the *goorie* then stopped.

'All right, thank you, Sister Rani. Believe me, it is only a trivial matter, of course, but you know what our Mehreen is like.'

'Yes, I know what she's like but at the moment she's down in the dumps,' she coolly pointed out to him. 'And desperately needs your love.' Liaquat reddened.

Rani had said her piece and declined the offer of tea from Rasoola, standing with a tray in her hand.

'But you do appreciate our house situation, don't you, Sister Rani?' Liaquat drily reminded her.

'If you're talking about the *goorie,* I'm sure your Ismail can well look after his wife,' she coldly replied, wanting to get out of the building, not quite ready to forgive her nephew yet for jilting her daughter. All those journeys to the bazaars in the heat for wedding gifts! Suddenly feeling bitterly tearful she blindly pushed past Rasoola with the tray.

In the courtyard, she had the misfortune to glimpse the 'golden-haired foreign woman' standing at the basin.

'OK, Sister Rani, I'm glad that you two sisters will spend time together, but do tell her that I'm coming to bring her home the day after tomorrow.'

Rani's eyes lingered on her daughter's *sokan.* Was it those gold strands, glinting in the sun, that had captured her nephew? Without saying goodbye, Rani strode out through the gates, silently mourning, 'This was meant to be my daughter's home!'

*

Liaquat stood in the middle of the guest room, his fingers raking through his thick grey hair. 'Now I've made enemies of both her sisters – how did this come about?'

Walking out into the courtyard, he felt as if he was crossing unfamiliar territory. There was no wife at home. Instead, a strange woman was there. Daniela had nervously glanced at him and quickly returned to her room, her heartbeat quickening, the baby stirring inside her. The hostility was still there, but she had glimpsed something else in her father-in-law – the look of a lost man.

And where was Ismail's mother? She had not seen her since yesterday afternoon. A middle-aged woman servant appeared to be hovering everywhere she went. If she went to the basin to wash her face the woman was giving her a toothy grin, eagerly offering clean towels. Last night, she had come in with a glass of milk and some *kashoo* nuts.

Daniela walked into the room, depression suddenly hitting her. Ismail was scanning the pictures he had taken that day with their digital camera. Daniela, finding everything so different, had made him take lots of photos of the food and spice stalls and looking highly embarrassed, Ismail had obliged.

'I've made things very difficult for your family, haven't I, Ismail?' Daniela told her husband. 'Your father can barely look at me. Your mother is aggrieved, never mind Saher's mother! I really do wish now that I had never come.' She sounded so forlorn that Ismail swept her up in his arms, with a tender look sweeping across his face.

'Don't be foolish, Daniela, I'm now actually glad that you came. I was a coward and should have told them a long time ago, and also about our baby.'

'But not like this!' she ruefully offered, nestling her face against his throat.

'Hey, stop giving yourself a hard time. What about your parents? Haven't I caused a rift in your family? Now your father has problems with your mother and you've not seen your mother for two years – how do you think I feel about that?'

'Please, Ismail, don't mention my mother. We both know she's a racist.'

'And my father isn't? In fact, neither of them is able to accept us as partners for their children. Colour seems to be an issue here … I'll never forget your mother's expression … her jaw dropping on seeing a brown man standing holding her daughter's hand outside her door. Your mother adores you, yet she was horrified when she learned that you were marrying a man from another ethnic group and faith. It's the same for my parents – with you being the "white woman" in their midst, and they have a lot of stereotypical perceptions about Western women, especially relating to sexual matters. It's this that has coloured their view of you.'

'Yes, I know. I'm the *goorie* who not only sleeps around but has stolen their beloved son!' Daniela bitterly laughed.

'OK, if we're talking about stealing, then I've stolen you from your parents, but I'm not repenting – I'm very happy to have done the stealing. What about you?'

'Guilty! Been stolen and have stolen,' Daniela giggled against his ears, pulling his hand against her abdomen.

'Ismail, just put your hand here – feel your child kick!'

'You know the sex of the baby, don't you?' he responded, a speculative gleam entering his eyes.

'Sure … This household is going to have a grandson.'

She buried her face against his chest. Ismail tenderly held her against him, but his thoughts were with the people he had let down. His mother had dreamt of a grandson, but the only difference was, she had been expecting one from Saher, not from a foreign woman who couldn't even speak her language.

CHAPTER 37

The Kiss

Ismail was not on Saher's mind; her thoughts were elsewhere. Arslan's words to his mother, 'I'll stay if ...' went round in her head.

Pressing her warm face against the pillow, she squeezed her eyes tight. Unable to sleep, she reached for her phone to text a message. A minute later the phone rang.

'Hello,' she nervously greeted, startled.

'Yes. Is everything OK, Saher?' Arslan enquired.

'I ...' Heat rushed through her face; he couldn't see her but he sensed her discomfort at the other end.

'Yes?' he prompted, not making it easy for her.

She stuttered to explain. 'I was wondering whether you could keep me company? Mother has gone to take Aunt Mehreen back to her home and has decided to stay there for the night. Only the servants are here. You can sleep in the guest room, but I would feel much safer if you were in the building.' It was a strange request and they both knew it.

Unable to bear his silence, she switched the phone off, chiding her stupidity for calling him.

'To hell with you, Arslan!' Saher slid back into the cool linen, closing her eyes.

*

A bell rang somewhere in the house, but Saher was floating away. Arslan was sitting beside her on the bed, his face getting nearer. Saher smiled, her lips parting to welcome his mouth.

Something warm touched her cheek. Her eyes fluttered open

and then widened in shock, clashing head on with those of the man she had been dreaming of. His hand was gently caressing her cheek as in her dream!

He was smiling back at her; face only inches from hers. Her dazed eyes traced the counters of his jawline. Letting go of her cheek, he sat back on the bed.

'When did you come?' she stammered, wetting her dry lips, voice hardly audible.

'A short while ago.' He looked steadily at the painting on the wall, allowing her the privacy to cover her body properly. Grateful for his thoughtfulness, she plucked her pashmina shawl from the chair and draped it carefully over her female curves. For the first time in her life, she felt very conscious of her body. The thin muslin night *kurtha* hid very little.

Heat rushed into her cheeks, recalling the last time he was in her room, when she had first wept in his arms and then had thrown him out. Her gaze lingering on his profile, she willed him to look at her. Then startled him by pulling off her shawl and throwing it across the room.

He chuckled at her flushed face and angry eyes. This was the Saher he knew, passionately ranting at him one minute and then touching him affectionately on his face the next. His wilful eyes lazily caressed her hair, the well-defined features, the creamy column of slender throat, dipping to the shadowy valley between her breasts. Their fullness, etched against the thin fabric, had him looking him away. Reddening, Saher pulled the quilt up to her neckline.

'Which room do you want me to sleep in?' He slid off the bed.

'The guest room.' Voice distant and polite, her eyes remained carefully lowered.

'OK.' He was walking away.

'Thanks!' she murmured. 'Please don't go!' The urgency in her tone arrested him.

Sweeping around, he shot her a questioning look. Her heart was in her eyes, but he wouldn't read them.

Instead, he deliberately exchanged a blank stare, mouth hardening. Did she not realise the effect she had on him? That it was impossible for him to stay another minute in the room without pulling her into his arms. Was she so naive where he was concerned, or a tease or just deliberately cruel?

'Please don't go!' she cried, uncaring of the naked look on her face or the fact that the quilt had fallen off her body.

'Saher, please!' he muttered, breathing ragged, his eyes pained. What was she expecting him to do?

'Please!'

'Saher, I have to go …' he appealed, and then found his legs carrying him back to the bed.

Face level with hers, he knelt down on the marble floor, his arms resting on the edge of the bed and a wicked smile curving his mouth. 'Saher, I can't sleep here with you!'

Electric shock jolting through her, she put a hand to her throbbing cheek, as if shielding herself from him, and pulled the quilt back over her shoulders.

'I didn't mean that, silly!' she gruffly reprimanded, too embarrassed to look him in the eyes.

Arslan watched her face with interest, joy flooding through him. His sleeping beauty had at last woken up. One of life's little triumphs. Wanting to enjoy her discomfort, his fingers moved lightly over the soft skin of her palm lying on the edge of the bed.

'Then what did you mean?' he coaxed. Fascinated, she watched his fingers playing with her hand.

'I meant that I didn't want you to go back to America.'

Taken aback by her words, his smile disappeared: 'Saher, don't become my mother's ambassador. As you know there's nothing here for me in the village.'

'Everything is here for you!' she chided.

He got up, poised to leave, but her brimming eyes arrested him.

'Please don't go!' she urged.

'Saher …' He turned his head.

Desperately she whispered, 'But everything is here!' Her voice was thick with tears.

He shook his head, feeling dejected. 'I'm not going to argue with you, Saher. I don't know why I bothered coming at this time of night.'

'Then go! Go back to where you came from!'

He strode across the room and pulled the door open. Outside in the courtyard, it was dark with the cool night breeze brushing his face. Suddenly, he turned and sprinted back to Saher's room. It was in semi-darkness, only the bedside lamp was on. With her face pressed down on the pillow she didn't hear him enter. Softly he padded to the bed and whispered, 'Saher, you said everything is here for me.'

Shocked to hear his voice, she raised her head, cheeks wet.

He looked away, not wishing to embarrass her. 'Please explain, Saher, what you meant.'

She lay there, staring up at him. 'What do you think, Arslan?'

He grimly reminded her, 'I'm too afraid to hope and think, Saher.'

Cheek dimpling and joy rushing through her, she smiled, reaching for his hand, tracing the outline of his thumb. 'I'm here!'

'I know!' His eyes were now playing with hers. Breathless, she enjoyed looking at him, holding his gaze. He watched her playful fingers weaving their magic on his palm.

'I know you are here. So what?' he challenged.

'If I asked you to stay, would you not do it for me?' she challenged, eyes now lowered.

'Only if …' he stopped.

'If?' she eagerly prompted.

'You know, Saher.' His tone was flat.

Silence. Only broken when he was about to rise.

'If you'll not stay, then take me with you!'

His eyes bored into her. She lay back on the pillow, a coquettish smile spread across her face. Confident and in control, her warm eyes caressed him, waiting and watching.

'Why?' he had to ask, yet afraid of her answer.

'Doesn't the wife normally accompany her husband!' she triumphantly threw at him, stunning him into silence.

Heart soaring, he shuttered his eyes, shielding his joy from her, deciding to play her game. Bending down, his face only inches from hers, he stated, 'Yes, normally she would – that's if she was a wife!' his voice as light and warm as the summer breeze passing through the valley.

'Then the answer is simple. Make me your wife!' she teased, holding his gaze steady.

'So that you can go with me?' he taunted, his eyes darkening.

'No, so that I can keep you here,' she tartly returned.

'Why? For my mother's sake?' he parried. She sensed his with-drawal and responded, letting her hand reach up to his cheek, the most natural of her gestures since childhood, but now her eyes caressed him with a new light.

'No, for my sake!' she whispered, pressing her fingers against his lips, smiling and in full control.

'OK, Madam Lawyer, wish granted. I'll stay for your sake, but only if you share my bed!'

Shocked, she pulled her hand back.

He laughed, enjoying her discomfort. 'Only after you've become my wife, that is,' he continued. 'And as you are not my wife yet, I've no right to share it now, have I? So please, Saher, let me leave this room, before we do something that will embarrass us both!'

Saher blushed, colour sweeping high in her warm cheeks. Dispensing with the teasing, he murmured, 'Do you know how happy you've made me?'

She nodded her head. He pressed on, still not quite con-vinced. 'Are you sure, Saher? If you change your mind tomor-row, I'm going to wring your lovely neck or drag you away with me wherever I go.'

'Then why don't you marry me now, so that I won't change my mind?' she mocked, the coquettish look reappearing. 'Then you can share my bed!'

'You just don't know how much I wish that could be the case. Unfortunately, we both know we are not going to find a *maulvi* at this time of the night to wed us.'

She nodded, letting him lift her hand and pressing it against his mouth.

'How beautiful you are. I adore you!'

She inwardly mocked herself, 'For so long I have ignored him, pretending that there was nothing between us.' His hand was now on her throat, making her shut her eyes to the sensual touch of his fingers.

She slid down on the pillow. No hiding or veiling. She owed it to him; to let him carry on brushing his eyes across her face, throat and shoulders, feeling the scorching warmth of his gaze, wondering at how many shades of colour it had brought to her cheeks.

Aloud she answered, 'I know.'

'I'm glad. Do you know you've twelve years to make up to me?'

'What if I don't – will you make me do it?' He vigorously nodded his head.

The urge to kiss her was so strong, forcing him to utter, 'Please, Saher, marry me quickly! Do you know what it's been like for the last five years, knowing that you were going to become someone else's bride?'

She mutely stared back, only able to imagine his heartache. She had just woken up, had just tasted the pain – the pain of losing him.

'I'll marry you tomorrow, if that's what you want, Arslan. I want no grand weddings. A simple *nikkah* ceremony is more to my taste. In any event, my trousseau is already packed, remember? Only the groom has changed. Instead of one home, it'll go to another.'

'Indeed!' Arslan agreed. 'I was so angry with Ismail for jilting you, now I feel I should worship him. You know how painful it has been for me.'

'I know … I'm glad that Ismail has married Daniela – you have been my affectionate shadow for so long. How could I possibly live without my shadow?'

Marvelling at the tenderness in her voice, he happily continued feasting on her beauty.

Then surpising both herself and him, she pulled his head down and kissed him hard on the mouth. He kissed her back, assuaging years of need. It was he who pulled away feeling himself going crazy with the need to carry on kissing her.

'No more, Saher! Please! Let me go!'

Blushing hard and looking away, Saher nodded. He stood up, breathing hard, trying to maintain a normal heartbeat.

'I'm glad you called me. If you hadn't I was planning to leave for Islamabad tomorrow. I think after our kissing and for your reputation's sake, my darling, it's best that I don't sleep under the same roof as you until we're married … best that I return home. I can't trust myself. Your mother, too, will not be pleased, you know that! Aunt Rani has always known how I felt about you. She definitely saw what you failed to see.'

'Yes, I was blind! And yes, you must go back home. I'm fine now … I was just upset about losing you,' her husky voice wooed, not ashamed of having kissed him, finding herself alight with passion.

Smiling and nodding at her, he got up to leave, noting the brazen smile curving her lips.

His hand was on the door handle when he heard her whisper, 'I love you! As a man! You know that now!' A triumphant smile slashing across his face, Arslan let himself out of her room.

CHAPTER 38

The Making-Up

'Massi Fiza!' Rukhsar's eldest daughter called, peering down from the rooftop gallery of her house into Massi Fiza's small courtyard, stacked with an assortment of baskets and bags of laundry.

In the middle of it all was Massi Fiza in full swing with her washing, her agile mind assessing each article of unwashed clothing in the basket in front of her. An agonising debate going on in her head rested on whether to dip the sweetmaker's syrup-sodden shirt into the same water as his daughter's delicate lawn *kameez*.

Massi Fiza's honesty and fair play as always ruled the day. Allah Pak had blessed her with a conscience of which she was immensely proud. 'Allah Pak is watching … he sees everything you do,' she took care to brutally remind herself when occasion-ally she was tempted to economise on detergent. Her commit-ment to quality work dictated that it would be a crime to let such a delicate article of clothing touch a stained one. Sighing, she swished aside the sweetmaker's greasy overalls.

She hated this part of the day – the horrible chores of boiling pots of water, and then dipping, lathering, kneading and the painstaking task of rinsing the sodden clothes with her bony arms.

'Auntie Fiza,' Rukhsar's daughter called again from the roof terrace. She could just make out their neighbour leaning over a large, red, plastic tub and listening to another one of Nusrat Fateh Ali Khan's *qawalis*. The dust-encrusted audiotape ran at least four times a day. Fans of Nusrat's *qawalis* knew where to go just to hear his voice in the village. Many stalled their pace outside Massi Fiza's courtyard wall to chant the long 'Allaho Allaho' qawali.

Massi Fiza glanced up, face brimming with pleasure, then immediately she straightened it, her mouth becoming a tight slit; remembering that she was not on speaking terms with the household next door. Then just as quickly she relented, chiding herself that it was the mother she had fallen out with, not the girls – they still remained her 'darlings'.

Cupping her hand over her lined forehead to shield her face from the beating sun, she warmly called back, 'Yes, my daughter?'

'Auntie, could you please wash the yellow *haldi* stain off my white silk party suit? I won't risk sending it to the other laundry house!'

Speechless, Massi Fiza blinked up at the young woman, peering over the shoulder-high brick wall.

'Yes, of course, Shabnum dear!' Her generosity made her quickly offer. 'Bring your suit down in an hour's time ... I'll have cleared this tub of washing by then.'

'Oh, you are wonderful, Massi Fiza!' Shabnum excitedly called before disappearing.

Massi Fiza waited for an hour but there was no sign of the girl. Shrugging her shoulders she continued with her washing – imagining that Shabnum had changed her mind.

*

Shabnum was still desperate to have the *haldi* stain washed from the suit that she had set her heart on wearing to her friend's engagement party. The truth behind her non-appearance was her mother's obstinacy and being caught in the act of smuggling the suit out to Auntie Massi Fiza's capable hands. It was the manner in which the girl's chiffon *dupatta* was fully draped down to her waist that gave the game away to her observant mother.

The goldsmith's daughters were incredibly fashion conscious and prided themselves on setting fashion trends in their village. Young teenage girls often copied and quoted their samples for dresses to their tailors. Moreover, the girls were not much given to modesty when it came to covering their head or their chest area, unless really necessary – during prayer times, and those moments were rare: only on Eid days or during the month of Ramadhan. The youngest, mimicking the urban fashion trends, even had the audacity to have a sleeveless dress made, causing Gulistan's tailor-mistress to gossip to her other clients: 'Can you imagine it, not even two inches of a sleeve – totally sleeveless! Those goldsmiths' daughters are setting outrageous fashion trends for our modest village daughters. What next? Will they start showing their legs or their ankles off as those shameless presenters sometimes do on TV?'

When her mother pulled off her *chador* to see what she was hiding under it, Shabnum had looked first guilty and then sullen.

'I'm taking the dress to be washed, to Massi Fiza!' she defiantly yelled at her mother, not wanting to succumb to her mother's scathing chastisement.

'Don't you dare!' Rukhsar angrily ordered.

'Oh, Mum, this is so stupid. That new *dhobi* of yours has ruined two of my delicate suits already – the seams on my taffeta dress have come apart and on Father's shirt two buttons have gone missing. As you saw for yourself, your lovely deep-purple suit is now sun-bleached to a horrible bland colour! I'm not risking this silk suit. Look! Only Aunt Fiza can remove this!' Shabnum held up her dress to show the yellowish fat stain.

'You bone-idle girl!' Rukhsar firmly blocked the doorway. 'You've got hands. Wash it yourself! None of you ever scours any pots – you let them lie around the sink until lunchtime waiting for the maid to clear them away.

'And guess what? I'm to blame for spoiling you all, for making you into lazy women. How will you survive in your future homes? There will be no guarantee that you will have dozens of maids doing your bidding! Why is it that you think you girls are so special and that all the housework needs to be done by someone else?' Rukhsar ranted, seriously worried about her daughters' capacity to survive in their in-laws' households – and who would be blamed? She! Their mother.

'Mum! That's so unfair.' Shabnum hated the long waffly lecture but did not know how to stop it.

'I tell you that you are going nowhere near that woman, do you hear me?' Rukhsar shrieked, snatching the dress off her daughter.

'Mother!' Shabnum cried, nearly in tears. 'I want to wear it to my evening party!'

'You've got a wardrobe full of clothes, madam! Half of your father's gold income goes into dressing you girls in the best of outfits, and you are going to have me insulted – by that woman!' Rukhsar aggressively shepherded her daughter back into the living room.

Sullen and fed up, Shabnum fled to her room and sprawled on her bed to enjoy a good sulk – hating her mother for her petty attitude.

After two hours of flicking through two magazines and a *Readers Digest* romantic saga, and listening to the latest Bolly-wood songs, Shabnum suddenly remembered Massi Fiza.

'Oh, no!' Scrambling off the bed, she sneaked upstairs to the roof gallery to peer down over the brick wall into their neigh-bour's laundry house.

'Massi Fiza,' she called softly, afraid of her mother hearing her, and just about spotting Massi Fiza amidst the washing lines of coloureds and whites criss-crossing the small courtyard.

Dismayed, Massi Fiza was looking at a dripping red *dupatta*, its bright reddish colour dyeing the brickwork of her veranda floor. Every evening she had to scrub out some dyes or other. Today it was the stubborn red one.

'Shabnum, the water … the bucket of clean hot water I put aside for your suit has gone cold … still waiting, darling.'

'So sorry, Auntie,' Shabnum hastened to apologise, shame-faced, 'but I couldn't come.'

'Couldn't? You should have sent your sister.'

'She couldn't come, either,' she replied, blushing.

'Why? Are there guests in the house or is there a big necklace order?'

'No, Auntie,' Shabnum stammered, and then blurted out

the truth to their dear neighbour, who had known them since the day they opened their eyes, had washed and pressed their clothes as well as colouring their days with visits and basketfuls of gossip. 'Mother said that I could not bring my suit to you,' she miserably admitted.

'I see,' Massi Fiza muttered, her thin-lipped mouth fallen open, the colour ebbing from her sunburned face.

Crimsoning in regret, Shabnum disappeared from the railings.

Massi Fiza dropped the dripping red *dupatta* into the bowl, ignoring her cold, wet *kameez* streaked with a red gash straight down its front, and kicked the bucket of soapy water she had prepared for Shabnum's clothes aside. She knew for sure that her sugar levels had dropped; feeling the slight faintness coming on, she grabbed one of the *ladoos* from her sweet plate.

Not bothering to lock her door, she shot up Rukhsar's staircase from the street entrance. 'Nobody would ever think of stealing anything from your house, Massi Fiza – the stench of the washing itself is a deterrent,' Rukhsar had once joked, much to Massi Fiza's shame.

Upstairs, her heart thumping, she aggressively thrust open the door straight into Rukhsar's living room. Instead of her friend, it was the goldsmith who greeted her. He was being served his lunch by his wife, who was seated beside him on the sofa. Both were taken aback by Massi Fiza's rude entrance and the hardened glint in her eyes. Outraged, Rukhsar's jaw dropped, unable to speak. It was thus left to the goldsmith to gobble down his big morsel of *kofta* meatball and find his tongue.

'*Assalam alaikum*, Sister Fiza – I've not seen you for a long time,' he affably offered, unaware of the prickly tension hovering across the space between the two women, their eyes falling at his words. The mutinous look on his wife's face bemused him as he popped another chunk of the meatball into his mouth.

'I think I know what has happened,' he chuckled. 'No wonder that young son of the *dhobi* has been cockily bringing our washing back. Have you two, the best of friends, with over 20 years of "sisterly" friendship, by chance fallen out with each other?' he mockingly commented.

'Yes, we have!' Massi Fiza jumped in to answer first. 'Your wife has become very childish and mean-spirited late in life, brother. She stopped your Shabnum from bringing her washing to me.'

'What?' the goldsmith gasped, the second meatball gripped between his fingers as he turned to his wife. Rukhsar was purple with rage. How dare that *dhoban* call her childish and mean-spirited?

'Yes!' Rukhsar screeched.

'Your girls are like daughters to me, Rukhsar! How could you do this to me? I wanted to wash Shabnum's suit – she had especially asked me to.' She turned to appeal to the goodness of his heart, 'Your wife can send her washing to India, or China, if she wants, but if your dear girls want me to do theirs, I'll not turn them away – not even at midnight. I've stitched their zips and tucked in the hemlines on their college jeans on my trusty old sewing machine – but I have always done it because I love them. Is this how your arrogant wife repays my friendship?'

'I've come for Shabnum's suit. Just you try and stop me, Rukhsar!' Massi Fiza threatened, eyes appealing to the goldsmith. 'Brother, you decide as to who's in the wrong and who's in the right?'

'Sister Fiza,' he began, his appetite now truly ruined as he concentrated hard on trying to appease his irate neighbour. 'Nobody will stop you from doing all our washing. Please take it! Take it all!'

He turned to stare with disgust at his wife. 'Fancy stopping Sister Fiza from taking the laundry, Rukhsar-ji! Are you OK?'

'It's her! She gave me the cold shoulder first!' Rukhsar snapped.

'Well, you thought I was going to steal your gold necklace!' Massi Fiza blurted out, still deeply affronted and rattled by that incident.

'It's all in your silly head! I never accused you of anything, did I?'

The goldsmith pushed aside the tray of food in front of him and leaned back on his sofa, lazily glancing from one to the other.

'But your eyes did!' Massi Fiza shot back.

'Oh dear, oh dear!' the goldsmith laughed, suddenly springing to his feet, feeling that physical intervention was now required. 'Women, their imaginations and their petty squabbles, it's all beyond me. I must say, however, Massi Fiza-ji, that you've got it wrong this time. Please believe that I'm not trying to defend my wife. Of course we can trust you. Who else can we trust? You have practically lived half of your life with us and, in fact, you are an extension of our family.

'So this is a storm in a teacup, stemming from an overactive imagination. I'm truly disappointed in both of you. Please, Fiza-ji, don't fret, you can take Shabnum's suit to wash. In fact, take three of mine, too. I never did like that cocky son of Master Dhobi. His starch makes my legs and arms itch all day. How can we possibly take our business away from you Massi Fiza? It would be immoral!'

'Your wife did!' Massi Fiza jeered, making her friend bristle all over again.

'When I went to your home, you refused to speak to me!' Rukhsar bitterly hit back.

'Ladies, ladies! I don't want to take any sides. Come, make up and hug each other, please,' the goldsmith urged. Then his jaw dropped open, astonished to see how quickly both the women fell into each other's arms. Bemused, his gaze rested on their joined bodies. He giggled – Massi Fiza was practically clutching his wife's shoulders.

'After everything they've said! It was all a matter of foolish pride at the end!' he told himself.

Rukhsar called her daughter, Shabnum. Massi Fiza, smiling, now very much at home, stayed to enjoy her favourite cup of milky coffee. Tucking Shabnum's suit under her arm, she took her leave. Both friends still felt slightly raw, but they had crossed one major bridge today. And would cross another one tomorrow, before they fully reverted to their former camaraderie.

From the door Massi Fiza offered quietly, 'Rukhsar-ji, if you've any suits of your own that need washing, do send them down, I'll happily do them for you.'

'Yes, of course, Massi Fiza-ji,' Rukhsar stammered, touched

by her friend's generous offer and deliberately adding the term 'ji'. They were fast reinstating each other within the parameters of mutual respect.

That evening, Shabnum had her suit returned; washed, neatly dried with a hot iron and the *haldi* stain removed – all courtesy of their 'special aunt' next door. Massi Fiza-ji had missed the social chit-chat with Rukhsar and wondered whether the gold-smith's wife had the good grace to acknowledge how much her dear neighbour was worth. Apart from the cups of coffee and an occasional meal, there was very little she took from them. So the scales were definitely tipped on her side.

CHAPTER 39

The Feast

Upon her return to her home Mehreen felt wretched. Biting her lower lip, she headed straight up to her bedroom. Rani, unable to cope with meeting the Englishwoman who had ruined things for her daughter, had departed, saying she had to visit one of her friends. Rasoola gently knocked on the bedroom door and waited with a panting heart.

'Rasoola, Sahiba-ji,' she dutifully announced before entering her mistress's room.

Mehreen, her back to the door, was removing her sandals for her *wudu* ablutions. She glanced up, carefully shielding her eyes from the crafty woman's all-knowing gaze.

'Good to have you back, Sahiba-ji.' Rasoola smoothly declared.

'Thank you, Rasoola,' was the polite answer.

'Dinner is ready. Will you be joining Daniela and Ismail?' Mehreen was not cowed by the bold question and peeped at the mirror; it merely reflected her panic.

'It would be good to spend time in the company of your son and daughter-in-law,' Rasoola firmly advised, knowing she was playing with fire. 'They'll be going back soon, Ismail was saying. I can't speak *Engrezi,* but I can communicate through gestures pretty well with his English bride – she's really nice, Sahiba-ji.'

'Thank you, Rasoola,' Mehreen coldly cut in, now quite cross. Rasoola had a knack for trespassing social parameters and family matters. This woman had started her nightmare!

'So will you join them?' Rasoola pressed, determinedly.

'Yes, Rasoola!' Mehreen swung round to glare at her housekeeper. 'Now leave me alone!'

'Right, the table will be ready in one hour,' Rasoola softly informed her before taking her leave, a smug smile hidden behind her hand, and satisfied at achieving her goal of getting her mistress out of her room to join the family. She was very aware of the rift between her master and mistress – her mistress's swollen eyes spelt it all.

These 'big' people had everything to their name – everything that the world could possibly provide, yet they still wept in misery like everyone else. Her mistress's arms were weighed down by dozens of *tholas* of gold bangles; yet, that gold did not halt her tears.

For Rasoola, to stay in the cool of an air-conditioned room in the heat of the summer season was a blessing indeed in life. But for Mehreen, that air conditioning did not cool the burns that scarred her inside.

Once downstairs, Rasoola cheerfully announced to Ismail that she was making pasta for the 'bride', as she liked to call Daniela, *kheer* rice pudding for Ismail, chicken *biryani* for her mistress and for the master it had to be *shami* kebabs. Ismail's mouth was already heavily salivating from the delicious freshly ground mint sauce she had given him to taste.

Rasoola gleefully entered her kitchen. A feast she was going to provide for this family of hers!

'Whether or not it is a good idea to interfere in this family's affairs, I have done it out of the goodness of my heart,' she happily told herself.

*

A silent group, gathered for Rasoola's feast, were surreptitiously eyeing each other. Daniela nervously watched her father-in-law with a lowered gaze, sitting opposite him at the round table. Liaquat was openly staring with hostility at both his wife and his daughter-in-law. Mehreen was looking down at her plate, risking the occasional furtive glance at her husband. Only Ismail seemed to be relishing his meal.

Nobody dared to leave the table – and so they hung on for tea. All four reluctantly accepted the need for bridges to be built in their household and in their relationships. Otherwise their lives would become insufferable.

Liaquat was bent on avoiding eye contact with Daniela. By the end of the meal, he had arrived at a turning point. The compass of reason dictated that he had to accept this foreign woman as his son's lawful wife and into their lives. Similarly, he needed to forgive his errant wife for her stupidity and impulsive ways. No matter how hard it was, he needed to pass this test and really well! Draining his hot tea to the last drop, he left the table. The two women raised their heads.

In the office safe, Liaquat's hand stalled on a pile of six velvet jewellery boxes. Taking them out, he flicked the latch of the largest one, lifted the lid and stared at a heavy sparkling gold and topaz necklace set. 'These are my Saher's!' he murmured, feeling his eyes filling up. He'd had them lovingly designed by the best goldsmith in the city. Lifting another box he did the same, until he couldn't bear to look at the last one.

Determined, Liaquat returned to the dining room and stood behind Daniela. She glanced up, fearful of the look of hostility she expected to see on his face. Pushing aside a jug of water, he placed the six velvet boxes on the table in front of her. Daniela turned a blank stare at him, wondering what was going on whilst her husband and mother-in-law gasped, knowing what the boxes contained.

'Ismail, take them! These should now belong to your wife. Please tell her!'

His voice rough with emotion, Ismail translated his father's words to Daniela. Mehreen paled, staring at the boxes, waiting for an explanation. Was her husband mad, passing all that gold to a foreign woman?

'Daniela, my father is giving you these gold necklaces as a wedding present. They are all yours, so open the boxes and look inside, my darling!' Ismail instructed, voice rich with tears, overwhelmed by his father's generosity.

Daniela could not believe either her ears or her eyes. Pleasure rushed through her as her husband flicked open the lid of the first jewellery box. All three stared down at its contents

– a delicate, three-layered choker set, studded with rubies and pearls.

Daniela rose to her feet. Taking the older man totally by surprise, she planted a warm kiss on his cheek; so quick and sudden that Rasoola, returning with a tray of fruit, was rooted to the spot. The foreign woman had kissed her master in the presence of everyone – God forbid!

Mehreen and Ismail, too, were frozen into stillness as Liaquat's mind blanked out. He looked across at his wife, who was sitting there, laughter tugging at her mouth. Relaxing, his eyes fell in embarrassment; his daughter-in-law had just proved how big the cultural gap was between them. 'Which Pakistani daughter-in-law would leap up to kiss a man, even if he were her father-in-law?' he wondered.

Daniela opened each box, one after the other, marvelling at their contents. Saher had fussed about the items and the designs, whereas this woman wore a childlike look of wonder on her face. Over the fourth box containing an emerald necklace, gold earrings and matching bracelet, Daniela broke down and sobbed – startling the other three around the table.

'These are the people I've hurt with my unexpected entrance into their lives,' Daniela mocked herself. 'Now they are honouring me with all this gold – I don't deserve this.'

Mehreen's special look compelled her husband to obey her signal. His hand lifted to pat Daniela's head. His gentle touch startled Daniela into raising her tear-smeared face to him. Her smile and her emerald eyes, swollen with tears, were his undoing. He relaxed his mouth. Each basked in the other's smile: Daniela, out of gratitude, no longer afraid of this tall, fierce-looking man, and Liaquat, dutifully, and because he simply couldn't help himself liking his English daughter-in-law and her reaction to his gifts.

Mother and son looked on, happiness spiralling through them. Smiling from cheek to cheek at Rasoola and with his heart soaring, Ismail revelled in the look on his father's face; it was equivalent to six boxes of gold and precious stones.

Mehreen, humbled, shyly smiled a 'thank you' from her eyes. She was not sure what it was for, for the gold or for that kind gesture in patting his daughter-in-law's head. When her husband's smile lightly brushed Mehreen's face, the world was shining and inside she was singing.

CHAPTER 40

The Mission

'Your wish has been granted!' Arslan coolly announced to his mother as he entered the dining room in the morning. Gulbahar looked away from his forbidding face. 'Did you not hear me, Mother?' he teased, a hint of warmth creeping into his voice. Gulbahar fearfully lifted her eyes. 'You have your wish,' he repeated.

Begum wheeled in the breakfast trolley with a steaming *siri pai* curry dish, setting Arslan's stomach rumbling for the sheep's trotters.

'Have you got your special baked *naan* bread, Begum?'

'Of course, my prince.' Begum was aggrieved at the question. 'How can you possibly have *pai* without my special *naan* bread – I've made four piping hot ones and dripping with *makhan* fat.'

Gulbahar looked on dispassionately – her son's last breakfast at home – still waiting for his explanation. Love swimming through his veins, the kiss still fresh in his mind Arslan took pity on his mother. Getting up, he hugged her from behind. She froze as his arms circled tightly around her shoulders.

'I'm going to stay on, Mother,' he quietly informed her.

Eyes incredulous, Gulbahar swung round to face him. 'And there is more ... I'm going to marry Saher – and very soon.'

'*Such much* – really!' she exclaimed in wonder, eyes brimming with tears.

Kissing the top of her head, he spoke in a voice warm with laughter. 'Yes, she's agreed and she's mine! I'm taking you with me to Aunt Rani's house, so that we can formally ask for Saher's *rishta*.'

Gulbahar's eyes shone with pleasure as she nodded, savouring and letting the moment wash over her.

'How did this come about?' she whispered.

'I gave her an ultimatum that I would only stay if she married me.'

'I see. So you would rather stay because of Saher and not because your own mother begged you to?' Gulbahar quietly stated with resigned acceptance. Would any man passionately in love listen to the request of his beloved or his mother? She felt an overwhelming joy as she realised that it solved everything, as well as poor Rani and Saher's heartache.

Arslan had stepped away and sat down to enjoy his breakfast. A moment later, catching his mother's uncertain look, he moved his plate aside. 'But, Mother, I'll only stay in Pakistan if my sister and my niece are brought back home! Do you hear me, Mother?'

Gasping for breath, Gulbahar nodded. Then bitterly burst forth, 'I hear you! I understand you! Don't shout! Continue with your breakfast,' she commanded.

Why was their son always their accuser? Did he think that it was easy for her to watch her granddaughter walk out of their home?

He broke off a piece of the *naan* bread. 'Mother, won't you have some?' Gulbahar shook her head, one thought only on her mind.

The dead had to be replaced with the living.

*

Gulbahar had her own mission in the west wing of the *hevali*, a place she rarely visited – the office area, where the male clients were entertained and land deals discussed. A traditional landowner, Haider had embedded strict rules in his household. This included the door to his office quarters remaining firmly shut, protecting the privacy and sanctity of his domestic world and of his wife's quarters in particular. He was an enthusiastic believer in the notion that women should neither be seen nor heard by strange *ghair* men. If his business counterparts brought their wives with them, then Gulbahar would entertain them. Only the extended family members and servants had access to the rest of the *hevali*.

Looking over her shoulder with trepidation, Gulbahar walked down the veranda, afraid of interrupting her husband in the company of other men. The familiar sight of Ali coming out of the *bethak* brought a sigh of relief to her lips.

'Mistress? Anything wrong? You should have sent Begum,' Ali asked, surprised.

'Ali, is Master-ji alone in his office?' Gulbahar smiled at their *munshi*.

He nodded. 'The accountant is coming later this afternoon – I'm going to take Master-ji to the bank.'

'Thank you, Ali.' Gulbahar stalled outside the door, to straighten her shawl around her shoulders and to still her thumping heart. Gently pushing the door open, she recalled the last time she had entered – two years ago precisely – to inform her husband of the death of one of his cousins.

'Gulbahar!' The blue eyes immediately frosted, questioning her presence in the 'business' domain.

Emboldened by her mission and ignoring the changing, slightly hostile, landscape of his face, she approached his desk. He had been examining his accounts, ticking items off with his expensive gold pen in his business ledger. His appointment diary with its scrawled entries lay open on one side of the desk and a jug of water stood on the other.

'Haider-ji,' she began, 'Arslan is leaving tomorrow – you know that, don't you?'

'Yes.' Haider was mightily displeased and lanced his wife for reminding him. Apparently Gulbahar had come on an errand for their errant son. Gulbahar steeled herself, determined not to be intimidated by his cold manner. She reacted by coldly staring back, her new-found strength enabling her to stand up to her husband and fight on her daughter's behalf.

'Then you will know what his ultimatum is for staying?' she firmly reminded him, her tone still gentle.

'I'll not be blackmailed by that scoundrel, Gulbahar!' Haider raged, rising from his leather seat and throwing his pen on the table. Gulbahar flinched, but didn't cower in front of her husband's aggression; instead she raised her head tall to start her rehearsed speech.

She began, 'Haider-ji, if you don't bring my daughter and granddaughter home, you may as well bury me within these four walls, for that's all I have now.' She paused, scanning his face carefully. 'Nothing else to live for. I slew a daughter in my heart ten years ago. I callously let our beautiful, innocent granddaughter stride out of our lives ... I said and did nothing! I'm now faced with the loss of my only son, after five years of absence. Forced to give up both my children! What's my ultimate test of endurance to be, Haider-ji, to prove to you, above all, that I'm a good, faithful wife – but a heartless mother? Should I become a loving mother or a rebellious wife – in either case I cannot win, can I, my dear husband? To which fate will you have me assigned, Haider-ji? Yet I love you – you know that.

'For so long, I have stood by you and supported all your decisions. Don't break my heart now by letting my beloved son walk out of our lives. I beg you! Don't make a mother choose a husband over her son! Mehreen and her husband are learning to accept a woman from another country, another race, another culture into their lives, and Mehreen tells me that Liaquat has handed all the gold meant for Saher to their English bride.

'Have we not got enough humanity in our hearts to accept a fellow, Pakistani Muslim villager? What makes us so special! From which earth, *mitthi*, have we sprung? What right have we got to reject another human being?'

Her husband's clapping stopped her short.

'How beautifully you string your words, and make me out to be the wicked demon in all of this! You'll make a great advocate in Saher's court, my dear wife!' Haider cynically lashed out at his wife.

'You know well, Gulbahar, what Jubail and Laila did, or have you so conveniently forgotten? Do not attempt to condemn or isolate me – or hold the moral high ground. I'm not a wrongdoer, as you well know. I'm a fair man and I gave you the choice then, to do what was best for you. It was your decision, Gulbahar, to turn your back on your daughter, remember? It was you who insisted on removing all traces of her from our home.' The earnest rebuttal spelt to Gulbahar that she had hurt her husband with her words.

'No, I've spoken to remind you that I've always been a faithful wife to you and have supported you in all decisions.'

'It was not just a question of being faithful and supporting me, Gulbahar,' he harshly reminded her. 'Your decisions were dictated by your personal belief in what you were doing. You knew what we did was right at the time. If what you believe in now is different – in other words, that I should now embrace my daughter and her family and bring them into our midst, into our home, then so be it.'

He was confronted by her blank stare, as Gulbahar tried to make sense of his words.

'You'll … you'll bring back our daughter?' she stammered in disbelief.

Eyes skirting her anxious face and his own, a tight, sad mask, Haider nodded.

'I lost a daughter a long time ago and a son to another land. Arslan's deep-rooted hatred of us and what we did is suffocating everyone. I can't afford to lose a wonderful wife, too. Gulbahar, whatever you wish will happen, my dear.'

Gulbahar rushed around the desk to cross the space to the man who held her peace of mind and happiness in his big masculine hands. Laying her head against his chest, she wept tears of anguish and joy.

Haider hugged her tightly, mouth grazing the top of her head, unable to bear hurting his beloved wife, wittingly or unwittingly. Bleakly, he stared at the space in front of him, contemplating. A high summit had yet to be climbed.

The sobbing abruptly stopped.

'I haven't told you the good news – Arslan is to marry Saher!' Gulbahar excitedly blurted, eyes shining with delight.

'What?'

She nodded, her soft fingers lovingly caressing his face.

'Yes, Saher has agreed. Isn't it marvellous?' For the first time, she saw his face relax as he grinned down at her.

He sighed with happiness. At last, something good was happening in his household. There could not be a better bride for their son than Saher. And with her strong influence over him she would definitely keep him here.

'I'm going to Rani's house today to ask for Saher's hand.' Gulbahar shyly peeped up at him, catching the warm tender look in his eye. Haider was about to kiss her hard, there and then, but he reluctantly let her out of his arms; the office was the wrong place and his accountant was due any minute.

*

A few minutes later in the large kitchen, Gulbahar couldn't hold back her joy as she exchanged another tight hug with her housekeeper; her aching cheeks remained plumped into a broad smile. All afternoon Ali had been despatched on so many errands. Some he dealt with on his mobile phone, but the important task still remained – to collect the tastiest fresh sweets in special trimmed decorative baskets. Gulbahar's most treasured item of jewellery, a *gulaband* necklace set embedded with real *kundan* gems from Delhi, was plucked out from her jewellery safe. Originally, it had been set aside as part of Laila's trousseau, but now it was to honour Saher's throat.

In the afternoon, Gulbahar drove out with Ali and Arslan into Attock's main shopping bazaar. Mother and son hopped in and out of sari department stores to sample yards of silks and chiffons. With so many delicate and colourful fabrics rolled across the tables in front of them and the portable fans purring away at their sides, Gulbahar was unable to decide either on the colour or on the embroidery design. In the end her son happily came to her aid, his eye caught by one colour, imagining the sensuous and softest of chiffons in sky-blue moulded around the contours of his beloved Saher's body.

'But it has no embroidery on it, my son,' Gulbahar chided, aggrieved at his very 'plain' and 'simple' choice.

'It doesn't matter, Mother. Plain and simple is best and this is the one I want to see her in – she'll love it, please believe me!'

Gulbahar laughed, shaking her head at him.

'But if Saher and Aunt Rani don't like it, blame it all on me, Mother. Just relax, please!' Joy threaded his voice, bringing a lump to Gulbahar's throat. The burka-clad woman sitting on the other sofa seat, also purchasing a sari for her daughter, smiled behind her *niqab*, eyes peeping over the fold held up to her nose.

'Good choice, sir!' the shopkeeper politely commented, disappointed that he had not been able to sell one of the more expensive gem-encrusted saris that the older woman had been thoughtfully fingering. They also purchased a similar one for Daniela, as a gift.

'Now, the ring!' Gulbahar reminded him, stepping into the goldsmith's shop next door, bringing an eager smile to the lips of the middle-aged owner, delighted to show off his wares. Arslan hastily shepherded his mother out of the shop, much to the disappointment of the jeweller.

'I've got the ring already, Mother, so please don't fret.'

'What? When did you buy it?'

'I bought it in New York. It was meant to be my wedding present for Saher. A diamond ring, in fact. I'll show it to you later – you'll love it. Let's go, we need to reach Auntie's house before evening.'

Gulbahar chuckled at her son's eagerness and reached out to hug him yet again.

*

Humming to herself, Begum took the breakfast tray up to her mistress's bedroom. From the top of the wrought-iron balcony outside her mistress's bedroom, Begum saw father and son, dressed in their outdoor jackets, apparently waiting for Ali to bring the Jeep round to the front door of the *hevali*.

Heart and step immediately lighter, Begum thrust the door wide open with her foot. '*Assalam alaikum*, Sahiba-ji!' Her loud, cheery voice had her mistress sitting up in bed, face creased in condemnation.

'Begum!' Gulbahar scolded her housekeeper.

Begum brazenly proclaimed, 'You are going to eat everything

on this tray, Mistress Sahiba, because you have a wonderful day ahead of you! Please believe me!'

'Have I, Begum?' Gulbahar asked, pushing her thick, curly, greying strands of hair back from her face.

'Yes, Mistress, indeed you have.' There was no let-up on the cheeky note as she placed a tray on the table. 'You see, your beautiful fairy is coming with her mother,' she dropped the bombshell.

'Begum?' Gulbahar whispered, lips parted, wanting so much to believe Begum's words but too afraid to entertain the idea in her head.

Perched on the end of the bed, Begum searched for her mistress's feet under the quilt. The effect was immediate; Gulbahar relaxed, revelling in the magic of her housekeeper's calloused fingers. It was a ritual that always drew the two women into close intimacy, a prelude to a warm heart-to-heart chat. It was at such times that the mistress was not the mistress and the housekeeper was not the housekeeper. Closing her eyes, Gulbahar relished the pressure from Begum's nimble fingers.

'Mistress, Master Haider and Master Arslan are, at this moment, on their way to Islamabad to bring our Laila back home.'

Gulbahar's eyes widened in delight.

'You'll now ask me as to how they know where Laila lives. Well, I have a confession to make, Mistress – I'm sorry. Today, I can share the guilty secret that has been eating away at me for so long. I stayed with our Laila for two days. Please don't look so shocked. Ali would have killed me if he knew! It was the time when I was gone for a week to visit my elderly aunt, who lives in a village outside Islamabad.' She stopped, looking shamefaced. 'I'm sorry, Mistress, but I had to … love Mistress Laila!'

Gulbahar didn't know what to say. Though dismayed, she was unable to reprimand her housekeeper.

'Thank you, Begum,' she murmured, trying hard to soften her expression. Then the image of the fairy zoomed before her eyes and her face split into a wide smile.

'Oh, Allah Pak! Bless you, Begum, for bringing me such wonderful news!' she cried. 'What am I doing sitting in bed, if my *pari* is coming to her grandparents' house? We must prepare a special room for our fairy. The *halvie* must make piping hot *jalebis* for my fairy. A very big tray! You told me that she loves *jalebis*?' Grinning, Begum nodded, delighted at her mistress's childlike response.

'When will the men be back, Begum?'

Gulbahar slid off the bed, standing tall, poised for a long day of activities and a special dinner menu to plan.

The joy on her mistress's face had Begum sobbing into the fold of her *chador*. 'I'm so happy for you, Mistress. At last this will be a normal house. For years I've wept for my Laila. I was her "second" mother. You parted company with her willingly – I did it under duress. This is indeed a joyous day for us both, Mistress!'

Gulbahar wryly nodded her head and, placing a comforting arm around Begum's shoulders, she hugged her tightly. 'You're indeed a mother to our children. I appreciate very much the love you've lavished on them, Begum. At times, I think you are more of a sister to me than my own, for they have both turned against me.' Gulbahar could not disguise the bitterness in her tone.

'Mistress?' Begum prompted, wanting to know more but too afraid of prying further. She heartily blessed herself with the fervent words, 'My mistress is one in a million.'

'Nothing, Begum,' Gulbahar replied, shrugging her shoulders as if to shrug aside her sisters and the stress they brought into her life. She wouldn't let Rani's latest poison cloud her day. How did one count the minutes and the seconds whilst waiting for loved ones?

'Come, Begum. Call two extra maids for the day. A lot of work ahead of us!'

'Yes, of course, Mistress!' Begum enthusiastically chanted.

PART FOUR

CHAPTER 41

The Visit

The heavy midday traffic in Islamabad was punctuated by the loud blaring of car horns. In a side street, Haider's Pajero stood parked outside a small house, referred to locally as a *quarter*, its whitewashed wall grimy with graffiti, road dust and layers of dried moss.

With beating hearts, Haider and Arslan knocked on the door indicated by Ali, dutifully standing a few paces behind. In both their heads the same thought hammered – would it be their Laila or …?

The door was slowly pulled open and to their surprise a small figure in a lemon cotton frock stood in the doorway, ready to bid *salaam*, but the greeting died on her lips as she caught sight of the red-haired man. She stepped back, leaving the two men at the door stunned.

The door left open, the girl was now running across the small courtyard, giving the visitors their first glimpse of Laila's marital home; a modern house, with a courtyard the size of the smallest storeroom in their *hevali*.

Standing in the doorway of the living room, her face red, Shirin seared her mother with an accusing glare, having just realised that there was some sort of connection between her mother and those people from the village.

'Daddy, the old man with red hair from the village is here,' she declared, mouth falling open as her mother stumbled to her feet from the sofa, nearly tripping over the small coffee table in front of her. Barefooted, Laila ran out into the courtyard, the words 'surely it cannot be!' ringing in her head.

When she caught a glimpse of her loved ones' dear faces shyly peeping into her home, the world and time stood still, incoherent sounds of joy and sobs choking her. At the sight of his daughter's joyous face, as if by magic, Haider's arms lifted. Laila dived straight into them, happily letting them become a tight band around her waist and sinking her face into her father's chest.

Her bemused brother stood by, eyes smarting with tears. Jubail had now come out with Shirin in tow. He was galled by the tableau before him. Across the small space, his gaze clashed head on with that of his father-in-law. Those blue eyes still lanced him but the strong arms were loath to let go of his daughter.

'What's Mummy doing in that horrible man's arms?' Shirin demanded, standing by her father's side, one hand placed possessively on his leg. The urge to pull her mother out of the red-haired man's arms was strong but her father's tight grip held her back.

At last Laila raised her sobbing face, 'Mother?'

Arslan hastened to explain, anticipating the direction of her thoughts. 'Don't worry, Laila, Mother is fine. We've come to take you home.' The hesitant words produced an awkward silence. Laila warily peeped up at her father.

Eyes steadfast and solemn, Haider nodded. Face alight with joy, Laila looked over her shoulder at her grim-faced husband and scowling daughter. The smile slipped, the light in her eyes immediately dimmed. Gently withdrawing from her father's arms, she called to her daughter, 'Shirin, come. Meet your grandfather and your uncle. Say *salaam*,' she coaxed.

Her small mouth wedged into a mutinous line, Shirin sidled closer against her father's leg and reached her slim arm up to his waist.

'Shirin!' Laila called, but her daughter had run off into the room, banging the door shut behind her. Laila stood in shock under the small veranda with its two colonnades and yellow peeling plasterwork.

'Jubail, please!' she appealed to her husband to intervene.

Jubail's answer was an angry scowl before he, too, disappeared into the room, banging the door behind him, echoing his daughter's action. Haider and his son were shocked by what was taking place in front of their eyes. Laila desperately willed the door to open and for her husband to appear to welcome the guests.

Seconds passed. Shirin had inherited her father's stubborn streak. Laila raised her tearful face to her loved ones.

'You've left it too late, Father!' Opening out her hands, palms up, she signalled defeat. Her two special guests stood frozen.

'Will you not come with us, Laila?' Arslan urged.

'Not without my husband and daughter – please forgive me!' she begged, her face ravaged by pain. Haider merely stared. 'Forgive me, Father … I didn't expect this reaction from them. I can't bear your humiliation at my door! Please go! I don't know what else to do or say!' Leaning against the veranda pillar, she loudly sobbed, her body doubling over.

His cheek muscle ticking away, with a glazed look, Haider strode back to his Jeep. It suddenly dawned on him that he had not properly entered his daughter's home. Bewildered, Ali and Arslan silently followed him.

Laila ran to the door and watched the vehicle drive off.

In the living room, without glancing at either her daughter or husband, Laila went straight into the adjoining bedroom. They heard her turn the lock inside.

'Daddy, has that nasty man gone?' Laila heard her daughter softly ask.

'Yes,' came the gruff reply.

*

'Mistress, the Jeep is back – I can see it!' Begum excitedly shrieked from the rooftop gallery. For the last hour she had stationed herself on the rooftop terrace, where she could have a long view of the road leading to the village.

Gripping one of her loose flip-flop *chappals* tightly with her big toe, Begum ran down the marble stairs.

Gulbahar was nervously cooling her hand in the clear fountain spray and sprinkling a few drops on the garland of flowers, lovingly threaded for her beautiful fairy. A large tray of hot *jalebis* was propped on the aluminium patio table. Gulbahar had deliberately not told her sisters about Laila. She wouldn't let them blight her golden moment – her daughter's homecoming – with their paranoia and twisted minds.

In her head she sadly mused, 'What will I say to a daughter callously deleted out of my life for ten years and a granddaughter never acknowledged?' She decided she would let her arms, hands and kisses say it all for her.

Begum's excited squeal set Gulbahar's pulse racing again. She checked her earlobes for the diamond studs, a wedding gift from her Haider-ji's trip to Lucknow. For her daughter's arrival, she had made a special effort with her appearance by wearing a silk suit topped with a delicate silk shawl. A touch of blusher on her cheeks made her translucent complexion come alive, giving her a youthful appearance. The elegant French pleat, so loved by her daughter, would inevitably bring out that mischievous, sensuous sparkle to her husband's blue eyes as they fell on her hair.

'Hush,' Gulbahar happily chided Mithu, swinging in his birdcage, making cheerful noises, as she waited for the sound of the Jeep.

'Who will come in first? Laila or Shirin?' she excitedly wondered.

'Are they here yet?' Gulbahar impatiently asked, peering over Begum's shoulders.

'Yes! The Jeep is here … oh!' Begum abruptly stopped.

'Begum, who's stepping out of the car first – Laila?' Gulbahar's tear-ridden, excited voice demanded to know from behind her.

'Mistress …' Silence.

Gulbahar clutched the handle and pulled the door wide open – only to collide with Arslan striding through it, his face set. Immediately behind him was his father, with an equally set face.

'Arslan!' Gulbahar called, staring at their backs, both disappearing, Haider to his office and Arslan into his room.

'Begum?' Gulbahar enquired, heartbeat accelerating, her voice now faint with dread.

Ali stood in front of his mistress with his head down. Words weren't necessary. He merely raised his arms in defeat, keeping his eyes carefully averted, unable to bear his mistress's suffering.

'Ali!'

'Mistress, she did not come,' he dully echoed – the only sound in the courtyard was the gurgling of the water from the fountain. Mithu, too, sat still on his swing.

'Ali!' Begum too found her tongue. 'What are you saying?'

But her mistress was already walking away, her shawl slipping off her shoulders. It was Begum who had the honour of hearing the full sordid tale.

'She chose her husband over her family!' he spat. Begum gasped, deeply affronted, pressing her tight fist against her mouth.

*

The loud thuds on the outside door startled Laila. Jubail had fed his daughter, left a tray of food for Laila beside the bed and then left for work. A shamefaced Shirin, on her father's instructions, tried to coax her mother to leave her bed, but to no avail. Laila merely stared across at the wall and the cornice with delicate ropes of cobwebs dangling from them.

The front door opened. Laila sat upright, listening with mounting excitement. Surely her ears were playing tricks on her. Then the bedroom door was thrust open.

'Begum,' Laila gasped, joy leaping through her body at the sight of the woman who had done so much for her.

The smile died on her lips, the harsh outline of Begum's face intimidating her. Shirin glared at the rude woman with grey hair who had dashed in with no *salaam*, immediately recognising her as the woman from the big house.

'Begum,' Laila repeated, reaching for her *dupatta*.

Begum was looking around the room, turning up her nose in distaste. The place was only a little better than the potter's hovel in the village.

'Yes, it's Begum!' she scoffed. Laila's eyes widened, taken aback by the housekeeper's hostile tone and demeanour. Guilty flags of colour etched her fair cheeks.

'They came to take me home.'

'I know!' Begum jeered. 'Everything! You are a selfish destructive cow!'

'Begum!' Laila was deeply offended.

'You deny turning your "mighty" father and "loving" brother away from your door?'

'I had no choice, Begum,' Laila meekly explained.

'No choice!' Begum strode to the bed and taking her by the shoulder, shook her hard, venting her rage.

'Take your hands off my mummy,' a fierce, little voice commanded from behind. Both turned to stare at the small, fuming figure standing by the bed.

Begum giggled, her anger deserting her, and reached out to the 'beautiful vision' as she'd always called Shirin in her head, pulling the reluctant, wriggling bundle of flesh into her arms, hugging her tightly. Shirin tried to escape from the tight band of the 'awful' woman's arms.

'Mummy!' she wailed for help.

'Shirin, this is our Begum – a very special lady. Stop being silly,' Laila reassured her, laughing.

Shirin was not at all amused. Begum let her go. The girl stared back with hostility.

'This is not a social call,' Begum stiffly informed Laila. 'But to remind you of the new destruction you have heaped on your family. Your poor mother is heartbroken. All day she worked so hard … sorting out a room for your *beautiful fairy* – dressing up for you … clung to the outside door, for that first glimpse of you … Imagine what it has done to your proud father. You threw him out!'

Laila's wet cheeks had no effect on their housekeeper.

'I had no choice, Begum! Please don't rush to condemn me. Neither my husband nor this little madam would even say *salaam* to them. How could I go with them, if Jubail or my daughter wouldn't?'

'I suppose those two matter more to you than your own parents!' Begum bitterly accused. 'You had begged me, on your knees, over the years to get your parents to take you back. I never thought I'd say this, but nobody deserves a child like you, Laila. And I take full responsibility ... I'm to blame ... I've spoilt you. As my Ali always says, you've used me many times – but today I'm washing my hands of you! Don't look at me like that, for you've made your choice. Stick with the potter's son and I wish you luck with it! Even your brother, who clamoured day and night for you to come home, has thrown you out of his life.'

'Begum, please stop. I didn't know what to do – I'm so unhappy!'

'Happiness walked to your door, but you blew it, Laila! Good day!'

'No!' Laila screamed. Begum was already striding out of the door. Barefooted, Laila scrambled after her, alarming her daughter.

'Begum!' she shouted. Begum didn't turn round.

'Wait! Wait!' Panicking and bareheaded, with no shawl around her shoulders, Laila ran out onto the street to the car.

Alarmed, Ali turned to his wife's tight face, seeking an explanation. Begum coldly commanded, 'Ali, let's go!'

'Ali, please wait, I'm coming with you, with or without my daughter or husband – I don't care.' Laila ran back inside. Ali and Begum exchanged a quick glance, joy spreading across their faces.

Inside the house, Laila, ignoring her sullen daughter, pulled out her suitcase from under the bed.

'What are you doing, Mama?' Shirin asked in trepidation, watching her mother fill the case with some of her clothes. Young as she was, Shirin was acutely aware that something was afoot and it was to do with the visitors who came yesterday.

Her mother's determined face frightened her.

'Shirin, we are going back to the village, to stay with the two men who came yesterday and my mama, the lady who called you *beautiful fairy* over the phone. Come!'

'No, Mummy!' was her daughter's rebellious answer.

'OK. I'm writing a note to your father to explain. I'll leave you with our neighbours and your father will collect you from there.'

'You are going to the red-haired man's house, aren't you?' Shirin accused, her little chin defiantly raised.

'Yes, that's my father and your grandfather!' Her mother angrily turned to her packing.

'Then I won't go.'

Her mother closed her suitcase shut. 'Then stay! I'm not dragging a silly little girl with me. I don't know when I'll be back, but I'll phone you.'

Shirin was panicking as she watched her mother scribbling a quick note for her husband.

'Mummy, put my dresses in, too. I'm coming!'

'Good,' her mother quietly answered, smiling, her back to her daughter.

*

Begum returned alone to the *hevali,* wanting to give herself time to prepare her master and mistress for their daughter and granddaughter's entrance into their lives.

'Begum, where have you been all day?' Gulbahar angrily greeted her housekeeper as she stepped into the *hevali.*

'On a special errand. Sorry!' Begum took Mithu's cage from her mistress, remembering that it was their pet's bath day, and not relishing the task of chasing the lovable bird around the courtyard.

'I hope your errand was worth it. I tried to cook the monkfish the way you make it, but still burned the bottom layer. Please, Begum, go and check!'

'I will, Mistress, but I think that today we need to prepare a special feast … and with hot *jalebis.*'

'Why?' Gulbahar asked, tone monotonous, shoving seeds into Mithu's reluctant mouth.

'Because …' Begum positioned herself in front of her mistress to savour the look on her face '… there's a beautiful fairy you might want to feed instead of Mithu today. She's here, Mistress!'

Fingers trapped in the slender metal bars of Mithu's cage, Gulbahar gasped for breath, eyes aching for the sight of the fairy.

'Really?' she cried, joyful, yet so terribly afraid.

'Yes, Mistress. Mother and daughter are in my house, getting ready to meet you.'

Eyes wide in disbelief, Gulbahar shouted to her loved ones through her trembling mouth, 'Arslan! Haider-ji!'

'I will phone the *halvie* for the *jalebis*,' Begum merrily added, staring up happily at their Mithu. The bird's days were numbered; for he now had Shirin as a rival for Mistress Gulbahar's affection.

As if in a dream, Gulbahar slid onto a chair, her eyes fixed on the outside door for that first glimpse of her loved ones.

*

'Mistress, are you ready now?' Ali politely hovered in the doorway, embarrassed by the homeliness of his bedroom with its peeling plaster and clothes hanging on hooks on the wall, as he watched Mistress Laila pulling at her daughter's unruly curls. He was sure she had combed Shirin's hair twice already.

'Yes, Ali.' Laila deposited the comb back in her handbag. Wetting her dry lips, she shyly requested, 'Is it OK if we leave our things here for the time being? Just in case they turn me away!'

'Of course they won't, Mistress.' He was stunned by her request and comment. 'Regard this as your home. It's your father's home anyway. He owns it.'

'Good, let's go!' Nervously she stepped out into the sunshine of the village lane, savouring the smell of fresh coriander and spinach in the field outside Begum's home.

'Come, Shirin – today you'll see your mother's home.'

Petulantly, Shirin offered her hand to her mother, not at all happy at entering the home of that 'horrible' man.

*

Laila's legs buckled beneath her outside the door of her parents' home, and she leaned against the wall for support, hiding her face in the fold of her *chador*. How could she possibly enter it?

'Mistress Laila?'

'I can't go through this door, Ali!' she sobbed.

Ali's mouth fell open. 'But, Mistress, it's only a door!'

Laila shook her head, wanting to run back to Ali's house.

'Silly Mummy, it's only a door,' Shirin loftily scoffed, bringing a smile to both their lips.

Letting go of her mother's hand, she pushed the tall, heavy wooden door with her body. In the courtyard, with bated breath, Gulbahar saw the fairy step in. A bold, little figure stood before her, head moving from side to side, her bunches of curls swinging as she looked around with interest. Then her eyes fell on the older woman, sitting straight on a chair under a large birdcage with a green parakeet swaying inside it.

As if in a dream, Gulbahar walked towards her fairy; a strange shy look on her face. Her arms opened wide. Shirin watched the approaching figure with trepidation. The woman was smiling but, like her mother, also crying!

'*Assalam alaikum*, my beautiful *pari*, welcome home!'

Shirin nervously blinked up at the older woman. The kind dark brown eyes melted Shirin's reserve and she let herself be folded in a tight hug, hearing very clearly the woman's thumping heartbeat against her ear. The woman's wet cheek was now pressed against her face.

There was a sound from behind her. Gulbahar raised her head and looked straight into her daughter's tearful eyes; an awkward, nervous figure clutching the fold of her *chador* against her wet cheeks. Ali stood protectively behind her.

Laila fell into her mother's arms, and both hugged and wept. Shirin watched on, bemused, and felt a warm, big hand slip into hers. A tall, smiling man stood beside her. Instantly, Shirin knew that this was her uncle and her face happily split into a grin, with one pink cheek dimpling. The next minute, he had swung her high up in the air and kissed her on her head before returning her to the floor.

Then she saw the older man with the reddish-brown hair. The look in the eyes, the mutinous line of the mouth and the speed with which she had swung her head the other way hit Haider badly. His outstretched arms dropped to his sides.

Inside Shirin's head the panic-ridden words drummed, 'If he hugs me, I'll scream!'

He did not; instead he turned to his daughter. When Ali had phoned to inform him that mother and daughter had arrived, Haider had immediately abandoned his business guests in his office and sprinted out to the central courtyard, an air of excitement about him.

Both mother and daughter felt his powerful presence. Reluctantly, Gulbahar let her daughter slide out of her arms. Laila, her eyes studiously lowered, fell into the welcoming band of her father's masculine arms. Haider squeezed his eyes tight, stopping tears from spilling, as his daughter sobbed against his shoulders.

Gulbahar led Shirin into the drawing room.

'Wow! What a lovely room!' Shirin squealed in excitement 'So big!'

Her grandmother brimmed with pride.

'Your room is big, too. Begum!' Gulbahar called her housekeeper, her voice trembling with joy.

Begum, within seconds, materialised in the room, holding the big china plate of hot sweet *jalebis*.

'Here, Mistress, you can now feed your fairy yourself.' Shirin's eyes fell longingly on the hot crispy rings of sweets drenched with syrup. Gulbahar plucked one from the plate and handed it to her granddaughter. Both giggled as some of the warm syrup trickled out of Shirin's mouth and down her chin. Gulbahar lovingly wiped it away with the end of her expensive shawl. It was her granddaughter that mattered. Not the shawl.

Begum left them both giggling over their sticky mouths and fingers. 'What a blessed day, Allah Pak!' She promised herself firmly to say her special *nafl* prayers in between her cooking chores. Her body ached but her heart was soaring to the clear, blue skies above. Unknown to her mistress, she had also been busy on the phone. Between cries of joy she broke the news about Laila's arrival to Mistresses Mehreen and Rani, but warned them against visiting that very day.

*

After dinner, and holding on tightly to her uncle's hand, Shirin had excitedly toured the *hevali* and her grandfather's office, and had marvelled at the size of her mother's old room. There, pulling open the drawers of the dressing table, she found a stack of Laila's old photographs. She giggled, unable to connect the young girl and boy in the pictures with her mother and uncle.

Laila remained downstairs and asked Begum to phone and let her husband know about her visit to the village. Trying not to dwell on her husband's possible reaction, Laila instead concentrated on the people around her. So much to talk about and so much pain to share. Gulbahar found it easier to relate to her granddaughter than to talk to her Laila. Bitterness persisted on both sides. One man divided them and both were loath to mention his name.

At last she uttered. 'I'm sorry, Mother, for everything.' Gulbahar pulled her daughter's head into her lap and planted a kiss on her cheek. Haider had left mother and daughter together, wanting no part in their personal conversation, afraid of the unpleasant memories. When he had hugged his daughter, Haider sadly realised how much he had missed and still loved her. The topic of her husband would remain a taboo. Yet the wretched man had to be invited.

'We've one choice, either to accept him into the family or to lose our daughter,' he bitterly reminded himself. He had learned from Begum that it was she who had persuaded Laila to come home; otherwise she would have stubbornly remained by her husband's side. Strangely, he admired her for her marital loyalty. Would he not expect a similar response from his own wife? Now, would Arslan tell them whether he was going or staying?

Nostrils flaring, Haider squeezed his eyes shut in nausea, imagining the potter's son sharing his daughter's bed in the *hevali*. He strode out, seeking fresh air in the fields; to think, and to suppress his former feelings of hatred towards the potter's son, who was now a graduate and had a good job in Islamabad.

Later, when he went back to the guest room, his wife's face was against Laila's cheeks. Haider walked across the room and, bending down, planted a light kiss on his daughter's forehead. Laila's eyes opened wide in shock. He smiled gently, his eyes a startling shade of blue, but Laila was unable to bear the smile or the look and started sobbing.

Gulbahar wound her arm protectively around her daughter's shoulders. Haider gently brushed away her tears.

'This is no time for weeping – you'll both be ill,' he chided.

With love shining from her eyes, Gulbahar ardently thanked him, 'Thank you for giving me back my daughter.'

Lost for words, Haider reprimanded, 'Laila is my daughter, too, Gulbahar', his voice raw with feeling. Gulbahar nodded, hugging her daughter once more. She couldn't get enough of her.

'Where's Shirin?' Haider asked. Laila stiffened against her mother's chest.

CHAPTER 42

The Proposal

Haider saw them. Arslan was seating his giggling niece up on the white horse.

'Arslan!' Haider's authoritative tone startled them both. Shirin swung her head round at the sound of the man's voice, her face once more tight and rebellious.

Haider slowly walked across the paddock, eyes on the little face, tracing Laila's beautiful features. His granddaughter's gaze didn't fall, strangely pleasing him. The child had spirit – her mother all over. 'Arslan, give your niece as many rides as she likes. Tomorrow we'll buy a special pony for her!' he announced.

Unimpressed Shirin continued with her frosty stare.

'Did you hear that, Shirin?' her smiling uncle prompted.

Shirin hesitated.

'Do you want a pony, Shirin?' Haider now directly addressed the girl.

Shirin vigorously nodded her head, eyes on the horse's neck.

Now standing by the horse, Haider laid his hand on Shirin's. She froze, wanting to snatch her hand away, but found herself instead looking into the eyes that had haunted her for so long.

'Yes, please,' she politely murmured, gently drawing her hand out of his grasp. Haider's arm fell to his side, the smile slipping. He stepped away.

'Arslan, take Shirin round the fields,' he commanded.

'Yes, I was going to do that.' Arslan beamed a smile of gratitude. His father was definitely trying his best.

Haider watched the horse canter away, laying the palm of

his hand that had touched his granddaughter against his cheek. 'One step at a time!' he reminded himself.

*

Saher was overjoyed by the news, delighted at Arslan's achievement in bringing Laila home. 'So, Begum, he has done it!'

Hearing the sound of the doorbell, she rushed onto the veranda. Her mother had arrived.

'Mother, guess what has happened in Auntie Gulbahar's house?'

'Don't know and don't care!' Rani snapped, stiffening at the mention of her elder sister's name. 'But no doubt you are going to tell me.' Her voice dripped with sarcasm.

'Mother!' Saher peered into her face.

Eyes averted, Rani brushed her daughter aside, heading for the dining room.

'I'm hungry and tired from shopping! I hope that the table is laid for dinner?' Rani swept into the dining room.

'The good news – Laila has come home, Mother!' Eyes lit with pleasure, Saher scanned her mother's face, expecting a similar reaction. Rani's gaze was on the plates, wanting to hurl them against the smooth creamy walls.

Rani felt the chill of her daughter's gaze and wanted to escape. Saher, however, was determined to get to the bottom of what ailed her mother.

'Did you hear me, Mother?' she coolly mocked. 'Laila has at last come home with her daughter. Will you not call Auntie Gulbahar to congratulate her?'

'I heard!' Rani hissed. 'I'm not deaf!'

'Good! Then let's go.'

'No.' Her tone flat, Rani turned her back. 'I'm tired.'

'Mother! What's wrong?'

'Nothing!' Eyes evasive and tone belligerent.

'Something is terribly wrong, Mother. Your behaviour tells me that a major crisis is taking place inside you!'

'You'll not marry him!' Rani exploded on cue.

Saher was shocked into silence, horrified by the rage in her mother's eyes.

'Mother! What're you saying?'

'You heard me!'

'What?'

'You know!' Rani accused, itching to slap her daughter's face. Did she think that she was dense?

'What's going on, Mother?' Saher hardened.

'Mother and son came for your hand in marriage,' Rani contemptuously threw at her daughter.

'And?' Saher coldly prompted, rage reddening her cheeks.

'And …' Rani repeated, 'and I turned them away. What did they expect?'

Saher was stunned into silence.

'They had the cheek to come, carrying baskets of *mithae* and boxes of saris for you. What do they think we are? A charity case! That my daughter could be jilted by one man and then would stoop to marry another – one who is *younger* than her?'

'Mother!' Saher cried, trembling with anger, pulling a chair out from under the dining table to sit on.

Rani was now in a spitting mood.

'How dare they!' she fumed, eyes glittering with rage.

Saher could not contain herself any longer. 'They dared because I had told them to come,' she stated in the tone of supreme authority she used in court. Her mother's eyes grew wide in disbelief.

'Saher!'

'I've heard enough of your poison, Mother. I'll marry whomever I want! I had instructed Arslan to place my *segan* with you.'

'You are mad!' Rani exploded, feeling betrayed. 'I've just been arranging your *rishta* with a top lawyer!'

'To hell with your *top* lawyer. I want to marry Arslan, and I love him very much, Mother. If that's hard for you to accept or understand, then that's your problem, for marry him I shall!'

'The thought sickens me!'

Dismayed, Saher gave up, walking away. 'You sicken me!' she cried, turning to give her mother a long, pointed stare. 'You have harboured a lifelong hatred for your two sisters. Arslan has never done anything to harm you. If I'm going to marry anybody, it'll be him. If you push me too far, believe me, Mother, I'll desert you! I'm so ashamed of the way you think and behave. I'm going to my aunt's house. If you want to play a part in your daughter's wedding plans, you may.'

Saher stepped out into the sunshine of the flower-scented courtyard, trying to stabilise her breath. Her phone was ringing. It was Arslan. A tender smile spread across her face.

'Hi, I think that we've a few things to discuss ... including the *mithae*. After all, if I cannot eat at my own engagement celebration, when else can I do it?'

'I gather that you know we came, Mother and I? Knowing my aunt I was prepared for that reaction of hers. So we just ignored it and came home,' Arslan tentatively explained.

'Yes I know ...'

'And ...?' he prompted, letting her finish the sentence.

Hearing the dining-room door open she chose her words with care, 'Please come. You have chosen the blue sari. I love it! But I'll choose my wedding dress – is that understood, Arslan? By the way, how are they? Laila and Shirin? I'm so glad for all of you.'

'It's fantastic to have them at home. Laila is eagerly planning for our wedding. Come and visit them now. I want you so much, Saher!' The husky tone made her blush. Both were recalling the kiss.

'Yes ... we've wasted too much time already.' She glared over her shoulders at her mother. 'If some people can't be happy for us, then that's their problem.'

Rani angrily brushed past.

CHAPTER 43

Time of Need

'Massi Fiza!' Shabnum shouted down from the rooftop, her hand aching from opening the two heavy padlocks on the terrace door. There was no sign of their neighbour from amongst the rows of washing lines. Or was she squatting in one corner of the veranda?

In fact Massi Fiza was in her room, lying on a *charpoy*, her forehead tied with a band of *nala* string and eyes squeezed shut. She heard Shabnum and groaned in dismay, the vision of more stitching panicking her.

'Why can't these girls leave me alone?'

Hearing another shout, she pulled herself out of bed and cupped her hand over her forehead to keep the daylight from her eyes. Her neck ached.

'What is it, Shabnum?' she called flatly from the middle of her courtyard, face raised and eyes tightly shut. 'I'm not well today! But I'll do what you want tomorrow!' Without waiting for a reply, she scuttled back to the bliss of the darkened room with its old wooden window shutters closed. Her parched lips ached for some pink *sabz* tea, but the challenge of brewing it in her little aluminium pot was akin to climbing K2.

Massi Fiza thought she had imagined the thudding sound from her outside door. It was past midnight. When the noise continued she draped an old woollen shawl around her shoulders and went to unbolt her outside door.

'Who is it?' she called, afraid.

'Mam, open the door!'

Massi Fiza swung open the door to her eldest son, heart

skipping a beat at his appearance. He was dressed all in black – a black *shalwar kameez* suit topped by a bulky, black turban, and he sported a long black beard.

'Why are you dressed like this?' she asked, alarm bells ringing.

Her sons were always keen on wearing Western jeans, and now he looked like one of the Afghan Taliban. Locking the door, Fiza rushed inside after him, scanning his face in the dim light.

'What are you doing, Maqbool?' she watched him tip the contents of their battered old leather suitcase onto the floor and rifle through her clothes. When understanding dawned, she pulled at his arm, but he pushed her away, and she fell with a thud against her bed, moaning in pain. Barely glancing at her, he pocketed the contents of her small leather purse.

'Leave my money alone, you wicked boy!' Fiza shrieked.

Her son turned on her, the wild look in his eyes frightening her. 'I need this.'

'Why?'

'I'm going far away.'

'Where? With those few hundreds!'

'It's enough.'

'Where are you going?'

'Over the mountains …'

Massi Fiza's eyes opened wide, fear clutching at her. 'You are not one of them …?'

'Yes!' he finished with a sneer. 'I'm fighting a jihad – for a purer state of Pakistan, not run by America!'

'But the Taliban are bombing and killing people. What are you doing, my son? Are you mad?'

'I'm leaving for the Afghan border. I don't know if I will come again and don't tell anyone that I've been here … The military are after us …'

'Have you killed anyone?'

'You are daft, Mam. How do you win any wars without killing?'

Massi Fiza felt faint, watching him in despair. He was now opening another suitcase, and pulled out a T-shirt and a pair of jeans. Then with his back to her, he changed his clothes. As her eyes fell on the shining blade of a knife and a gun hidden inside his clothes, Fiza backed away.

'I never want to see you again!'

'You won't have to! I'm destined to be a martyr!'

'A martyr!' she bitterly scoffed. 'Which heaven will receive you for killing innocent women and children? If that is what you are intending. Why did Allah Pak curse me with a child like you? There I was – planning your *rishta* with the goldsmith's daughters. Would they give their daughters to evil people like you?'

'Those sluts, with their naked arms and bare heads! If one of them was my wife I would …' he spat, his wild look of disgust shooting through Fiza. She loved those girls.

'What would you do?' she jeered, anger emboldening her. 'Kill her for her bare head? You beast! Is my son only good at bullying and tyranny? You yearned for a look from those girls … you stupid boy.'

Her son was already out on the veranda. At the door he whispered, 'And don't tell anyone that I was here. Many of my friends have died – others have fled into the mountains and across the Afghan border. I'm following them to fight the Americans.'

Massi Fiza stood for a long time under the light of the stars in the small courtyard, bemused at her thoughts and feelings. Why did she not feel any fear for her son's safety? When did she become such a hard woman? The answer came fast. 'Because I don't know him any more!'

*

Massi Fiza felt a gentle touch on her arm. Alarmed, she lifted her head, sleep vanishing in a second. Rukhsar was standing by the side of her bed.

'What are you doing here?' Massi Fiza squeaked, flustered, her eyes opening and closing, worried in case Rukhsar had seen her son and ashamed of her overcrowded and cluttered surroundings.

'To see how you are,' Rukhsar gently replied, keenly aware of Massi Fiza's discomfort. Politely, she kept her eyes off the stack of four battered leather suitcases and the pile of her son's clothes strewn across the floor. This was Massi Fiza's entire domain – the place where she slept, lived and hoarded all her worldly goods. Her sons, when at home, slept in the smaller room annexed to the kitchen. Rukhsar brutally crushed the urge to make a quick exit.

'I ...' Massi Fiza sat up, holding onto the tight *nala* band around her head.

'Shabnum told me last night that you aren't well. Tell me what's wrong, my friend?' Rukhsar softly coaxed, noting her friend's flushed cheeks and the reason behind them – embarrassment.

'Just not feeling well – a bit of a headache,' Massi Fiza stuttered, plucking at the frayed ends of an old embroidered flower motif on her pillowcase that her Aunt Noor had stitched two decades ago. She had always prided herself on her bedding, but today, to be caught sleeping on an old pillowcase was unforgivable! Then she blushed beetroot at the sight of the yellowy oil stain spread across the middle from her head massage. She strategically shifted her arm over it, whilst following Rukhsar's eyes to the four tins of starch powder, her sons' old portable beds stacked one on top of the other, her two wooden dowry chairs, one with a missing leg. Her good-for-nothing sons had never got it mended.

The contrast between her friend's well-to-do home, with its foreign silk rugs, modern quality furniture, two maids and three college-educated daughters looking after it, and her own humble solitary existence was indeed unfair. Then to be caught like this when she was feeling at her lowest! Massi Fiza burst into tears, burying her face in her muslin *dupatta*.

'Massi Fiza, what's wrong?' Rukhsar was nonplussed, gingerly resting herself on the rounded wooden leg post of Massi Fiza's bed. Then she eased herself down on the jute section, ignoring its rough texture chafing the soft flesh of her thighs through the *Benarasi* silk fabric of her *shalwar*. Apparently, Massi Fiza did not use the under mattress, *thaliée,* on her bed. In Rukhsar's house they had modern beds with thick mattresses and huge, fancy headboards. The portable jute beds were only used for visitors and were always neatly kept hidden away. The poverty and the squalor of her neighbour's house depressed Rukhsar.

Massi Fiza pulled her legs up, making space for her friend, head bent, still sobbing into her shawl, agonising over whether to tell her friend about her son.

'Something is obviously wrong?' Rukhsar gently prompted. 'Please tell me. Aren't I your friend?' Her gentle tone and kind words melted Massi Fiza's reserve.

'It's my sons. I'm worried about them.' She offered a half-truth.

'What?' There was a pregnant pause.

Rukhsar wasn't surprised. The selfish behaviour of her neighbour's two sons had always disgusted her, and everyone in the village speculated that they would end up as criminals.

'The elder came home last night and took everything – down to my last rupee.' Massi Fiza decided to tell this much, but nothing more.

Rukhsar diplomatically kept silent. 'I'm sorry,' she offered again, her heart going out to her friend.

'Thanks,' Massi Fiza muttered, now regretting telling her neighbour and too ashamed to raise her head and show her smarting red cheeks. Who would ever offer their daughters to her criminal sons? Rukhsar certainly would not.

Not that her sons had ever had any hopes of success in that direction. From their childhood days, those trendy, fashionable, chauffeur-driven, young women, living upstairs in the house next door, were in a different league. Daughters of a well-off goldsmith, blessed with not only good looks but a college education from the nearest city, their attitude to fellow villagers oozed snobbery. With their style of dressing, mannerisms, the way they spoke, they were 'city girls' at heart; eager to marry urban men and escape to the glamorous and, in their words, more 'civilised' world of the city.

Massi Fiza's boys on the other hand had barely made it to the eighth class. The shame of being two loutish lads stuck in the seventh class for two years in a row, sitting amongst younger children, was deeply mortifying for both them and their mother. So when they sidled out of school via long absences, their mother squeaked not a word of protest, secretly hoping that they would now take over the laundry business. The boys had other ideas, immediately absconding to the capital, seeking migration agents and their fortune. And they only occasionally came back, usually to rob their mother of her hard-earned cash from the laundry business. Whilst their mother was a favourite with the girls next door, the boys were treated with sneers.

'And he didn't even stay the night,' Massi Fiza mourned.

'I hope you won't mind me saying this,' Rukhsar had dispensed with diplomacy. 'As we are good friends, we should be able to exchange honest views. Do you agree, Massi Fiza-ji?'

Massi Fiza looked up, fearful of what Rukhsar was about to say. 'Yes,' she answered meekly, ready for a lecture.

'Right, first let me tell you that you have wasted your life away on your good-for-nothing sons – pardon my blunt words. I speak not to offend you, but as a concerned friend. I'm worried about your health. Your work hard to earn a living and support your two sons but, in the end, they are just as bad as their father, aren't they? Please let me finish.' Rukhsar saw Massi Fiza's mouth open to defend her family. 'The miserable gits have all abandoned you and used you! Your husband may well be abroad. You think he's dead, don't you? But God knows what he has been up to for all these years – women, drink or even worse. He has just disappeared off the face of the earth … Despicable man!' Seeing her friend's mouth open again, she hastened to add, 'Please, Massi Fiza, don't even jump to his defence!'

'Has anyone ever come home? Most of your Eids are spent alone. If they deign to visit you, they arrive late at night and by morning are gone. Do they hold you and the village life so contemptible? Please, Massi Fiza …' she continued. 'I don't speak out of malice … to hurt you … but to gently remind you of the reality of your sons' lives.'

Massi Fiza dejectedly nodded. In her heart of hearts she agreed with everything.

'They are ashamed of me – this home … my work! How do you expect them to come and stay here in a house piled with dirty laundry? As poor children they have an inferiority complex – that's the problem.'

Rukhsar's heart melted at her friend's predicament.

'Your sons have turned out to be little snobs, Massi Fiza-ji! Should our children be ashamed of the very parents who have brought them into this world and worked so hard to raise them? We all work, Massi Fiza, to earn our livelihood. There's absolutely nothing demeaning or wrong about any kind of work … For I believe all work is honourable if it puts food into our children's mouths and if we provide a service for the well-being of society.'

'Oh, Rukhsar-ji, so kind of you to think like that, but you know very well that some work is more *honourable* than others. For instance, yours is better than mine …' her voice trailed away.

'I'm not going to discuss this further, for you're falling into the same trap as your sons. I value your work. We all work in some context or other, whether out in the fields or at home making quilts. Apart from the *zemindars'* wives, the landladies like Gulbahar or those supported by their menfolk working abroad, all women work pretty hard in the village, don't you agree?'

'Yes! Thank you,' Massi Fiza gratefully mumbled, appreciating what her friend was trying to do, but inside she was still drowning in her grief and regret.

'Rukhsar-ji, I wish I had a daughter. She would not have done this to me.'

'Yes, Massi Fiza-ji, a daughter remains a daughter for life. Now, please get up, bring a suit or two with you – you're coming to stay with me. Don't look so surprised. My girls and I are going to look after you – you are overworked and highly depressed.'

'But …'

'Your washing can go to hell for a few days! Just rest … If you like, you can thread some pearls for me!'

'Rukhsar-ji?' Massi Fiza's voice trembled, touched by her generosity.

Rukhsar pulled her friend up – Massi Fiza's chapped fingers were rough against her soft palm – eager to be off, unable to stand the musty smell of detergent any longer.

*

In the goldsmith's guest room, Shabnum hovered near Massi Fiza's bed with a bowl of chicken soup, graciously offering it to their *unwanted guest*.

Very rarely did the three sisters agree on anything. Today, they unanimously doubted their mother's wisdom in bringing their *lowly* neighbour to stay with them. And, horror upon horrors, letting her sleep in the guest room on the soft king-sized mattress. They all grimaced at the thought of Massi Fiza's oily head knocking against the creamy white velour of the headboard. When their mother overheard their conversation, she was mortally aggrieved and being a God-fearing woman earnestly touched her ears and beseeched her Allah Pak to forgive her daughters' arrogance in referring to another human being as *lowly*.

'As human beings we need to treat each other with respect,' she had passionately beseeched while her daughters had mocked her with a look of pure bewilderment.

'Mother, she's like a servant! How can she be our equal?' Shabnum blurted. Which planet did their mother live on?

'You callous snobs, all three of you!' Rukhsar bitterly lashed out, chilled by their statement. 'How would you like it if somebody called you lowly? In the social hierarchy, the goldsmith is at the lower end, for your information! The sun also rises and sets for all people.' That sobered the girls.

Their mother continued with her lecture. 'In the eyes of our Allah Pak, we are all equal! Doesn't everyone pray together in mosques and perform Hajj together in Mecca? And you are complaining about a woman who has done so much for you spoilt girls.

'So, enough of this *lowly* nonsense! Fiza-ji may wash people's clothes in our village but she's my best friend and I'm not ashamed of her. But I am *extremely* ashamed of you all, for harbouring such wicked thoughts.' She turned her back on them.

'But, Mother. Everybody thinks like us – not like you!' Shabnum boldly reminded her mother.

'Does that make it OK? I thought I had you well educated, my girls, but apparently those women's magazines have only taught you fashion, make-up tips and to text "twits" on your phones.'

'Tweets, Mother!' Ruhi corrected. They all laughed – their mother was catching on to the use of social media.

Their mother was not amused. 'Twits or tweets, now, go and be nice to your Aunt Fiza. And put those damn phones away, girls! Can't you keep your hands free from them for even a few minutes?' Smiling, all three sisters vigorously shook their heads. Their phones and iPads were their link to the big 'outside' world.

Rukhsar had made the soup herself, with the right quantity of chilli seasoning, and had even thrown in some new potatoes which Massi Fiza loved.

'Shabnum, it was Massi Fiza-ji who embroidered the lace on your *dupatta* at midnight once!'

Chastised thus, Shabnum dutifully carried the tray to Massi Fiza, pinning a pleasant smile to her lips. She sat with their guest for up to an hour, trying her very best to entertain her while inside she cynically wondered what a boarding-school and college girl could have in common with an illiterate older woman? In any event, poor Aunt Fiza was quite depressed and her mouth had a permanent downward tilt, no matter how many jokes Shabnum told her. When her mother finally walked in, she let out a sigh of relief.

Rukhsar was determined to get her friend out of this dismal mood.

'Massi Fiza-ji,' she began, 'I bring you some good news. The baker's wife has just told me that Mistress Laila and her daughter have returned and both are now at her parents' house. Can you believe it?'

Massi Fiza's head shot up from the pillow, her round eyes alight with interest.

'Really!' she croaked.

'Yes, really! Apparently mother and daughter came the other night. It was our sweetmaker who kindly informed the baker's wife after getting a large order for hot *jalebis* for the granddaughter.'

'What, Rukhsar-ji! They have accepted the potter's brat into their home!'

'It's their grandchild, don't forget, Massi Fiza!' Rukhsar coldly reminded her. Massi Fiza was just as bad as her daughters for putting people down.

Massi Fiza was now sitting up. Excitement was to be found elsewhere and there was nothing to be gained in moping around in bed. Fancy Rukhsar bringing her some news for a change!

'Rukhsar-ji, I'm well enough now! I would like to thank you for your hospitality ...'

'You're going nowhere!' Rukhsar chuckled, reading her friend's thoughts very accurately, and gently pushing her down on the bed. 'Not until you've fully recovered your strength. I know you want to see what it's like at Master Haider's home, but you'll leave when I say so! Is that clear, Massi Fiza-ji?'

Massi Fiza, bemused, dumbly nodded.

She persisted, however. 'Please, Rukhsar-ji, ring Begum and tell her that I'll be down in the *hevali* for their washing tomorrow morning.'

'OK, *acha baba*. What do you think will happen if the potter's son ends up on their doorstep? Will they take him in or not?'

'I don't know, Rukhsar-ji, but I'm so pleased that Mistress Laila is back at home. I can't wait to see her daughter walking around the *hevali* – that's if Begum lets me in ... She's always telling me off for spreading rumours. As if I would!'

'Yes, as if you would!' Rukhsar chuckled.

'Well, I gossip, and mainly with you. And it's quite harmless ... you know that.' Massi Fiza looked aggrieved. 'I'm not a malicious person and would never speak ill of anyone.'

'Yes,' Rukhsar agreed with alacrity. 'You're an honest, gentle soul.'

'Thank you, Rukhsar-ji.'

'Well, you can show your gratitude by drinking this wonderful soup. I used a full chicken – not skimped on anything ... so that you can gain your energy back!'

Touched by her friend's kindness and with shiny, tearful eyes, Massi Fiza noisily slurped down the bowl of soup, picking at the tender chicken meat with her chapped fingertips.

Rukhsar watched her friend happily, shrugging aside the thought of work on the big necklace for the lecturer's daughter's wedding. Massi Fiza had given so many hours and days of her life to her family.

CHAPTER 44

The Potter's Son

Nobody in Master Haider's household was prepared for Jubail's arrival two days later. 'Daddy's here!' Shirin came running into the central courtyard.

Laila's heart plummeted, the pea-pod shell popping out of her fingers. She was sitting under the veranda, giving Begum a hand in preparing the vegetables for the evening meal and enjoying the breeze from the water cooler. Her mother, engrossed in the chopping and quartering of lemons and raw green mangoes for the pickle, sat up straight in her chair, the small knife poised in mid-air, and exchanged a nervous glance with her daughter as the outside door was thrust open.

Jubail stood in the doorway, body tall and stiff, eyes quickly locating his wife and coolly resting on her face. Laila coloured, noting the rigidness of his face and his hostile gaze, now on her mother. Spellbound, Gulbahar was caught in the moment, taking her fill of the man who had stolen their daughter and blanketed their lives with misery for over a decade.

Jubail could not quite fathom his mother-in-law's expression. There was neither hostility nor welcome. He scrutinised his wife's demeanour, seeking telltale signs.

Then his daughter joyously flung her small arms around his waist. Laila glanced down at the bowl of peas. Bile rushed through Jubail – she had finally chosen her family over him.

They all heard the footsteps on the marble staircase. A ball of nervous energy spiralled through the three women, their hearts thudding and breath held.

Haider had taken his afternoon nap and was on his way back

to the office for a meeting with two of his tenants, unprepared for the sight in the courtyard. On seeing Jubail, he stood still, reading carefully the scene in front of him, noting his daughter's bowed head and the mixture of dread and appeal on his wife's face. A petrified Begum leaned against the marble pillar, her two fingers, gripping a pinch of birdseed, stuck in the parakeet's cage. And there, just inside his courtyard, stood the 'beast', with his arm protectively around his own daughter, eyes defiant.

Sensing the tension in the courtyard, Shirin's timid gaze flitted from one adult face to the other, hands clutching at her father's jeans. It was that little action alone that brought home to her grandfather exactly what was at stake.

The girl.

Laila was drowning, distressed by her divided loyalties – pulled between parents who had suffered so much and a hostile husband about to walk out of her life.

Haider strode to his daughter's side, placing his arm protectively around her shoulders. Laila's head shot up. Bemused, Jubail's fingers lovingly threaded through his own daughter's curls.

Laila's mouth fell open as Jubail, pulling his daughter behind him, headed for the door. He had his answer; his wife had chosen her family.

'Welcome home, my son. Will you not stay?' Haider's cool, authoritative voice sliced across the courtyard, shocking everyone into a strange stillness, freezing Jubail's hand on the door handle. Tears of gratitude pricked Laila's eyelids and a sob caught in her throat.

Gulbahar remained sitting, etched against the marble pillar. Surely it had to be a dream.

For Begum it was no dream; she came alive, rushing to take up the cue from her master. 'Please, Jubail-ji, come inside, you are welcome!'

Lost for words, Jubail stared at them blankly, unable to make sense of the scenario facing him.

Haider, firmly in control of the new tableau he had created, gently came to his aid. 'Laila, my dear, please take your husband upstairs. He will need to rest after his journey.'

Laila struggled to her feet. Gaze lowered, mouth dry, she found herself uttering the words she had fantasised over for so long, but had lost all hope of ever using.

'Jubail-ji, let me show you to our room,' she coaxed in her husky, trembling voice, feeling him stiffen as she crossed the courtyard and gripped his arm hard, making him realise that if he snubbed her father's welcome and walked out, it would all be over for them, the ten-year-old battle between them concluded. She never forgot her parents and he never forgave. Laila wouldn't let her family down twice and Jubail knew that, but he also knew that he was walking a tightrope. Grateful for the cue, he followed, gently pulling his daughter with him. He would do it for his daughter's sake; she was the glue holding them together.

'Daddy, let me show you my room – I've this really big room,' Shirin excitedly hopped ahead, bringing a smile to everyone's lips, relaxing all in the central courtyard. Mouth softening and gaze lowered, Jubail exchanged a shy smile with the three adults. They watched him cross the courtyard. For the first time ever, he was going to the first floor. When he worked with the horses, he had respectfully remained outside the private quarters of the *hevali*, in the horse's paddock.

*

Gulbahar beamed at her husband, treating him to a warm smile of gratitude. 'Thank you.' Again Haider's gentle words chastised her.

'She's my daughter, too, Gulbahar!'

Begum, tears of joy streaming down her face, dashed to her master's side, startling him by grasping his hand and printing feverish kisses all over it.

'Oh, thank you, Sahib-ji,' she echoed. Chuckling and touched by their housekeeper's reaction, Haider teased, 'You're going to be even busier, Begum – not that you're not already! See that our daughter, her husband and especially our granddaughter are well looked after.'

'Erm, yes, of course. I've dreamed of this, Master-ji, for so long that I don't care if my limbs fall off my body from exhaustion. I'll never tire of lavishing my love on this family.'

Haider gently withdrew his hand from her grasp, feeling the texture of her chapped fingers. 'You're a good woman, Begum.'

'Forgive me, Master, for my past mistakes,' Begum pleaded, sobbing. The need to repent and beg forgiveness was swamping her.

'Hush, Begum, there's nothing to forgive,' Haider gently consoled their treasure of a housekeeper, who was simply indispensable. 'You're a good soul, Begum. Let's forget the past, shall we? It's the future that matters.' Then he walked off towards his office quarters.

Flushed with joy Begum reached out to her mistress, hugging her tightly, revelling in the moment, their eyes automatically looking up to the top gallery.

CHAPTER 45

The Farewell

Mehreen stood watching her son and daughter-in-law packing a suitcase, feeling bereft. Many bags of gifts, collected from different bazaars and city shopping malls, littered the floor. Only two more days left of their stay. Ismail was now trying to make space amongst a pile of clothes for two pairs of traditional *khussa* shoes and a box of six dozen multi-coloured glass bangles for Daniela.

'Please wait. Rasoola!' Mehreen called her housekeeper standing outside the door. 'I've something for Daniela.'

Ismail looked up, exasperated. 'Mother, we've already far exceeded the weight limit.'

Mehreen looked away in embarrassment from the shape of Daniela's breasts pressed against the fabric of her tight dress. Could her son not advise his wife to wear a padded bra or a shawl around her shoulders? Thank goodness her husband was not with her.

Rasoola entered with an armful of clothes.

'What's this, Mother?'

'Your wedding presents, especially suits for Daniela.'

Daniela quickly asked, 'What's your mother saying?'

'These are all for you, my darling. But how are we going to take them?'

Overwhelmed, Daniela watched Rasoola, grinning from ear to ear, place a pile of velvet, silk and chiffon outfits on the embroidered bedspread.

Tearful and feeling very lonely, Mehreen left them to finish the packing. Despite her show of generosity that night, Gulbahar had not phoned once. What had hurt the most was that she had learned about Laila's arrival from Rasoola.

'Gulbahar hates me so much that she could not even be bothered to share such wonderful news with me,' Mehreen mourned, wanting so much to visit her niece.

Instead, she had phoned Rani, whose strident tone tore through the phone line, quickening Mehreen's heartbeat.

'No, I was not told about Laila and I don't care!'

Mehreen had no inkling that for her middle sister, the pining had begun again; the desperate longing for Rashid and the heartache that went with it.

The last thing Mehreen wanted was to jeopardise the fragile bond they had recently cemented as sisters. Gulbahar was now the blessed one, with both her children at home. Mehreen crushed the envy rushing through her, reminding herself how much she owed her elder sister.

'Shall we visit Gulbahar? Did you know that Laila is back?' she asked her husband later in the evening, standing in front of him.

'Mehreen, if we've not been informed, then is it right for us to foist our company where it's not wanted?' he stiffly reminded her, turning away, his eyes cool.

Thanks to her paranoia and idiotic runaway tongue, she had had him banished from her sister's side. How he missed Gulbahar's company!

Unhappily, Mehreen slipped into her own bed with no expectations of her husband joining her.

CHAPTER 46

The Cry

On the rooftop terrace, Rani gazed up at the stars, letting the warm, late-evening breeze brush her wet cheeks. She was at the lowest point of her life, with thoughts of Rashid totally swamping her. Hearing steps, she stiffened. Saher stood awkwardly behind her mother, willing her to greet her.

'Mother?'

'Leave me alone.' Rani slumped down into the chair.

'I can't,' came the low, stubborn reply.

'What do you care?' Rani bitterly accused.

'Of course I care.'

Rani shook her head and then, to her daughter's horror, burst into gentle sobs, head bent over her lap.

'Mother!' Saher pleaded, distressed. 'Do you hate Arslan so much that you don't want me to marry him?'

Rani shook her head. 'No! It's not that.'

'Then what is it?'

Saher put her arm protectively around her mother's body.

'I'm so lonely, Saher,' she uttered, stunning her daughter into silence.

'Mother, please explain. Lonely? I'll have to leave this home sometime, but if I marry Arslan then I will be able to see you every day! Arslan is staying and is planning to enter politics. If I had married Ismail, I would have gone to another country, and if I had married in the city you would not see me for months. Don't you agree?'

Rani nodded.

'Then why this sad mood?'

'You've no idea what it's like to live a wretched life of widow-hood,' Rani whispered, caving in and stunning her daughter.

'Mother, I'm so sorry! I didn't know!'

'Of course, nobody knows! I'm supposed to be coping well with everything,' she returned bitterly. 'I've everything, according to the world: wealth, acres of land, a wonderful home and a loving daughter to keep me company.'

'Yes,' Saher offered tentatively.

Rani burst into tears again, recoiling in self-loathing. What was happening to her today? All she knew was that Mehreen's phone call about Laila's arrival had triggered a personal crisis; pain and envy rushing through her.

'Mother, I know it must have been a hard life without a husband, but please talk to me. It will help.'

Rani was crying and nodding at the same time, stuttering out the words in a rush, baring her soul to her beloved daughter.

'To become a widow at 24, with a two-year-old daughter, is not a fate I would wish upon anyone else. Then in the following years to see your own two sisters blossoming, their youthful lives and bodies pampered in every way, their loving husbands at their sides. How I hated them and their lives. To always remain on the periphery has been so cruel and painful, Saher.

'Gulbahar loved Mehreen and lavished so much attention on her, but she never quite appreciated that I needed more attention than my spoilt, young sister.'

'But, Mother, you've rebuffed everyone with your cold attitude!'

Rani's bitter laugh echoed around them. 'That cold attitude was my armour, to protect myself. I needed no one.'

'But you did though, didn't you? Is that what you are really trying to say?'

'I needed everyone to …' Rani hiccupped, her cheeks shiny with tears, '… to get past my cold front, but nobody bothered!' she bitterly mourned.

'Why didn't you marry again? I gather there must have been a *rishta* or two?'

'At first for your sake, my darling, I was afraid that perhaps the other husband might reject you …'

'Oh, Mother! Was there any man?'

'Yes. One man took pity on me and wanted to marry me.'

'Why didn't you?'

'He was already married. I could not enter another woman's household or bring a strange man into my household. I let him go … and now he is out there with the army leading the soldiers against the Taliban …'

'Oh!' Saher was startled by her mother's revelation. 'What's his name? Why didn't you tell me?'

Rani looked down, lost in her thoughts of Rashid once again.

'Mother?'

'No one knows about Rashid. And after one or two attempts nobody bothered to ask or advise me to marry again. But if only somebody had arranged it for me … if only my sisters had realised how much I was missing a life companion.'

'Oh! Mother. I wish you had married.'

'My sisters enjoyed male companionship, while I had no one, apart from the servants.' Rani continued, determined to speak her heart out to her daughter today. 'They had total freedom in life. I had none. Not that anyone stopped me from doing anything. I gave up wearing makeup. Lipstick, in particular, something I so dearly loved since my teens … I loved collecting expensive lipsticks, top Western brands. I was supposed to be the most attractive of the three sisters. Then at the age of just 24, I became inhibited, afraid to let any colour touch my lips or cheeks, afraid of the prying eyes. If I did dare to smear a dash of it on, I would guiltily smudge it off, afraid of wagging tongues, sputtering, "Why is she made up? Which man is she trying to attract?"

'From a confident, fashionable, young woman who held herself in high esteem, I became a dowdy, middle-aged woman before my time. Reluctantly, I parted with my shapely, short-sleeved dresses, and swapped them for drab, long-sleeved baggy *kurthas*. The elegant, flimsy ropes of crushed chiffon and silk *dupattas* that I casually threw around my shoulders were dispensed with. Yards of fabric smothered me from the male gaze, even from family members, for I had no husband to attract to my youthful, female shape. Check all the photographs, Saher. I stand out like a dowdy tent.

'I did it willingly, though grudgingly at first. My veiling soon became second nature. If the shawl accidentally slipped off my head or from my shoulders, I felt naked and hastened to sort out my clothing. My sisters, on the other hand, were careless about veiling themselves and often remained totally bareheaded. Gulbahar only took to covering her head in her forties, after Laila's elopement.

'Gulbahar freely enjoyed Brother Liaquat's company and he frequently visited her any time of the day – forever in and out of her home. Why? Because Gulbahar was chaperoned by her husband, even if he wasn't there physically! At times, I've seen him looking at my sister with a wistful look of admiration, though I doubt that saintly sister of ours would ever notice that male look anyway! It was strange that her husband has never noticed it. Poor Liaquat, however, could never visit me alone, especially in the early years, for fear of compromising me and my honour.

'When you grew older, my life became more bearable. For you became my sister, daughter, friend, my companion and chaperone, all rolled into one. The need to talk to another adult, however, has always remained. I could not, of course, communicate with the servants. Social parameters have prevented me from doing that.

'Now, Saher, I've lost you to Arslan. I know you've chosen him and he may well be a good husband but my unhappiness will remain my daily companion. Also …'

Rani stopped, gaze lowered.

'Also …' Saher prompted, unable to take in everything that her mother had painfully poured out.

'Also, I am mourning the man who could have been my companion and I turned him down.'

'I know there's a real need in you for male companionship. I alone cannot fulfil that but I wish you had spoken to me earlier. If only you had remarried.'

'It was not to be.'

'Please give me your blessing to marry Arslan. He adores me!'

'Yes, he's crazy about you all right,' Rani laughed bitterly. 'All his life! His eyes were forever on you, whenever you weren't looking, with that possessive look which I so hated. It's so strange, my daughter, how naive you've been, not to spot the passion in his eyes. I've watched two men in love, Liaquat with our Gulbahar and Arslan with you, yet stupidly neither of you two women saw it.'

Saher blushed, not wishing to discuss her feelings for Arslan, remembering the feel of his mouth again.

'You've got it wrong about Auntie Gulbahar and Uncle Liaquat – what a thing to say, Mother!' Rani shrugged her shoulders and let the matter rest for the sake of her sister's *izzat*.

'Why were you so against Arslan?' Saher challenged.

'I don't know. I hated him for feeling this way about you, as if he was defiling you. So I felt the need to protect you from him.'

'Is that why you were happier to get me married to Ismail instead?'

'At least he was older. You treated Arslan as a child – you always bossed him, remember? How can you marry a man you feel that way about?'

'He's not a child any more, Mother. And what we feel for each other now is very much grown-up stuff.' She lowered her gaze, cheeks a fiery shade of red.

'Then I'll have to give you my blessing.'

'Oh, Mother!' Saher buried her face in her mother's lap. 'Thank you, I'm so glad,' she cried, raising her tear-smeared face up to her mother.

'He has to promise me to let you stay one night every week with me.'

'He will, Mother, he will!'

After a while, basking in the warmth of her daughter's kisses, Rani drew away.

'Come, we are both tired and there's a lot to be done tomorrow. I want to do it before Ismail goes back to the UK. Also Laila is back, and I want all my sister's family to join me in my celebration. Enough time has been wasted and spent in isolation. I need to bond with both my sisters, especially with poor Gulbahar. I'm so ashamed of my behaviour over the years, always imagining that she was slighting me because I was jealous of Mehreen. And now she'll become your mother-in-law and I'm really pleased. For in my heart of hearts, I respect that sister very much!'

'I'm so happy, Mother!' Saher hugged her. Then, 'Mother, about Rashid ...' Her mother stiffened.

'Let's go down. I'll tell you more about him, one day,' Rani stood up tall, face shuttered, pain chasing across her features.

Rashid.

She did not want to think of him now, of all times. Life was back in her body – head full of tasks for a full-blown wedding instead of an engagement party, so that Ismail and his English wife could attend it, too.

CHAPTER 47

The Wedding

'Rukhsar-ji, I'm not going to miss out on this wedding! Enough of this lying around in bed – with your pampering, you are going to give me bedsores,' Massi Fiza teased her friend.

Every minute was precious – the quicker she got to the *hevali* the better her chance of joining Master Arslan's wedding entourage. Surely Mistress Gulbahar would be kindly disposed towards her, for had she not done many errands for that family over the years?

Ignoring her friend's mocking gale of laughter, Massi Fiza had scuttled down her friend's staircase to her home. From her rusty, steel trunk, she dragged out a neat bundle of fabric – her best party outfit, wrapped in a muslin shawl. Squatting on the floor, she hurriedly ironed her peacock green taffeta and satin garments on the jute *dari* mat.

With a nervous heartbeat, coupled with a cheeky grin, Massi Fiza duly presented herself to Begum, the domestic goddess of 'power' in the *hevali*. She would see who won today – Massi Fiza or Begum.

'Please, Begum …' she began earnestly. 'I'll help you to clear up everything tomorrow and do all your washing, if you'll let me join this wedding party.'

Begum's mouth dropped open at the woman's appearance in a *gota kinari* peacock-green satin and taffeta suit, which boxed her thin, wiry body. She was late with the tea and here was this mad woman with the cheekiest of requests!

'And what will you do at the wedding party, Massi Fiza, may I ask?' Begum frostily demanded, her thin eyebrows arched in disdain, cheeks swollen in secret laughter at the laundrywoman's audacity in presenting herself as a guest at Master Haider's only son's wedding!

'You see,' Massi Fiza stuttered, 'I can carry some of the presents, the baskets of *mithae*, for example.'

'What! The presents are already there – we are only taking the sweets and chocolates. Mistress Laila is now back at home and will do all the ritual carrying, not any of us humble servants. Definitely not you! The *goorie* will also be carrying one of the bridal sweet baskets.'

'Please, Begum – take me with you!' Massi Fiza cried, the vision of the *goorie* lending more urgency to her request. 'I beg of you!'

Melted by Massi Fiza's genuine longing, Begum relented and stiffly reminded the laundrywoman: 'It's not an engagement, but a wedding party. As Master Ismail and his English bride are leaving the day after tomorrow, it was decided to have this *nikkah* ceremony today. The bride and groom don't want any fuss at all – it was as if they wanted to tie the knot this very evening!' Begum stopped, mentally chiding herself for confiding so much of family matters to the laundrywoman.

'Oh, wow, Begum!' Massi Fiza marvelled, her eyes lighting up. This was even better. Reaching forward, she grabbed Begum's hand and gave it a walloping kiss.

'Please, Begum, you've got to take me with you. I'll even catch a *tanga* just to get there! Allah Pak is my witness – I'll do all the housework for you! I'll be your personal maid at the ceremony … Please, all I want is a glimpse of how these people get married and what happens in these big mansions. Also, I'll wash all your Ali's clothes for free for two months,' she added, still holding fast onto Begum's hand.

'OK. You can go … Let go of me, you silly woman!' Begum screeched, pulling her hand back, shocked by the woman's idiotic behaviour.

'Oh, Begum, you are an angel!' Begum feared the woman would swoon on her kitchen floor.

She ordered, 'You might as well make yourself useful right now. I'll get Ali to take us both in the Jeep.'

'Thanks, Begum. You are simply wonderful!'

'Stop the buttering! Don't make me regret it. Mind you, you'll have to stay the night at Mistress Rani's house, as she'll need our help in clearing up after the party tomorrow.'

'Of course,' Massi Fiza's smile now strained from one end to the other of her narrow face. This was even better – to spend two days at a wedding in Mistress Rani's mansion! Wouldn't it be wonderful to see how that haughty, middle sister lived!

'Now, nip out to the sweetmaker's house and check if the *mithai* is ready ... Their phone is busy all the time.'

'I hear that Salma, the quiltmaker's daughter, is leaving for Dubai. Bano, the seamstress, has been busy stitching all her suits. Keeping everyone else waiting. The baker's wife is livid as the stitching for her daughter's trousseau is being neglected!'

'Never mind the baker's wife! Now go ... You are a bad influence, Fiza. You've got me going, too – gossiping!'

*

'Take the tray, you daft woman!' Begum cried, grabbing hold of Massi Fiza's taffeta *dupatta* as she was about rush out of the kitchen in Rani's *hevali*.

'The dancing, Begum! I've got to see ... the sisters are dancing in the drawing room.' And then she had shot off. Begum, curious herself, sprinted after her. Over Massi Fiza's shoulders, she peered into the room where the female members of Gulbahar's clan were gathered, watching Mehreen do a traditional footstool wedding dance to celebrate her nephew and niece's wedding. The small *peeri* propped on one shoulder, Mehreen's stout body dipped and swayed in different directions to the *dholki* music played by two women seated on the floor and accompanied by the energetic chanting of folk songs by a group of women singers from the village.

Panting and giggling, Mehreen called to her smiling elder sister, sitting next to the groom and the bride. 'Baji Gulbahar, see, this is how I danced at your Arslan's birth. Don't laugh, everyone! Of course, I was much slimmer then!' Smiling, she grimaced down at her waistline, padded with rolls of fat, and reached to pull her sister, Rani, with her stiff body and deadpan expression, into the dancing circle.

'Come on, Rani. Cheer up, for God's sake! It's your daughter's wedding day. Let's celebrate. Laila, my darling – come and join me!'

Glad to dance at her brother's wedding, Laila gracefully swung into the circle of dancing women, swirling her maroon chiffon sari around her body to the delight of the younger women, wanting to see more modern dancing than Mehreen's clumsy movements. It was a much prettier sight to watch than Mehreen's wobbling waist. Laila elicited loud clapping and cheering from everyone.

'Mummy, can I dance too?' Shirin excitedly pulled at the *phallu* of her mother's sari. Flushed, Laila nodded. 'It's your uncle's wedding – of course, my princess.' Arslan, sitting happily beside his bride, beamed his approval at his niece.

Gulbahar, full of love, stood behind her middle sister and squeezed her hand. 'Happy, Rani?' Rani nodded, and on impulse planted a kiss on Gulbahar's cheek before she got cold feet. Gulbahar's arm closed around her sister.

'*Mubarak*, Rani. I'm so thrilled to have your Saher come to us, but she remains your daughter always. So don't think you have lost her.'

Rani smothered silent sobs against her sister's shoulders as she desperately tried to thrust aside the image of Rashid, and then felt Mehreen's arms encircling her. Everyone watched the three sisters clasping each other and weeping with joy.

Daniela, sitting beside Saher, happily looked on. Dressed in an elegant cream chiffon sari, given to her as a wedding present by Gulhahar, she had smiled her way through the entire evening. Enjoying every minute of this novel experience of attending a Pakistani wedding, she had learned about the different rituals and customs. She was in awe of the gold jewellery draped around the women's upper torsos and admired the colours, textures and styles of garments worn by over 30 women and young girls from Haider's clan.

Many stealthy glances lingered on the foreign bride, as the

guests marvelled at her Western beauty, her lustrous, shiny hair. They found her friendly manner so engaging; the way she stood up to embrace them, her sweet *salaams* and smiles to all were so endearing.

'An enchanting creature she is!' Mehreen proudly boasted to one of her cousins, who had come for the wedding from Karachi, her eyes often resting on her daughter-in-law with pride. 'This is Allah's way! He knows best!' Who would have thought that her only son would marry a foreign woman! 'And see how well she has blended with us and embraced our customs and way of life!'

Begum first lightly tapped and then poked hard on Massi Fiza's bony shoulder.

'Stop showing your funny teeth, you silly woman, we are here to serve dinner. The men have already been fed in the marquee. It's the women's turn. I know you want to stand here all evening gawping in admiration at the brides, but we are not the *bharathis*, the guests ... Are you listening to me, you daft woman?'

Begum gave up, confronted with the dreamy look in Massi Fiza's eyes. The *dhoban* was in seventh heaven. To be part of the landlord's family wedding entourage and to witness the whole of the wedding reception, from the arrival of the groom from the other village in a limousine, and a atop white horse for the last few hundred yards, to the solemn *nikkah* ceremony, to the lively exchange of presents and milk-giving and money-bartering rituals and finally to watching the women's dancing celebrations, was pure bliss.

'How lucky I am! Thanks to you, Begum-ji! Wait until I tell Rukhsar all this – she'll be so envious! If only I had a camera ... Oh, God, I must get a picture with the two brides, especially with the *goorie*. I overheard that she's leaving soon for London. I want to sit beside her and say something to her in *Engrezi*. If only I could. Alas, an illiterate woman like me is not destined to speak that language. Did you see the presents she's been getting all evening and the wodges of money, Begum!' Her tone had now switched to envy.

'Shut up!'

Pulling Massi Fiza by the wrist, Begum led her out on the

veranda, to the table laden with food by the village chef and his staff on exquisite china platters, trays and bowls. Massi Fiza feverishly counted in her head the number of dishes being offered. Three she could not recognise. Meat, as expected, was plentiful, consisting of chicken, lamb, pigeon and fried fish. Overwhelmed by the experience of being amongst people of wealth, the upper classes, Massi Fiza turned a tearful glance at her friend.

'Begum, thank you for letting me come here!'

'Thank me later, you silly woman.' Begum hissed. 'Serve the drinks in the crystal glasses from Mistress Rani's dining room. And don't break any! Mistress Rani is not Mistress Gulbahar, you know. She might even charge us for any breakages!'

Giggling, and straightening their multi-coloured taffeta shawls fringed with golden *gota kinari* lace over their heads, they modestly lowered their gazes and stepped aside when the male guests filed past them for their tea in the dining room.

Haider lingered on the veranda, peering into the room through the open door and catching a glimpse of his grand-daughter circling around the room in a brisk dance sequence, with the women energetically cheering. Haider caught his daughter's eyes over the heads of the women guests. A poignant smile was exchanged. Feeling tearful, he moved on. Then, at the door he stopped, hearing steps behind him, and waited for his son-in-law. Jubail, disconcerted by this gesture, humbly entered the room. Begum and Massi Fiza exchanged a pointed glance beneath the fringes of their shawls. The potter's son was honoured by his father-in-law in front of all the guests. Begum dreamily gazed at the retreating figure of her master. 'How wonderful he is.' At times she thought she must be in love with him, for his generosity and kindness to folk like herself and that traitor, Jubail.

Then they saw Mistress Rani come out of the deawing room, a mobile phone to her ear, eyes wide. She walked to the other end of the veranda, head lowered, talking in hushed tones. As Begum went to pass the hostess with a tray of drinks, she glimpsed tears and distress on Mistress Rani's face.

Later when she mentioned it to Fiza in the kitchen, the latter shook her head.

'Those tears were not of happiness, I tell you. Mistress Rani was highly distressed. I wonder who had called her and why?' As Fiza nodded, she continued, 'I saw her go up to her room, tearful cheeks hidden behind her *dupatta*. I guess it has all been too much having her daughter wed. Why are we gossiping again? The tea still has to be served to the ladies. Now pass me that round china pot and don't drop it, for goodness sake!'

'Please, stop bossing me!' Now that she had seen the whole wedding, Massi Fiza had the temerity to challenge her new employer.

It was much later in the night, after the food had been served, that Massi Fiza's dream came true; she had had her photo taken with the *goorie* bride, and by a professional photographer, too. It was Gulbahar who drily told the photographer that these women were 'special' in her household, catching a glimpse of disdain in the young city photographer, used to shooting pictures of glamorous models and fashionably dressed city women. He politely nodded, hiding a smirk as the two frumpy-looking women fiddled with their shawls, looking harassed and pursing their mouths even more when he asked them to smile. Massi Fiza would not obey him, bent on hiding her crooked teeth. After the photos had been taken, Massi Fiza went to call Mistress Rani from her bedroom. There she found mother and daughter hugging, with Rani sobbing over her daughter's shoulders, 'Do you understand what I have told you? I have to go to Rashid!'

'Of course, you must, Mother! You have my blessing,' Saher affirmed,

Shy of intruding on their intimacy, Massi Fiza closed the door. Her eyes were alight with speculation. Who were they talking about and where was Mistress Rani going? Her first question whilst scouring the pots in the kitchen to Begum was, 'Who's Rashid? Is Mistress Rani's husband not dead?'

Begum looked mystified and then hotly scolded her helper. 'Forget Rashid, whoever he is! Get on with your scouring!'

CHAPTER 48

The Reunion

Elizabeth was enjoying her glass of sherry in her study, eyes closed, listening to a heated debate on Radio 4 when there was a knock on the door. Dave was ready to join his mates at the local pub to watch Wigan, his favourite team, playing football.

Frowning, Elizabeth got up; they were not expecting anyone. Daniela and her husband stood outside, two suitcases on the ground beside them. Elizabeth's gaze was the first to drop. Ismail nervously turned his head, unable to look at the woman who had made her dislike so clear to him on their first meeting and then had refused to even acknowledge his presence in her daughter's life. Face straight, Daniela shot a challenging look at her mother.

Love welling up for her daughter, Elizabeth pulled the door wide. But both her visitors remained standing. Elizabeth's eyes slid off Ismail's face. 'Come …' she said, her voice faint and roughened with emotion. She had not realised how much she had missed her daughter.

Daniela stepped into her parents' home, after three years. In the living room they waited, exchanging surreptitious glances, whilst Elizabeth disappeared into the kitchen to make tea for them, her hand shaking whilst she sliced a carrot cake. Then she heard Dave's loud exclamation, 'Daniela, my pet!' and smiled wryly at the delight in her husband's voice.

'Dad!'

A few minutes later, Elizabeth wheeled a tea trolley into the living room. Ismail rose to help her, reaching for the trolley bar, his brown, suntanned hand near her white one. He glanced at her and then let go of the trolley.

Daniela was animatedly showing pictures from her digital camera to her father, explaining who the different people were: 'This is Ismail's mum, Mehreen.'

'Let's see, my pet.' Dave peered at the small screen and then passed the camera to his wife. Bemused and heartbeat quickening, Elizabeth stared down at the overweight, Pakistani woman in a turquoise suit with her head and shoulders draped in a matching shawl, standing beside a colonnade in a courtyard. 'This stranger – this woman – is now linked to my daughter,' she bitterly echoed in her head, pressing the button to flick across more photos, steeling herself at the sight of another world cascading before her eyes, mind reeling at the unfamiliar faces and scenes.

'These photos are of the wedding of Ismail's cousin, Arslan. This is Laila, dancing at her brother's wedding, and that lovely little girl is her daughter – Shirin, I think,' Daniela looked at her husband to confirm. 'Ismail has such a big family. So many relatives and big houses. It was lovely, Mum.' Her voice petered away, assessing her mother's face with interest, diving into her thoughts. Cheeks warming under her daughter's scrutiny, Elizabeth recovered her poise and smiled, noting her daughter's animated face and flushed cheeks. She had indeed lost her daughter to another world – to people of another race, faith, colour and culture.

As Daniela excitedly described some of the places she had visited and showed her father the printed photographs, Elizabeth stole a surreptitious glance at her son-in-law. She could tell that he was nervous and was bent on avoiding eye contact with her. So she was surprised to hear herself addressed by him: 'How is your PhD research going, Elizabeth?'

Father and daughter exchanged a pointed glance. Elizabeth coolly answered, 'Fine,' eyes sliding off the brown-faced man who had stolen her daughter's heart. Daniela pulled up her large handbag and drew out the jewellery boxes that her father-in-law had given her. Flicking the lids open, she startled her parents with their contents. Elizabeth stared at the line of blue and red velvet boxes containing the gold and silver gem-studded necklace sets, lying on her Persian silk rug.

Daniela drily informed them: 'These are my gifts from my parents-in-law, Mother ... All this gold is mine ...' Elizabeth stared back, chafing under her daughter's mocking gaze, and politely uttered, 'They are lovely, darling ...'

'Let's have a proper look.' Dave had plucked out a set and was smiling at Ismail. 'What a lucky girl you are, Daniela. These are lovely, mate. Thank your parents for this.'

'I will,' Ismail beamed in pleasure and then disappeared out of the room. He returned a few minutes later with a small silk rug in his arms.

'This is for you both. We bought it in Murree, a lovely hillside resort. I hope you both like it!' Squatting on the floor, Ismail unrolled it over the other rug. Elizabeth's face spread in a look of pure joy, her eyes marvelling at the rustic landscape of trees, deer and birds, cleverly woven with silk thread.

'Thank you,' she softly offered, bending to trace her finger over the shining, soft, silk surface.

Bent on impressing her parents, Daniela went out into the hall and, zipping open her suitcase, she pulled out the suits that Mehreen and Rasoola had helped her pack.

'These, too, were given to me as gifts.' Daniela happily thrust the pile of suits into her mother's lap. Elizabeth stared at the Asian outfits of all colours and textures. Daniela pulled out one of her favourites. 'This long skirt, Mother, is called a *lengha* and there is a tunic and a matching scarf. Look at the embroidery and sequin-work – see how fine it is. And these are real zirconi crystals on this sari. I wore it at the wedding. I've got photos of me wearing it. Here, let me show you.' Overwhelmed, Elizabeth dumbly nodded, gazing wryly at the photo Daniela had thrust in front of her and the people in it who had crowded into her daughter's life. 'These two are Ismail's aunts – Gulbahar and Rani. Gulbahar is nice, but Rani never smiles and ...' Daniela stopped. She was about to add: 'I know Rani hates me.' She would never tell her mother about Saher, the fiancée, and that nightmarish experience during the first few days of her visit to Pakistan.

'And these are some of their servants. This is Rasoola, the

housekeeper in Ismail's home. In this photo is the laundry-woman called Fiza who works in Ismail's aunt's home. She kept babbling on about wanting to sit next to me at the wedding and having a photo taken.' Elizabeth nodded.

An hour later, after tea and more small talk over photographs, their jewellery items packed away apart from one silver necklace which Daniela presented to her mother as a gift, Ismail rose to leave.

'We need to go, Daniela. You need to rest. We came straight from the airport to say hello,' Ismail explained.

'I'm glad that you came to see us first, Ismail! Delighted to have you both back!' Dave shook Ismail's hand. 'Thanks for looking after my daughter. We were worried at times … but it looks as if she had a marvellous time.' Ismail and Daniela exchanged a special look, remembering the early days.

Dave hugged his daughter. Elizabeth rose and gathering her daughter into her arms pressed a kiss at the side of her face. Daniela kissed her back. The two men looked on, Dave's eyes filling. It was exactly three years since mother and daughter had been in the same room. Dave offered to drop them off home.

At the door, Elizabeth shyly invited, voice unsteady, 'Come for lunch on Sunday and stay for the day.'

Both stared. Ismail was the first to reply.

'Elizabeth, why don't you come to our house for dinner?' he invited, a challenging look in his eyes. A pregnant pause, then a nod from Elizabeth. It was the nod that prompted Daniela to impulsively explain to her mother. 'I have decided on a name for my son, Mother – Ibrahim. In English it is Abraham.'

'That's nice,' Elizabeth politely commented, her gaze falling as she retreated to the living room.

Outside, after the luggage had been placed in the car boot, Daniela whispered to her father, 'How are things between you and Mum?'

Dave shrugged. 'On some days everything is normal, on other days there is no real communication. And you know what, pet – I really don't give a damn. Perhaps now that her relationship with you has improved, she might well lose some of her hostility towards me, too.' They saw Mrs Patel getting out of her car with bags of groceries from Tesco and vegetables from the local Asian supermarket.

In the house, Elizabeth was fascinated by the elegant silver necklace set that Rukhsar had personally studded with zirconi and black gems whilst gossiping with Massi Fiza about Jennat Bibi and her superstitious beliefs. Elizabeth peeped at the necklace many times that evening, and finally decided that it would go really well with her favourite black shift dress. Inside she was wrestling with different thoughts and feelings, including names for the baby. Daniela had mentioned a Muslim name for her son. Did that mean her daughter had adopted the teachings of that faith and adapted her life accordingly? She closed her eyes, recoiling at the sudden image flashing across her mind; a scarf wrapped around her daughter's head. What if Daniela took to wearing the veil? Then the question: how brown would her grandchild be? Light brown? Olive brown? Or just brown like the father? Surely with her daughter's colouring, the child had to be creamy white?

'What am I thinking?' Elizabeth reined in her racist thoughts, bitterly recognising the uncomfortable truth. 'I have gained back my daughter. And I will see her in two days' time.'

A few minutes later, Elizabeth pushed aside a copy of Euripides' tragedy *Hippolytus* and strode to the wall mirror to try on Rukhsar's handiwork, the silver necklace originally designed for Saher's neck. Pulling up her hair to get a better view of her slim neck, she smiled. The necklace, wherever it came from, was exquisite.

CHAPTER 49

Rashid

Rani could not make up her mind as to which sister to speak to: Mehreen or Gulbahar. In the end, it was her elder sister she honoured by her visit and insisted on privacy, shuttling her sister up to the roof terrace. Unlike Gulbahar, Rani trusted no one, especially not the servants. The matter she was about to divulge was too personal, only to be entrusted to the bosom of a loyal sister. Begum had served refreshments and was then dismissed.

'I've something to tell you, Gulbahar … ' Rani solemnly began, sitting at a patio table facing her sister, finger circling the rim of a cool glass of sherbet.

Gulbahar waited, steeling herself for some bad news. Gaze faltering, Rani began, 'I'm going to do something …' Eyes on the basket of petunia hanging from the marble colonnade of the rooftop veranda, she continued, 'Not that I need your or anyone's permission. But out of respect, I've come to you.'

Gulbahar stared, still none the wiser.

'Rani …' she coldly prompted.

'Today … this afternoon … I'm defying convention, abandoning the customs of female modesty …'

'Rani?' Gulbahar's heart was thudding. What was her sister trying to say?

In a steady voice Rani announced, gaze falling, 'I'm visiting a man …'

Seconds ticked away. Gulbahar's lips parted, breath caught, staring at her sister.

'Visiting a man?' she queried, trying to make sense of her sister's words. 'What are you saying, Rani? Which man? And why?'

To her horror, Rani's face folded in distress, silent sobs shuddering her body.

'A dying man!'

Eyes wide, Gulbahar reached for her sister's hand across the round table, watching a red and white kite sway over the rooftop terrace and the black crows diving down from the sky to perch on the railing wall, spreading their glossy, black wings and then flying up again, one after the other.

From the courtyard downstairs, Gulbahar could hear Begum chanting, 'Mithu! Mithu!' Mouth parted, 'Rani …' she prompted, standing behind her sister, hand poised but afraid to touch in case she was rebuffed.

'A man … whom I should have and could have married, but did not …' She stopped, sobbing afresh, '… is in hospital.'

'Oh!' Gulbahar's face paled, heartbeat quickening. This was not what she was expecting. A man linked to her widowed sister? Rani, who had led such a sheltered life, shielding herself from all men, at all times. Where had this man come from? How and when? Nausea spiralling through her, Gulbahar recoiled from the image of her sister with a man.

Rani raised her head, accurately reading the fleeting expressions chasing across her sister's face.

'One day, I'll tell you about him and how much he means to me … Today, I neither want to nor have the time.' The agony in her sister's husky voice sheared Gulbahar. Dumbfounded, she continued staring.

'I came not to explain my actions but to inform about my whereabouts, in case anyone was looking for me.'

Gulbahar nodded, dismayed. Her sister had become a stranger. When exactly was it that they had drifted so apart, that she, the elder sister had no inkling of such a happening in their Rani's life. Who was this man? And why did Rani not marry him? Nobody would have stopped her. Rani cynically dug into her sister's thoughts.

'I know what you are thinking and feeling, but I don't care. I need to go … to be with him … for whatever time he has left. I don't need your permission or blessing, and I don't care about anyone's opinion.' Her voice had risen, eyes bitterly assessing the shadows of unease chasing across her sister's face. 'I'm a mature adult, able to make my own decisions. I hope you'll understand the serious nature of this visit. I gave up so much, Gulbahar ... my youth ... Bartered my personal chance of happiness for years of loneliness, and now it's too late!' Her mouth quivering, Rani was bitterly sobbing again.

'I can't bear to lose him! If only I could turn back the clock. Why did I give him up? Please pray for me, Gulbahar ... that I'm not too late ...' Rani mourned against her sister's body, before pulling herself away.

'I will,' Gulbahar softly promised, letting go of her. From the stairs, Rani cried, 'I'll be at his side ... No man or woman will be my judge. I know Allah Pak understands my pain. Whatever I do will be for Rashid's sake!'

'Do what you have to do – my love and support is with you.' Gulbahar softly asked, 'Does Saher know?'

'Yes.'

From the rooftop gallery, Gulbahar watched her sister's Jeep drive out of the village and turned her face up to feel the sun on her face. Life would never be the same again. Her sister was running to the side of a *ghair mard*, a man with whom she had no legitimate relationship and no right to be with. Who was this Rashid? Was he the captain friend of Rani's husband who came to inform us of Yacub's death? It must be. He had visited them a number of times after Yacub's death. What had happened? What was there between that man and her sister? Only time would tell and she would let her sister tell it all.

Aloud she cried, 'Rani! Rani! I spent all my life protecting Mehreen's marriage and I never gave your widowhood a thought and you never let me. What pain or sadness have you been hugging to yourself all these years!' Behind her eyes there strayed the image of Rashid talking to her sister at one of their social gatherings. Harmless social interaction; when did it transform into something else? And why did her sister give him up?

Rani's secret would remain safe, drowned in the well of her sisterhood. She could just imagine Mehreen's likely comment:

'What? Our sister has run away to the side of a strange man! Has she no shame – no *sharm*? And at her age! And her daughter has just got married. Is she mad?'

'Why is everyone revolting against the norms? First Laila with the potter's son, then Ismail marrying a foreign woman. Now Rani, a modest woman, leading a pure life, running to be with a strange man with whom she has no marital links. What madness has struck our family?' In her heart of hearts Gulbahar knew. Love.

To her husband, Gulbahar uttered not a word about her sister. If anyone asked, the answer would be, 'Rani is visiting some friends.'

✳

Rani's driver was aware of his mistress's distress, but social parameters forbade any enquiry. He glanced at her often through the rear-view mirror, wondering why his mistress was so upset and why they were going to a hospital in another city and with a suitcase full of clothes. As she had told him to take extra clothing for himself, he was wondering about his own family and work schedule. When would he return to the village? Mistress Rani had not specified dates.

Rani, sitting at the back, had her face pressed against the car window, looking out at the passing scenery, eyes swollen with tears, shawl pulled low over her head.

'Why? Why did I do that?' How many times had those bitter words rung through her head?

Simple words, 'Please do not contact me again,' chosen with care and uttered on impulse, spurred on by the sound of the other woman's voice on another continent. The words, 'Rashid, who are you talking to?' had sent terror chasing through Rani, making her question her own motives.

The thought of trespassing into another woman's life and home, and sharing her husband, sent waves of nausea through her. With those words, she had cut herself off from the man whom she had begun to care for, the man who offered her a way out of her misery, an opportunity to lead a fulfilling life. Her decision to turn him away would haunt her for years and cause her to shed many bitter tears.

'Why? Why?' she had cried. She was the loser. 'But I cannot enter into another woman's life and cast my shadow!' was the painful realisation. Only five years ago, she found out that he had separated from his wife and children, and returned home from Canada. Then her bitterness turned to him. 'Why did he not get in touch? Why not let me know that he had divorced … I gave him up for her!'

Of course, she did not know that pride had forbidden him from approaching her again. She had rebuffed him and in very clear terms – he would not cloud her horizon again.

She could still recall the excitement, the rush of adrenalin on hearing his voice and the moist feeling of her palm as she cradled the phone against her ears. She had been incredibly happy to receive that phone call.

Then his proposal – shocking her. A glorious feeling of joy washed over her, wanting to reach out to him And the agonising silence; he waiting, she recovering – holding onto the phone and her breath. The joyous words, 'I don't know what to say … Yes! Yes!' never left her mouth or reached his ears. For her own ears had picked up another voice, a woman's voice, unwittingly staking her claim over the man on the phone. It hit Rani in the head as nothing else could have done. She had to contend with that person, that voice. The joy was quashed there and then. He was not hers – but belonged to another. Her personal happiness spelled misery for the other woman. She could never be the second woman in his life, the despised second wife, who had usurped and 'stolen' the role of the original wife. The thought of confronting his children, as their 'new mama', froze her.

She often had wondered over the years how her life would have been if she had not heard that woman's voice. She knew she would have said yes and married him. The voice was her undoing, intimidating her into withdrawal, afraid to even catch a glimpse of the other woman, let alone share Rashid with her.

She often thought of their walk in the orchard, her most cherished memory of her time with Rashid. The raw excitement of youth, the tingling warm blushes she could still experience, as they had strolled alone, behind the group of other strollers from Rani's family. Without realising or intending, their pace had stalled, the distance between the others widening. They were still discreet, still in sight, but enjoyed a degree of intimacy that they both welcomed and were reluctant to part with.

On both sides there were blushes, stammered words, pregnant pauses, eager, shy looks as they hungered to know more about the other: what films they watched, what books they read and what they did when they were bored; the bout of giggles when Rashid shyly revealed he took showers and she added that she put on red lipstick. That day she was wearing red lipstick and glad that she was, knowing how becoming it was on her face with its flushed creamy cheeks, and matching her elegant white and red *shalwar kameez* outfit.

She walked confidently on her white high-heeled mules, having wanted to look her best that afternoon. Though she did not admit it to herself at the time, later she knew she had dressed with care that day, spending extra time in choosing her jewellery and doing her hair. It was the first time she had let herself dress as she used to before she became a widow. Why? She had asked herself so many times. Now she knew. She was loath to show herself as the 'dowdy' widow, her beauty hidden.

Just before they separated to enter the house, with his voice and head lowered, he shyly offered her the compliment, 'I've enjoyed talking to you. I hope we get a chance to do so again!'

Blushing, she had nodded and reluctantly had followed him inside. They parted into different rooms; Rani to where the women were gathered and he, after refreshments, went out onto the lawn. Through the window, she often found her gaze straying to the lawn. Once he had looked around and caught her eye. She returned the gaze and shyly moved back.

Later in the comfort of her bedroom and her bed, Rani faced the naked truth. Surprisingly, there was no shame in acknowledging that she was falling in love with this man, a friend of her husband's.

Then the waiting began. No communication. Just hope. Hope

that he would get in touch. She had faith in her intuition; his body language signalled both his interest and his enjoyment in her company.

'We are nearly there, Mistress Rani,' her chauffeur announced, stealing into Rani's thoughts.

*

Rani had insisted on her driver waiting in the hospital car park. She had gone to see the consultant who had contacted her on her daughter's wedding day and broken the news about Rashid's accident. Rani was one of the people the patient had requested that the hospital authorities contact. Mouth dry, Rani had listened to the consultant's words, her heart flying with hope as he said that they were trying their best; that he would recover fully, but they could not save one of his legs. She had eagerly interrupted to ask, 'Can I see him?' At his nod, she had hastened out of the office, clutching the paper with details of Rashid's room.

Head lowered, heart beating fast, Rani took no notice of other visitors, nurses, doctors, patients in wheelchairs or the lively children walking down the hospital corridor. Ahead of her, down the corridor, a woman came out of the door. Rani turned round and walked down the stairs, heart thudding, afraid of coming into contact with his relatives. Who was that woman and what relationship did she have with Rashid? She returned to the car, a terrible, hissing noise in her head. The driver left her with her thoughts and went out for a meal.

Rani returned to her memories, to arm herself for the encounter with him. Rashid had got in touch a few days after their walk, though indirectly. There were no mobile phones or emails in those days, and no obvious reason or excuse for him to visit a widow. He communicated with her through a book of poems by the philosopher and poet, Rumi, with a page marked on a poem:

My heart is like a scroll,
from here to eternity

Sent in the post as a parcel, the book was to be opened by her. There was no name or address of the sender. She just knew, holding the book against her chest, that it was from him. Later in the evening she had memorised not only that poem, but others he had highlighted. Then she waited. She could not get in touch with him herself and her mind would not entertain the thought of his wife and children. It was only a week later when she visited the army headquarters to check about her husband's salary matters that she found her feet walking to Rashid's office. He was busy with three guests. Shyly she was about to exit, but he stopped her.

'Sahiba-ji, we sent some books of your husband's home. I hope you received them?'

This was a blatant lie. Her husband never read poetry nor would he have purchased any such books. This was her cue and she happily took it to convey to him her thoughts and feelings.

'Yes, Rashid-ji. Many thanks. I have read many of those poems. In particular, I liked the one about "a scroll". So beautiful! I loved it! It's exactly how I feel.'

'I'm glad. I will speak to you soon after this meeting. Please wait.'

She did not. She had achieved what she had set out to do: to let him know that she had received the books and that she felt the same. The rest was up to him.

It was two months later before he contacted her again by telephone, and it was then he had proposed. Two months that had decided for him that he wanted this woman in his life and two months of misery for her waiting to hear from him. She wondered then how this illicit attraction, this interest in the other, had started. Perhaps on the day he had entered her home to announce her husband's death?

She could still remember the crushing anguish. He, too, lived the naked grief of this woman as she heard the news. That moment forged the link between them. He was shaken by her anguish and his own instinct to protect her. She was picking something from the floor and rose to greet him with a smile of welcome, her beauty accentuated by a fashionable outfit and an immaculately made-up face. An attractive woman, at the height of her beauty and youth, about to have the joys of her life snuffed out.

The next time his eyes fell on her she was cloaked in white from head to toe. Face naked, brutally stripped of any makeup. His heart mourned, not just for his friend who had died in a car accident but for the woman whose life was destroyed, too. What option did she have, but to lead a sterile life of widowhood, stripped of all the things that most women took for granted.

The thought was unbearable. At the end, it was not his passion for her but the teaching of their Prophet Mohammed who encouraged men to marry and look after widows, that prompted the thought of marrying her, especially as his own marriage was failing. Not that Rani had any money worries. She was an extremely rich woman from her father's inheritance. It was more about offering her companionship. And she had rejected him. He had never forgiven her for that.

Half an hour later, Rani retraced her steps back onto the hospital ward, nervous but determined. She was afraid of no one. She had come on a mission and would complete it.

She slid open the door and saw a man lying on his side on the bed, facing the other way. Rani froze. Not ready.

Breath held she pulled the door shut. She stood outside in the corridor, looking out of the window, her hand clutching the folds of her *chador* around her head. She caught the shadowy reflection of her face in the glass frame of a picture of the gorgeous Swat Valley hanging on the wall.

'Will Rashid even recognise me?' she mourned. She was older, not made up and her hair was grey. The woman he knew – the youth, elegance and beauty from her twenties – was gone. What became of her? An empty, bitter shell of a woman.

'No, I am not alone and will not be alone!' Rani vowed, turning to the door once again. Hand trembling, she turned the handle and stepped inside.

Rashid still had his back to the door. From the gentle sweeping movement of his chest under the white cotton sheet, it appeared that he was asleep. Rani sighed, tiptoeing across the room to sit in the armchair beside his bed. She could tell that it was no ordinary room, but a well-furnished, private suite, and wondered who was paying for it. The army or his family?

The desperate longing to catch a glimpse of his face had her rising but then sitting down again, shy of meeting his eyes. With her own, she lovingly traced the shape of his head. The springy thick hair was now partially grey and shorter in length. She could wait no more.

Heart thudding, she circled the bed, standing in front of him. Thankful that he was asleep, she took her fill of him. Time had done its duty, gently drawn its faithful marks on his face; faint lines and soft creases on the forehead and around his mouth, his complexion darkened by the sun. The rest, the shape of his high cheekbones, the jutting chin displaying stubble, the full-lipped mouth and the straight nose were the same. The stubborn frown wedged between his eyebrows had her wanting to reach out and smooth it away.

Holding her breath, she leaned forward to touch him, to caress his cheek, ready to welcome and meet the eyes of a man she adored. She had dreamt of this moment for so long, letting her fingers lightly trail over the side of his right cheek.

Heavily drugged, Rashid's eyelids fluttered open and focused on Rani's waist. Imagining it to be one of the nursing staff, he closed his eyes again, hating to be disturbed for another examination. Rani sat down on the chair next to the bed, levelling her face with his, staring at him, waves of excitement fanning through her body. Her eyes could not get enough of him.

'I'm here. And he is alive! God help us!' How she had longed for this moment. To see him alive! The doctor had said something about an injury to one of his legs and a shot in the stomach. She didn't yet know the details.

The urge to touch him so strong, Rani tenderly pushed back the stray lock of hair that had fallen on his forehead. Rashid's eyelids gently lifted and he stared straight into a pair of dark brown eyes and a face that appeared familiar. His mouth worked to say something, his tongue slipping out to lick his dry lips. Rani's gaze faltered, colour flooding into her cheeks, her hands trembling on her lap.

'Rani?' Voice hoarse, Rashid was sure he was hallucinating due to the medication he had taken.

'I am here ...' she softly replied, voice laced with longing and tenderness, head shyly lowered, cheeks burning and mortally ashamed of her faded looks. Why had she not dyed her hair or at least added a touch of colour to her mouth. Gentle though it had been with her, time still had dealt a blow. What did he think of her? Was he shocked and disappointed?

Rashid did not know what to think. Her looks were not on his mind. Surprised to see her; joy shot through him. He tried to lift himself up, but was gripped by another dizzy spell and clutched at the cotton sheet. Rani bent forward, pulled the sheet over his bare chest. Watching his face crease in pain, she trailed her fingers across his cheek; it was the most natural thing to do.

'How are you?' she asked in a quivering voice, attempting to smile. Mentally, she accused: 'Why did you never call again? I waited for you! Why punish me with such a long silence?'

Rashid was having his own poignant conversation with her in his head. 'Why did you do that to us? Cruelly turn me away? What have you gained from that wretched life of loneliness? Why punish us both?'

Aloud he politely mouthed, 'Fine,' masking his physical pain from the shrapnel wound behind the weak smile. So much to say and share but neither knew how to begin. In their hearts they meant so much to each other but outwardly they were still strangers; their only interaction had been in public places, and limited to mundane social exchanges.

Seconds ticked away and the silence continued. Rashid was glad that she had come to see him, but was none the wiser as to what her presence entailed. Instead he let his eyes go on caressing her. It was left to her to make the first move. Rani understood and happily took the cue.

She did it not with words but with her hands and mouth. She let them say it all, let them be her passionate messengers of her joy, grief and regret. She reached for his arm and, tenderly cradling it against her face, she pressed her mouth to it. Rashid held her gaze, spellbound. Rani continued with her passionate kisses, pouring out her longing for him, brushing her lips against the side of his arm, around his wrist and then on the back of his hand and palm, savouring the feel of his warm, moist flesh. Her eyes whispered, 'I want to go on kissing you, my darling.'

It was then that the door opened and a nurse entered the room, surprised to see Rani holding the patient's hand against her face. What relationship did this woman have with the patient, she wondered. Was she the wife? A sister would not have held the hand against her mouth in that way. And that unfazed look in the woman's eyes. Her gaze politely lowered, the nurse moved into the room, mumbled a greeting, keenly aware that the woman did not let go of the patient's hand.

After checking the medical notes, her eyes briefly sweeping across the two figures still caught up with each other, she announced, 'I'll be back later!' and slipped out of the room, giving them the privacy they needed, noting with interest that the woman had shown no sign of embarrassment in being caught in such an intimate scene.

Rashid's tender and poignant gaze warmed Rani's face and heart, making her smile. He mouthed the word 'Why?' She had surprised him with her action; in compromising herself and her *izzat* by kissing him, and then being caught doing so by someone else.

'You belong to me! You are mine!' she murmured, smiling shyly, and then to demonstrate she pressed the back of his hand to her mouth and let her lips communicate once again. Inside she vowed, 'I'll not leave you, my beautiful darling.'

Touched and gloriously happy, Rashid offered his own response. 'I am happy to belong! But for how long you have me, I do not know, nor can I promise. I'm sorry.'

'I'll not give you up again … for anyone or anything!' was her passionate reply, bathing under his tender gaze. When his hand tentatively reached for her face, she basked in the feel of his fingers. Nothing mattered; neither her appearance nor the parameters of female modesty, just the human need to serve, to touch and to have. Then she was shedding bitter tears of regret for all those years lost, head buried against his arm on the bed.

'Why were we so stupid, Rashid? Why did we let pride divide us? I thought I was doing the right thing! But for whom?'

'*Kismet* ...' was Rashid's low answer, now in physical pain and unable to enter into proper discussion with her. 'Hush, we are together now ...' His eyes too mirrored her regret. If only he could turn back the clock. He did not want it this way – to see her after so long and as an invalid with a missing leg. He would live each day that God blessed him with.

*

'I need to phone your Aunt Rani in Islamabad to see when she's coming home, or I might visit her myself,' Gulbahar let slip the information.

She had not told anyone in her family what Rani was doing in Islamabad for the last few days. Her last phone conversation with her sister had ended with Rani fervently saying, 'Either I stay with Rashid and look after him or bring him home. I'll not part with him, Gulbahar! If something happened to Haider-ji, would you give up on him? For that is how I feel about Rashid. Whether it is right or wrong, I no longer care!'

Gulbahar had a mission. To support and bring back her sister and Rashid – she did not know how to describe this relationship. Rashid and Rani were not friends, lovers or spouses. Yet Rani's actions, words and feelings made all three legitimate. Something had to be done or suggested. *Nikkah*. Her sister had to marry the man. How she was going to break the news to the rest of the family daunted her. How to explain to her Haider-ji? First Liaquat having a crush on her and now Rani with Rashid. Heat rushed into her cheeks at the gossip that would ensue. She could just imagine the laundrywoman's wagging tongue, going around the village saying, 'Can you believe it! Mistress Rani gets wed after her daughter! What's happening to our world? Does no one feel shame, *sharm,* any more.'

Gulbahar thought of the years that her sister had pined for Rashid. The recent long phone conversation between them had given her an idea of Rani's suffering after nobly turning away the man who had held out a hand and offered a world of happiness to her. 'If only we had communicated. Rashid has lived alone all these years, since his wife divorced him and migrated to Canada. We were both stupid. I for rejecting him and he for never approaching me again. Out of pride! Tell me which person on earth would try and separate us now? Do we both not deserve to snatch what time we have to be together. All I want to do now is sit with him and touch him. To feel him, that he is there! I want to be with him, Gulbahar! I never want to leave his side!'

Gulbahar listened with a sinking heart. Morality was no longer an issue for Rani, for she had trespassed into forbidden territory, well beyond the parameters of female modesty, lost in the love of this man. It was up to her, as the eldest sister, to guide the reins of Rani's life in the direction of her sister's wishes. Gulbahar shuddered. How far did their touching go? Did passion have any limits? Her sister had compromised herself. As the eldest sister she had to protect her sister, both her love and her position in the world. Love alone was not enough. Marriage remained the only logical answer and as decreed by their faith. Rani could not live in sin with a man in an unwed state; she had suffered too much to cope with prying eyes, gossiping tongues and social ostracism.

CHAPTER 50

The Door

In Gulistan, in the quiltmaker's house, there was mayhem. The taxi was on its way. Zeinab was rushing around her house doing the last-minute tidying-up before their departure to Dubai – distributing fresh vegetables, jute bags of rice and flour to her neighbours. Her prized electrical items were neatly locked away in her bedroom to prevent anyone using them. Years of darning quilts had furnished her humble home well. And she had every intention of returning to Gulistan once her daughter was settled in Dubai.

Zeinab clambered up the mud-veneered staircase to her rooftop to get her darning table and heave it down to the veranda. The crunching sound of car wheels outside the door made her panic.

'Salma!' Zeinab shouted.

Salma sat stooped on her bed, staring into space, clutching a cotton coat with a suitcase by her side.

'Come on, my silly girl. The taxi is here. Let's go,' Zeinab coaxed, looking at her daughter, 'I'm really excited about getting on a plane.'

The girl lowered her head further.

'I'm abandoning my home, my work and my village for your sake so don't you sit there looking glum,' she gently reminded her, the doctor's words of advice ringing in her ears. 'Salma is going through a terrible period of post-natal depression. Please be gentle with her … She needs your support and understanding. Harsh words and rebukes will not solve anything.'

Salma's piteous cry 'I don't want to go' had Zeinab pointing the pencil she was holding in her hand at her daughter.

'You silly girl! Of course we are going! We need to seek medical help for you and to leave behind this village of silly women and their superstitions. *Gulistan* – what a name! This is no rose garden city! But a village of thorns!'

Clutching her handbag, Salma rose to leave.

'Paper? I need paper.' Zeinab was riffling through an old pile of her daughter's college notebooks and tore out a sheet of paper from one of them. Educated to tenth *matric* class, writing posed no problem for Zeinab. With the blunt pencil she scribbled some big bold words across it in *Nastaliq* script. 'Salma, have you seen the sticky tape?' Her daughter shook her head.

Dashing into her own room, she rummaged through her darning basket for two small needles and a black felt-tip marker that she used for drawing lines on the quilts. Smiling and putting the items in the side pocket of her long *kurtha* she locked her bedroom door with an aluminium padlock.

'Are we ready to go?' Salma's husband, Yunus, politely enquired from the courtyard. Mother and daughter nodded, letting him drag their suitcases to the car in the street lane. An excited, bedraggled group of children was circling the car. After peering into it, the children sidled away in disgust; just another ordinary car and one with a little dent. It was the monstrous Jeeps and tall Pajeros owned by the migrant families and the wealthy landlord that elicited wistful looks.

Inside her small courtyard, Zeinab tearfully looked around, eyes grazing the rooftop where most of her darning took place in the warm weather, then down to her humble kitchen with its *tandoor* where she slapped in *chappatis* against the hot mud-baked surface. All the crockery was stacked away in her wooden cabinets. Her three *charpoys* stood under the veranda for her neighbour to borrow for her guests. She was locking her daughter's room when her neighbour came in to bid them goodbye.

'Here, Resham – our key. You can use my *tandoor*, those *charpoys* and all the crockery in the kitchen.' She omitted to mention the two locked rooms. Both understood. Zeinab would take the keys for those with her.

'Don't worry about anything!' her friend reassured her, hugging Zeinab.

'I don't want to leave, Resham, but I have no choice. Alone, Salma will be lost in Dubai, especially when her husband is out working,' Zeinab ended tearfully. She very rarely left the village.

'It will be good for you and Salma … *In'shallah* our prayers are with you, Sister Zeinab.'

Salma's husband Yunus was waiting, quietly listening to their conversation. Salma was already in the car. From the car, Zeinab instructed: 'Salma, please wave to your Aunt Resham.' Salma obeyed, waving a limp hand.

'Let's go!' Yunus said, checking his expensive watch purchased from the Dubai gold *souk*. They still had to visit his family in the town before they flew off.

As the taxi passed Jennat Bibi's house, Zeinab shouted to the driver.

'Stop for one minute!' Salma froze, staring at the door of Faiza's home – the friend who had betrayed her. Zeinab scrambled out. They looked on, fascinated. Standing tall before the door, Zeinab pulled out the three items from her *kurtha* pocket. Holding the paper against the sweetmaker's door, she pinned it to the wooden surface with the two needles. Then, not taking any chances, in case the paper flew off or was pulled down, just below it she scrawled two sentences in big, bold, *Nastaliq* Urdu with her black marker.

The driver and Yunus read the bold writing, and looked away when Zeinab sidled back into the car.

'Let's go,' she instructed, ignoring her daughter's piercing look, a smug smile dashed across her face.

The car wound out of the village lanes and into the open space of the communal mosque square flanked by sugarcane fields, and headed towards the city of Attock.

✳

That evening, returning from his sweet shop, Jennat Bibi's husband came to an abrupt stop outside their wooden door and pulled out his reading glasses from his jacket pocket. A paper was stuck to it and he read aloud the words 'Don't enter! Beware of *perchanvah* in this house. Keep away from Faiza's evil shadow,' streaked across the middle of the door.

Blood rushed to Javaid's face. It could only be the quiltmaker. He went to check and was greeted by a padlock hanging outside Zeinab's door. Smiling and whistling to himself, he entered his own home.

The following mornng, he read the notice again and sauntered off to his sweet shop, stealing a look over his shoulders; their milkman was now peering at the notice. Cheeks bulging with laughter, he braced himself for his wife's reaction, but first he protected himself by switching off his mobile phone.

Jennat Bibi had no idea that her front door had been defaced. It was much later in the day that her best friend Neelum reported it to her. Many other passers-by had read the notice, including Massi Fiza, who scurried off to tell Rukhsar about it.

'Jennat-ji, I think you should see this,' Neelum pulled her friend away from the kitchen stove where a pot of milk was simmering for the *barfi* sweets. Jennat stopped dead outside her door. Flushed red, she was ready to explode.

Just then the baker's wife cheekily sauntered back to read the notice for the second time that morning. Smirking and ignoring Jennat Bibi's venomous look, she went on to cheerily explain, amused at Jennat Bibi's reaction:

'That notice has been there since yesterday afternoon. I saw Zeinab stick it up.'

Jennat Bibi tore off the paper, ran inside and returned panting with a wet broom and began her boisterous scrubbing of the wooden surface. Some of the ink from the writing got smudged. The rest stubbornly remained visible. Everyone could still make out the words.

'Neelum, how I hate my Javaid!' Jennat Bibi raged. Neelum sheepishly looked down. 'That rotten husband of mine has been through this door so many times, but did not bother telling me. I bet he loves this! Just see what I will do to him when he gets home, Neelum.'

'Don't worry, Jennat-ji. It's not his fault,' her friend mollified her, eager to lower Jennat Bibi's blood pressure. When the sweet-maker returned home, he saw their village carpenter busy fixing a new door, hammering the nails in.

He requested of the carpenter, 'Please pretend to take this old door away when my wife looks out, but leave it standing after she has gone'. The young man was surprised but very happy to oblige. Smiling and winking at the carpenter, Javaid handed him a 50-rupee note as a form of compensation in case his wife took her wrath out on him later.

That evening, just as Salma and her mother were settling into their third-floor apartment in Dubai, peering at the traffic down below, after a day of sightseeing on the Jumeirah Beach, Jennat Bibi shrieked at her husband: 'You knew about the door and you did nothing!' He smiled his way through her verbal abuse. When she finished, exhausted, Javaid quietly sauntered off to take a look. The original door was still there, propped against the wall next to the new door.

Literate passers-by could still read the message pretty well. Smiling, he went back inside.

Epilogue

Shirin was at her second favourite spot, nimbly balancing her small, mule-clad feet on a thick branch of the gnarled old tree in the middle of the two paths with its ropy, thick roots jutting out of the dusty ground.

Her mother, busy packing to go back to Islamabad had no inkling about Shirin's tree-climbing adventures. Her uncle and Saher had just left for a holiday in Paris. Begum was making her special breakfast of spinach *paratha* and her grandmother who kept calling her 'fairy' was crying because everyone was leaving at the same time. Hugging her grandmother tightly Shirin had promised her that she would visit them again during the holidays, but was now eager to see the new home that her grandfather had purchased for them in Islamabad. Gulbahar herself was leaving to visit Rani in the hospital accommodation; she had not seen her since the wedding. Saher had already visited her mother twice with Arslan, and had met Rashid. Liking him very much, she insisted with her Aunt Gulbahar that her mother's *nikkah* be delayed until they returned from their honeymoon in Paris.

The sound of horse hooves startled Shirin. Her foot slipping, she gripped the branch to stop herself falling. Twisting her neck, she peered over her shoulder and saw two horses coming up the path. With a beating heart, Shirin recognised the riders; her grandfather and Ali. The horses came to an abrupt stop a few yards from the tree. Paling and with their breath caught, the two men exchanged glances.

Haider instructed his *munshi*, 'Ali, you ride ahead,' eyes on his granddaughter, fearful for her safety.

Ali, winking at Shirin, peeping at them from above the branch, obeyed his master.

Shirin nervously watched her grandfather's horse's bared teeth get nearer, now only two feet away.

Soft mouth parted, Shirin was terribly afraid, hating the man and his beast. Bemused, Haider watched her little face with interest, noting the fear in her eyes and the angry flush spreading fast through her cheeks.

'Hello there!' he softly greeted, reining to turn the horse's head the other way. Only a branch separated them.

Shirin didn't answer his greeting, her gaze on his collar, willing him to disappear. Body straining and afraid of falling, she gripped the branch harder, bruising her palms on the rough bark. Her mouth remained a mutinous line. This man and his horse had made her fall before; she wouldn't let him do it to her again!

Unafraid of him or his long-faced horse, Shirin raised her small chin, a defiant tilt angled at her grandfather, openly glaring at him.

'Would you like to ride this horse?' Haider gently wooed, taking her by surprise, reaching his hand towards her. Mouth dry, Shirin stared at his hand and then looked away. Haider's eyelids swept down; hiding the disappointed look, he tugged sharply at the horse's reins. Ready to turn, he then saw her slide her left hand off the branch and hold it out in front of him. Eyes widening and a smile splitting the harsh planes of his face, Haider's fingers eagerly grasped the small hand in a tight fist. Inching the horse nearer, he grabbed her around her shoulders and lifted her onto the horse in front of him.

Gasping for breath, Shirin's little heart thudded, her body held against her grandfather and secured with the protective band of his arm. She froze, frightened of both the horse and the man holding onto her as they rode out of Gulistan.

Resting his chin on her soft curls, Haider's words fanned into her ears, 'Would you like to ride out into the fields?' There was an odd appeal in his tone which, as a child, she missed.

'I know you will enjoy the ride.'

He nervously waited for her answer. At last a small voice squeaked, 'Yes.' Then she tentatively added, 'Please,' remembering her mother and her manners.

His heart alight with joy, Haider kicked the animal into action, the little bundle of warmth in front of him grasping his arm tightly.

'Hold on, my *chand*, my beautiful star,' he tenderly urged, as the horse sped away.

Shirin relaxed, nestling against his chest, feeling the thrill of the moving animal under her body, the warm, morning air on her cheeks, her hair flying back and into her eyes.

'Good?'

'Yes,' she affirmed, giggling, watching his handkerchief flutter away in the wind, and turning to look at him. Haider laughed aloud into her eyes, glimpsing the first smile meant solely for him. Heart soaring, he kissed her soft curls, hugging her even tighter against his chest.

She let him; strange, but comforting.

'Your mother, too, loved horse riding,' he confided, his chin resting against her hair.

THE END

Glossary

Acha baba: An endearment used to pacify someone. 'OK dear!'
Adhan: The call to prayer for Muslims.
Akros: Vegetables – ladies' fingers.
Assalam alaikum: Muslim greeting.
Athar: Traditional fragrance used as scent by men in the Arab and Muslim world.
Atta: Flour.
Badmash: Someone of not good character.
Baesti: To be shown up and degraded.
Baesti: To lose one's honour and social standing.
Baji jan: An endearing way to address an older sister or relative.
Baji: A title offered in respect to signify older woman or sister.
Bakra Eid: A celebration that is held annually after Hajj is performed as part of the Muslim calendar.
Barfi: An Asian sweet, like a Western fudge sweet.
Bavarchikhana: Kitchen.
Bechari: Pitiful.
Befakuf: Foolish.
Benarasi: A rich gold threaded fabric, often used for saris.
Besharm: Shameless.
Bethak: Lounge.
Bhaji: An older sister or female relative.
Bhangra: A dance often performed to the beat of the *dhol* drums.
Bholi: Innocent.
Bismillah: Form of greeting. 'To begin in the name of Allah'.
Boker: A broomstick, made out of little thin sticks to sweep away dust and cobwebs.

Chador: A large shawl-like garment used by women to cover themselves.

Chaki: A large stone-grinding implement used to mill grain such as wheat.

Chana halwa puri: A brakfast delicacy made from chickpeas, semolina pudding served with a fried bread.

Chand: Moon.

Chappals: Traditional sandals.

Chappati: Flatbread served with meals.

Charail: Witch.

Chardevari: Four walls.

Charpoy: A bed used in rural areas with wooden legs and woven jute.

Chillah: A period of 40 days after the birth of a child when women are traditionally resting and being cared for by their family.

Chirag: Light – a lamp.

Chooridaar pyjama: The trouser part of the traditional outfit worn by women, like tight leggings which ruffle at the bottom.

Chothi pari: A small fairy or angel.

Chumkay: Dangling earrings.

Daigs: Big pots for cooking large quantities of food.

Dal: Lentils.

Dari: Jute woven mat.

Deira: A farmstead with cattle etc.

Desi: Traditional.

Dhai: A birth attendant – a local midwife.

Dhoban: Woman who washes clothes for a living.

Dhobi Ghat: Laundry house.

Dholki: A small drum used by women whilst singing traditional wedding songs.

Dhols: Drums.

Divas: Candle-like lights.

Du'a: Prayers and good wishes.

Dupatta: A scarf used to complete a tradtional outfit.

Eid: A celebration held by Muslims to celebrate the end of the month of fasting or the Hajj.

Engrezi kitab: English book.

Engrezi: English language.

Fajr: The first prayer of the day for Muslims – morning prayer.

Gajar halva: A sweet dish made with carrots and milk.

Ghair mard: A male relative apart from father, husband and son that a Muslim woman is forbidden to interact with on her own.

Ghair: Forbidden.

Ghusl khanah: Bathroom.

Goorie: A white person – girl or woman.

Gora: A white person – boy or man.

Gota kinari lengha: A traditional outfit of a skirt-like garment embellished with gold trimmings.

Gujjar: Tribe or clan of people who are traditionally involved in the dairy business.

Gulab jamuns: A sweet – normally round and brown in colour.

Halal: Allowed according to Islam.

Haldi: Turmeric powder used in cooking.

Haleem: A tradtional dish made of mutton and lentils.

Halvie: A person who makes the traditional Asian sweets and confectionery.

Halwa: A pudding made with semolina.

Haqiqa: A function held to celebrate the birth of a child.

Haram: Forbidden, not 'Halal'.

Hevali: Mansion.

Hijab: A scarf that is used by Muslim women to cover the head.

Hum loothey ghey: 'We have been robbed or looted'.

Izzat: Personal and family honour.

Jaan: An endearment. 'You are my life.'

Jalebis: A sweet shaped like a ringlet served during clelebrations, normally orange or yellow in colour, fried and dipped in syrup.

Jamaat: Class.

Jamounoo: Purple.

Jamuni: Purple.

Juma: Friday.

Kajal: Black eyeliner used in South Asia.

Kala kola: Name of black dye used to colour hair in India and Pakistan.

Kamal hai: 'How strange or how wonderful!'

Kameez: Traditional outfit worn in South Asia by men and women.

Kara: A gold bangle.

Khabardor: Means 'Don't you dare!'

Kheer: Rice pudding.

Khuda Hafiz: A common greeting to say goodbye. 'God be with you'.

Khussa: Traditional leather shoes with embroidery and embellishments for both men and women.

Khusroos: Transvestites.

Kismet: Fate.

Kofta: Meatballs.

Kundan: A type of Indian jewellary involving particular stonework.

Kurtha: A shirt-like garment.

Ladli: Beloved, special girl i.e. daughter or neice.

Ladoos: Asian sweet, normally round and yellow.

Lassi: A drink made with yogurt and milk.

Lengha: A skirt, part of a formal outfit worn mainly at weddings.

Machlis: Dangling bits of earrings or necklace sets.

Mafi: Forgive.

Maghrib: The East.

Mahals: Mansions.

Makhan: Butter.

Mala: A necklace.

Malai: Cream.

Manhous: Cursed.

Matr malas: A gold necklace made with small pea-like gold balls.

Maulvi: A religious scholar.

Mela: A fair.
Merlas: Unit of measurement of land.
Minar: Tall tower of a mosque.
Mithai: Asian sweets and confectionary.
Mitthi: Soil.
Mubarak: Congratulations.
Munshi: Manager of estates and lands.
Naan: A bread.
Nakhra: Snooty/displaying airs.
Nallah: Special string to tie the trousers (shalwar).
Nastaliq: A form of Arabic script used in the Urdu language.
Nazak: Delicate.
Neem: A tree bearing the neem fruit.
Nethu Pethu's: Any Tom Dick or Harry.
Nikkah: The marriage ceremony according to Islam.
Niqab: face veil – partially covering the face.
Noor: Light.
Pagaal: Crazy.
Paisa: Money.
Pak: Pure.
Paratha: A bread that is made with butter, normally eaten at breakfast.
Patesas: A sweet – normally dry and creamy-white in colour with delicate crumbling layers.
Peeri: A footstool.
Perchanvah: Evil shadow.
Phutley: A puppet – used by puppeteers for entertainment.
Piari shahzadi: A beautiful princess.
Pir: A devout man who gives guidance on religious matters.
Pleat: Unclean (opposite to 'pak').
Puris: A fried bread, like a pancake.
Qawalis: Musical, spiritual, devotional pieces.
Rakah: A unit of the prayer offered during the five obligatory prayers.
Ressmeh: Customs or rituals.
Rewarian: A sweet.
Rishta: A proposal of marriage.

Runak: Celebration – a merry atmosphere.

Sabz: Green.

Sahiba-ji: A title given to the lady of the house by subordinates.

Sak: special wooden/herb stick used for brushing teeth, which leaves an orangey stain on the lips.

Samoses: A fried savoury pastry filled with meat and potatoes.

Segan: presents for the newly engaged or wed.

Shaitan: Devil.

Shalwar: The baggy trouser part of the traditional outfit worn by men and women in South Asia.

Shami: Name for round meat kebabs.

Shan: Social standing and respect.

Sharm: Shame.

Shukria: Thank you.

Siniaran: Wife of a goldsmith.

Siri pai: A delicacy comprising the trotters and head of goats or sheep.

Sokan: A second wife, a rival in love.

Takht paush: A special prayer table used for offering prayers.

Tamasha: An altercation/dramatic incident for other people to watch and enjoy. Also means entertainment in a theatre.

Tandoor: A clay oven.

Tangas: A horse and cart used as transport in mainly rural areas.

Tava: A flat iron pan used to make chappati and other breads.

Thalie: A plate or tray.

Thola gulaband: A gold necklace of certain ' thola' weight.

Thola: A weight measurement for gold.

Tikka: A piece of jewellary that adorns the forehead worn by Indian or Hindu women.

Tofa: A present.

Tweez: A religious amulet worn around the neck by some people.

Vakil: Lawyer.

Velat: Abroad.

Velati: Foreign people or things – from overseas.

Wudu: To wash before offering the prayers according to Islam.

Zemindar: Landlord.
Zuhr nafl: An extra prayer that is said apart from the five obligatory prayers.
Zuhr: The afternoon prayer.

Acknowledgements

I would like to thank the following people for all their hard work, support and sheer interest and guidance relating to *Revolt* and my other works of fiction:

John Shaw, Margaret Morris, Gary Pulsifer, Karen Sullivan, Angeline Rothermundt, James Nunn, Rosemarie Hudson, Sabiya Khan, Kate Lyall, Shaheeda Sabir, Dr Afshan Khawaja, Anora McGaha, Prof. Akbar Ahmed, Prof. Abdur Rahim Kidwai, Dr Salim Ayduz, Amanda Challis, Barbra Bos, Jen Thomas, Sameena Choudry, Asad Zaman, Nikki Bi, Jonathan Davidson, Aditi Maheshwari, Sobiya Gondal, Mohammed Anwar, Rahila Bano, Shashi Pandey, Manorama Venkatraman, Tahira & Mohammed Amin, June Rosen, Heather Fletcher Jackie Harrison, Jackie Lewis, Sarah Kemp, Bob Day, Jonny Wineberg, Warren Elf, Angharad Reed, Prof. Lynne Pearce, Dr Robert Crawshaw, Dr Graham Mort, Dr Corine Fowler, Dr Claire Chambers, Prof. Liesel Hermes, Prof. Karin Vogt, Rudi & Roswitha Rau, Ingrid Stritzelberger, Angelika Hoff, Felicitas Freisenhaus and Winfried Rohr.

My husband Saeed and my beloved sons Farakh, Gulraiz and Shahrukh for their everlasting support – with Mama's globe-trotting, busy lifestyle!

I also want to thank the British Arts Council for the award I received to support this writing project.

Last but not least, my main family – my dear brothers Dr Suhail, Dr Zulfikhar and Dr Waqar, my sister Dr Farah and sister-in-laws Sajida and Dr Naushine, and my beloved father, for all being there in my life; for their love and long-lasting support.